A. J. WRIGHT was born in Wigan and educated at Leeds University. He has been shortlisted for the CWA Debut Dagger Award and won the Dundee International Fiction Prize for his murder mystery *Act of Murder*. His writing is inspired by his two major interests: all things Victorian, and classic works from the Golden Age of crime fiction. He is a former English teacher, GCSE English Literature examiner and education consultant. He lives in the beautiful village of Croston in Lancashire.

By A. J. Wright

Striking Murder
Elementary Murder

ELEMENTARY MURDER

A. J. WRIGHT

Allison & Busby Limited
12 Fitzroy Mews
London W1T 6DW
allisonandbusby.com

First published in Great Britain by Allison & Busby in 2017.
This paperback edition published by Allison & Busby in 2017.

A CIP catalogue record for this book is available from
the British Library.

10 9 8 7 6 5 4 3 2 1

ISBN 978-0-7490-1959-4

Typeset in 10.5/15.5 pt Adobe Garamond Pro by
Allison & Busby Ltd.

The paper used for this Allison & Busby publication
has been produced from trees that have been legally sourced
from well-managed and credibly certified forests.

Printed and bound by
CPI Group (UK) Ltd, Croydon, CR0 4YY

For my younger brothers Billy and Stephen, who shared a great childhood with me in the ironically-named All Saints Grove. I should also like to dedicate this novel to all the friends I made at St Benedict's RC Primary School, Hindley, and Blessed John Rigby Grammar School for Boys, Gathurst, Orrell.

If only we had a time machine . . .

George Street Elementary School, Wigan
Extracts from school log book September 1894
[Completed by Mr R. D. Weston, Headmaster]

Monday 10th September
Billy Kelly, Standard 6, given three swipes of the cane for spitting at Albert Parkinson in class. Later given six swipes of the cane for swearing at Miss Ryan in the playground. Absented himself from the school buildings at 3:20 p.m.

Tuesday 11th September
Mrs Kelly demanded interview with me. Her son unable to carry out his duties at Cartwright's Rolling Mill on account of his hand. Mrs Kelly was informed firstly that the boy's inability to collect scraps of wrought iron from the floor of the foundry was a direct consequence of his inability to behave himself in class and in the playground. Secondly, that in any case it was against the law for her to send her son to work at Cartwright's or anywhere else. There ensued a most unseemly scene in front of girls' drawing class. Police informed.

Wednesday 12th September
Albert Parkinson absent – third Wednesday in a row.

Friday 14th September
Letter received from school inspector based in Blackburn. He will visit next week (the 21st) which is also the date of the interview for new assistant teacher to replace Miss Rodley. We must make a concerted effort to impress upon the inspector how far the

school, and especially Standards 1 and 2, has come in terms of spelling and arithmetic. Last year's report spoke of 'lamentably weak performances' in those areas. We must also be sure to let the inspector know of our high hopes for sewing: it is hoped the successful candidate next week will build on the excellent work Miss Rodley has done with the Standard 6 girls in this area.

Monday 17th September
Arthur Clayton, Standard 2, and Edna Clayton, Standard 4, not in school all day. Attending the funeral of their father who was killed in the pit last week. I observed Miss Mason's spelling lesson with Standard 1; our pupil-teacher is making very good progress and will doubtless be an asset to the profession.

Wednesday 19th September
The four Macfarlane children sent home on account of infant sibling suffering from scarlatina.

Thursday 20th September
Lady Crawford paid a most unexpected visit this morning to see the work of the sewing classes. Her Ladyship was most complimentary and gave a short address to the staff, graciously praising their work with 'such inferior material' and paying tribute to the efficient leadership enjoyed by the school.

Friday 21st September
A most curious day. The school inspector, Mr Henry Tollet, spent almost the whole day in school, during which time he attended several lessons. He was most impressed by Standard 4 boys' geography, and he commented favourably on Standard 5 girls'

penmanship which, he observed with humour, flowed far more fluently than their speech! He expressed surprise and delight at the work of our pupil-teacher, Miss Mason. There were points of dissatisfaction, especially the behaviour of some of the children, and his subsequent report will enumerate in more detail his concerns. However, it is sufficient to say that on balance his observations weighed more heavily towards the favourable.

Unfortunately, the interview for a new teacher to replace Miss Rodley did not end satisfactorily. The applicant, a young lady named Miss Dorothea Gadsworth, had spoken well enough when with myself and some members of my staff, and in spite of an initial lack of firmness and distance when observed with Standard 6, she eventually acquitted herself quite well. Later, in the staffroom, she was overcome by a fainting spell, a circumstance made all the more awkward as it coincided with the entrance of Mr Tollet on one of his peregrinations around the school, accompanied by our school manager Reverend Charles Pearl and myself. Rev. Pearl and I were both in melancholy agreement that such sensibilities would be unsuitable for the hurly-burly of teaching at George Street and at her interview informed the young lady accordingly. She was most distressed.

I have arranged for a short staff meeting Monday morning before school to discuss the inspector's preliminary (verbal) findings before the official report is issued.

Monday 24th September
It is with the greatest regret that I must record the dreadful events of this morning. Upon unlocking the school buildings and prior to firing up the stoves, our caretaker, John Prendergast, made a terrible discovery. In Standard 5 classroom, he discovered the body

of a young woman. I was shocked to discover that it was the body of Miss Dorothea Gadsworth, whom we had last seen on Friday and whom we were compelled to dismiss as a candidate for Miss Rodley's position.

The police were sent for and I took the decision to close the classroom. Standard 5 were placed with Standard 4 for the day. To a very great extent the pupils behaved with commendable gravity, with only a few exceptions who were dealt with as befitted the solemnity of the occasion. I spoke at length with the police detective who was most impressed by the way the school had comported itself on this most unfortunate of days. The aforementioned detective conducted several interviews with members of staff at the end of the school day and he complimented the manner in which the school had risen to the challenge of a very trying day.

CHAPTER ONE

'What the bloody 'ell's up wi' that lot?'

The concerned citizen had paused on her way to the shops when she heard what she thought was a full-scale riot emanating from the schoolyard of George Street Elementary School.

The old woman she was addressing lifted her shawl a little and glanced across the street, shaking her head.

'Should be inside an' learnin' summat,' she said. 'Goin' to the bloody dogs, that place. They let 'em run wild. I'm glad my young uns are out of it. Didn't learn 'em owt anyroad.'

'It's makin' the little buggers stay till they're eleven,' an older man added as he approached the two women. 'When I was their age I were down t'bloody pit pushin' tubs.'

As if to emphasise his disgust at the recent raising of the school leaving age, he spat forcibly into the road before shuffling his way into town.

The two women watched him go, then, with a sniff, returned

their attention to the unholy racket from the schoolyard, where they could see several children violently shoving each other in what seemed to be a desperate attempt to climb up to the windows of the school building facing the street.

The old woman chuckled.

'At least when my lot went yonder they fought like buggery to leave the place. Them little sods look like they're fightin' to get back in!'

'Eyup!'

The first woman elbowed her companion and nodded towards the upper end of George Street, where two police constables, standing either side of a man in plain clothes, were marching purposefully along the pavement. All three had grim expressions on their faces.

'Some bugger's for it!' she said. 'Probably *'im.*'

She raised a gnarled finger and pointed at the sign outside the building, its lettering faded and the paint flaking where the wood was rotting:

George Street Elementary School
Mr Richard D. Weston, Headmaster

She was slumped near the door, one arm stretched out as if she had been reaching for something, while her other arm lay loosely by her side. She was wearing a small hat that rested slightly askew on tight curls, and the small outdoor coat was still buttoned tightly at the front to highlight her trim waist. Nearby, there was a pool of congealed vomit, and stuck in the centre a single sheet of paper. Fighting back a wave of nausea, Detective Sergeant Michael Brennan stooped low and carefully plucked it from the rancid mess. Although the paper was damp, he could still make out the only thing written there: in spiderish letters the word FAILED.

He stood up and turned to the man standing in the doorway. The caretaker, John Prendergast, had found the body early that morning, as he opened the building. He was around forty, with thick greying hair and a scar down his left cheek. He stood there now, staring at the woman's body with a mixture of pity and revulsion on his face.

'You say the door was locked?' Brennan asked him.

The man nodded and wiped his mouth. 'Aye. It were. When I looked through the glass in the door an' saw her lyin' there I had to break the lock.'

'You didn't have a key?'

He shook his head vigorously. 'These classrooms are never locked. I keep the keys in the storeroom back yonder.' He pointed towards the end of the corridor and a small door that lay half open. 'I ran back there for the key but it weren't where it should be.'

'So you broke in?'

'Aye. I didn't know what else to do. She might've been alive still for all I knew. I thought she might be drunk.'

Brennan looked around the room. 'Was the door locked from the inside?'

'Aye.'

'How do you know? It could have been locked and just left like that, leaving the woman still inside.'

As if by some sleight of hand, John Prendergast pulled something from his pocket. When he held it out towards him, Brennan could see it was a key.

'That's the key to this room, is it?'

'It is.'

'I thought you said you couldn't find it?'

'I never said that. It was found after I broke in. It were on

13

t'floor over yonder. Reverend Pearl spotted it when he came in.' He pointed to a space behind the door.

'Are you saying the door was locked from inside?'

'Aye. Key must've dropped out when I broke t'lock.'

Brennan gave a long sigh. 'What did you do after you found she was dead?'

'I went for Mr Weston. He came along, with all the others followin'. . . '

'Others?'

'Aye. All the staff. And the vicar. They'd got in early for a meetin', after the inspector's visit last Friday. Seein' what he'd had to say in his report, probably. Anyroad, when Mr Weston saw for himself, he asked the reverend to escort 'em all back and said I were to make the room secure. Though how I was supposed to do that wi' yon lock hangin' off . . . I just shoved a bench in front of the door. That's when he must've sent for you lot.'

Brennan thanked him. 'I'll need to speak with you later, Mr Prendergast. But that'll be all for now.'

When he'd gone, Constable Jaggery, who had been standing outside the classroom with the other constable to ward off any prying eyes, came in and gazed down at the body.

'Why do they do it, Sergeant?'

'Do what?'

'Suicide. She seems pretty enough.'

'Let's see if we can get some answers, then, shall we?' With that, he told Jaggery to stand outside the main entrance, while Constable Hardy waited for the wagon to arrive for its melancholy cargo.

In the normal run of things, Richard Weston regarded his study as his inner sanctum, a sacred place where he dispensed the necessary punishments, oversaw the work of both scholars and teachers, and drew up his weekly list of materials to be introduced to the children for their Object Lessons as advocated by Mr Currie and his worthy tome *The Principles and Practice of Common-School Education*. In such a venerated place, he ruled.

Today, however, he sat in his study feeling rather unvenerated, and tried hard to keep his hands still. His face was pale, a consequence of standing over a body and, with his caretaker watching on, ascertaining that indeed the woman was dead and declaring this was a matter for the police.

'Suicide is the most heinous of crimes, in my opinion. A selfish, wicked act.'

'And you are convinced it was suicide?' asked Brennan, sitting opposite him.

'Well,' he began with the same patient tone he would use with a backward child, 'there's the small matter of the note she left.'

'Of course,' said Brennan, placing a hand against his inside pocket, where the slip of paper lay folded inside his handkerchief.

'Added to the fact that she locked herself in the room so she wouldn't be disturbed.'

'I see.' Brennan thought for a few seconds then said, 'Perhaps you could tell me who the woman is and how she came to be found in a classroom?'

Mr Weston leant forward and picked up a pen, turning it around and examining the dry nib.

'As to your second question, I have no answer, Sergeant. Mr Prendergast, our caretaker, assures me he locked the school on Friday night – only two doors, front and rear. How the woman got into the school is beyond me.'

Beyond the closed door of the headmaster's study, they could hear the shuffle of feet along the corridor where the woman's body was being carried in the cheap wooden coffin to the wagon waiting outside. They must have opened the large double doors that formed the entrance to the main school buildings, for immediately from inside the headmaster's study, they could hear the loud screams of nervous and excited children who would be gathering round the coffin eager to steal a glance and terrified of the consequences.

'Get back you snivellin' little sods!'

Brennan smiled thinly. He could rely on Constable Jaggery, whom he had left on duty in the schoolyard, to maintain the safety, if not the dignity, of the melancholy transportation. He looked at the headmaster's bowed head and gave an audibly provocative sigh.

Finally the headmaster began to elaborate.

'Her name is Miss Dorothea Gadsworth. She was here in school on Friday.'

'Why?'

Mr Weston took a deep breath, as if he were about to dive in a freezing stretch of river, and said, 'She had been invited for interview. We are soon to have a vacancy, you see, as Miss Rodley is leaving us. She is engaged to Reverend Pearl, our school manager, and as such it would have been inadvisable for Miss Rodley to continue in her post.'

'Now, tell me what happened on Friday.'

With a frown, he looked up at Brennan and said, 'From an inauspicious start, everything was going quite well, Sergeant. Until the poor woman fainted.'

Dorothea Gadsworth stood at the front of the class – Standard 6 – and cleared her throat before speaking. Thirty-seven pupils –

girls and boys – stood before her behind desks that had seen better days. Their faces were, for the most part, quite clean, although Dorothea could make out smears of dirt just below the hairline on many of the boys. Occasionally there was a chorus of sniffling, and she noticed several of them using their sleeves to wipe their noses. She had been told beforehand of the nature of this particular group – 'prone to silliness' had been the view expressed by Miss Jane Rodley, the teacher whose position she hoped to take – and so she adopted the stern expression they had been encouraged to develop at training college.

'Good morning, Standard 6.'

There was a ragged chorus of 'Good morning, miss' mainly from the girls. The boys stole furtive glances at each other and some covered their mouths to hide their sniggering, unaware that such an action served only to highlight, not conceal, such rudeness.

'Now you may sit. In SILENCE!'

Although she had a slight, demure figure, her voice was loud and forceful. It had the desired effect, for now the whole class were sitting quietly behind their desks.

'My name is Miss Gadsworth, and I am here to teach you arithmetic this morning.'

There were the beginnings of a communal groan that were immediately stifled when the schoolroom door opened and the headmaster, Mr Weston, entered, followed by the school inspector, Mr Tollet. The children all rose and stared directly ahead, their faces now expressionless, a contrast with the rather apprehensive frown that had suddenly appeared on Miss Gadsworth's forehead.

'Sit!'

Mr Weston's voice was hard and splintery, rather like the long cane he carried under his arm.

It took Miss Gadsworth a few seconds to re-compose herself, but she lifted her head in a superior manner (again following the guidelines set by her training) and leant forward on the teacher's desk in what she imagined was an attitude of authority.

'As you are no doubt aware, I am new to the school and would like to spend a minute getting to know you. I am told you are a very bright set of children.'

There was a sharp cough from Mr Weston, who had by now moved to the back of the room, Mr Tollet beside him.

Miss Gadsworth moved away from the front of the classroom and began to walk between the rows of desks. She raised a hand and pointed to a small girl seated halfway along.

'Name?'

'Elizabeth Paxford, miss,' the girl replied in a faint voice.

'Elizabeth. I want you to tell me what you want to be when you grow up.'

The girl looked at her curiously.

'Do you understand me, girl?'

'Miss?'

'Well? What do you want to be?'

It was clear that the girl was under great pressure, for her cheeks reddened and she looked down at her desk.

Undaunted, Miss Gadsworth pointed to a young boy seated at the back of the class, a few feet away from Mr Tollet.

'You. What is your name?'

'Albert Parkinson.'

'Miss,' she added as a reminder of his manners.

'Miss Albert Parkinson,' came the instant reply to an accompaniment of sniggers.

The hopeful applicant took a deep breath, glanced to the rear of

the classroom where the headmaster and school inspector sat with
expressionless faces.

'And what do you want to be when you grow up, Albert?'

The boy looked at a red-haired boy near him and said loudly, 'A
carrot, miss. Just like Billy.'

There was general laughter, which threatened to reach a riotous
crescendo until Mr Weston stepped forward and gave the joker a
resounding slap around the head.

The headmaster gave a paternalistic sigh.

'She made two basic mistakes, Sergeant. After the lesson –
which went off quite well after that wicked boy's attempts to
derail it – I told Miss Gadsworth that she must always remain at
the front of the classroom, either seated at her table or standing
behind it. That provides a commanding focus of attention,
and she can see at a glance any child who fidgets or otherwise
misbehaves. A lighthouse, I told her, never moves but shines its
light in all directions. A warning and a guide. That is what she
must be. Secondly, a teacher must never try to *make conversation*
with the children. They aren't her friends, they are her charges. A
lighthouse may benefit all within its compass, shall we say, but it
never encourages vessels to sail close. I mean, asking them what
they wish to be? It encourages dissatisfaction. Besides which, the
question was superfluous.'

'Why?' Brennan asked.

'For the simple reason that there is very little doubt about these
children's futures. Mapped out, Sergeant. The girls will work in the
mills and get married and have children of their own, or they'll
work on the pit brow screening coal and wearing those ridiculous
trousers. The boys will go down the mines or work at the iron

works. One or two might even run away to join the army. Why encourage flights of unreachable fancy?'

Brennan had a fleeting image of his own six-year-old son Barry and the dreams he had spoken of.

'She should have made them recite their times tables,' the headmaster went on. 'Much more productive. And harmonious.'

Brennan shifted in his chair. He wasn't here for a lesson on lessons.

'You said Miss Gadsworth fainted?'

'Yes, indeed. After her lesson I left her in the staffroom and asked Miss Rodley – whose class she would have been taking over – to speak with her and give her some words of encouragement. Miss Mason and Mr Edgar were already there – they are in charge of Standards 1 and 5 respectively – and they made a very pleasant table fortified by tea and coffee. By this time it was playtime and all the children were outdoors. The boys in their playground and the girls in theirs, of course. Miss Gadsworth seemed to be getting along with everyone. So I left to have a word with our school manager Reverend Pearl, who had arrived a few minutes earlier and whom I had left looking after Mr Tollet.'

'And who's Mr Tollet in charge of?'

Mr Weston gave a wry smile.

'I suppose in a way the answer is all of us.'

Brennan frowned, so Mr Weston explained.

'Mr Tollet is our school inspector. Occasionally we're graced with an inspection. It was just unfortunate that poor Miss Gadsworth chose the moment we entered the staffroom to faint. Mr Tollet was most gracious – indeed, most concerned for her welfare. He ordered her to be laid flat on the floor of the staffroom and the windows opened. She recovered enough to ask if she might be excused for half an hour to *take some air*.' He gave a half-smile. 'She hadn't spent much time in this town, obviously.'

Ignoring the condescending attitude to his town, Brennan asked, 'She left the school?'

'And returned within the half hour, looking a little more composed. Mr Tollet later assured me that the incident would form no part of his report. Out of respect for his position I asked if he wished to sit in on the interview later in the day. I would have welcomed his views on the girl. But he pleaded a prior engagement. Of course by that time . . .'

The headmaster spread his hands open and left the rest of the sentence unspoken.

'By that time, what?'

'Well, considering she was an applicant for a position here, it would have been unseemly to confirm her appointment.'

'Why?'

Weston seemed to take umbrage at the question. 'Apart from her initial lack of firmness in the classroom, and although she acquitted herself quite ably for the remainder of the lesson, it would have been folly itself to appoint someone who fainted in front of a school inspector. What would that say about our judgement of character, Sergeant? The Lord Himself knows what she would have done if he *had* agreed to stay for the interview. Perhaps a more histrionic attack of the vapours?'

Brennan, who found himself now feeling a certain sympathy for the deceased, shook his head. Mr Weston took that as an affirmation.

'I would be grateful if you could give me a list of all those staff who came into contact with Miss Gadsworth.'

'Might I ask why, Sergeant?'

'Because I wish to speak with them.'

The headmaster flushed. 'What I meant was, why do you wish to speak with them?'

'Because I have a desire to,' Brennan replied with a smile.

The expression on Mr Weston's face contained elements of shock, outrage and protest. Clearly, he was unaccustomed to such prevarication in his own office. When he spoke, his lips barely moved.

'I shall furnish you with a list, Sergeant. Of course. Though as to why you should wish to prolong this unfortunate incident . . . However, may I ask that you speak with my staff when school finishes for the day at five o'clock? The school is already facing disruption.'

Brennan considered the request and gave a nod. 'And the address of the school inspector, Mr Tollet.'

Mr Weston stood up. 'Is that really necessary?'

'Part of the investigation. No stone unturned.'

'But an investigation into what, for goodness' sake? The poor woman was obviously distraught at failing her interview and came back here to take her own life. There is absolutely no need to bring Mr Tollet into this. No need whatsoever.'

Brennan, too, stood up. 'We'll see. And now I'll set about my business while you set about yours. I can hear the children getting restless.'

As he opened the door he paused and turned. 'Just one more thing, Mr Weston. Out of interest.'

'Oh?'

'Once your caretaker found the woman's body and reported his gruesome discovery to you, why didn't you close the entire school? It would have made our job all the easier.'

The headmaster smiled at last. 'My responsibility is to look after the pupils in my charge, Sergeant, not clear the way for what appears to be unnecessary officiousness. Besides, letting them loose at nine in the morning would create far more work for you and your constables than you could ever imagine. Think of a pack of monkeys swinging around the market hall, not to mention the howl of anger from parents who'd got rid of them till midday. I took the decision with the full support of Reverend Pearl who was here this morning.'

'So I gather. He took the staff back to the staffroom.'

'Yes. The sight of that poor girl was most distressing.'

'The reverend didn't stay?'

'Why should he? Once we'd secured the room, there was no reason for him to stay. He had only come to discuss the inspector's visit, and we could hardly do that with a dead body down the corridor. Besides, he had parish duties to perform.'

Brennan grunted and stroked his moustache. 'This afternoon will do, Mr Weston.'

'For what?'

'The list of people who met Miss Gadsworth. If you could ask your staff to remain behind when school ends.'

'Yes.'

'Oh, and that will be a good time to pick up Mr Tollet's address.'

Brennan could see the man's hands were now shaking as he leant on his desk for support, and he was almost through the door when the headmaster called out, 'You never answered my question. An investigation into what?'

'The circumstances of Miss Gadsworth's death.'

'But I thought she had taken her own life. Surely the evidence . . .'

'A possibility, of course. And from the blue colouring of her skin and lips I'd say it *was* poison of some kind.'

'There you are then.'

'But I have some questions first, Mr Weston. Before I can accuse the poor woman of suicide.'

'Questions? What sort of questions?'

'The sort that need answering. And if you'll . . .'

The detective's sentence was left unfinished. There was a sudden commotion from outside. And in the midst of a tremendous cheering and screaming from what sounded like the hordes from hell, he could hear Constable Jaggery's ferocious roar, threatening to *rattle the arse* of anyone who threw another thing.

Albert Parkinson was ten years old. Along with the rest of the school, he'd watched as the policemen carried out a long wooden box with grim expressions on their faces. It was obvious what the box contained. Some of the girls had begun to whimper, prompting the lads to sneer at them and warn them that the body in the box would rise up any second and eat them.

The girls had screamed and hugged each other for protection. Soft sods.

Every Wednesday, instead of going to school, he helped his uncle deliver coal, heaving hundredweight bags from the back of the cart and dragging them along the back alleyways to make his delivery. It was grimy work, coal dust often billowing from the badly-tied bags, and gave him a cough which he never seemed able to get rid of. The work, though, gave him a sturdy physique, which, along with his usual surliness, meant the other pupils at George Street kept a wary distance from him, unless he saw fit to include them in his occasional bouts of mischief. In which case many of them became his temporary if reluctant allies, unwilling to endure his wrath if they refused him. He took particular delight in ridiculing Billy Kelly, who was the only one in the class with red hair, and who was also the only one to stand up to him. Not that it did him much good: such defiance usually ended with Albert triumphant and Billy in tears. But Billy had always been told by his dad to fight back if anyone picked on him, and he knew that any reports of cowardice would get back to him – Billy was much more afraid of his dad's temper than Albert Parkinson's thuggery. Sometimes he even gave a good account of himself. Trouble was, Albert's strength far outweighed Billy's courage.

But Billy hadn't shown up at school this morning, a fact that required some elaboration as they waited for permission to enter the school building.

'Cos I snotted him Friday night. Ran off like a mouse, skrikin'. That's why 'e daren't show 'is face, the gingerknob bastard. That right, Joe?'

In such scathing tones Albert dismissed his arch rival's absence: there was room for only one cock of the school.

The other boys looked at Albert's right-hand pal, Joe Marshall, a small ferret-faced child with a permanently glistening nose and a fierce temper. None of the others had witnessed the altercation, and it fell upon young Joe to offer confirmation.

'Aye. Like a mouse. Albert snotted 'im all right.'

There was a communal groan. It was a great pity they'd missed all the fun.

With this most recent testimonial to his ruthlessness, Albert urged several of the boys to leave the school entrance, where the large policeman stood guard scowling at them like a gargoyle, and follow him to the rear of the building, to the trapdoor that led down into the cellar where the coal was stored for the classroom stoves. The lock on the door was faulty. Everyone knew that. The plan was simple: each boy was to fill his fists with lumps of coal and return to the front of the building where they would hurl their missiles at the uniformed bully stopping them from entering.

He lifted the trapdoor and ushered them down. Once their clogs were crunching the coal beneath them, he gave his rallying call to his troops. 'It's our bloody school. He cawn't stop us gooin' in. Fat bastard.'

Some of them nodded, more in agreement with his depiction of Constable Jaggery than their leader's uncharacteristic desire to enter the building. Outside was much more fun.

'Besides,' Albert added, standing atop the mound of coal and now appealing to their sense of family loyalty. 'Them bastards battered me dad in the lockout last year. Be bloody good if we clod some o' these at 'em!'

He held up the lumps of coal in his fists. They all nodded at the retributive fitness of such missiles, each one of them mindful of the darkest period in their lives the previous year when the five-month miners' strike almost brought the town to its knees, and hunger ran rampant. Several of their fathers had been involved in various scuffles with the police, and they had long, vengeful memories. But it was the hunger they remembered the most.

He watched the others clamber up the coal pile and into the bright morning air and followed them more slowly.

He gripped the two lumps of coal and felt the black grit bite into the palms of his hands. As he strolled purposefully now towards the front of the school, a smile slowly spread across his face.

* * *

The three men moved with exaggerated slowness, weighed down by the cumbersome protective clothing they were forced to wear. Each of them was clad in thick iron boots, barely visible beneath the wide leather aprons and the shin guards that restricted their movements as they approached the strangely-shaped puddling furnace. The heat in the large workshop at the Cartwright's Rolling Mill was intense.

Tommy Kelly, the principal shingler of the three, felt the ferocity of the furnace's heat more than the others, not least because of how he was seething inside. He cut a large, almost superhuman figure beneath the clothing, an impression enhanced by the square mask of iron with its narrow slits for his eyes that made his head appear to sprout impossibly from his broad shoulders and bypass altogether the bull neck that lay beneath.

It was Tommy's job, now that the pig iron inside the furnace had finally become molten, to damp down the fire that had burnt with such ferociousness before stirring the iron with a puddling bar in order to allow as much air to reach it as possible, while at the same time ensuring it kept well clear of the carbon from the flames.

He forced the bar into the well of the furnace with more than usual vigour and scuttled it around to disperse the molten iron, feeling the sweat pour down his forehead and into his eyes. He cursed out loud at his inability to wipe away the salty sting that blurred his vision.

The two other men, standing a few yards behind him with their heads free of the stifling iron headgear, gave each other knowing glances. They knew better than to speak to Tommy when he was in such a mood, although they knew full well what was causing it. It had nothing to do with the heat, or the strained effort it needed to puddle the iron sufficiently. No, they'd been told at the beginning of their shift that morning what had put the big fella in such a 'heat'.

'Shithouses!' he had said to them as they booked in at seven that morning.

'Who, Tommy?' one of them had asked in a voice that carried a slight tremble of uncertainty.

'They'll not speak to my missis like that again in a fuckin' hurry! Sendin' the bloody police round cos she made a stink.'

The others had looked at each other with smiles of relief, happy in the knowledge that it would be the pig iron, and not they, who would suffer the big man's wrath.

Later, as the three of them sat in the small yard outside the workhouse and ate their snap, he seemed to have brought his temper under control.

'Can be a little swine, our Billy, I know that. But yon bloody headmaster's gettin' too big for his boots. Needs choppin' down.'

'They're all t'same,' said Gilbert Barlow. 'Put 'em in a suit an' they reckon they're a cut above the likes of us.'

'Aye,' Fred Dunn added. 'He wipes his arse like the rest of us.'

'I'll wipe his arse wi' me puddlin' bar if he talks to my Edith like that again.'

Then all three of them laughed at the vision big Tommy's words had conjured up. After a few minutes' silence, the big man spoke again, this time with a surprisingly low voice, as if he were afraid of being overheard.

'T'wife reckons that's why he's done it, all this trouble at school.'

'Done what, Tommy?'

'Our Billy. T'wife reckons 'e's 'ad enough.'

'Aye, but what's 'e done?'

Tommy Kelly swirled a mouthful of cold tea around his mouth to clear the remains of his egg butty, spat it out and watched as it soaked into the ground.

'Our Billy buggered off Friday night. Not seen the little sod since.'

CHAPTER TWO

One of the problems of meeting with the Chief Constable of Wigan, Captain Bell, was the unpredictability of his moods. Normally a stern, rather humourless figure who ruled the force with a military firmness, he nevertheless drifted off occasionally into a more reflective state of mind. Today was one such occasion.

Detective Sergeant Brennan had given his superior the bare outlines of the unfortunate discovery at George Street Elementary School and had informed him of his intention to regard the death as suspicious until he could prove otherwise. But instead of a cursory 'Carry on' or even an expression of doubt as to the desirability of continuing with the investigation, he merely sat back and placed his hands together on his chest, a dreamy glaze in his eyes.

'When I was in India, visiting Jeypore, Sergeant, I took a stroll in the public gardens.'

'Really, sir?'

'A fascinating place. There's an educational museum there. Believe it or not, it's housed in a building they call the Albert Hall.'

He paused, waiting for the amused glint in Brennan's eye that never came.

'There's a department of crime in that museum, you see? They have little puppets, very life-like they are too. They re-enact every crime you can think of. From drunkenness to murder most foul. They even have models showing the most efficient way of disposing of a murdered person. One way was to cut the poor chap up into little bits and drop them in a postbox.'

'Ingenious, sir.'

'Evil beyond measure, Sergeant.' Captain Bell's eyes flashed a cautionary glance in his direction. 'Another group of figures shows a Thug throttling a British soldier. The poor fellow's face is purple like a bursting plum.'

Brennan, who couldn't think of anything remotely appropriate to say, kept silent.

'The point I'm coming to, Sergeant Brennan, is this. In the museum's courtyard there's an inscription – a saying of Akbar's.'

'Akbar, sir?'

'The one buried at Sikandra. The Emperor.'

'Oh that one.'

Captain Bell blinked but carried on. 'It read, "I never saw anyone lost on a straight road".' He paused, waiting for the wisdom of the maxim to permeate his sergeant's brain.

'I see, sir.'

The chief constable unfurled his fingers. 'Quite plainly you do *not* see. I was merely trying to point out that you have a tendency to deviate into all manner of byroads and pathways when the simplest way is forward. Forward on a straight road.'

'You wish me to accept the woman's death as suicide?'

'What makes you think otherwise? The note she left would seem to be conclusive. Her failure to secure a position. The shame of going home jobless. The inescapable fact that she locked herself in the classroom so she wouldn't be disturbed. What more evidence do you want?'

'It's nothing very definite, sir. It just seems strange that Miss Gadsworth should choose to end her life in a school rather than the confines of a hotel room. Why go back there at all? And how did she manage to enter a locked building? Furthermore, how did she know where the classroom keys were kept?'

'She wished to torture herself in the place where she suffered rejection,' Captain Bell offered with a frown of understanding and conveniently ignoring the subsequent questions altogether. 'The surroundings gave her the impetus she needed to do the deed. Poison, you suspect?'

'Indeed, sir. The signs were unmistakable, though we'll see what the post-mortem tells us.'

'Well then.'

'I'm still rather curious as to how she got into the school in the first place. According to the headmaster, there were no indications of a forced entry.'

Captain Bell looked through his window for an answer. 'Loose window?' he suggested with little conviction.

'A possibility, sir. I suppose.' He examined his fingers before adding, 'And another thing. Why did she faint?'

'Faint?'

Brennan explained.

'Isn't it obvious? She wasn't up to the job. And seeing a school

33

inspector walk in . . . well, shrinking violets don't like the heat of the sun.'

It wasn't a saying Brennan had heard before, but he gave a short nod as if he had.

'Well, Sergeant. It's clear you haven't finished your enquiries yet.'

'No, sir.'

'But I wouldn't want you to spend an unprofitable length of time on what appears to be a sad case of a woman scorned. Not by love, on this occasion, but by her own inadequacy. Very sad, but if people took their own life whenever they met a rejection, where would that leave us, eh? A melancholy mountain of bodies, Sergeant.' He shook his head as if the vision were set clear before him. 'But remember what I said. The straight road, Sergeant. The straight road.'

Brennan took the wave of his thin hand and the slow shaking of the head as signs of dismissal. He stood up and left his superior gazing through his window, but whether he saw the tram shuttling its way up King Street, some resplendent garden in India, or a pile of rotting suicidal corpses it was difficult to say.

By the time Brennan and Constable Jaggery returned to George Street later that afternoon, a sizeable crowd had gathered. Pupils, home for their dinners, had spoken of classrooms filled to the rafters with bits of dead bodies, and word had got round the town that something serious had taken place at the school. Passers-by, curious as to what was going on, had been given increasingly gruesome distortions of the grim truth through the school railings by children eager to show they were at the centre of events.

A woman wi' 'er eyes cut out . . .
I 'eard she'd been etten by rats . . .

34

Aye, 'er ears an' nose bitten off . . .
And 'er 'ead . . .
Wi' 'er innards all over t'floor.

Most of the parents were at work – down the mine or in the mill – but others had taken their place and muttered darkly of the *poor little buggers* being taught in blood-stained classrooms, and what the hellfire did that headmaster think he was doing letting a murderer loose near the littluns anyroad?

The two policemen ignored the more salacious questions hurled at them. Brennan paused at the railings to make a short and terse statement.

'A young woman has died. She isn't a teacher at the school. If any of you are waiting for your children, they'll be out at the usual time.'

There were mutterings, but the way Constable Jaggery clutched his truncheon and faced them with his considerable bulk subdued the more vociferous.

Once inside the building they were immediately met by the headmaster, who, Brennan supposed, had been spying out for their arrival. Along the arched corridor were a number of classrooms, each with its door firmly shut. From one classroom – the nearest – they could hear the lacklustre chanting of times tables.

One times two is two
Two times two is four
Three times two is six
Four times two is eight
Five times two is ten

As they walked along the corridor towards the headmaster's room, Brennan overheard a loud clatter from another classroom.

He glanced through the upper window of the closed door and saw a class of around thirty very young children seated at their desks, all of them watching with interest a confrontation involving a young girl – around five years old – who was standing defiantly before her teacher. The teacher herself seemed very young and looked uncertain what to do.

'I said pick it up, Sadie Gorman.'

'No!'

'You have broken your slate!'

'You said take away six from three.' The young girl's voice rose in anger.

'I said no such thing. I told you to take three from six.'

'You can't take six from three.'

Mr Weston gave an apologetic cough. 'Excuse me, Detective Sergeant. I may have to intervene. Miss Mason is a pupil-teacher. An excellent one, but not quite the finished product yet, I'm afraid. Should have another teacher in with her but as we're so short-staffed . . .'

Before Brennan could reply, the headmaster burst into the room with all the force of a gale. The pupils immediately stood up. Brennan saw the young teacher swirl round to face Mr Weston. He noticed the glimmer of tears in her eyes as she briefly turned her face to the window. Her eyes widened in what looked like shock when she caught sight of Constable Jaggery's uniform.

A brief exchange took place between herself and the headmaster. After a few seconds of listening with her head bowed low, Miss Mason gave a sharp nod and, with the presence of such reinforcement to support her, she raised her head and once more instructed young Sadie to pick up the cracked slate. The pupil gave a furtive look in the headmaster's direction and then stooped low to do as she was told.

'I trust you will deal with this she-devil in the appropriate manner, Miss Mason?' said Mr Weston in a loud voice that carried to the back of the room. 'Violence, vandalism and defiance – an unholy trinity indeed in one so young, Gorman.' He then glared at the rest of the class as if they were somehow equally to blame. 'Today of all days!' he said darkly. 'Today of all days!'

With that he breezed past the tearful Miss Mason and slammed the door shut behind him.

'No *idea* how to behave,' was his only comment to the two policemen as he led the way to his study at the end of the corridor.

Brennan wasn't sure whom he was referring to.

The hand bell was clanging at the far end of the corridor, the boy from Standard 6 heaving it from shoulder to knee with great gusto. Within seconds there was a communal scraping of chairs; doors the length of the corridor were flung open and children of various age and size came rushing out. As they neared the outside doors held open by the caretaker, the noise increased until the playground became a frantic blur of bodies running, jumping, scuffling and kicking their way to the school gates, where a larger than normal group of onlookers – including some parents – were waiting to greet and interrogate them.

Richard Weston stood at the window and gazed out at the noisier than usual scene in the playground. He refrained from commenting, however, and turned to face Detective Sergeant Brennan, who was scrutinising the sheet of paper he had presented to him.

'I see Mr Tollet, the school inspector, lives in Blackburn.'

'That is his address, yes. It is what you asked for.'

'It certainly is. I see that the vicar isn't down to speak with me this evening?'

'Unfortunately, according to Miss Rodley, Reverend Pearl has other commitments to carry out, so he is unavailable for interview. I'm sure you can make alternative arrangements?'

Brennan grunted his assent.

'You'll notice that I have placed Miss Mason first on the list, Sergeant Brennan. She is, as I explained, a pupil-teacher, and she has an hour's study from five o'clock until six. I am helping to prepare her for the Queen's Scholarship Examination.'

'What's that then?' Constable Jaggery, who was standing by the door in readiness for his role as usher, looked puzzled. 'She's a teacher, ain't she? Thought examinations were done with by the time you pick up a stick o' chalk.'

Mr Weston gave a condescending smile. 'At the moment she is merely a pupil-teacher. Until four years ago she was herself a pupil in this school. Then she became a monitor. One of the very brightest children I have ever met, despite her rather harrowing background. The man who called himself her father was a profligate and the only favour he ever did for her was to die. The poor girl's mother died, too, soon afterwards, and her grandmother has taken sole responsibility for her upbringing. She has few friends now – her former classmates seem to have frozen her out because she chooses to work in a school instead of the cotton mill. And yet, despite all that, the girl shows great promise. In other schools they allow the children to address pupil-teachers by their Christian name. You may notice that does not happen here. She is always *Miss Mason*. Once we iron out some of her verbal lapses, *and if* she passes the Queen's Scholarship with a first class, she will be able to go to training college for two years. With my assistance.'

'She might be wed by then,' Constable Jaggery added. He was about to make further pronouncements on the general desirability of women to become mothers at the earliest opportunity when he caught sight of Brennan glowering at him.

'Very well,' said Brennan. 'If you'll be so kind as to bring the child in, I can begin.'

'She isn't a child, Sergeant Brennan. For the purposes of her standing in this establishment she is not to be referred to as anything other than a teacher, albeit a pupil one.'

With that, he left the room.

Constable Jaggery gave a chuckle. 'Touchy bugger, Sergeant.'

'A man under pressure, Constable. It's not something they train you for in headmaster school. Finding dead bodies in a classroom.'

'Didn't know they 'ad schools for 'eadmasters an' all,' said Jaggery with a shake of the head. Humour, unless of the vulgar and violent sort, often passed him by.

A few minutes later, they heard mumbled whispers from the corridor, before the door swung open and Mr Weston escorted the young pupil-teacher into the study.

Brennan stood and moved around the desk to sit in the headmaster's chair while indicating with an outstretched hand that Miss Mason should sit facing him.

'Thank you for agreeing to see me, Miss Mason,' Brennan began. But before he could go any further there was an irate cough from Mr Weston, who was glowering at him.

'Ah,' said Brennan, understanding at once the reason for the interruption. 'I won't be occupying your chair for long. And as you won't be staying . . .'

'What?'

'It's better I speak to the staff alone.'

'But they are *my* staff, Sergeant. They may need support.'

Constable Jaggery, standing in his usual position by the door, also gave a cough, but its genesis lay more in concern for the headmaster's well-being.

'They're answering a few questions, Mr Weston, not facing a mob.'

During the brief exchange, Miss Mason kept her eyes cast down. It was clear she had never heard the headmaster being spoken to in such a way.

Constable Jaggery held the door open.

'In that case I shall be in the staffroom. Unless, of course, you have an objection to *that*, too?'

'None whatsoever.'

With that, the headmaster left with his head held high.

Once Jaggery had closed the door, Brennan leant forward and gave Miss Mason a reassuring smile.

'As I said, just a few questions, Miss Mason. I'm trying to build up a picture of what exactly happened to the unfortunate young woman who was found this morning.'

At last she raised her head. Close up, Brennan was struck by how young the girl looked. *She's really no more than a child herself,* he reflected, and recalled the look of panic in her eyes when faced with a naughty child and the wrath of the headmaster. Although her hair was tightly braided, a few strands had slipped free, giving her a somewhat harassed appearance. She was pretty, though, he thought.

'It was horrible,' she began in a low voice. 'I only caught a glimpse of her lyin' there this mornin' but . . . after seein' her so full of life only last Friday . . .'

He gave her time to recover. For such a young girl, the sight of death in such incongruous circumstances, a room normally associated with all the spirited exuberance of life, must indeed have been a shock.

40

'Mr Weston said she'd took her own life,' she whispered, her words low and tremulous.

'Well no one knows that for sure,' Brennan said gently. 'That's what I'm trying to find out.'

The girl frowned. 'But if you find out she didn't take her own life, that'd mean . . .'

He held up a hand. 'Let's see what we can find out, eh?'

She gave a short nod, clasping her hands together.

'The woman's name is Dorothea Gadsworth,' he began. 'She was here on Friday to be interviewed for a position in the school.'

'Yes. I was introduced to her then.'

'What can you tell me about her?'

The question seemed to flummox the girl.

'I only met her proper that once. At playtime.'

'Did you speak with her?'

'She said she hoped I would pass me scholarship. That 'er time at training college was the best time of 'er life. That she'd met such wonderful and interesting people there.'

'She was pleasant with you then?'

'Very.'

'What mood was she in?'

Miss Mason thought for a while before replying. 'Seemed all right. I remember thinking how she'd be in class. Y'know, stood in front and getting them in order. She said Standard 6 had been a handful but they weren't as bad as some she'd taught over in Salford.'

'Were you alone with her?'

'Oh no. All the others were there – the other teachers, that is, and Miss Rodley, o' course. She was showin' her round t'school. It's her job she was here for. Miss Rodley's leaving, see? Gettin' wed to the vicar. Reverend Pearl. We spoke to each other no longer than a couple of minutes.'

'You were there when she fainted?'

'It was a shame. One minute she was, like, happy an' then 'er legs buckled.'

'This was when Mr Weston, the vicar and the school inspector Mr Tollet came into the staffroom?'

Her brow darkened. 'Aye. He'd make a donkey faint, I reckon.'

'Who?'

'That inspector bloke. One o' them as is all smiles an' all the time makin' notes. You don't know what he's puttin' down, see? Mr Edgar reckons all inspectors should be drowned at birth.' She gave a shy smile and looked down at her hands.

Brennan had some sympathy with the view. He recalled ruefully the visit of Sir Herbert Denman, Her Majesty's Inspector of Northern Division, earlier in the year. Captain Bell had put all of them through a torturous course of drill in the week leading up to the visit and had made it clear that any member of his force letting him down would suffer a fate of biblical proportions. He had given Brennan the dubious honour of showing the great man the cells which had been scrubbed overnight, a fact that Sir Herbert's nose detected at once.

'You clean the cells with borax, Detective Sergeant?'

'Not personally, sir.'

'It kills vermin, you know. I would have thought you'd be putting the miscreants at risk, eh? Can't have the devils dropping dead willy-nilly, eh, Sergeant?'

'Indeed not, sir.'

Oh how he had laughed at the inspector's droll humour.

He blinked himself back to the present and jotted a few points down.

'You had no further conversation with Miss Gadsworth?'

'No, sir. I was back in the classroom an' taught all afternoon. Saw her at the end of school though back here in the staffroom, but I didn't get the chance to speak to her then.'

He thanked the girl and she left with what Constable Jaggery thought was an unnecessary curtsy.

'It's all my fault, Sergeant Brennan. Absolutely.'

The woman sitting before him – Miss Jane Rodley – was in her late twenties, early thirties, Brennan guessed. Unlike the pupil-teacher who had just left, this seemed to be a much more confident and able member of the profession. Her white blouse, set off by a black and white cameo brooch pin at the neck, gave her an aura of modesty and competence, and he could well imagine her commanding respect and even devotion from the Standard 6 pupils in her charge. She was also something of a looker, too, he reflected. Her dark brown hair immaculately pinned back, penetrating green eyes and a firm, rounded mouth, he was hardly surprised that she should now be engaged to be married, and to the vicar too. She'd be a great asset to his parish work.

'And how do you work that out, Miss Rodley?'

She thought for a few moments. 'If I hadn't been leaving, then the poor girl wouldn't be here in the first place.'

'That's hardly . . .'

'*And* in the second place, after her fainting spell I should have consoled her far more than I did. Than we all did. Mr Weston seemed to be more concerned about the impression we made on Mr Tollet, the inspector, than the welfare of Miss Gadsworth.'

'But she recovered quickly, did she not?'

43

'She did. I'm ashamed to say Mr Tollet showed her more concern and tenderness than any of us.'

'In what way?'

'He acted with commendable speed. Issuing orders to have her laid quite flat on the floor. Asking me to expose her neck and chest as much as was seemly. Opening the windows, that sort of thing. He even asked if we had any chloric ether in the school, but of course we have nothing of the sort here.'

'He seems remarkably well-versed in medical emergencies,' Brennan observed.

Miss Rodley smiled. 'Afterwards, he appeared to be quite embarrassed by his actions. Said he had made common ailments a particular study. A hobby, I suppose. At any rate he appeared to have succeeded in bringing Miss Gadsworth round. He took her into a corner of the room and spoke very gently to her. She seemed very anxious to reassure him she was fine.'

Brennan thought for a moment, then asked, 'Your conversations with Miss Gadsworth? What was she like?'

'I liked her. She spoke of her excitement at the possibility of working at George Street. She'd done some preliminary teaching in Salford and I gather the extreme poverty she came across there had not only appalled her but fired her enthusiasm for doing good.' She paused and gave a half-smile. 'This would have been her first appointment, you see, and *any* post would feel like that. I felt much the same way five years ago. She'd eventually find her enthusiasm tempered a little by experience, but not much. It's a wonderfully rewarding job, Sergeant, despite the challenges set daily by our little charges.'

'Would you say her enthusiasm was so great that a disappointing outcome to the day might . . . discourage her deeply?'

'Make her kill herself, you mean?'

Brennan gave a nod of acknowledgement. This was a woman who spoke plainly. Perhaps she might have to temper *that* when she becomes the vicar's wife.

She thought for a while. 'I can't really judge. She was excited, not excitable. But I didn't speak with her after she was given the verdict by my . . . by Reverend Pearl and the headmaster, so I can't say how she took it. I'm sure she was bitterly disappointed. She had been looking forward to working here so much. I just wish I could have spent some time with her afterwards, given her words of encouragement. But I never saw her again. Until this morning . . .'

Her voice tapered off into sombre reflection, and Brennan allowed her a few moments.

'I gather you are engaged to be married? To Reverend Pearl?'

She flushed. 'Yes. Next June. You know my fiancé?'

'Not personally, no. He's vicar at St Catharine's in Scholes, I gather.'

'Yes.' She noticed the trace of a smile on his face. 'The church with the crooked spire, before you mention it.'

He nodded. Many people knew the reason for the leaning spire at St Catharine's. The church was built on land riddled with coal mines, and around thirty years ago there had been major subsidence, causing damage to the church's west wing. His father – a bricklayer – had told him the story of how local collieries with workings beneath the church contributed to its repair, and how his father himself had worked on repairing the building. He even recalled the joke he'd repeat when drunk:

Sure I expected any minute to be struck be a bolt o' lightnin', Michael, me helpin' to fix a protestant church with each brick a mortal sin. Or a mortar sin, eh, son!

'It will be necessary for me to speak with him at some point. I gather he has parish work to carry out.'

'I shall be seeing him later. There's a meeting to discuss his forthcoming series of lectures on a range of topics. He believes firmly in the benefits of an education that doesn't stop at the school gates. Then he has choir practice. You can see him any time after that.'

'Very laudable.' Brennan wondered what the uptake for the lectures would be in Scholes, not the most enthusiastic area of Wigan when it came to stimulating the mind. Stimulations of another kind altogether were more in their line.

'Perhaps if you came along after seven tonight. You know of course where Lorne Street is?'

'Of course.'

He knew every street, every yard, and every alleyway in the Scholes district. Hadn't he scoured the place only last year during the miners' strike, and the murder of Arthur Morris, the most hated of the colliery owners?

'Then if you'll be so kind as to forewarn him of my attendance?'

She smiled. 'Be careful, Sergeant. My fiancé can be quite persuasive. He might well draft you in as a guest speaker on the causes of crime.'

Her eyes flashed with humour, and once again he could well imagine how the good vicar had been struck by her beauty.

Lucky beggar, he thought, then felt an immediate stab of guilt as he pictured his Ellen stirring a pot of stew and wondering where on earth he'd got to.

It was a source of wonder to many of their neighbours in Diggle Street how Edith Kelly had managed to stay alive. She was a few inches over five feet tall, with thin, shrewish features and narrow bony arms. There was steel in her eyes, though – Mrs Arbuthnot a few doors down had once joked that she got that look from her husband Tommy who must have brought home some shavings from the rolling mill and shoved them in her eyes.

If her glare was sharp, then her tongue was sharper, as more than one of the neighbours had found out to their cost. She had a way of cutting them down with her bitter words, and if they didn't work she always had her poker, which she often brought out to settle street disputes.

But her Tommy was a big bugger. His red hair – which his only son Billy had inherited – only served to enhance his reputation for a fiery temper, and surely to God, the neighbours reasoned, he could swat her away with one sweep of his huge arms as soon as she started on him, which she did on a regular basis. And yet she not only lived but ruled.

Tommy Kelly might hammer the living daylights out of any man in any pub in Springfield or even up Scholes on the other side of town for that matter where the real hard men lived, but when it came to facing down his beloved wife it was an entirely different tale.

So when they heard yelling from inside number 23 at teatime, apart from the odd sniff and raised eyebrow, the conversations on the street went on as normal. Those with husbands who hadn't yet come home took the opportunity to have a last minute chat, each woman leaning against her own doorway in case his lordship should happen to appear suddenly from the direction of the union workhouse which dominated the area and which they all shunned like the plague.

Inside number 23, however, the atmosphere was far less conducive to either idle or meaningful conversation.

'Don't slouch there like an overfed pig, get off thi backside an' get out lookin'.'

Tommy looked at the welcoming glow of the coal fire, felt its warmth tingle his stockinged feet. "E'll come back when 'e's ready. When 'e's clemmed.'

'Bound to be bloody well clemmed if 'e's not eaten since Friday night. Summat might've 'appened to 'im. An' that lot out there are beginnin' to talk.'

'Bloody *hellfire*!' Tommy cursed and spat onto the coals, watching his phlegm sizzle on the grey coating of ash. 'I'll go, woman. But if I see the little bugger I'll tan his arse. Upsettin' us like this.'

Nathaniel Edgar was the teacher in charge of Standard 5. He sat before Brennan with one leg crossed over the other and his hands resting gently on the desk between them. With his dark well-groomed hair, he was quite handsome in a rugged kind of way, with well-formed cheekbones that were accentuated by his clean-shaven appearance. As the interview moved along, Brennan noticed the expression in his eyes alternate between wry amusement, aloofness and the occasional flicker of melancholy.

'Yes,' he began in answer to the detective's question, 'I spoke with Miss Gadsworth.'

'Can you recall any details from your chat?'

He uncrossed his legs and leant forward. 'I remember she was very excited about the day itself. This was her first interview and she wanted to acquit herself well.'

'Go on.'

'She told me she'd be the first teacher in her family. Her father owns a pharmacy in Bolton, I believe, and has encouraged her most keenly to join our profession.'

Pharmacy, thought Brennan. *Interesting*.

'Anything else?'

'She spoke about how she had enjoyed her training at Manchester. How she felt a curious closeness with the children she taught over there while on practice.' He thought for a moment. 'Ah, yes. She felt close to them because of the poverty they endured. She actually started to tell me one tale about a child she'd taught in Salford who lived in the most appalling of hovels and who came to school with maggots actually crawling out of her hair. I could almost detect tears in her eyes as she spoke. But then Mr Weston came in with the inspector and the vicar and she fell silent.'

'Why?'

'Seemed to me she was the sort of girl – woman – who is intimidated by authority. It can be a hindrance in our profession, Sergeant. One minute you're ruling the roost – or should be – in the classroom, the next minute you're tongue-tied in the presence of such figures.'

'But when the headmaster came into the staffroom with the others, Miss Gadsworth had already met him, hadn't she? Mr Weston, I mean.'

'Oh yes.'

'Is he – as you say – intimidating?'

He shrugged. 'Not to me, no. I know what lies behind the mask. But to someone just starting off . . .'

'What do you mean, you know *what lies behind the mask*?'

For the first time the man's confidence faltered.

'Just an expression, Sergeant. I mean, don't we all have masks of some sort?'

'Do we?'

'Again, in our profession we have to adopt certain roles – fierce upholders of discipline, gentle words of encouragement . . . you know the sort of thing. You also need a broad back.'

He felt the need to dig a little further.

'But what exactly does Mr Weston have lurking beneath his mask?'

Nathaniel Edgar crossed his legs once more and gave a superior smile. 'Generosity of spirit, Sergeant. A strict disciplinarian on the one hand, and a conscientious mentor on the other.'

'Mentor? You mean with the pupil-teacher, Miss Mason?'

Edgar nodded. 'Sometimes he hides that generosity well, but it's there nevertheless. He's most assiduous in helping young Emily get the start in life she deserves.'

'So. When Mr Weston entered the staffroom with the inspector and the vicar, Miss Gadsworth dried up?'

'Yes.'

'Did she tell you anything else? Before they came in? Or after, for that matter.'

'No. Our conversation lasted no longer than ten minutes. We spoke about the usual things of course – the weather, the children, what Wigan is like – that sort of thing. But as for anything personal, no. I'm afraid that's it.'

'You were actually present when she fainted, I gather?'

'Yes. I suppose I'd seen it coming.'

'How?'

'Well, she looked rather pale – not flushed with enthusiasm as much as that morning. I'd heard about the awkwardness she'd faced in lesson. It must have had more of an effect on her than we thought. At any rate, she was quite subdued and then when Mr Weston and the good reverend came through the door with the school inspector . . . She seemed to mutter something, but I couldn't really tell what she said. I was too busy catching the poor girl.'

'Try.'

Edgar thought for a moment. 'Well, I'm not sure, you understand, but it sounded something like, *Of course . . . Let's wait . . .*'

'*Let's wait?*'

'I know. It sounds meaningless, really. Perhaps it's the sort of gibberish one says when swooning.'

'I see. Well, thank you Mr Edgar. That's been most helpful.'

Brennan gave a sigh. Couple of little snippets to go on, but not much there, he thought as Nathaniel Edgar left the room. Not much at all.

Brennan sat opposite Miss Alice Walsh and registered at once the woman's defiant gaze. She was very pretty, he observed, although that was muted somewhat by the suggestion of hostility in the way she regarded him. It was almost as if she were daring him to find her attractive. Nevertheless, with her dark hair, dimpled cheeks and absorbing brown eyes she did exude an appeal that many would find alluring. He had a fleeting memory of his old teachers, and the comparison with what he'd seen today did them no favours.

'Miss Walsh, you're in charge of Standard 3, I gather?'

'Yes, I am.'

'Just a few questions, miss, about last Friday.'

'Go ahead.'

'Did you have any conversation with Miss Gadsworth at any time?'

'Yes.'

Brennan let a sigh creep out. He said slowly, 'And can you tell me what your conversation was about?'

Miss Walsh pursed her lips. 'You,' she said simply.

Brennan looked shocked. 'I beg your pardon? You talked about *me*?'

'About *men* in general,' she explained. 'Miss Gadsworth told me she'd done her training in Manchester and I asked her if she had been to any political meetings.'

'Why?'

'Because it is in Manchester that Emmeline Pankhurst lives. I wondered if she has met her, as I have. She has established a branch of the Independent Labour Party there. More importantly she formed the Women's Franchise League. You're familiar with the suffrage movement, Detective Brennan?'

Brennan found his seat a trifle uncomfortable. This woman was fast turning the tables on him and he needed to restore the natural order of things.

'So you discussed women being given the vote?'

Alice Walsh laughed. '*Being given* says it all in a nutshell.'

'Was there anything specific that you discussed that might help me build a picture of what took place here last Friday?'

'Tax.'

'Tax?'

'John Stuart Mill, whom I am sure you've heard of, once said that women paid tax, and those who paid tax were entitled to have a say in how their taxes should be spent. In other words – or perhaps I should say, in *his* words – "taxation and representation should be co-extensive". So, I asked her if she felt it was right that she would be paying tax as a member of the teaching profession without the right to vote. She couldn't answer.'

'I see.' Brennan felt as if he'd been harangued from a soap-box.

Perhaps Dorothea Gadsworth had felt the same. 'And were you present when Miss Gadsworth fainted?'

'I was not. Myself and Miss Hardman were outside in the girls' playground and Miss Ryan was overseeing the boys. She is Mr Weston's deputy, and apparently that means she holds more sway with the boys. Nonsense, of course. Her frosty demeanour cuts no ice with some of those boys, if you'll forgive a rather lame metaphor.'

She waited for him to say something but he remained silent.

'When we returned to the staffroom before lessons resumed, we saw the poor girl recovering and that inspector tending to her.'

'I see. Well, if there's anything else you can tell me, I'll be most grateful.'

She stood up, but before she left she said, 'I hear she drank some poison?'

'I really can't tell you anything, Miss Walsh.'

'Because I'm a woman and need to be protected from such horrors?'

'No, miss. Because I'm a detective and need to consult a pathologist. Good evening.'

She turned and left the room.

CHAPTER THREE

Tommy Kelly hadn't gone far in search of his son, missing now for four days, when he caught sight of his workmate Gilbert Barlow leaving the Pagefield Hotel on the corner of Park Road and Gidlow Lane. Unlike Tommy, whose wife always insisted on a prompt return from work with none of that 'I were thirsty nonsense', Gilbert had stopped off for a livener before heading home for his tea. Once Tommy had made his presence known, it was inevitable that both men would see the rationale of a drink in the vault. Women, of course, weren't allowed in the pub's vault, and Tommy needed some fortification before embarking on his futile quest to find Billy. As for Gilbert Barlow, it made more sense to agree to the big fella's invitation than risk a confrontation in the street.

'Not turned up yet then?' Gilbert asked as they stood at the bar, frothing pints of bitter in hand.

Tommy shook his head.

'You know what young 'uns are like, Tommy. He'll be back when his belly's empty.'

'Aye. That's what I told 'er.' He took a long gulp of his pint, and then licked off the froth from his thick moustache.

'Happen it's just as well 'e weren't in school today anyroad.'

'Why?'

'You not 'eard?' Gilbert took a long, slow draught in the confidence of a one-sided knowledge.

'Don't bugger me about,' Tommy snarled in a low whisper.

His mate swallowed quickly and spent the next five minutes explaining in vivid detail the gruesome discovery only that morning of a woman's mangled corpse at George Street Elementary School.

'Took 'em all mornin' to find enough of the poor wench to put *in* a box,' he added by way of colouring in the drab truth of the incident.

Tommy looked long and hard at his drinking companion. 'They sure it *were* a wench?'

''Course they're sure, Tommy owd lad,' said Gilbert with a reassuring tap on the big man's shoulder. ''Course they're sure. Even the bloody bobbies can't get that wrong.'

Tommy gulped down the rest of his drink and slammed it down on the brass counter, occasioning a furtive but silent glance from the landlord. 'That bloody school!' he snapped, before storming out into the half-light of early evening.

Gilbert Barlow breathed a sigh of relief and beckoned to the landlord, lifting his empty glass. 'Might as well,' he said to no one in particular.

Brennan had left the school caretaker till last. He would normally be the last to leave the premises anyway, and the poor man had been the one to suffer the greatest shock that morning when he'd discovered the lifeless body of Miss Gadsworth.

His interviews with the rest of the George Street staff had elicited nothing new: Miss Hardman and Miss Ryan, who took charge of Standards 2 and 4 respectively, hadn't even met Dorothea Gadsworth, seeing her only in passing during the day. Both were on playground duty along with Miss Walsh and could tell the detective sergeant nothing more revealing than 'she seemed a very nice young woman'.

He'd been struck, however, by Miss Ryan, who apparently was Mr Weston's deputy. She gave the distinct impression that his leadership qualities were lacking somewhat.

'There is one member of this staff who gets away with murder,' she told him, qualifying her observation only when she realised what she had said. 'I shall name no names, Sergeant, but the headmaster is a frequent turner of the blind eye.'

She refused to elaborate further, and, reluctant to engage in staffroom politics, he dismissed her.

Mr Prendergast, on the other hand, seemed quite eager to impart everything he could about the morning's sombre discovery, along with his own background.

'This,' he said, pointing to his scar as soon as he sat down opposite Brennan, 'in case you're wonderin', is summat I copped in Egypt. I were in the Yorks and Lancs Regiment at Tel-el-Kebir. Cut me face an' me leg.' He tapped his right leg. 'Invalided home. Invalided out. Two scars an' a medal. That's what I've got to show for servin' Queen an' country.'

Brennan let him talk. Perhaps it was the shock of what he'd found that made him so garrulous, or perhaps this was the natural way of things. Eventually, Brennan's silence registered with the caretaker.

'Take me through the events of this morning again, Mr Prendergast. From the moment you opened up.'

'I always open the school up at seven-thirty. Never late. Army, see? I always go down to the cellar, bring coal up for the stoves, then fire 'em up. Which I did. Then I usually go round all the classrooms, open the windows wi' me long pole, an' unlock the front doors.'

'The front doors were definitely locked?'

'Aye.'

'How do you get in?'

'Back way.'

'And that was locked too?'

'It were. I always lock up on a Friday night. It's what they pay me for. Why they call me a caretaker. Cos I take care.'

'And the classrooms. Do you normally lock them before you leave?'

'Never.'

'You told me you keep the keys in the storeroom.'

'That's right, but there's never a need to use 'em. What's the point if I'm lockin' the school up anyroad?'

'Did Miss Gadsworth happen to visit the storeroom last Friday on her tour of the school?'

'Not that I know of. Hardly the sort of place you'd take visitors.'

Brennan rubbed his thick moustache before resuming. 'Tell me about finding the body.'

'I told you this mornin'.'

'Tell me again.'

For a few seconds Prendergast reached forward and stroked his right leg. Then he spoke. 'Like I said, the room were locked so I broke in when I looked through the glass an' saw the woman lied there. I remember it stank. Foul smell. Then I saw the sick. Dried up but still stinkin' to high heaven. I bent down but I could tell straight off she were dead. That's when I saw the bottle.'

Brennan leant forward. 'What bottle?' He looked across at Constable Jaggery who gave an elaborate and baffled shrug. 'You didn't mention a bottle this morning.'

'Must've forgot. It was a bottle of Scotch. Brown's Special Scotch, if I'm not mistook. It had been supped almost dry, anyroad. 'Bout half-inch left. Just lyin' on the floor under the teacher's desk. That must've been why I thought at first she were drunk.'

'And what happened to this bottle?'

'Dunno.'

Brennan scribbled something down in haste. Constable Jaggery, standing by the door, read the signs right enough.

'So. You found the body – and the Scotch. What then?'

Prendergast sighed. 'I've seen dead bodies aplenty, Sergeant Brennan. Some wi' bits cut off. You name it. But I never seed a dead *woman* before today. Somehow it's worse. She'd frothed at the mouth, an' it had dried. I don't think she died well, if you ask my opinion.' He sat silently for a few moments before continuing. 'Anyroad, I went to fetch Mr Weston and Reverend Pearl from the staffroom where they were meetin' the rest of the staff an' told 'em what I'd found. We all went straight back an' Mr Weston went mad cos they all walked in to take a peek. He asked the vicar to take 'em all back. That's when I pointed at the bottle an' the piece of paper all covered in sick an' said, "Looks like she needed a bit o' courage an' all". He said I were bein' disrespectful to the dead an' told me to wait outside while 'e checked the room.'

'Check it? For what?'

'No idea. Then he comes out an' just tells me to make the room secure.'

'Did he have the Scotch with him?'

'No.'

Brennan wrote more down in his notebook then asked if there was anything else the caretaker could remember.

'Only the cellar,' he said.

'What about it?'

'Well, when I got in it to get the coal, summat weren't right.'

'What?'

'I always leave things as they should be, Sergeant. No mess. Army trainin', see? But when I went down that cellar this mornin' I seed stuff I'd not left there Friday night.'

'What stuff?'

'Bits o' wood scattered about. Near the bottom of the coal mound. An' scraps o' paper stuffed in between 'em. If I were a bettin' man – which I ain't – I'd say somebody were tryin' to light a fire down yonder. But Mr Weston said I were lettin' me imagination run riot.'

There were any number of places his son could have gone to, Tommy Kelly reflected ruefully. In the past, the first place he would surely have sought out would have been his grandma's in Clayton Street. But since she died during the miners' strike last year, the house had remained empty. Still, it was worth a look – the little devil might have hidden himself away there for some reason known only to himself – so he increased his pace with a greater conviction. It was quite a walk, but as he thundered along Frog Lane the darkening expression on his face meant that those who would normally greet him with a nod and a word kept their distance.

The big fella was best left alone when he had that sort of mood on him.

* * *

Brennan looked through the window and saw the sky darkening. He glanced at his watch: 6:10 p.m.

'Get his bloody lordship in, Constable. Tell him there's a few supplementaries.'

Constable Jaggery looked puzzled. 'A few what, Sergeant?'

Brennan scowled. There were times . . . 'Just get him in. Now!'

'Yes, Sergeant.'

A minute later, Mr Weston was seated opposite Brennan, his hands clasped and a friendly smile on his face.

'I presume you've completed your . . . investigation, Sergeant?'

'Almost.' Brennan sat back, his arms behind his head. 'Only one thing needs clearing up.'

'Oh?'

'It concerns you, Headmaster. And the deliberate suppression of evidence.'

The hands unclasped, the smile vanished. 'I beg your pardon?'

'A bottle of whisky was found by Miss Gadsworth's body.'

The headmaster flushed and coughed to clear his throat. 'Indeed it was.'

'You saw fit not to mention it earlier.'

'I didn't think it was relevant.'

To Constable Jaggery standing by the door, it looked as though Micky Brennan was about to explode. Instead, with what he thought was admirable control, the detective sergeant leant forward and spoke softly.

'A bottle of Scotch beside the body? You don't consider that relevant?'

Richard Weston sat upright, his chin jutted forward defiantly. 'I considered its implications.'

'Which were?'

61

'The good name of the school.'

The look Jaggery gave his sergeant spoke volumes on what he thought of the school's reputation locally.

'With respect, Headmaster, that wasn't a decision for you to make.' He held up a hand as Weston was about to respond. 'I presume it's in that classroom somewhere. Just tell me where you put it.'

His shoulders sagged. 'In the cupboard where the slates are kept. At the back.'

Brennan nodded to Jaggery who was, for once, quick on the uptake. When he'd closed the door behind him, Brennan spoke once more.

'And you failed to mention the signs of disturbance in the cellar.'

For a moment, Weston appeared confused. Then he understood.

'Ah. Mr Prendergast has told you about the bits of wood and so on.'

'Indeed he has.'

'You must appreciate, Sergeant Brennan, that I have had a great deal on my mind today. It isn't every day a headmaster has a dead body turn up in his school. So please forgive me if I forgot to mention the scraps of wood. Besides, Prendergast isn't as efficient or as prone to tidiness as he makes out. He could easily have left the mess himself on Friday evening. I simply forgot to tell you. My apologies.'

Brennan stood up. 'I think that will be all for now, then, Mr Weston.'

He could hear Jaggery making his bovine way along the corridor. The door swung open and Jaggery held out the bottle. A small amount of amber liquid swirled around the bottom.

'Got it, Sergeant!' he said triumphantly.

'A masterful piece of detection, Constable,' said Brennan. 'Well done.'

'Thank you, Sergeant!' Jaggery replied with a smile of satisfaction at the headmaster, who had understood the ironic tone, even if Jaggery hadn't.

Even when his mother-in-law was alive, Tommy Kelly had never liked visiting her house in Clayton Street. It stood only a few doors away from the slaughterhouse, and the stench that emanated from the place was bad enough in winter, but in the hot and steamy days of summer it was overpowering. Now, in the early days of autumn, the smell was still foul and stomach-churning as he walked quickly past its slumped wooden roof and ramshackle gates. Somehow, the light seemed to fade faster here, as if the fetid odours swirling along the street had somehow managed to infect the very air itself. He always reckoned that's what sent her to the idiot ward at the infirmary.

'The stink affected the old bitch's brain,' he told his mates when his wife was well out of earshot.

When he came to the house, he peered through the front window, but it was smeared so thickly with grime that it was impossible to see anything inside. There was no light, though, and the house itself looked dark and forlorn. He tried the door handle but it refused to give. He saw three or four women standing in their doorways, leaning idly against the jamb and watching him with a bland curiosity. It was worth a shot.

'Any of you lot seen a young lad hangin' about?'

The woman nearest said, 'Aye. There's lots of 'em on t'canal bank. Tha can take thi pick yonder.'

The other women laughed, unafraid of his size or the menacing scowl he gave them.

He stepped back onto the pavement. 'Piss off inside an' cook thi husband's teas!' was his parting shot as he swung to his left, heading for the ginnel that would take him to the alleyway at the back of the row of houses. He'd get inside that bloody house if it killed him.

Once he was through the narrow passageway and into the long winding alley at the back, he turned to his left and passed a row of common privies. The smell from there was almost a welcome relief from the slaughterhouse. He pushed his way through the back gate of the house and into the tiny yard, picking his way through an assortment of mouldy boxes, an upturned dolly tub with its peg hanging loosely to one side, and a rust-coated bucket, until he came to the back door. It was hanging at an angle, the lock evidently forced and dented. He pushed against the door and it easily yielded to his weight. The light was fading now, and it was difficult to see anything other than vague shapes in the small kitchen. He stepped past the table resting against the wall opposite the door and banged his elbow on the slopstone beneath the curtainless window.

'Bastard!' he mumbled as the pain shot up his arm.

Once he got to the front room and looked round, he saw only scraps of what had once been the old bat's furniture: a couple of slats from her wooden chairs, a long white pipe she used to smoke sitting by the fire, a cracked earthenware bowl she'd use to soak her feet in. The smell of damp filled the place, plaster peeling along the walls and ceiling.

'Billy!' he shouted.

His voice bounced around the entire house, but there was no response.

'Billy, if you're upstairs bloody well get down 'ere this minute!'
Silence.

'Bloody *'ell*!' he rasped and made for the stairs, careful not to step on any that had rotted away with the damp.

When he reached the top he moved into the front bedroom where the old bitch used to sleep. The number of times she'd poked her head through that front window and screeched down at her Edith standing on the doorstep with Tommy wrapped round her body . . .

Happy bloody days.

There was nothing in the room save the dilapidated bed frame, and a framed legend that read 'Nearer God to Thee' hanging skew-wiff above the bed.

He moved quickly into the next room – Edith's old room where, before they rented their own house in Diggle Street, the two of them had started their Billy. Be bloody funny if the little sod were hiding in here, he thought to himself as flashes of their lovemaking came back. He'd almost suffocated Edith with his huge fist when she began to scream out in pleasure.

The light was even poorer here at the back of the house, and the floor seemed empty. He knew the bed had gone because he'd taken it himself, enlisting the support of Gilbert Barlow to drag it all the way back to Diggle Street at the insistence of his wife who'd told him it still had plenty bounce left in it, a comment which Gilbert later shared with the entire vault of the Pagefield.

'Billy!' he said, this time lowering his voice almost out of respect for the room where the lad was conceived.

Silence once more. Only the slamming of a privy door from the alley beyond the window, the gruff rattle of a cough and the more distant clanging of clogs from the street at the front.

Then, just as he was about to turn away and leave the room, he spotted something. In the corner of the room, below the window. A dark, motionless shape, like a body curled in on itself. His heart began to beat faster now as relief, expectation and dread swirled around inside him. He moved closer, leant slowly towards the shape, and saw a head resting on the bare boards.

'Billy?' he said softly, but the body remained still. He reached out and carefully raised a forefinger before touching the back of the head.

It felt cold, damp, lifeless.

CHAPTER FOUR

In a fit of generosity, Brennan had acceded to his constable's request to finish for the day.

'It's past me knocking-off time, Sergeant,' Jaggery had argued, 'an' I don't reckon I'd be any use sittin' in a vicar's house suppin' tea wi' me little finger stuck in the air, like.'

'Bright and early tomorrow then, Constable. You hear?'

'As ever, Sergeant. Ta.'

And so it was that Detective Sergeant Brennan found himself standing alone at the back of St Catharine's Church in Lorne Street, Scholes, waiting for the vicar, the Reverend Charles Pearl, to conclude his work with the small gathering of boys in the chancel by the altar who he presumed formed the church choir. Candles flickered along a small stand nearby, and as he caught the last snatches of the hymn 'There Is a Land of Pure Delight', he realised with some surprise that the boys' voices seemed smooth and almost angelic, an effect, he told himself, of the half-light and the sanctified atmosphere of the church.

Could we but climb where Moses stood,
And view the landscape o'er,
Not Jordan's stream, nor death's cold flood,
Should fright us from the shore.

It was with some amusement that he watched the choir troop past him when they'd finished. Some of them he recognised as young toughs from Scholes, and they were clothed in their usual scruffy garb with slim neckerchiefs covering filthy necks, each boy holding his folded cap as if it were something holy. Still, there was something about them, the way they walked with an unaccustomed slowness, heads bowed lower than normal, that made Brennan look back at the vicar still standing at the altar with admiration. If he could work such miracles with this gang of ruffians . . .

As the choir reached the heavy wooden doors, he saw them revert to what he'd expect – a sudden bout of pushing, shoving and cursing as the doors fell open and they stumbled out into the darkening world outside – and he wondered if his impression a few moments ago had been a self-deluding illusion.

'Detective Sergeant Brennan?'

He turned back and saw the vicar approaching along the aisle.

'Yes, sir.'

He wasn't quite sure how to address a protestant vicar – *Father* wouldn't do at all, he told himself as the Reverend Pearl escorted him out of the church and into the vicarage next door.

'Who the fuck are you?' the shape said.

The man – for man it was – had taken some prodding, but eventually he shifted his position on the bedroom floor and slammed himself against the wall. In the darkness, all he could see was a huge figure looming over him.

'An' who the fuck are *you*?' Tommy Kelly asked, regaining his equilibrium quickly after the initial terror of seeing what he thought was his dead son transform himself into a filthy-looking fellow whose wild and staring eyes were just visible in the gloom from the window.

'I sleeps 'ere!' the man said, not taking his eyes off this lumbering intruder.

'Not any more tha doesn't.'

'It's God's will.'

'It's not my bloody will!'

Tommy Kelly was both relieved and angry. Billy was still missing, but he hadn't found the little bugger dead. Instead he'd found a mangy flea-bitten beggar dossing down in his saintly mother-in-law's home.

He grabbed the filthy specimen by the neck and dragged him to the top of the stairs.

'Up to thee,' he said. 'Tha goes willin' or I clod thee down.'

Faced with such a brutal choice, the beggar hobbled his way down the stairs and slammed up against the front door, only to find it locked.

'Back door!' Tommy snapped.

Within seconds the man had vanished into the back yard. He heard him shuffle his way through the gate and into the alleyway. Once he was safely away from the house, the man yelled up, 'May the Lord judge between thee an' me, and may the Lord avenge me upon thee. Yer big fat bastard!'

Then he scuttled off, muttering further curses until he faded into the distance.

Tommy sat at the top of the stairs and leant forward on his elbows.

The darkness had descended now, and he suddenly felt the damp and the chill of the night creeping around him. The house was as silent as death.

Where are you, you little sod?

'Most of my parishioners are colliers and their wives, Sergeant. They are rough and ready, and sometimes it is the poor children who suffer as a result. My housekeeper, Mrs Flanagan, makes sure that every Sunday there are cakes to be handed out as the children leave church.' Reverend Pearl sighed ruefully and held his hands open. 'Invariably we have cakes left over. My congregation can be quite sparse at times.'

They were seated in the small living room of the vicarage. A small but ornate fireplace lay unlit. Along the walls hung a number of framed prints of the countryside, and Brennan was struck by the wildness of the scenes: the grand sweep of a mountain topped by thick clouds; sparse landscapes, narrow waterfalls emerging mysteriously from thick wooded hillsides, a huge expanse of lake reflecting the hills on the far shore, a dying sun rendering a small fishing boat melancholy and insignificant, its oars hanging limply in the water.

'Ah, I see you find them of interest?'

Brennan smiled. 'A weakness, sir. Can't say I understand them, but I do like a good picture.'

'They're particular favourites of Jane, my fiancée whom I gather you spoke to earlier.'

'I did indeed.'

'She loves the wildness of the countryside. Says it's only there she can truly feel the hand of God and have a sense of His grand design. In the classroom, and the signs of suffering in some of those children at George Street, she feels the design of an entity quite different. I'm blessed, you know.'

Brennan presumed he was referring to his relationship with the retiring schoolteacher and not the Almighty, although he had to admit, the good reverend was right in a more personal respect. He was quite a handsome fellow, early thirties, he'd guess, and it was easy to see the attraction for the similarly attractive Miss Rodley: he sported jet-black hair that was just the respectable side of long; he had what might be regarded as craggy features – cheekbones that were prominent and a nose that had at one time been broken – with eyes that were a piercing blue. They made an attractive couple.

'She tells me you wish to speak to me about the terrible events of this morning? I shall never forget the sight of that poor girl . . .'

Brennan shifted in his seat. 'Dreadful business, sir. I gather you were with the rest of the staff when Mr Weston went along to the classroom.'

'That is correct.'

'And the caretaker tells me you found the key to the door?'

'Yes. It was lying a few feet away. Obviously the girl had locked herself in before she threw away God's greatest gift.'

'It would appear so.'

'I see.' He gave Brennan an inquisitive look. 'You don't accept that the poor girl committed a grievous sin upon her own person?'

'I'm not sure as yet, sir. I don't like jumping to conclusions.'

'From what Jane tells me, there seems to be only one conclusion to jump to.' There was a subtle change in the man's expression that suggested he'd overstepped the mark. 'Forgive me. What is it you wish to know?'

Brennan paused then said, 'Last Friday. Your contact with Miss Gadsworth. What did you speak about? Even your observations of her would be of help.'

Reverend Pearl took a few moments to gather his thoughts. He steepled his hands to aid contemplation. Finally he said, 'Before I met her, I remember being most impressed by her letter of application. Good penmanship, excellent qualifications and just the right spark of personality that suggested a lively, fresh approach. Sadly, when we met her in person . . . well, let us say the pen was mightier than reality.'

'In what way were you disappointed?'

'I was told her classroom presence was good, despite some early hesitancy, but when I met her in the staffroom, admittedly after that unfortunate fainting spell, she spoke falteringly, with little of the authority or the vivacity one had come to expect from her letter of application. Of course I wouldn't have expected sparkling wit or mature conversation after such a thing, but still, you'd expect to see traces, wouldn't you?'

Brennan said nothing.

'At any rate, Richard Weston described her as "milky" and I see no reason to contradict his judgement.'

'Did you speak with her personally at any time?'

'I had intended to speak privately with her at dinner time after the hurly-burly of her lesson, but that was pre-empted by her fainting spell when we came into the room.'

'The school inspector, Mr Tollet, administered to her?'

'He was most expert, issuing orders and aiding her recovery. By the time she'd gathered her wits, I deemed it ill-advised to impose myself. It was quite clear to everyone that she was not suited to the tribulations of George Street.'

'Do you have any idea why she fainted?'

Reverend Pearl frowned. 'I should imagine it was her brain's way of telling her she was incongruous.'

'How so?'

'People faint for a number of reasons, Sergeant. I knew a woman parishioner once who fainted whenever she smelt a rose. Not in *this* parish, you understand,' he added with a smile. 'Roses are in short supply in Scholes.'

Brennan raised his eyebrows in agreement.

'But there are those who faint because of an inability to cope with the situation they are faced with. And I think that was the case with Miss Gadsworth. She simply realised, after sampling the delights of Standard 6, that a Wigan school was not for her.'

'I was told she acquitted herself quite well for the most part.'

'Perhaps she saw glimpses of the devil lurking amongst them? Who knows?'

'You and Mr Weston later interviewed her?'

He shook his head sadly. 'According to Mr Weston, it was as if the light she had shown earlier, during her teaching, had been extinguished. She was almost monosyllabic in her responses and didn't do herself any favours at all. It was, sadly, an easy decision at the end.'

'She took it badly?'

'Oh there were tears just below the surface, I suspect. She thanked us and left in quite a hurry, as if she was desperate to be out of the place. Most curious.'

'As the school manager, sir, you have responsibility for the appointment of teachers?'

'Among other duties, yes.'

'So you would naturally receive the various letters of application?'

'Yes.'

'Might I see Miss Gadsworth's letter?'

Reverend Pearl shook his head. 'Alas, no, Sergeant. Once the decision was taken not to appoint, we destroyed it.'

Brennan looked crestfallen.

'Why do you need to see it, if I might ask?'

'Her address, sir. It's the only way we have of knowing where she lived. To inform her next of kin, you understand? And to examine her handwriting.'

'Handwriting? Why?'

'To compare it with the note beside the body.'

The vicar raised his eyes to Heaven. 'We are given self-discipline by God Himself, and when we cast that aside, why, we lose self-control and the devil takes over. It's always fascinated me that no one leaves a note explaining why they *haven't* committed suicide.' He closed his eyes for a moment, then opened them and stood up briskly. 'But I can give you her address, Sergeant. It was I myself who wrote back to her inviting her for interview. I have it in my desk.'

Brennan watched him walk over to the small bay window where an oval desk fitted snugly into the recess, the leather chair with its back to the windows. He opened a drawer and took out a single sheet of paper.

'Here it is. You may keep it, of course. I have no further need for it.'

He handed the sheet to Brennan who glanced at it – an address in Bolton – before folding it in two and placing it in his inside pocket.

'If there's nothing else, Sergeant?'

'No, sir. You've been very helpful.'

As they stood in the hallway, Reverend Pearl placed a friendly hand on his shoulder and said, 'The next time we meet, Sergeant, it's perfectly acceptable to address me as "Vicar". "Sir" makes me feel like a knight in shining armour!'

'I'll do that, sir,' Brennan replied unthinkingly.

Tommy Kelly had slouched back home, downcast and apprehensive, ignoring the wary greetings from those he passed who were making their way to any one of a number of local hostelries. He knew he'd have to face her sooner or later, and there was little point in his trudging round the streets of the town looking for Billy. He could be anywhere. Besides, it was growing dark now. Perhaps the little devil was already home, squatting down in front of the fire and gloating about where he'd been and what he'd been up to.

When he opened the front door, his heart lifted for a few seconds as he heard voices from the kitchen, but it sank almost immediately.

Edith was sitting in one chair with Dolly Marshall seated in the other across the small table. Both were drinking tea, and both glared at him as he approached.

''Ere 'e is, bloody useless lump. Empty-'anded, I see.'

'Dolly,' he mumbled with a nod in their visitor's direction. He turned round and was about to move back into the front room when his wife forestalled him.

'Oh no you don't. You'll stay in 'ere an' listen to what Dolly 'as to say.'

Despite himself, there was something in her tone that made him stop and face them both. 'What?'

It wasn't difficult to see where Dolly's son Joe – who was Billy's age – got his ferret-like looks from: she had teeth that stuck out a little too much, and small eyes either side of a sharp, pointed nose.

75

She gave a sniff and folded her arms, confident of his attention. 'Our Joe saw your Billy Friday night. Pushin' an' shovin' wi' Len Parkinson's lad like two turkey cocks.'

'Feytin'?' Tommy frowned. Was Billy lying injured somewhere?

'Aye. But our Joe reckons your Billy wouldn't 'ave 'im a do. Reckons your Billy just ran off.'

Tommy clenched his fists. 'My lad never run away from a feyt in 'is life.'

Edith Kelly felt it incumbent upon her to support her husband's judgement. 'I reckon your Joe might've got that runnin' away bit wrong.'

Dolly sniffed again. She was torn between her fear of Edith's temper and her desire to defend her son's veracity. She chose the latter. 'Not in the 'abit o' tellin' lies, our Joe.'

For once, Edith allowed the pursuit of facts to outweigh her lust for violence.

'Whether or not our Billy ran off – an' as Tommy says that's a bit bloody far-fetched, knowin' our Billy. But that's by-the-by. Fact is, your Joe saw 'im Friday night. Did 'e tell 'im or that Parkinson brat where he was off to?'

Dolly shook her head. 'Our Joe reckoned the two of 'em 'ad words right enough, but 'e couldn't make out what they said to each other. Then off he runs.'

'But where was he goin'?' Tommy's voice betrayed his growing sense of exasperation.

Dolly Marshall held out both hands palms upwards on the table like a card player with no hand left.

'Well where did 'e run off to? Which direction?'

'Up towards town, that's all our Joe said. So when I 'eard your

Billy were missin', I thought to meself, it might be summat you could tell t'police.'

'Police?' Tommy whispered the word. 'Why the 'ell should we tell them men? The lad's buggered off before now an' come back with his tail between his legs.'

Dolly shrugged. 'Your Billy's been missin' for four days.'

Edith looked at her husband. He could see a new expression in her eyes: fear.

Moses Reed had waited a long time to get *Septimus* filled to its limits. He'd stood on the canal bank alongside his son Bart, watched the pit lasses high above riddle through the coal to clear it of any dirt before tipping it into the screening chute, where it would slide its way down into the belly of the barge. There, he watched more pit lasses levelling the mounds of coal to spread the weight evenly. But the time they took! He'd shouted up at the supervisor, who cupped his ear against the crashing noise of the coal, then made a great show of taking out his fob watch and holding it up. The light was fast fading, and he was sorely looking forward to the first pint in the Woodhouse's.

'Might as well polish the bloody coal while they're at it!' he said to young Bart, who was busy feeding Goliath before their last pull of the day.

Still, once the base coal was levelled onto the boat, and a sufficient mound of coal built up to capacity weight, he signalled his relief with a less than cheery wave at the supervisor and a shrill whistle to his son waiting on the towpath with both hands on the harness. A sharp tug, and Goliath gave an angry snort, stamped his hooves on the cobbled stretch of the canal bank, and heaved his way forward. Once the barge had pulled away from the bankside and the towpath's surface changed from cobbles to dirt, enabling the spikes hammered into the horse's shoes to take a firm grip, the load became easier. He gave another snort, of satisfaction this time, as they set off down the Leeds–Liverpool Canal towards their destination on the outskirts of Wigan.

Occasionally, Bart would whisper words of encouragement to Goliath. Although he was only twelve years old, the boy had grown attached to the huge beast in the three years he'd been working with his dad on the barges. But even so, he'd seen a gradual deterioration in the horse's strength, manifesting itself in slower, more laborious progress, the occasional whinny of pain as the harness dug deep into his broad shoulders, and the look in his eyes sometimes – a pleading, heartrending expression of misery. When Bart had tried to explain all this to his dad, he'd been met with a single, dismissive comment of 'Bloody years left, yet. Bloody years.'

Still, he'd said nothing when Bart had persuaded his mother to sew together some cloth ears to protect Goliath from the clouds of flies that buzzed around the canal's surface during the hot summer months.

As they approached Pottery Bridge, near Poolstock, Bart brought the horse to a halt. The towpath dwindled to nothing beneath the bridge, and it was necessary to unshackle the horse until the barge was safely through the archway of the bridge and out on the other side, where it would be tied once more to its cumbersome load. Carefully, Bart unbuckled the harness and freed it from the rope linking it to the barge.

'Hurry up, young 'un!' Moses shouted, almost tasting the froth on his promised pint.

'Done!' came the reply. Bart led the horse up the narrow pathway, wincing as he saw it struggle to gain footholds on the steep slope of the path.

Once he saw the horse stand on the road's surface above him, Moses stepped onto the mound of coal and leant backwards until he was lying on top of the coal a matter of inches from the slime-ridden under-roof of the bridge. Then he raised his legs and began to heave against the roof, straining with all his might and forcing his legs to push the barge forward.

He'd done it a hundred times and more, but he always seemed to miss a couple of footholds at least as his clogs slipped against the treacherous brickwork. Eventually, though, he saw the orange glow of the evening sky emerge from the darkness of the bridge and sat up blowing hard, wiping his brow before clambering down the coal heap and standing once more at the stern of the barge.

Bart was waiting for him on the towpath which now widened again to accommodate the horse. He gave the lad a cheery wave.

'I'm spittin' feathers!' he shouted.

But his son stood stock-still, one hand on the horse's harness and staring back at the dark tunnel of the bridge as Moses grabbed the tow-rope and hurled it out to him.

'Wake up, young 'un!' he shouted.

Bart raised his free hand and pointed back, to where the barge had just emerged.

Moses followed the direction of his son's pointing finger. He gave a gasp.

A body was slowly drifting from the darkness of the tunnel, face down and arms stretched outwards, as if it had been trying desperately to reach the bank of the canal and had failed to do so.

CHAPTER FIVE

Len Parkinson worked as a dataller in the Douglas Bank Colliery, near Woodhouse Lane. He was paid a daily wage, unlike the contracted work of other men who laboured in the mines, and his job consisted of repairing roadways damaged by the coal tubs pushed along laden with coal. Occasionally he worked the night shift, and this morning, as he clambered out of the pit cage and shielded his eyes from the glare of the early morning sun, he looked forward as usual to the pint of porter his wife would have waiting for him, cooling in the shade of the alley wall where he lived in Frog Lane.

As he walked down from Woodhouse Lane, he saw a familiar figure making his way towards him. Under normal circumstances, he would greet him with a gruff wave and a guttural *Owdo*, but this morning felt anything but normal.

For one thing, Tommy Kelly started work at Cartwright's Mill at seven-thirty, and it was now just after half-six. For another,

Tommy lived in Diggle Street, and that was back towards Woodhouse Lane, the opposite direction from where the big bugger now approached. But the things that really roused Len Parkinson's curiosity, not to mention his concern, were the menacing gait, the ferocious scowl, and the two ham-sized fists that were now clenched and ready for action.

'What's up, Tommy owd lad?' he shouted as Kelly drew near.

Before he knew what was happening, he found himself rammed hard against the wall of a house with one rough hand gripping his throat and the other lifting him clean off the ground. With his coal-blackened face highlighting the whites of his eyes, he looked like a man who'd come face-to-face with a ghost. His snap tin rattled into the gutter.

'Tommy! . . . I cawn't . . . breathe.'

'What's 'e done wi' my lad?'

Kelly's voice sounded like the low, savage growl of a beast about to attack.

Parkinson swung his legs, trying to regain some footing to relieve the tremendous pressure on his throat. The grip merely tightened. He felt his head grow light, and his eyelids began to flicker.

Suddenly the pressure lifted and he dropped to the ground, doubling up and clutching at his bruised windpipe.

'Ast' gone soddin' mad?' he gasped when breath finally returned to his lungs.

'Dost want some more?'

He looked up. The man's huge frame was blocking the sun. He could see, further down the street, curtains move apart ever so slightly. A door opened, and someone emerged. Parkinson knew who it was.

'Tommy, I've not got a clue what tha're on about. What's who done with thi lad?'

'I got told thy Albert 'ad a do wi' my Billy Friday night.'

'Just young uns scrappin'.'

'Well my young un never came 'ome.'

Gauging it safe to stand, Parkinson reached forward to pick up his snap tin before facing his assailant.

'Look, all I know is they 'ad a bit of a do. Tha knows what them two's like, Tommy. Allus 'avin' a go. Our Albert said Billy ran off.' When he saw the big man clench his huge fists once more, he added hastily, 'But not cos 'e was scared or owt. Our Albert reckoned 'e was in hurry, like.'

Suddenly, Kelly felt something sharp pressing against his neck.

'Touch 'im again, ye big bastard, an' I'll stab thee to buggery.'

Tommy turned round, very slowly, and the point of the carving knife followed him, almost breaking the flesh. The woman facing him, gripping the knife firmly, was taller than most, with brown hair strewn wildly around her pinched face, and green eyes that glared with anger at the sight of her husband reduced to a cowering wreck.

'An' good mornin' to thee, Doreen, love.'

If he felt any fear he didn't show it. Rather, the presence of the knife at his throat served to calm him, but it was a very cold calm indeed. He looked directly into her eyes.

'I want a word wi' your Albert.'

'Oh aye?' she said, maintaining her grip on the knife handle.

'About our Billy.'

'What about 'im?'

''E's missin'. An' your Albert might know summat.'

At that moment, a voice from across the street yelled out, 'Mam? What's up?'

Doreen Parkinson diverted her eyes for a second at the sudden sound of her son Albert's voice, but it was time enough for Tommy to make a grab for the knife. She winced as the huge fist forced the knife from her fingers and then pushed her towards her husband. Now he had control, Tommy turned to Len Parkinson, and said, 'We'd best go an' speak to the lad, eh, Len? Find out what's what.'

A few minutes later, the three of them were seated around the kitchen table, steaming mugs of tea in their hands, with Albert Parkinson standing with his back to the window, ashen-faced.

'You sure that's what our Billy said?'

'I am. Said 'e'd done a bad thing an' he didn't want to be hanged for it.'

'Hanged for what though?' Tommy asked, the fire inside his belly now replaced by a slow, pervasive chill.

Albert shrugged. 'That's what I asked but 'e just said I was to keep me trap shut.'

Doreen Parkinson watched the steam rise from her mug. She'd always said the Kellys were a washout. Perhaps after this folk would listen.

Later, that Tuesday morning, although the sun was shining and birds were cooing on the rooftop of the town hall, which incorporated the police station, Detective Sergeant Brennan's mood could hardly be characterised as summery. His first quest of the day was a meeting with his chief constable, Captain Bell, during which he was to request permission to travel beyond the borough boundaries to interview Mr Henry Tollet, the school inspector who lived in Blackburn. The request would be met, he knew, with at least two obstacles he needed to surmount: one would be the inconvenience of the chief constable sending a telegram of courtesy informing his counterpart in the Blackburn Borough Police Force that one of his detectives would be making inquiries in the town. The second objection would be merely a repetition of the previous day's conversation, that to continue the investigation into Dorothea Gadsworth's death would be a waste of his time, that it was obvious the poor wretch had taken her own life after the disappointment of failing to gain the teaching post.

Jaggery was waiting for Brennan on the station steps. He knew better than to engage him in any sort of social chat, going from the expression on his face, so the two of them entered the station in silence. A giant of a man in rough working clothes was standing at the front desk, hands on hips, and glaring at the uniformed desk sergeant.

'I told you,' the sergeant was saying, 'I've taken down all the details and we'll see what we can do.'

'Tha'll not find my lad sat there on thi arse!' was the man's rejoinder.

'I'll mention it to my constables before they go on their beat, Mr Kelly. That's what we do when a child goes missing.'

'Well I reckon it's that bloody school what's made the little sod run off.'

'You've already said, Mr Kelly.' The desk sergeant gave Brennan a weary gaze. 'But schools have to punish them if they don't follow the rules. It's like everything else. We need rules.'

'Well I'll bloody rule 'em if I go down there! I'm already late for me shift, else I'd go down yonder an' see if they fancy canin' *my* arse.'

Tommy Kelly slammed a large fist on the desk, rattling the inkstand and causing the papers to rise and flutter as if a sudden breeze had caught them. Then he turned and stormed through the door, giving both Brennan and Jaggery a murderous scowl and a valedictory, 'Shithouses!'

Jaggery, never one to ignore an insult, took steps to accost the man, but Brennan grabbed his arm.

'We've work to do,' he said before approaching the desk sergeant. 'What was all that about?'

The sergeant nodded at the door behind him. 'Tommy Kelly. His lad's gone missin'. Only it's not the first time an' it won't be the last. Not exactly home sweet home, if you get me meanin', Mick.'

Brennan gave a wry smile. Sometimes, when the feelings in a house reach boiling point, the children either take the blows or get out of the way. Every week in the police courts next door, cases of casual brutality against either the wife or the children – or both – made a predictable and mournful appearance.

The sergeant consulted what few notes he'd written down. 'Reckons his teachers made his life a misery. I'd say it was t'other road round, but anyway. Meladdo yonder reckons his son's buggered off on account of the punishments. Apparently the little sod's had a few last week. Still, can't be too difficult to find him. He's got red hair for a start. Not many red-headed runaways knockin' about!'

Brennan returned the man's smile and glanced at Jaggery, who gave a non-committal shrug.

At that moment, he felt a hand clap him on the shoulder.

'Sergeant Brennan. I was about to take my morning stroll around the town. Would you be so good as to accompany me?'

Captain Bell, resplendent in his uniform replete with helmet, stood there with an incongruously ingratiating smile across his face.

What the bloody hell is all this? Brennan thought before replying, 'Of course, sir. A pleasure.'

Jaggery saluted his chief constable and headed for the station canteen.

It had been a difficult morning.

The previous day had been an exciting one for the children, there was no denying. They'd found out within minutes the reason for being forced to remain in their respective playgrounds, and they'd spent the rest of the day – once they were allowed back into the building – in an excitable and silly mood, making classroom control quite a task. Today, though – Tuesday – their mood had if anything intensified.

Several of the boys swore they'd seen a woman's ghost passing their classroom, and every creak of the floorboards, every shifting and settling of coals in the classroom stove, every blast of wind against the windows was given a supernatural provenance. Some of the girls began snivelling, especially when Albert Parkinson told them the ghost was after fresh blood now and would be waiting in the girls' playground to get it.

As a consequence, Richard Weston's entire morning had been taken up with disciplinary measures of one kind or another as pupil after pupil was marched into his study and a whole catalogue of misdemeanours recited before the inevitable clearing of accounts.

Now, as the screams and yells from outside informed the casual passer-by, even if he or she were blind, that the children were let loose for playtime, the headmaster sat back in his chair and gazed at the ceiling. He had yet another unpleasant task to perform, and this time pupils were not involved.

'Of course you know what the problem is?' he asked Nathaniel

Edgar who sat facing him with a mug of steaming tea before him.

'They're overwrought?'

Weston laughed, a harsh, rueful sound. 'Parents,' he snapped. 'They're the problem. You can bet they pumped their little angels dry for any salacious detail they could salivate over. Then the fathers could repair to the nearest alehouse and contribute their own little ha'porth of garnered tittle-tattle to the intimate seminars that would have been held the length and breadth of the town. And instead of reading their little dears a bedtime story from the *Arabian Nights*, they'd have urged them to dig and dig for anything else for the whole of today to satisfy their ghoulishness.'

Edgar chuckled. 'It's called human nature, Richard. You can't do anything to hold back the waves of curiosity.'

While not appreciating the veiled allusion to Canute, he accepted the truth of the observation.

'It's not enough having Her Majesty's Inspector turn up and probe into our workings; now we'll have the whole of the town keeping an eye on us, waving the finger of speculation. The wretched woman took her own life. How could that have been prevented?'

It was a rhetorical question, and Edgar responded by lifting the mug to his lips.

Suddenly the headmaster's brow darkened, his tone sombre. 'You know why I asked to see you, Nat?'

Edgar shuffled uncomfortably in his chair. He said nothing.

Then, just as Weston was about to continue, there was a timid knock on the door.

'Enter!' Weston shouted.

The pupil-teacher, Emily Mason, came in. When she saw Nathaniel Edgar sitting there, she flushed a deep scarlet. 'Oh, I'm sorry, Headmaster, I . . . I'll come back later.'

A flicker of annoyance swept across Weston's face, but it was immediately replaced by a professional smile. He stood up. 'Nonsense, Miss Mason. The daily review of your teaching notes. I completely forgot, what with . . . At any rate, Mr Edgar here was just about to leave. We'll discuss that matter further later,' he said with another smile.

Nathaniel Edgar gave a nervous swallow but accepted the hint gracefully, bowing elaborately at the girl he used to teach before leaving the study, closing the door ever so gently as he did so.

He knew very well what the headmaster had been about to say.

For a while, the two of them didn't speak. Rather, Captain Bell spent time acknowledging the greetings of shopkeepers and passers-by as they strolled along King Street towards Wallgate. The sun was shining, and Brennan thought of the contrast with the previous year, the hardships of the miners' strike, the bitter cold of November, and the scowls that greeted each policeman, seen then as the extended arm of the colliery owners. A perception he, personally, found abhorrent.

He caught sight of a couple of beggars loitering outside the premises of William Daniel, Saddler and Harness Manufacturer, with hands thrust outwards whenever someone passed them by. *Shrewd location for begging*, thought Brennan, as Daniel's carriage trade would be rather more prosperous than those frequenting the pawn shop further along. They took one look at the splendour of his companion's uniform, its silver buttons gleaming in the morning sunshine, and made an instant decision to seek out newer, less menacing pastures. Captain Bell raised his baton and pointed it in their direction.

'Vermin of the worst sort,' he said.

'Yes, sir.'

'Remember those we caught last year? At the height – or should I say depths? – of the strike? Devils going round with handcarts begging loaves of bread from shopkeepers, only to turn the corner and set up a stall themselves, undercutting the very people who'd just shown them Christian charity? An obscenity, Sergeant.'

'Yes, sir.'

'I've *seen* beggars, Sergeant. Genuine beggars in the narrow, stifling lanes of Benares, on the banks of the Ganges. Dreadful, sweltering place. "The City of Trampled Flowers", they call it. And rubbing shoulders – quite literally, I might add – with the fakirs and the ascetics with faces and hair rubbed white with ashes, are the beggars. Blind, lame, stinking creatures, many of them ridden with leprosy. Those are beggars, Sergeant. Not that filth over yonder.'

Finally, as they headed right towards Market Place, the chief constable broke the silence.

'I think you were right, Sergeant.'

Brennan blinked. Had he heard right?

'About what, sir?'

Captain Bell watched a tram shuttle its way past them up the incline to Market Place. Several of the passengers gave him hostile looks.

'This affair at George Street Elementary. You had doubts about the poor woman committing suicide.'

'Yes, sir.'

'Well then. You must pursue the matter with your usual tenacity.'

'Of course.' He wondered what had brought about this change of heart.

He soon got his answer.

'A report came in this morning. A body was fished out of the canal in Poolstock last night. It seems to have a connection, at least, with that school. And I am well aware that you are no great believer in coincidences.'

For some reason, Brennan thought of the giant of a man he'd seen haranguing the desk sergeant only a few minutes ago, demanding an immediate search for his missing son.

'And what is the connection, sir?' he asked.

Captain Bell heaved out his chest and watched the passengers emerging from the tram that had stopped ahead of them. 'According to a heavily soaked visiting card discovered on his person, the body was that of a Mr Henry Tollet. I believe he was a school inspector who attended George Street Elementary last Friday.'

CHAPTER SIX

'Well there's one thing, Sergeant.'

'Oh, and what's that?'

Constable Jaggery, hastening to keep up with his sergeant's urgent pace and giving each nurse he passed along the corridor a friendly smile, said, 'At least you don't have to go all the way over to Blackburn to interview this Tollet bloke.'

'I can do it right here in the infirmary, is that what you mean, Constable? While he's lying face up on a mortuary slab? Very thoughtful of him. Doubt I'll get much out of him, though.'

Even Jaggery accepted the impossibility of such a course of action.

'Aye, it's a bugger.'

As they passed the Idiot Ward they heard someone scream, a long piercing sound that ended in a sobbing whimper.

'They should keep that lot chained up,' Jaggery said with a nod in the ward's direction. 'Bloody nurses deserve a medal.'

Brennan said nothing. He was more concerned with what Dr Monroe was about to tell him concerning the post-mortems he had just completed on the bodies of Dorothea Gadsworth and Henry Tollet. Captain Bell had apparently pressed the good doctor to treat both as a matter of great urgency, and for once Brennan was glad that his superior had seen fit to throw his weight around.

Captain Bell was right – he had no time for coincidences, and he harboured a deep suspicion that the answer lay with George Street Elementary School, with things he had yet to discover. But he was like his bricklayer father in reverse, he told himself as they entered another long corridor which led to the mortuary downstairs. His da spent all his working life placing one brick on another until the structure was complete; he, on the other hand, spent his time dismantling the lies and the facades others had built until there was nothing left but the foundations.

'Demolition, Constable,' he said with a cryptic smile at his nonplussed companion.

Jaggery, who knew better than to question such bizarre utterances, slowed down at the top of the steps leading down to the mortuary. 'I'll stay up 'ere, Sergeant. On guard, like.'

Brennan knew how much the big man disliked the sight of eviscerated bodies on a slab.

'I'll be back soon,' he said as if he were addressing a child on the steps of a drinking den.

'Don't be afraid, it's me.'

He blinked, his eyes struggling to get used to the glare from the oil lamp which now illuminated the small cellar. He saw the flaking plaster and the uneven brickwork that lay beneath. When he'd first been brought down here, *for his own good*, he'd had the lamp lit for ages and it had given off a sharp, not unpleasant smell as the oil burnt in its brass base. He'd spent some time, once he was assured of his safety, trying to work out patterns in the flaking plasterwork – he'd seen a dog there, sitting on its hind legs and begging, but when he reached out to pluck away at an incongruous piece, a more sizeable chunk fell away and beheaded the dog. Then he saw it with different eyes, and it had become a stormy sea – or what he imagined a stormy sea would look like – with sharp-crested waves soaring up to a darkening sky of damp.

He was handed a couple of biscuits, which he devoured greedily. He couldn't remember the last time he'd had something hot. '*But maybe next time?*' he asked and was reassured by a determined nod.

But the lamp had to be removed – '*in case anyone sees the smoke,*' he'd been told. '*We don't want that, do we?*'

No, we bloody well don't, he thought. It had been made very clear to him what would happen if anyone found out exactly where he was. No, after all that business on Friday night, he'd cop it good and proper and no mistake.

So the lamp went and for hours he was left in darkness.

Which didn't bother him one bit, him being ten and all.

'In the order of their demise, then?'

There was a sombre tone to Dr Donald Monroe's voice. He and Brennan stood in the centre of the examination room, where two bodies draped in white sheets lay a few feet from each other. Monroe had been house surgeon at the Royal Albert Edward Infirmary for sixteen years, and he was a highly respected figure in the community. Brennan found him rather cold at times like this, however, and he'd never got used to the man's subdued, doleful manner. He was more accustomed to the brash openness of the people he encountered in the normal run of things: the obscenities, the volley of abuse he endured on occasion, all had that raw spark of life in them that this man lacked. He could never imagine Dr Donald Monroe slapping his thigh and roaring out a 'Come All Ye' at a wedding or a wake for that matter.

Still, he was damned good at his job.

'If that's convenient, Doctor,' Brennan said and stood back as Monroe reached out and drew away the white sheet on the first of his two corpses: Dorothea Gadsworth.

'Convenient isn't the word I'd use, Sergeant Brennan. Alexander Bell presumes too much. It's not really convenient to have two possible murders filling my time when I have a wealth – if that's the right word – of cases from smallpox to cholera to deal with upstairs with the, as yet, living.'

'I do apologise,' said Brennan with some asperity.

'Hmm. Well now, this young lady.'

Brennan saw the girl's pained features once again. She had been quite a pretty thing. The smoothness of her cheeks and the delicacy of her nose and forehead delineated an innocence, too, that made him feel anger rising along with the bile.

Monroe held his hand above the face. Brennan had seen a stage magician perform the same action just before levitating his assistant. He admonished himself for the incongruous memory.

'You'll notice the cyanosis – the blue colouring of the skin – which is an indicator of arsenical poisoning.' He leant over her face and pulled open the jaw to expose her tongue. 'And the furring on the tongue, again a sign.' He gently closed the jaw and replaced the white sheet with reverential care. He gave a nod in the direction of a large metal bowl resting on a table by the wall, a cloth covering its surface.

Brennan swallowed hard. He knew what lay beneath the cloth.

'But of course it's in the contents of the stomach and the lining of the stomach that we find more conclusive proof. The lining was ulcerated and inflamed, and a substantial amount of arsenic was found in what remained in the stomach after the poor girl had vomited.'

'There was a bottle of Scotch found beside the body, Doctor. Only the dregs left.'

'Ah, yes. The bottle of whisky you sent me. Brown's, I believe.' He moved over to a small cupboard above the table and opened it, pulling out the same bottle that Jaggery had found in the classroom. 'I've examined the *dregs*, as you put it. Not something I personally would imbibe.'

'I should hope not.'

'Oh, not for the reason you're thinking, Sergeant. No, Brown's isn't to my particular taste. That's all. But there's nothing adulterated in this sediment.' He gave the bottle a swirl and Brennan watched the small amount of amber liquid cloud and settle once more.

'There's no arsenic in there?'

'None whatsoever.'

'And her stomach?'

'Large traces of yellow sulphide of arsenic. Produced during the process of putrefaction.'

Brennan watched as Monroe replaced the whisky in the cupboard. 'I must have got it wrong, then. I presumed she'd been poisoned by someone. I'd presumed she'd been given the poison in the drink – I know arsenic is almost tasteless so . . .' He screwed up his face in an effort to think clearly. 'Are you saying there was no whisky in her stomach?'

'None whatsoever.'

'But if it wasn't in the whisky . . . what else was there? I mean she's hardly likely to take arsenic on its own, is she?'

A rare smile almost flickered across Monroe's face.

'The arsenic was in the tea.'

'Tea?'

'This poor wee lass had taken a cup of tea with the arsenic. As you say, there wouldn't be much of a taste.'

'So she could have drunk the tea elsewhere? Before finding herself in the classroom?'

Monroe shook his head. 'Hardly likely. The impact of such a dosage would have been almost immediate. Not death at that stage, but immense suffering, vomiting, severe cramping. My guess – an educated one, mind – is that she could have suffered for a few hours before death finally brought relief.'

If she had locked herself in, thought Brennan, then why on earth didn't she unlock the door and seek help? Even if she had planned to kill herself, surely the intense agony of the poisoning would have compelled her to seek help from somewhere?

Unless she had no way of unlocking the door.

Furthermore, if Dorothea Gadsworth took the arsenic in her tea, then where was the cup? They'd seen nothing of a teacup in the classroom. Only the Scotch.

So what was the Scotch doing there?

The absence of the teacup meant that it had been removed after she drank from it. But if what Dr Monroe says is true she would have been incapable of removing it from the room herself, then returning and calmly locking the door so she could endure a long and agonising death.

Had the headmaster removed the teacup as well as the bottle? He'd make sure of asking him.

'And now for the male of the species.'

Dr Monroe stepped over to the draped form beside Dorothea Gadsworth. He removed the white sheet and stood back, allowing Brennan a good view of the deceased.

Henry Tollet, he saw, was a rather portentous individual. His jowls sagged onto his neck which was quite thick. He sported a close-cropped beard that contained specks of grey, and there were small areas of a slight redness dotted around his cheeks.

'This poor fellow drowned,' said Monroe. 'The face, as you can see, is quite calm. His tongue is swollen, as you can also see.' He had opened the man's mouth and Brennan could clearly see the swollen object flecked with tiny spots of foam.

'He wasn't attacked, then?'

'I didn't say that, did I, Sergeant? I said he drowned. But if you look here . . .' He pulled the sheet further back to expose the man's hands. Along the knuckles were irregular indentations, some of them deeply embedded in the flesh.

A sudden image shaped itself in Brennan's mind: Tollet, scrambling to heave himself from the canal. His assailant bending down and slashing at his hands with some object, possibly a heavy stone, or standing above him and stamping down hard with a clog or a boot, anything to prevent the poor fellow from dragging himself onto the canal bank and safety.

'He drowned, right enough, Sergeant. The lungs were distended and there was a considerable amount of water in his stomach, although with deeply submerged victims that isn't evidence of drowning in itself. There was froth in the mouth and nostrils. And you can see here, beneath the fingernails, traces of mud and minuscule fragments of plant life. He must have struggled very desperately to live. These wounds would seem to suggest an external force applied to keep him in the water, unless the damage was done by himself in some strange way – slamming his hands repeatedly against some hard object, for instance. It isn't very likely. But perhaps that kind of speculation belongs more properly to your sphere of expertise, eh, Sergeant?'

Brennan nodded and watched the sheet draped across the body of the school inspector once more. 'I don't like coincidences,' he said in a low voice.

'I beg your pardon?'

'Oh, nothing. Just thinking aloud.'

'There's what we found in his pockets.' Monroe was pointing to a small wooden box on a table at the other side of the room.

Brennan went over and lifted out the still-sodden contents: a leather wallet, a return railway ticket from Blackburn, and a monogrammed handkerchief. He flicked open the wallet and saw a few banknotes, several business cards he'd undoubtedly picked up on his travels, a booking receipt for the Royal Hotel, Wigan and a silver cigarette case whose contents had been ruined by the waters of the Leeds–Liverpool.

'Crocodile skin, if I'm not mistaken,' said Monroe who was now standing beside him, indicating the wallet. 'And the lining is calf skin.'

'Thank you, Doctor. I can't tell you how much that information will help me.'

Monroe's response to the sarcasm was a rare smile.

Brennan then formally thanked the doctor for his work and left the room.

'Ain't that the headmaster, Sergeant?' Jaggery asked as they walked up the slope of Standishgate towards the Royal Hotel.

Brennan saw in the distance a man walk quickly away from the steps of the Royal and turn to his left. The street was quite crowded, and the two of them lost sight of the figure as it moved quickly across the path of a passing tram and entered the Makinson Arcade.

'Looked like him, to be sure,' Brennan replied.

Once inside, they met the manager of the Royal Hotel, Mr James Eastoe, a small, dapper individual with a genial disposition. He was visibly shocked when told of the death of one of his guests, and led them to the room on the first floor where Henry Tollet had booked in for five days. Brennan gave him a sharp look.

'*Five days?* You sure?'

'The booking register does not lie, Sergeant,' he snapped back, his competence offended.

Various questions buzzed around Brennan's head.

Why didn't Weston tell me he was staying here?

Why give me his home address in Blackburn?

And what was Weston doing here not five minutes ago?

'Such a shock, a very great shock indeed. You don't expect your guests to be found in such a way. A very pleasant man,' said Eastoe as he unlocked the door. 'He arrived on Thursday evening and told me he was a school inspector here to look at two of our schools. One on Friday and one early this week. He said it gave him the opportunity to get out of – what did he call it? – the clang and the clamour of Blackburn. That's where he comes from, of course. As I say, a most pleasant guest.'

Brennan and Jaggery entered.

The room was overlooking Standishgate and the row of shops leading down the slope. The bed was unslept in, and the large wardrobe contained a few items of clothing, including a suit which he was doubtless planning to wear for the visit to his next school. Resting on the floor inside the wardrobe was a small tan leather briefcase, its flap-over buckles hanging loose and unfastened. Inside, Brennan found a sheath of notes pertaining to *George Street Elementary School – Inspectorial Visit 21st Sept. 1894.* A few sheets were clipped together under various printed headings: *Curriculum [including provision for physical exercise]; Discipline; Lessons Observed; School Attendance and Punctuality.* The last sheet of all had a heading different from the others: it was handwritten, and said mysteriously, *Reported Matters.* Beneath was a large question mark, but there was nothing else on the page. Brennan checked that the handwriting was the same as on the other sheets, which seemed to be filled with handwritten notes under each of the four headings. He placed all the sheets back into the briefcase, fastened it and handed it to Jaggery.

He then turned to the manager and said, 'Did Mr Tollet have any visitors?'

Eastoe thought for a while then shook his head. 'He only dined here three times, Sergeant. Thursday evening, Friday morning and Friday evening. His key was unclaimed on Friday night after he went out and it has remained on its hook behind the reception desk ever since. Unless, of course, you count Mr Weston.'

'The headmaster?'

'You've just missed him. He came to enquire about our guest, too.'

'What did he say?'

'He simply asked to see Mr Tollet and I told him he hadn't been seen since Friday night. He then left.'

'I see.'

Brennan exchanged a glance with Jaggery who gave a non-committal shrug.

'You say Mr Tollet went out on Friday night after he dined?'

'Yes. He hadn't long left the dining room to return to his room. He said he had some important documents to complete. Then someone left a message for him at reception and he seemed a little disturbed by it, so he left his key and went out. Hardly time to digest his roast beef and Yorkshires.'

'What was the message?'

Eastoe gave a professional frown. 'At the Royal we're not in the habit of reading personal mail of any description.'

A pity, thought Brennan.

The room held nothing of further interest. Brennan fastened the briefcase and tucked it under his arm. Eastoe seemed about to object then realised the futility of the exercise. His guest was dead, and Sergeant Brennan didn't appear to be the sort of man who would take any notice of hotel protocol anyway.

A cursory meeting with the curmudgeonly old man on reception told him nothing more: the note for Mr Tollet was left in an envelope on the front desk on Friday night when he was in the back office. No, he hadn't seen who'd left it and what did it matter anyway?

'I don't know what the world's comin' to, Sergeant.'

Brennan stood to one side as the pupils of George Street Elementary School swept through the school gates. As they whooped and yelled their way along the street, occasioning curses from a rag-and-bone man who was compelled to pull hard on the reins of his horse to avoid trampling a snotty-nosed child with its iron hooves, Brennan remembered well that feeling of elation, of freedom, albeit temporary, from the strictures and the scowls and the painful punishments they all endured.

'They're just letting off steam, Constable. Don't you remember what home time was like?'

Constable Jaggery frowned. 'But I weren't on about that lot,' he said with a finger pointed at the vanishing hordes. 'I were talkin' about meladdo in yonder.'

Brennan, accustomed by now to his constable's reluctance to give people their proper name or title, understood. 'You mean Mr Weston?'

'Aye. If 'is lordship's buggered about wi' cups o' tea t'same road 'e buggered about wi' bottles o' Scotch . . .'

'What indeed is the world coming to, eh, Constable?'

'Exactly, Sergeant.'

'Well, we'll soon find out.'

Now the children had vanished completely, Brennan led the way inside. As they walked along the corridor towards the headmaster's study, they caught a glimpse of Nathaniel Edgar, the teacher responsible for Standard 5, who was in the process of leaving the classroom. He looked surprised to see them.

'Sergeant Brennan? Are you here to see the headmaster, by any chance?'

'We are.'

'Then I'm afraid you're out of luck. He had to leave early this afternoon.'

'Oh? And why is that, may I ask?'

'We had a visit this morning from the headmaster at St Matthew's in Pemberton. Apparently Mr Tollet was due to pay them an inspectorial visit first thing this morning and he failed to turn up. As Mr Cumberland – that's the headmaster at St Matthew's – knew Mr Tollet was here last week he felt it his duty to seek the fellow out. Find out why he hadn't arrived. Mr Weston said he would look into it as a matter of courtesy. Mr Tollet is staying at the Royal Hotel, so I'm told, and the headmaster took himself off there. I do hope the fellow hasn't taken ill?'

Jaggery was about to say something but Brennan gave him a scowl.

'In that case I'd like to see Mr Prendergast. Your caretaker.'

If Edgar was surprised he didn't show it. He merely said, 'I'd be delighted to escort you. Please. Follow me.'

Once he'd taken them to the cellar beneath the main body of the school, he pointed out the caretaker at the far side, shovelling spadefuls of coal into a tidy heap. Then he left.

Before Brennan could take a step towards him, however, Constable Jaggery tugged at his sleeve.

'What is it, Constable?'

'Did you smell it, Sergeant?'

Brennan nodded. 'Yes, Constable. I smelt it.'

He must have dropped off to sleep. The screams from the street above woke him and he saw dim shadows flicker across the cellar ceiling. During the day the darkness wasn't total, and he could see different shapes shuffle past the tiny grid in the ceiling. But the screams were of those his age. It was too muffled to make out individual words or phrases, but he could tell they were running along the street, probably chasing someone – or being chased.

Never mind, he told himself.

I'm safe down here. As long as I stay here and don't let anyone know, I'll be safe. That's what I was told.

There were too many folk after him, ready to kill him. His dad, for one. His mam, for another. And worst of all the police. If they knew what he'd done, he'd be hanged.

But he had a saviour who'd promised to look after him. Which was a bloody big surprise all right, he told himself. There was something comforting in that, and the way the darkness wrapped itself around him like a blanket, keeping him safe and invisible where no bugger could get him.

The yells were already fading. From far off, he heard the rattle and hiss of a tram as it chugged its way along. Then the sounds settled.

If only he could have something warm to eat.

But his food wouldn't be long, he told himself.

'I could eat a flock bed,' he said aloud, echoing something he'd heard his dad say. Though he hadn't a clue what it meant.

'Didn't see a cup o' tea, no,' said the caretaker firmly. 'Didn't see anythin' other than what I told you. Bottle o' Scotch.'

The three of them were standing in the doorway that led to the cellar.

Brennan looked thoughtful. 'Was there anywhere in the school she might have drunk some tea – a canteen perhaps? The staffroom? The headmaster's study?'

Prendergast shrugged. 'Possible. But I can tell you this. There were no cup o' tea left hangin' around. I keep the place clean.'

'What about arsenic? Do you have any rat poison, for instance?'

The caretaker looked uneasy. He gave Constable Jaggery, who was standing by the door, a nervous glance before stepping back from Brennan and sweeping an arm around the cellar. 'All schools have rats. Not far from water round 'ere, are we? Stands to reason we get the little sods.'

'So you keep rat poison?' Brennan asked with dogged insistence.

'Aye. It's kept well away from pryin' eyes an' 'ands, though.'

'Where?'

With a melancholy shake of the head, he moved over to a cupboard opposite the door they'd entered by. He stretched out a hand and tugged at one of the two handles. The left-hand door swung open with a creak, displaying a row of boxes and bottles.

'You don't keep it locked?'

He nodded back towards the cellar door. 'That door's always locked. No bugger gets in but me.'

Brennan stepped forward and peered inside the cupboard. He saw at once a dark brown bottle with the label clearly marked: Barker's Rat Poison; Danger – Arsenic. Carefully he lifted it from the cupboard and examined it. 'Perhaps someone did get in, Mr Prendergast.'

But the caretaker shook his head. 'Who's to say whoever did for the girl didn't bring the poison with 'em?'

Brennan replaced the bottle and shook his head. 'You're absolutely right, of course.' He watched as the caretaker closed the cupboard door. 'You said last time we spoke that you suspected someone had been trying to build a fire in here. You found pieces of wood.'

'Aye. I did. But as I told you the headmaster said I was imaginin' things. Told me to keep the place tidier in future. But I saw what I saw.'

'I'm sure you did. Do you think it could have been any of the children who got in?'

Constable Jaggery, who for once saw the trap his sergeant had sprung, gave a triumphant snort. For the first time the caretaker hesitated. If he were to pursue that particular line, he'd be directly contradicting what he'd just assured Brennan – that the place was always kept locked.

'See up yonder?' He pointed to a small trapdoor that was level with the playground outside. 'If anyone got in, it was through that door. There's a lock on it but it wouldn't keep out a mouse. Or a rat,' he added in an attempt at humour.

'Then why not fix the bugger?' asked Constable Jaggery.

'Because Mr Weston and the good Reverend won't give me the money to buy the right sort of lock for it. They cost money, them sort o' locks do.'

'But there was no actual fire?'

Prendergast laughed. 'If there 'ad been, this place would've gone up like a bonfire. All this coal. These wooden beams. But no, it'd take a heck of a lot of flames to set this lot off. Coal doesn't burn straight off now, does it?'

Once they left the building, Brennan and Jaggery walked in silence for a while. It was Jaggery who spoke first.

'I reckon meladdo likes a tot.'

It took Brennan a few seconds to realise that his constable was referring not to the caretaker whom they'd just left, but the teacher they'd met when they arrived at the school: Nathaniel Edgar.

'I mean, his breath reeked of it, Sergeant. Ain't that against the law or somethin'? Buggered if we can drink on duty so why can teachers, eh?'

'It seems Mr Nathaniel Edgar might require some sustenance to get him through the day.'

Jaggery was about to protest at the basic unfairness of that, especially as far as policemen were concerned, when Brennan spoke again.

'Interesting, though, that the headmaster thought fit to hide the bottle of Scotch from view before we saw the body. And here we are, smelling stale whisky on Mr Edgar's breath. I wonder if there's a connection?'

Before Jaggery could add a comment, Brennan had increased his pace, and the big man had to move as swiftly as he could to keep up with him, a strain on his lungs under normal circumstances, but when his sergeant uttered the word 'Crofter's' the air seemed to taste sweeter, more promising.

It was over a year since Nathaniel Edgar's wife had left him, gradually worn down not only by his drinking – which had grown progressively worse – but by the ever-growing distance between them, often expressed through his condescension.

'I'm not one of your pupils!' she would say whenever they had words and she failed to come round to his way of thinking. He'd tried his best, though, but somehow, it seemed that as their rows grew more frequent, the more he sought out the comfort of the local bowling club, where members could sit and converse and be hearty without the glowering presence of women. He was by nature a sociable creature, and the other members liked him. Free from the oppression of home, he felt liberated and able to share the earthier humour of his fellow bowlers who never seemed to do much bowling. But each night, he felt that familiar sinking sensation in his gut as soon as he turned the corner of his street, knowing full well she would be lying in bed pretending to be asleep. Pretence, that's what they had been reduced to. So he would sit in the armchair before the dying embers and sip at his Scotch, and very often wake in the early hours feeling cold and wretched.

There were times when his life *was* illuminated, and not by drink either, but those occasions were becoming more infrequent now, especially since he'd refused to acquiesce fully to what was being demanded of him.

You lack courage! he'd been told.

Maybe so. But at least he could still hold his head high. And he thanked God that the truth had never come out. That would have destroyed everything.

Richard Weston had saved him.

One morning, a few days after his wife had left for good, Richard caught him slumped across his desk with Standard 5 in riotous mood. He silenced them, waking Edgar in the process. Later, in the confines of his study, Weston listened with genuine concern as he unburdened himself for the first time.

'If Reverend Pearl or any member of the school board hear of this, Nat, you realise you will be instantly dismissed?'

'And I'd deserve to be.'

'The good reverend has decided views on drink, decided views on any human weakness.'

'He's a God-fearing man, right enough. I know full well his views on Sin. He shares them every Sunday.'

'But you're an excellent teacher, Nat. That would be the sin – losing you. We've worked together for too long to throw everything away without a fight. If you can make me a solemn promise to repair the damage you've done today. To repair the damage to yourself . . .'

'Then you won't report this?'

The headmaster shook his head. 'I shall tell Standard 5 you are suffering from an illness.'

Edgar gave a bitter laugh. 'Well at least they'd recognise the symptoms. It's an illness shared with most of their fathers.'

Despite appearances to the contrary, Richard Weston was at heart a good man. If he had acted according to the rules, Nathaniel Edgar would have been out on his ear. More than likely he'd have been staggering around the streets of Wigan begging – or worse, leaping into the all-embracing chill of the canal.

The memory of that time, of that conversation, came back to him now.

That damn bottle!

It was foolish, bringing it to school in the first place. A gross error of judgement. And he had fully expected the headmaster to throw his hands in the air and surrender to the inevitable course of action he should follow. But no. When he returned from the school in Pemberton Richard Weston once again spoke to him with an almost fatherly concern, although they were both around the same age.

'I see no reason to let the police know why it was on the premises at all,' he'd said. 'As far as they are aware, it was brought into the building by that poor girl as a means of despatching herself along with the poison she took. But this really does have to be the last time, Nat. It really does. That fine line between respectability and ruin is growing thinner all the time.'

He nodded gratefully and made another solemn promise.

What Richard Weston's response would have been if he knew about the other thing – and what *she* had encouraged him to do – he shuddered to think. That was better left in the past where it belonged. He was just grateful that the man was in ignorance of one weakness, at least.

The Crofter's Arms, on Market Street, was a popular drinking place, its town centre location rendering it satisfyingly convenient for a number of people. Office workers, shop assistants and market stall holders rubbed shoulders with pitmen and foundry workers; not literally, though – the latter two would be found in the vault with its sawdust-covered floor rather than the optimistically named and carpeted 'Lounge', where the more suitably attired would repair for an early evening *livener*.

It was in the lounge that Brennan had found a table by the window, allowing Constable Jaggery, now divested of his uniform and in his civilian clothes, to make his considerable presence felt at the bar and return promptly with two frothing pints of Walker's Bitter.

'Just what I needed, Sergeant,' said Jaggery, wiping the froth from his mouth.

Brennan, having quaffed a sizeable amount, sat back and breathed out. 'What do you think, Constable? We've got a young woman failing to get a teaching post, found poisoned by arsenic two days later in the very room where she taught a class of Wigan's finest.'

Jaggery snorted, unaware of his sergeant's ironic tone.

'There's an almost empty bottle of whisky placed beside her but there was no whisky found in her stomach. What *was* found in her stomach – apart from the large quantity of arsenic, of course – was tea, but there was no cup beside the body. That's a bit of a mystery, eh?'

'It's bloody impossible, Sergeant, if you ask me. You say Doctor Monroe told you she'd've gone through agonies before she died?'

'Yes.'

'Then why didn't she unlock the door and call for help? I know she was tryin' to top herself but bugger me. You tellin' me she had the time or the strength to unlock the door, remove the cup from the room, stroll back and lock herself in again? Beyond belief.'

Brennan shook his head. 'Not beyond belief. Only beyond suicide.'

Jaggery took another gulp of bitter and digested both the beer and the implications of what Brennan had just said.

'Let's assume for a moment it wasn't suicide at all. Obviously

112

whoever gave her the arsenic-flavoured tea removed the incriminating cup soon after the poor girl drank from it. What I find puzzling is this bottle of Scotch. What was it doing beside the body if the girl never drank from it?'

'Happen that Edgar bloke left it there by mistake.'

'What? At the end of the school day?'

'Could've done.'

'If he's a secret guzzler during the day he's hardly likely to leave a bottle out in full view now, is he?'

'Not unless 'e'd been lushin' it that day.'

'We saw him earlier. Stank of stale whisky but perfectly in control. No, I think he's a steady drinker, not a drunkard. There's a difference.'

Jaggery took another gulp of bitter. 'So why did meladdo hide it then?'

'If you mean Mr Weston the headmaster, say so.' Brennan raised a hand to forestall Jaggery from following his instruction. 'Do we believe his claim that he hid it in the slate cupboard to protect the good name of the school?'

'George Street has a name but it ain't a good 'un.'

'Or did he hide it to protect his colleague?'

Jaggery looked surprised. 'You mean the 'eadmaster knows about Edgar's drinkin'? An' actually *protects* the bugger?'

'It's possible.'

'It's bloody outrageous, that's what it is, Sergeant. Teachers suppin' while they're teachin'? World's gone mad.'

Brennan smiled and continued. 'I'm also interested to know why Mr Weston didn't tell me that Tollet was staying at the Royal. I asked him for the man's address and he balked at giving it to me. Why not simply tell me where he was staying?'

'I don't reckon much to our Mr Weston,' Jaggery observed.

'Hmm. We're also told that Miss Gadsworth fainted when the headmaster, the inspector and the vicar entered the room.'

'They reckoned she were bad with 'er nerves.'

'Or she recognised someone.'

This possibility hadn't occurred to Jaggery. He blinked a couple of times to assimilate the implications, but the effort was too great.

'How do you mean?'

Ignoring the question, Brennan went on. 'And Edgar heard what she said as she fainted. "Let's wait", or something like that anyway.'

Jaggery grunted. 'When I've been in the ring an' clobbered some muttonhead I've 'eard 'em say all sorts, Sergeant. They don't think straight when they're on their way out, y'see?'

Brennan did see. He'd watched Jaggery fight in the ring on several occasions representing the Borough Police, and that thunderous left fist had scrambled quite a few brains.

'Still, if she *did* recognise someone and that caused the fainting spell, who was it?'

'You said three of 'em came into the room. Meladdo, th'inspector an' t'vicar. Must've been one of them buggers.'

'Logic would suggest that. But she'd already met the headmaster that morning. And apparently he and Mr Tollet observed her teaching a class. But Weston said that the vicar had only just arrived, which might suggest Miss Gadsworth hadn't yet met him.'

'You think it were the vicar she recognised?'

'*If* she recognised someone – and it's by no means certain – then it could well have been Reverend Pearl. Which means what, Constable?'

Jaggery gave the question some thought before responding. 'It means she'd seen 'im before.'

Brennan sighed. 'That's normally the case when you recognise someone. The answer I was looking for needed a bit more thought. But I'll tell you anyway. It means I'll have to go to church tomorrow. Ask a few more questions. That's what it means.'

After Brennan had been to the bar and replenished their pint pots, he took a long, slow drink, wiped the froth from his mouth then leant forward and spoke more softly. 'We don't believe in coincidences, do we, Constable?'

'No, Sergeant.'

'So how can you explain the drowning of the school inspector, Mr Tollet?'

Jaggery took a deep breath and then exhaled slowly to demonstrate how inexplicable the man's death was.

'Perhaps, Constable, we should call it murder, eh? The poor man was prevented from climbing out of the canal by someone stamping like hell on his hands. But what we have to work out is the link between what happened to Miss Gadsworth and Henry Tollet. We need motives.'

Jaggery put his hand to his head, an outward indicator that he was thinking hard. Then he said, 'You know this woman you say was murdered?'

'Yes.'

'Well I reckon you must've got that bit wrong.'

'How?'

'You said that door was locked when she was found Monday morning.'

'That is correct.'

'So if it were locked, then she'd locked herself in, hadn't she? So she wouldn't be disturbed.'

There was a lull in the conversation, filled by the raucous laughter of a group of clerks standing by the bar.

Brennan smiled. 'I said it was locked, not that she'd locked herself in.'

'But the caretaker Prendergast said the vicar found the key behind the door after he'd smashed his way in. It must've dropped out the keyhole.'

'Why? If we accept this was murder, then whoever locked her in the room needed only to keep hold of it and then drop the key behind the door when they all rushed into the classroom following Richard Weston yesterday morning, making it *look* like it had been locked from the inside.'

Normally, Constable Jaggery was slow on the uptake, but his eyes lit up with inspiration at that point.

'You saying that whoever killed Miss Gadsworth works at the school?'

'It's a possibility, Freddie. A distinct possibility.'

Constable Jaggery smiled at the use of his Christian name. He always knew when the ale was starting to have an effect on Micky Brennan.

The following morning, Brennan was preparing to leave the station and make his way to St Catharine's Church in Lorne Street, when there was a hesitant knock on the door of his small office. A fresh-faced young constable opened the door and said, 'You're wanted, Sergeant. At the front desk.'

'Who wants me, Constable?'

'There's two of 'em, Sergeant. Man an' a woman. They told Sergeant Prescott they wanted to see the man in charge of their daughter's murder.'

* * *

It was a part of the job he hated.

He'd known more than a few policemen who'd been able to harden themselves against feeling any kind of sympathy for the families of victims, whatever had happened to them. When he was still finding his feet in the force, one grizzled old constable had warned him against that sort of thing when they'd turned up at a lodging house in Douglas Road to inform the occupants of one of the rooms – a young couple whose three-year-old child had wandered off while they *had a minute to themselves* – that their little girl had been found cold and lifeless, having fallen down a nearby quarry. He didn't know what was worse – the wailing grief of the young mother who blamed her husband for his *bloody stinkin' appetite* or the silence, the dreadful pallid muteness of the young father. Their grief was intensified by the sense of guilt, an emotion Brennan, a Catholic, was well familiar with, and he spent many sleepless nights wondering how they were coping with the loss and the blame until, six months later, he heard they'd found the poor mother hanging from a tree overlooking the quarry.

He had told Ellen about it, about the depth of sorrow he'd felt then and since. And she'd whispered to him in bed, late at night, as they'd listened to their baby son breathing contentedly in the cot beside them.

If you ever stop feelin', Michael Brennan, then you know where the door is.

It had helped him, he knew. But now, in the cramped space of his tiny office, he still felt the emptiness in the pit of his stomach, an emptiness made more painful by the fact that there was nothing he could do to ease the suffering of these two parents seated before him.

Edwin Gadsworth was in his late forties. He was almost

completely bald, and there was a sad dignity about his bearing, enhanced by the dark mourning clothes he wore. His posture as he sat facing Brennan was erect and authoritative, his chin jutting forward as if to ward off the worst of the blows he was suffering. Brennan noted how gently, though, the man held his wife's black-gloved hand. Mrs Gadsworth was of medium build and had once no doubt been quite beautiful. But there were lines around her eyes as she raised the black veil, and her cheeks were pale not just with the grief she must be suffering but with something deeper – an illness, Brennan thought.

'We have just been to the mortuary, Sergeant. To identify our daughter's body.' He took a deep breath as a wave of realisation washed over him. Then he began again, this time more calmly. 'My wife hasn't been in the best of health, Sergeant Brennan. And what with the shock of – needless to say, we are devastated, sir. Devastated.'

'You have my deepest condolences, Mr Gadsworth.'

'I should like something more than that, Sergeant Brennan.'

Brennan blinked.

'My daughter was a God-fearing person, with deeply held views. The remotest suggestion that she took her own life – as we have heard from several quarters – would be a foul slander. She was murdered. I should like your assurances that whoever committed this foul crime will be brought to justice and the noose.'

'I can assure you of my unyielding efforts, Mr Gadsworth.'

He saw that Gadsworth was about to give some retort, so he said quickly, 'And to make sure everything possible will be done, may I ask you a few questions?'

Gadsworth took a deep breath, stroked his wife's hand very slowly, and said, 'Of course.'

'Your daughter lived with you in Bolton?'

'Yes. I own a pharmacy there. Off Churchgate. We've lived there since we moved from Leeds.'

'I see. She had ambitions to become a teacher?'

'Obviously, since she applied for a teaching post in this place.'

Brennan registered the sharpness in the man's tone.

Suddenly, Mrs Gadsworth spoke up. 'It was her lifelong ambition, Sergeant Brennan. Ever since she was a small child running through the streets of Headingley . . .' Her voice trailed off, as if she could see that selfsame child skipping innocently along all those years ago.

Brennan spoke quickly, to remove the pain of silence. 'I might as well clear one thing up before we go any further. It seems that a note was found beside your daughter.'

The implications registered on both their faces.

Brennan reached into his desk drawer and pulled out the soiled slip of paper. He slid it across the desk and they both looked down, neither of them touching it.

'Is this her handwriting?'

They both looked at each other. Then Mr Gadsworth said, 'A single word? In capital letters?'

'It isn't Dorothea's hand.' His wife's voice trembled, but there was a conviction there, too.

'You sure?'

'We're both sure,' said Gadsworth. 'So the fiend who poisoned my daughter wrote this?'

'It would appear so.'

Again they both stared at it, their eyes wide with horror.

Brennan quickly removed it and put it back in his drawer.

'You may not be aware that last Friday, at George Street School, Dorothea had a fainting spell.'

119

Edwin Gadsworth leant forward. 'Go on.'

'It may be that she felt ill – I believe that the lesson she taught was with a group of children that might be described as rather challenging.'

'When she was learning, our daughter taught in Salford, Sergeant Brennan. A hellhole, she described it. Filthy children. Filthier parents. She coped admirably then. I see no reason why she should fail to cope *here*.'

'I said it *may be* that she felt ill. There might well be other reasons for the faint.'

'Such as?'

'I don't know, to be honest. All I do know is that your daughter was very well looked after when she did faint. The headmaster, Mr Richard Weston, was most solicitous, as indeed were the school inspector Mr Henry Tollet, and the school manager, the Reverend Pearl.'

He watched them both carefully for any sign they recognised any of those names. But their faces remained expressionless.

Brennan sighed. 'When she'd recovered from the fainting spell, she left the school for some thirty minutes or so for some fresh air. Later in the afternoon she was interviewed. What I find most puzzling is this: why should your daughter leave the school after her interview, knowing that she had been unsuccessful, only to return later that same evening? Why not simply catch the train to Bolton and return home?'

Gadsworth held his gaze for a few seconds, then said, 'It's our belief she recognised someone.'

For a moment, Brennan was silent, a shiver of hope along his spine as they voiced his own suspicions. Before he could respond, Gadsworth reached into his inside pocket and removed a slip of paper.

'She left school after she had fainted to send us this. This is the reason we've come here today, Sergeant Brennan. Here. Read it.'

He handed it across. Brennan unfurled it. A telegram, bearing the short message:

Seen one responsible for Tilly's death. Past inescapable.

'Who's Tilly?' Brennan asked.

CHAPTER SEVEN

'Tilly Pollard.'

It was Mrs Gadsworth who took up the story. Her tone was sombre, but now and again, as the tale unravelled and the fondness of memories returned, there came a rare sparkle in her eye, like a flash of blue sky in a downpour.

'She was Dorothea's cousin, and her closest friend. My sister lived in Hawkshead, a small village in the Lake District. Tilly and Dorothea were very close, you see, had known each other since they were learning how to walk. It was a small community, a friendly one. Children were valued, Sergeant. Do you know what I mean? They were cherished, nurtured. And they gave such joy in return. Our families had watched the two of them grow, learn to talk, squabble, argue over dolls . . . They were both seven when it happened.

'We lived in Leeds at that time. My husband was working in his first pharmacy. Dorothea had begged us to allow her to spend the summer of '79 in the Lake District with Tilly.'

Mr Gadsworth interjected. 'I was quite busy with establishing myself – I began as a lowly dispensing assistant who didn't know the difference between typhus and typhoid, you see.'

He offered a self-deprecating glance which presupposed Brennan was fully aware of the difference.

'So,' Mrs Gadsworth went on, 'the chance to send Dorothea to her aunt's for the summer, giving Edwin time to complete his training and build up his reputation at one and the same time, proved opportune. And Dorothea loved the place. My sister and her husband, God rest their souls, adored her.'

Edwin continued. 'There was a girl in the village – she lived alone with her widowed mother, her father having died when she was very young – Julia Reece, her name was.'

He almost hissed the name, and Brennan noticed him hold his wife's hand tightly at this point.

'She was around seventeen, a flighty one, by all accounts, and no mistake. Still, according to Susan, my wife's sister, she seemed pleasant enough. Her mother Margaret had told everyone how her daughter had ambitions to become a governess or a teacher, because, as she put it, she was a *wonder* with children. If anyone ever needed her help in any way, if they thought a little education beyond what the children learnt in school would be required, why, Julia Reece would be more than willing to oblige. They all believed the woman. And apparently Julia *was* very good with the children – not just Dorothea and Tilly, but a few others, too. They all spoke of how enjoyable their time with the girl had been – the nature walks through Grizedale Forest or down to Esthwaite Water, and the casual learning they acquired. When we visited one time Dorothea and Tilly had a game where they'd try to outdo each other by reciting the silliest names of the things they'd been taught and had seen for themselves: bladderwort and sneezewort and knapweed and fleabane. And they'd double up in fits of laughter . . .

'Oh she taught them well enough. But then, so the story goes, she took up with a boy – around her age. He used to do odd jobs around the place and, although he lived over in Windermere and would catch the ferry across the lake, he became quite a popular figure. Likeable young chap, Susan said. Always willing to help. David, his name was. Never did get his surname. Anyway, he and Julia became fond of each other. She seemed to lose all sense of propriety.'

Edwin Gadsworth thought for a second, then added, 'They were like a poisonous compound. Individually, separately, harmless. Together, they were toxic.'

His wife said, 'She began to take the boy with her while she was in charge of the children. Susan caught Dorothea and Tilly giggling fit to burst one evening and when she asked them what was the matter they said they'd seen Julia and David *swapping spit.* They were seven, remember. And innocent.'

There was a pause, and Brennan felt the tension in the room now. It was clear the next part of the story was going to bring back painful memories.

Mrs Gadsworth sighed and gave her husband a wan smile before continuing. 'One day, a terribly hot day in summer it was, Julia gathered her little group together – Dorothea, Tilly and two others from the village – and told them that they were going to play a game of hide and seek near the church. That's the parish church in Hawkshead. St Michael and All Angels. Such a lovely place, too. Dates back to the fifteenth century. They say Wordsworth himself loved to sit and gaze at its beauty. Not a place for childish games, Sergeant.'

'No church is, Mrs Gadsworth.'

'At any rate, Julia took the children to the church grounds and told them that she would give them a good half hour to find the best hiding place they could, but that under no circumstances must they enter the church itself. It was strictly forbidden, she said. She had some jobs to do and would meet them in thirty minutes. Later it was discovered that the minister had asked David to clean out the belfry while he attended the funeral of a fellow minister over in Ambleside. The children, naturally, heeded her instructions, although that went only as far as the injunction to keep out of the church. After half an hour had elapsed, they became bored, and Julia hadn't appeared. And so, because it was a hot day, and the children thought they needed to cool down, Tilly suggested they go where Julia had taken them before – to Esthwaite Water. They say it's Windermere's little brother. But it's still a lake.'

Brennan waited as she composed herself once more. He could guess what was coming.

'They ran fully clothed into the water, for it's quite a distance from the church and the poor souls were even hotter when they got there. Apparently Julia had told them a tale about a water fairy who lived in the lake and Tilly said she wanted to find her. She waded out the furthest.'

She looked down, her lips quivering, but she said no more. Her husband finished the dreadful tale.

'Tilly disappeared into the water. Dorothea and the others thought at first she was pretending to be captured by the fairy, but then they saw a tremendous thrashing further out, and Tilly's arms rising and falling. Her head was thrust to the surface briefly. Dorothea said her face was turned to heaven, and her mouth gasping for breath. Then she vanished, and the water became still once more, and Tilly didn't emerge. They ran off for help, crying and in shock. The villagers, including Robert Pollard, Tilly's father, rushed down to the lake but there was no sign at first. Robert thrashed about wildly in the water until he stumbled over something. He bent low, and was heard to struggle for a while before rearing up from the water with little Tilly – dead – in his arms.

'As he carried her back, the children told the other villagers about Julia, and how they must keep out of the church. It wasn't a wild leap of the imagination to work out where the girl was and what she was doing. Still, some of them ran up to the church and found the two of them – Julia and David – up in the belfry. It wasn't the fact that what they had done was immoral. Not even that it was sacrilegious. No, by their evil actions, by Julia's dereliction and David's lustfulness, they had brought about the death of an innocent child. Hawkshead was a place filled with righteous fury. Julia and her poor mother Margaret were compelled to leave in an undignified haste. The boy David returned to Windermere and never caught the ferry again. Such a dreadfully sad time.'

There was a moment of heavy silence before Edwin Gadsworth broke it.

'That telegram suggests Dorothea saw Julia Reece after all these years. I'm convinced of it.'

Brennan frowned. 'But we've been informed that your daughter fainted when three men entered the room – Mr Weston, Mr Tollet and Reverend Pearl.'

Tactfully he failed to add that the only person she hadn't met from the three until that point was the vicar. No point yet in jumping to conclusions.

'And you have put two and two together to find it adds up to five, Sergeant? Isn't it at all possible that she had met someone earlier and the recognition registered only later?'

Brennan leant forward, handed the telegram back to Mr Gadsworth and nodded. 'As she fainted, she was heard to say something. She said, "Of course . . . Let's wait".'

The Gadsworths looked at each other in puzzlement.

'I'd presumed she'd fainted because she'd recognised someone who came into the room. But the words have puzzled me, I admit.'

Then something struck him.

'The name of the lake where the girl was drowned. What was it?'

'Esthwaite Water.'

Brennan gave a grim smile. 'Esthwaite. Sounds like "Let's wait". She must have said, "Of course, Esthwaite".' He thought for a moment. 'It's the "Of course" that's more significant though.'

'Is it?'

'It might suggest something had just struck her, that she'd been thinking about it and the answer had just occurred to her.'

'Answer? To what?'

'To where she'd actually seen someone before. Perhaps it had been playing on her mind all morning. You know the sort of thing? *I'm sure I know you from somewhere* . . . But quite often, remembering takes time. Which means it could be any of the people she had met that day at the school.'

'Such as Julia Reece?'

Brennan shrugged. 'With her name changed.'

Edwin Gadsworth stood up. 'Well then. What are we waiting here for?'

'I beg your pardon?'

'You have important new information, Sergeant Brennan. All you have to do is act upon it. Just where is this George Street School to be found?'

* * *

The liquid tasted funny, not altogether unpleasant. He could detect treacle – his favourite when his mam spread it on a butty – and something spicy.

'What is it?' he asked.

The bottle was thrust in front of him, but if he was supposed to read the label it was a hopeless gesture, even by the flickering light of the oil lamp.

'Godfrey's Cordial,' came the answer.

'What's in it?'

'All sorts to make you feel better.'

'But I'm not badly.'

'No. This keeps you from feeling badly.'

He took another swig from the bottle and wiped his lips. It wasn't a bad taste at all. Not at all.

'When can I leave? I don't like it down 'ere. There's all sorts. Rats an' all.'

A pause, the oil lamp raised so that the flame was level with his eyes. They were red and tearful.

'You been crying?'

''Course not.'

'Good. You need to stay strong, Billy.'

'But when can I leave?'

'When the police stop looking for you. It was a bad thing you did, Billy. A bad thing.'

'I know.'

Suddenly the lamp was removed, leaving him in the semi-darkness once more. He knew it wasn't night-time yet, but as to the time of day . . .

'Are you leavin'?'

'I have to. You know that.'

'Leave the lamp then.'

'No. Oil lamps smell. You'd be found.'

He heard the door grate open. There was an inrush of stale cold air before it was closed once more, and the bolt slid back into place.

He hunched his knees together and felt his head begin to swim. He could still taste the cordial on his lips.

It took all of Brennan's persuasive powers to keep the Gadsworths from storming down to George Street and demanding which one of them was Julia Reece.

'For one thing, everything we've said is pure speculation. "Let's wait" sounds like "Esthwaite" but it could equally be "Let's wait" after all. My constable is very well acquainted with the effects of fainting spells. He assures me people say nonsense words all the time. And for another thing, even if your daughter saw Julia Reece, who's to say she saw her in the school that morning? She could have passed her on the street, sat next to her on a tram, even been served breakfast by her that morning in a hotel. You see, we can't jump to any conclusions.'

Gadsworth muttered something about police doing the job they're paid for, but Brennan could see, as he escorted them from the station, that their ardour had cooled, at least for the time being.

'Are you returning to Bolton?' he asked on the steps of the station.

'We're staying at the Victoria Hotel,' Gadsworth said. 'Until we can make arrangements for Dorothea's remains to be taken back to Bolton. This place has done enough damage.'

'I see. Well if you can think of anything, however small, that you remember about Julia Reece and the events of so long ago . . .'

'Rest assured, Sergeant,' said Gadsworth sombrely. 'Rest assured.'

He turned to re-enter the station when Mrs Gadsworth said, 'My daughter's life was changed for ever in Esthwaite Water, Sergeant Brennan. Seven-year-olds shouldn't be seeing what she saw, should they?'

Gadsworth placed a firm hand on Brennan's sleeve. He spoke in a low whisper. 'This has grievously affected my wife's health, Sergeant. I fear the worst. It would be of some comfort to know her daughter's murderer faced eternal judgement before she does.'

Brennan watched them move slowly along King Street towards the Victoria Hotel beside Wallgate Station. Once he'd got back to his office, he was surprised to see the spectral figure of his chief constable occupying his chair.

'From their mourning attire I'd say that was Miss Gadsworth's parents?'

'It was, sir.'

'"And God shall wipe away all tears from their eyes". Isn't that so, Sergeant?'

Accustomed to the occasional reference to Scripture from Captain Bell, Brennan gave a melancholy sigh before giving him the gist of what he had been told by the Gadsworths.

'The telegram would seem to support your theory that she did indeed recognise someone,' the chief constable conceded.

'Yes, sir. I need to find out which of them – if any – has a connection with the Lake District, Hawkshead in particular.'

'A wise move,' came the reply with a slow nod of the head. 'By the way, I've read in the day's orders that a child has gone missing.'

Brennan gave him a curious glance. He recalled the huge brute of a man the previous day – what had the desk sergeant said his name was? Tommy Kelly, that was it. He'd been yelling fit to burst about his missing son.

'It may be something or it may be nothing, Sergeant, but this missing boy – William Kelly – attends George Street Elementary School.'

Brennan's heart sank. Another coincidence?

'According to Sergeant Prescott, sir, it isn't the first time the boy has run away. I gather both the father and the mother are quite brutal towards him.'

'Nevertheless, it might be something you could look into. I'm growing a little piqued at the mention of that place.'

'Of course, sir. No stone unturned, eh?'

Once the chief constable had gone, he muttered a curse under his breath. Not aimed at his departing superior but at himself. He really must find time to read the order notices of the day.

Billy Kelly had fallen asleep, but it wasn't a peaceful sleep. He dreamt of standing in a large wood, with huge, dark trees towering above him. There was a strong wind blowing, rustling the leaves and the branches which leant down after each powerful blast and whipped him on the cheek. He tried to run, but he could only move slowly, ever so slowly, his feet dragging on the ground and churning up deep ruts of mud and leaves in his wake. One tree suddenly sprang up in his path, as if it had grown at an incredible speed to catch him before he could find his way out of the black forest. Its branches grew wide apart as if offering a cold embrace.

Then he heard a sweet chirping, a high-pitched chatter that came from high above his head. He looked up, expecting at any moment to see a beautiful bird with blue and yellow feathers, but all he could make out at first was a thick branch stretching out to an impossible length.

Something scurried along the branch, stopped, leant over, then carried on. It wasn't a bird, he could see that. It had four legs and seemed in its own busy world. Then he saw it – a squirrel, with a nut clutched in its paws. It glanced down at him, and he saw a glimmer of kindness in its eyes as it stretched out, offering the nut. Suddenly he was very hungry and he reached up. He was on the verge of grabbing the nut when all of a sudden the squirrel gave a deafening screech and launched itself from the branch, sinking its teeth into his fingers.

He woke up at that point, to find a rat biting his hand.

Brennan decided to continue with his original course of action and pay Reverend Pearl another visit. Of the three men who entered the staffroom when Dorothea Gadsworth fainted, the vicar was the only one she hadn't already seen. Not incriminatory, of course, but it would be interesting now to ask him questions concerning his personal background.

He'd got the address of Tommy Kelly from Sergeant Prescott and would call there after he'd spoken with the vicar. He knew the uniformed constables would be keeping an eye out for the missing lad, and he hoped this really was a coincidence and that young William Kelly had simply run away.

When he knocked on the door of the vicarage, it was a middle-aged woman who answered.

'Yes?' she said, looking him up and down as if she were appraising his manner of dress. She was small, with sturdy arms and stocky build. The pinafore she was wearing, along with the duster in her hand, told him this was the housekeeper.

'Reverend Pearl?'

'Do I look like the vicar?'

'Not a bit,' he said with a smile. 'You've no dog collar, for one thing.'

She paused for a moment as if considering some sharp retort, but instead she said, 'Who is it?'

'Detective Sergeant Brennan.'

'Wait here,' she said and closed the door.

From within, he could hear a muted conversation, then the door reopened and the housekeeper stepped aside. 'You're disturbing him, but he's a saintly man. Come on in. Wipe your feet.'

As soon as he stepped inside, a tantalising aroma greeted him.

'I'll bet that's a beef stew,' he said to the woman as she closed the door. It never did any harm to get on a domestic's good side.

'Beef stew? With a chicken boiling away in the pot? Shin beef strained and chicken joints. That's cock-a-leekie, that is. Beef stew my eye!'

With an air of hurt pride at his culinary blunder, she brushed past and led him down a small passage. She gave a small knock on the door.

'Enter!'

Slowly she opened the door and said simply, 'Your visitor,' before ushering Brennan inside, closing the door behind her.

Reverend Charles Pearl was sitting behind a mahogany desk in what was presumably his study. He had a quill pen in his hand and had been in the process of writing with some vigour. He looked up and made an attempt at a smile.

'Sergeant Brennan. Please take a seat.'

'Thank you, Vicar,' Brennan replied, remembering the protocol.

As he sat down, he noticed an array of books and religious tracts lining the shelving behind him, and along the walls more prints of wild and rugged scenes similar to the ones he'd seen in the living room. But taking prominence on the wall by the window was a sizeable print of an elegant woman standing with a sad expression on her face and her left hand resting on a spiked wheel.

'I see you've been captivated by St Catharine,' said the vicar.

Brennan nodded. 'It was the wheel that gave it away,' he replied.

'Many people believe she died on that wheel. The Roman emperor's punishment for rejecting his proposal of marriage. In fact, the wheel miraculously shattered and she was finally beheaded. A tale of true courage, Sergeant. Saintly courage.'

'Quite so, Vicar.'

'Well, what can I do for you? As you see, I'm knee-deep in sin.'

Brennan blinked.

'My sermon,' came the explanation. 'There's little point in demanding my parishioners redeem themselves from sin if I don't tell them exactly what sinning is, how it corrodes the soul while cheering the flesh.'

'Indeed, sir.' As a child, he'd heard enough sermons like that at St Joseph's to scar him – or scare him – for life. He took a deep breath. 'Well, my visit is something of a quest.'

'Oh?'

'It appears that Miss Gadsworth may – and I emphasise the word *may* – have recognised someone she knew from the past and that may have prompted her fainting spell.'

'And what has this to do with her taking her own life? Or are you now convinced she didn't?'

'I'm convinced she was murdered.'

The vicar's eyes widened. 'You have proof of that?'

'We do indeed, sir. I can't explain the circumstances, but it's sufficient to say she was poisoned, and not by her own hand.'

'I see.'

'As I say, she may have recognised someone from the past.'

'And how can I be of assistance?'

'Well, this may sound a little presumptuous, but can you tell me something about your past?'

'*My* past? I thought it was Miss Gadsworth's past that was under consideration?'

'It is. And I'm trying to find out exactly what occurred on Friday morning. She sent a telegram to her parents that suggested she'd seen someone from her past. Someone who was involved in a child's death . . .'

Reverend Pearl carefully placed his pen in its stand. 'I have never seen that girl before in my life. That should be enough.'

'Just a few questions and I'll be going, Vicar.' Brennan reached into his side pocket and took out his notebook and pencil. 'Now, as to some years ago, fifteen to be precise. The summer of 1879 . . .'

'I was a mere youth.'

'Where were you living back then?'

The vicar shifted uncomfortably in his chair. 'I was twenty.'

Brennan gave him a patient smile. 'Not really the answer to my question.'

'Well I can assure you it wasn't me the girl recognised. I have never set eyes on her before Friday.'

'She would have been seven years old, Reverend Pearl.'

'Well then.'

'I'd still like to know where you were living at that time.'

The vicar shook his head resignedly. 'If you must know I was living in Somerset. A far cry from Wigan, I can assure you.' He gave a sacrificial smile then said, 'And I *am* in the middle of a sermon. You will have other enquiries to make, I feel sure.'

Brennan, ignoring the hint, remained seated. 'A little girl, Tilly Pollard, drowned fifteen years ago. It may be that Miss Gadsworth recognised someone involved in her death. This was in Hawkshead, by the way, in the Lake District.'

Reverend Pearl shook his head 'A beautiful part of the country, I've been told. But I've never had the good fortune to visit.'

Brennan stood and thanked him for his time. The housekeeper escorted him out.

Outside, he stood on the street gazing at both the vicarage and the church, playing the conversation over in his head. After a few minutes' reflection, he set off to catch a tram.

He'd be damned if he was going to walk all the way to Diggle Street. It was the other side of town.

The interior of Reverend Pearl's living room and study and the kitchen at Diggle Street couldn't have been more contrasting. Where the vicarage contained a whole plethora of landscape pictures showing nature at its wildest and most elemental, along with a host of religious volumes, the kitchen in which he sat facing Edith Kelly held not a single image nor a single book. Instead, the wall where the small range stood was smeared with dark soot stains from the tiny oven that formed part of the range. He saw the grey, cold ashes through an iron grill. In places the plasterwork on the walls had crumbled to expose bare brick underneath. A slopstone, badly chipped in places, held a number of unwashed plates, and behind the back door that led into a small yard a tin bath hung from a metal hook.

'Got an eyeful?' asked Edith Kelly, who had watched him survey her domain.

Brennan ignored the hostility in her voice. 'You must be worried sick, Mrs Kelly.'

'Never been gone this long. That's why we reported it.'

'And all the men have been told about him. Your husband gave our desk sergeant a good description of the lad. They'll keep a sharp eye out.'

'I'm sure they will,' she snapped in a tone that implied the opposite.

'William goes to George Street School?'

'Aye. An' it's *Billy*. William's the name he got give in church an' we don't go so we don't use it no more.'

'Your husband told us he'd been in trouble at school?'

She folded her arms and snorted. 'That swine of 'eadmaster walloped our Billy, all because he accidentally spat at someone. Then he gets another pastin' when that snot-nosed frosty-faced bitch Ryan catches 'im swearin'. He can wallop our Billy all he likes on his backside, but wallopin' 'is 'ands cost us money.'

'How?'

'Made 'em so sore the poor little sod couldn't work. Does the odd bit up at the rolling mill. Helpin' his dad. So I marched in an' told that stuck-up bugger just what I thought of 'im. Told 'im the only teacher in that place worth owt at all is leavin'. So 'e calls your lot in an' reports me.'

Brennan had seen the report, a visit from a constable with a warning for her to stay away from the school.

'And you think the punishment might have made your Billy run away?'

'Dunno. But 'e said summat daft to Len Parkinson's lad Friday night.'

'What was that?'

138

'That daft lummox went round to find out what was what. They told 'im our Billy wouldn't fight their Albert cos 'e'd done summat bad an' didn't want hangin' for it. Like I said, it were daft. That tannin' must've scrambled 'is brains. What goes on in that lad's 'ead is a mystery.'

'You said the only good teacher is leaving. Would that be Miss Rodley?'

'Aye. Teaches our Billy readin' an' writin'. First of the buggers to get through to 'im an' all. An' now she's taken up wi' that vicar.'

He thanked her for her time and promised to keep her and her husband informed if anything turned up. As he walked off he tried to assimilate all that he had learnt in his meetings with the Gadsworths, the vicar and the formidable Mrs Kelly. There was a thread linking them, he was sure, but where that thread would lead was still a labyrinthine mystery.

CHAPTER EIGHT

There were times, and this was most definitely one of them, when Emily Mason felt she would have been better off leaving school with the rest of them years ago and working in the cotton mill. Or even following those from her class who had taken on work in the colliery. It certainly wasn't shameful, working as a pit brow lass: she'd seen them from her bedroom window in the early morning, as they woke her with the *clack-clack* of their clogs on the pavement below, their bright red scarves, wider than normal scarves to keep the coal dust out; their expansive shawls and their white skirts with blue stripes, some of them wearing men's coats and even trousers!

She envied too their closeness, the friendship they seemed to enjoy in the mist-shrouded mornings when their voices seemed to drift from below, the easy laughter they shared at some coarseness.

But Emily had been encouraged to be different.

'Those girls have no ambition,' her mother had told her. 'They're nothing but sheep being led into the fold. What difference do they make to anyone's lives? Besides, you have a good brain, Emily. It would be a shame to smother it in cotton dust or coal dust.'

Emily heeded her mother's advice, absorbed her ambition and set her mind on becoming a teacher. When her mother became sick and lay dying – her mind wandering and restless a mere twelve months after the pig who called himself her father had died – the ambition had become something more, a determination to honour what her mother had set in motion. She had promised her faithfully to work as hard as she could to make her proud of her daughter.

Deathbed promises were all well and good, but as she sat in the headmaster's office now, waiting for him to return, she'd have given anything to be working a mule spindle or riddling coal. What did those old friends of hers have to worry about?

The door swung open and Mr Weston came in, accompanied by the teacher in charge of Standard 4, Miss Ryan.

Emily immediately stood up, but Weston signalled for her to sit back down. He held a chair for Miss Ryan before taking up his place behind his desk, facing the two of them with his hands clasped together.

Esther Ryan sat erect and stern-faced. She was thirty-seven, sharp of feature and with eyes that held the cold glimmer of marble.

'Now, Emily, you are aware of why I've sent for you?'

'Yes, sir.'

'Miss Ryan here has made certain complaints about you.'

'Yes, sir.'

'And she has asked me to speak with you.'

'Yes, sir.'

'It concerns the noise emanating from your classroom.'

For a moment, Emily hesitated. She said nothing but lowered her eyes to inspect her hands.

'Miss Ryan says her pupils in Standard 4 find such a noise distracting.'

There was a cough, and Esther Ryan spoke for the first time. 'Distracting is not the word, Headmaster. Perhaps *deafening* would be more apposite.'

'Emily? Is there a reason why your children are making such a disturbance?'

Emily glanced up. He could see there were tears in her eyes.

'It's the dictation, sir.'

'Dictation?'

'Yes, sir. They say I go too fast so I slow down and when I slow down they say it's borin' an' could I speed it up a bit. Then someone'll throw somethin' an' another'll do the same an' before I know it it's like a snowstorm in there wi' paper flyin' everywhere.'

She started to sob, a demonstration of feeling that brought only a sharp and impatient exhalation from Miss Ryan.

'In my view, young lady, you would be well advised to pull a few ears and smack a few hands,' was her advice.

Weston, seeing the tears flow freely now, had heard enough. 'Thank you, Miss Ryan. If you'd care to leave us now, I'm sure we can bring about a satisfactory solution.'

'It's a satisfactory silence I want, Headmaster. Nothing else.' With that she stood up, turned and left the room.

Weston stood up, moved to stand beside the weeping pupil-teacher, and placed his hand on her shoulder. 'Now then,' he said quietly. 'What's this all really about?'

* * *

143

He had no visitor for the rest of the day. And for the first time, he began to be really afraid once the total darkness came. The rat bite had frightened him. It had sunk its teeth in deep, in several places, and now the small wounds felt sore, and he was sure he could feel the skin swollen where it had attacked him.

The darkness seemed to press black thoughts into his head.

What if he were left here? No food any more, no visits. It might be, he thought, that the police were already close, sneaking up on him and ready at any moment to drag him out into the street above and hurl him into one of their black wagons.

But his mam and dad? What about them? He knew they'd already been told he was all right, that he was safe and out of harm's reach. They'd said as much, and they'd said he was forgiven. They'd asked for a message to be given to him, for him to make sure under no circumstances was he to go back home. Why, the police could well arrest his mam and dad if they took him back in.

'*Thanks very much for lettin' us know,*' they'd said. '*As long as 'e's out of 'arm's way, that's all we ask. It's very good of you. God bless.*'

Those were their exact words, he'd been assured.

And it seemed to fit in with the fragments of dream he'd been having, where his mam and dad were nice, and he could almost feel her stroking his head and singing to him in front of the fire, and his dad talking to him ever so nice, and the house was nice, and everything was nice . . .

But he wished someone would come. Even his mam. He wished everything was all right again and the police would go away.

And he wished the pain would go from his hand. It was throbbing now.

* * *

144

It had been a golden rule that he kept work in its place. Once he left the station and made his way home, he would normally feel the burden of whichever case was dominating his thoughts drop away with each step. He'd told Ellen once that she should imagine a coalman carrying a hundredweight of best cannel coal on his back, and in the sack there was a hole at the bottom. Every step he took would see a lump of coal drop out so that, by the time he got to his destination he had no coal left to deliver.

'Only when I get home,' he'd told her, 'I feel much better for shedding all that weight. I don't suppose the coalman'd feel the same way with an empty sack on his back!'

Tonight, however, as he made his way beneath the Wallgate Bridge, past Queen Street and Fisher's Yard before turning left into Caroline Street, it felt as though the sack had been mended and the weight remained constant.

A few people nodded at him, one or two of them exchanging the odd word of greeting, but he felt in a surly, uncommunicative mood as he turned the front door knob and walked into his front room.

'Dad!'

Little Barry Brennan scampered from the rug before the hearthstone and ran into his father's waiting arms. He squeezed his dad's neck tightly, until he gasped for mercy. It was a nightly ritual, and Brennan always cherished the moment between them. There'd come a time when it would transform itself into a gruff *hello* or a firm handshake, so he needed to make the most of his son's childhood.

Ellen came from the kitchen, wiping the flour from her hands onto her pinny. They kissed lightly. As he removed his coat and sat in his armchair before the fire, Ellen, who could invariably read his moods, said quietly, 'Not a good day?'

'Not really,' he said, ruffling Barry's hair as the boy settled back down before the fire to continue manning the small wooden fort Brennan had built him last Christmas, ready for the siege to come.

'Is it the missing boy?' She sat on the floor beside him, causing Barry to groan when she knocked over his dashing lieutenant.

Brennan looked at her curiously. 'What?'

'Billy Kelly. That's his name, isn't it?'

He sighed. He'd forgotten how effective the local gossipmongers were. 'That's the one, aye. Been missing since Friday night.'

She stroked his arm, leaving tiny particles of flour on his sleeve. 'The poor woman,' she said with a glance at Barry, now engaged in defending his fort against all manner of invisible attackers.

He said nothing. It wouldn't do for him to let her know what the *poor woman* was really like, a slatternly rough-tongued female it was difficult to picture showing any tenderness. Yet immediately he rebuked himself – Edith Kelly might be all of those things and worse, but he'd seen glimmerings of worry – just glimmerings but they were there nonetheless. Perhaps her feelings of tenderness had been ground down over the years, and any attempt to show them would be seen as feebleness and nothing else.

His reflections cast a gloomy expression to his features. Then, quite out of character, he found himself speaking his thoughts aloud. He told her about the information he'd been given concerning Dorothea Gadsworth and Tilly Pollard, and his conviction that she recognised someone – either the youth David or Julia Reece – last Friday.

'It stands to reason,' he said, staring at the flames that seemed to sway from side to side mockingly. 'So if she did recognise someone, then as far as the ages are concerned, the only ones who fit the bill are the headmaster, Weston, and the three teachers Nathaniel

Edgar, Jane Rodley and Alice Walsh. And the vicar, of course.'

Ellen's eyes widened. 'Dear Lord!'

They both remained silent for a while, the only noise being the crackling of sparks from the burning coals and Barry's idea of what gunfire sounded like. Then Ellen finally broke the silence.

'It seems that school's unlucky.' She rested her chin on his arm now, her eyes looking up at him, catching the glow and the sparkle from the flames in the grate. 'That poor mother. Imagine if our Barry had gone to that school and walked into the classroom to find . . . And then that school inspector, eh?'

'That's another thing. Why did he have to die?'

'Could that have been a separate thing altogether?'

'What do you mean?'

'Just him being in the wrong place at the wrong time. An assault gone wrong?'

He gave the idea some thought, then said, 'I don't believe in coincidences, Ellen.'

He stroked her head and nodded towards Barry, who had called a ceasefire and was now watching the two of them, aware that serious things were being talked about, because they always lowered their voices then.

She gave him a big grin and said, 'Your mam's silly, aren't I?'

A reassured smile crept onto his face and he returned to his men and the continuation of the siege.

'Happen we can talk about it after, eh, Michael?'

He picked bits of flour from her hair.

'Happen not,' he replied.

There were times when Alice Walsh could be very single-minded, so much so that everything else drifted into oblivion. Tonight, for instance, at the meeting of the Women's Franchise League at the public hall, she immersed herself so completely in the fervour of the speakers and the camaraderie of the audience that she lost all sense of time.

Even when the meeting broke up, she stayed behind and joined in the smaller discussion groups that spread themselves throughout the hall, where those who had earlier felt somehow intimidated by the large number of people in attendance now felt confident enough, in the intimacy of rearranged chairs, to express their own feelings and pass comment on the views presented from the platform.

Alice herself had spoken up on several occasions during the meeting proper, pointing out that words and speeches were all very well but what was needed was something a little more *startling*.

'*We need to win the argument before all else,*' the platform speaker had replied. '*And that's why I propose the petition to both Houses.*'

'*That should make their lordships quiver in their ermine!*' Alice had yelled in reply, to the satisfying echo of laughter in the hall.

Fired therefore by her call for more direct action to bring attention to the justice of their cause, others had joined her circle and listened eagerly to her stirring words.

But all meetings must come to an end, especially when the custodian of the hall began extinguishing the gas lighting as a tangible reminder of his desire to close the place up and quench his thirst in a nearby hostelry, and eventually Alice's group dispersed with heartfelt promises to continue at the next meeting. It was only as she left the building that she remembered where she had promised to be. And from the chimes of the parish church clock, she realised it was now too late. He would have to wait until tomorrow.

* * *

148

Sometime in the night, Billy Kelly began shivering. Not the sort of shivering you get when you're cold and a good thick blanket would shift it. No, this was a different type of shivering altogether, made all the worse by the terrible pain in his head. His mouth felt warm and sticky, and before he could do anything about it he vomited all over the cellar floor, hearing but not seeing it splash on the uneven flagstones. The stench was awful, and it made him retch even more. He slithered away from where he imagined the vomit was gathering, so far away that, in his haste and hampered by the absolute blackness of the place now, he tripped up and fell headlong into the wall, smashing his head so hard that he fell to the floor, all pain and shivering fading away into the unconsciousness that welcomed him into its cold embrace.

Emily Mason's grandmother, with whom she lived, was almost seventy, and she had lost her hearing suddenly one night when Sidney Mason had come in rolling drunk as usual and had started on Emily's mam. No parent would sit there and allow such wickedness to go unpunished, so her grandma had set about the animal with a poker, which he soon wrenched from her grasp and gave her a sound beating around the head. She lost all hearing that night, but as she declared later, it was worth it to save her daughter from yet another battering.

Emily, a mere four years old at the time, had sat under the table terrified. When he died a few years later, she felt nothing but relief that the dark shadow had gone from the house. When she started school at five years old, it seemed like a daily escape, a sanctuary from the wickedness at home. At school, grown-up people actually treated her quite well – better than her so-called father anyway, and she could never understand those in her class who complained about the punishments and the harsh regime of the classroom. Here at school, you were punished if you did something wrong: back home you were just punished.

Sometimes, though, she woke up in the middle of the night and imagined she could hear her late mother's screams or the sickening *thud* of knuckle on bone, and then the sounds just drifted back into the past where they belonged. But then she could hear nothing at all – no trams or horses' hooves or distant train whistles – and she had to hum a tune softly and listen out for her grandmother's harsh rattling breath to confirm she still had her hearing and to give her the peace of mind to return to sleep.

This morning though, as the headmaster sat at his desk with her lesson notes before him and a pile of her pupils' copybooks, she wouldn't mind just half an hour of her grandma's deafness, she told herself, just to block out the lecture she felt sure was coming her way.

'They don't look like words, Emily, do they?' he said, passing one of the copybooks across the desk. She opened it, looked down at the spidery scrawl that claimed to be lettering, and shook her head.

'No, sir.'

The school was still empty, and it would be a good half hour before the first of the staff members arrived, and half an hour after that for the pupils. Only the caretaker, Mr Prendergast, could be heard clattering about in the cellar directly below the open window in Weston's study.

'And this,' he said, passing across another book. 'Why, judging from the number of ink blotches on the page it would seem there's no room for writing of any kind.'

'No, sir.'

'I know it's difficult, Emily, but you need to exercise control first. Don't let them scribble away as if it's a drawing lesson. These are, after all, *copybooks*. I think perhaps I was wrong to ask you to give Standard 1 copybooks in the first place. It's entirely my fault. It might be better to return them to slate writing. We'd save gallons of ink that way.'

He'd meant it as a joke, for he could see her eyes were filling with tears. But Emily held her hands together tightly. No smile lightened her expression. Perhaps, she thought again briefly, she really would have been better off choosing the cotton mill or the pit brow.

There was a pause of some minutes while Weston read through her lesson notes. He nodded occasionally, and made approving noises as he turned each page. He looked up into her eyes, and she could tell he was softening. Not for the first time, she reflected on the huge difference there can exist between two grown men: Sidney Mason was a man, and Richard Weston was a man. And there the similarities ended.

'You see, your plans, your aims for each lesson, are good. It's just a matter of turning theory into application.'

Before she could reply, a knock came on the door.

'Enter!' he called out with a note of irritation in his voice.

The door opened and Prendergast stood there.

'What is it?'

Prendergast coughed and spoke over Emily Mason's head. 'You'd best come down to t'cellar, Mr Weston. See what I've found.'

When they reached the school cellar, Prendergast walked straight over to the dwindling pile of coal near the trapdoor. During delivery days, this door, once unlocked, was always held open with a catch while the coalman emptied the sacks of coal into the gap. Delivery was at two-week intervals, and today the coal supplies were low, with new supplies due tomorrow.

'There!' said the caretaker with arm outstretched towards the base of the coal.

Weston stepped closer. 'Where?'

'That book, curled up an' stuffed into the coal.'

Weston bent forward and saw that indeed a book was embedded into the coal.

'I left it yonder, in case.'

'In case of what?'

'In case it's evidence.'

A puzzled look flickered on the headmaster's face.

'But evidence of what?'

Prendergast sighed. He could see that his words were falling on deaf ears. He reached out and placed his index finger against the edging of the book. 'Arson, Mr Weston. This book 'as been singed round the edges. Looks like some swine tried to light it an' didn't have the sense to realise sheets o' paper packed tight like that won't catch. They won't catch, Mr Weston. That's what saved the school.'

Weston's expression had grown from puzzlement, to disbelief, and now horror. He stumbled over the coals and grabbed the offending book, dislodging it from where it was lodged and lifting it free. He stepped back, wiped the coal dust that blackened its surface and stared down at the front cover.

'It's someone's copybook,' he said, and flicked the book open at a random page. An elegantly pre-printed phrase ran along the top:

While beneath the legend a child's untidy scrawl showed feeble attempts to copy the saying on line after line, all the way to the bottom. On each line the pupil had misspelt *noisy* as *noisey*, and on several occasions the word *brooks* had been written *books*.

'Disgraceful!' was Weston's comment on both the penmanship and the spelling.

'Who's it belong to?' Prendergast asked with a firm nod in the book's direction.

Weston returned to the front of the copybook and saw *W. Kelly* written across the top.

At around the time the headmaster found his copybook, Billy Kelly was rubbing his eyes and touching the large bruise on his forehead. It was very painful, but the pain was muted by the awful smell of the place. He remembered being sick, and the number of times he'd done his business; he remembered shivering in the blackness, and he even remembered how he'd come to knock himself out. But he now felt a growing sense, not of fear – he'd felt enough of that these past few days – but of loneliness.

When was the last time he spoke to anyone?

He stood up and knew it was morning because he could hear, through the gap in the ceiling, the yells of children going to school, and the usual morning sounds that filled the streets: the shuttle of the trams as they swayed from side to side; the clatter of clogs and the loud, heavy coughing from older ones, men and women, who followed up their fits of coughing with a harsh gurgling rattle prior to spitting out huge globs of phlegm.

And people *talking* – as if everything was normal.

His hand, where the rat had bitten him, was throbbing even more today than yesterday, and he could feel now his flesh begin to prickle, just as it did last night before the shivering overcame him.

It was no use. He could stay down here no longer, police or no police.

What if he'd been forgotten about?

What if the shivering and the headaches and the throbbing from the bite got worse and worse until he collapsed in a heap and died?

What if the one who'd brought him here never came back? Been trampled to death by a horse gone mad. Would his body just rot away till there was nothing but his clothes?

Would the rats eat him?

'Sod that', he said out loud. It was strange hearing his voice now. It sounded hoarse, weaker than normal.

If he could get out of this cellar, then maybe he could go to the station – or follow the tracks to a place just outside the station where the train – any train – hadn't picked up enough speed to make it impossible for him to jump it. Then he could go to the next town and get off the train and beg for a bit. People would be bound to give him money; they'd feel sorry for him. Especially now he'd got this bruise. And when he'd got enough money he could go far away, to London, or even Manchester. Didn't need nobody's help.

And the best thing about that plan was the police from Wigan wouldn't have a clue where the hell he'd got to.

He was set, then. He needed no bugger, did he? He'd get out of this cellar and disappear. Just disappear.

Weston waited until all the classes had settled down to their work. It was normally his favourite time of the school day, for the children were, by and large, alert and some of them even willing to learn. Their restlessness was still lying dormant, and in his mentoring sessions with Emily Mason he'd advised her to take full advantage of their relative docility by getting them working on set tasks that would necessitate a great deal of writing or thinking: dictation, or arithmetic. With Standard 1, he told her, there was no more exciting sound than the rattle of abacuses as the pupils worked their way through their sums, and he did indeed hear the reassuring *smack-smack* of abacus beads as he passed Standard 1's classroom. Emily Mason, as well as the five-year-olds, was learning.

Today, though, he was concerned more about how he should proceed than the ambience of learning and diligence in his establishment. That wretched boy Kelly had left his copybook in the coal cellar, and it was obvious he – or someone else – had tried to light the scrawl-filled object with a view to burning the entire school down. Prendergast had found it, and it was therefore incumbent upon Weston to pursue the matter, even though a part of him would gladly consign the thing to oblivion. He'd had enough of police parading through his school as if they owned the place.

To make matters worse, Nathaniel Edgar had sent a messenger round to school just before the start of morning lessons to say that he would unfortunately be late for his class today owing to his neighbour falling ill and requiring his assistance.

Weston recognised it for the lie it was. He'd more than likely taken too much drink last night and was nursing a hangover. Still, it meant he'd had to arrange for Edgar's Standard 5 to be crammed into Standard 4 with his deputy, Miss Ryan. It was fortunate that she was quite capable of controlling such a large group despite the initial clatter as chairs were carried from one room to another. He would need to speak with Nathaniel Edgar when he had the opportunity —and when the foolish man had sobered up.

As he reached the classroom for Standard 6, he sighed, took a deep breath, and allowed all such thoughts to store themselves at the back of his mind. He swung the classroom door open and stood in the doorway. Gratifyingly, the whole class stood in silence at the sight of the headmaster in their presence, a tribute, he reflected, to the professionalism of Miss Jane Rodley, who stood at the front of the class with chalk in her hand and a set of grammatical exercises written in her usual exemplary copperplate hand. She would be sorely missed, despite her occasional lapse into mawkish sentimentality where the children were concerned.

'Miss Rodley? A moment of your very valuable time?' he said in a low, respectful voice that maintained the atmosphere of calm in the room.

'Certainly, Headmaster,' she said. She pointed to the list of ten sentences, each containing a grammatical error, and ordered the class to copy each one into their exercise books, making sure they put in the corrected version.

Some of the pupils looked puzzled at this; some of them shrugged and bent over their books to begin their work, while others, the entire back row, for instance, watched craftily with pencils raised, waiting for the moment the door closed behind Miss Rodley.

'Is William Kelly in there?' Weston asked. The corridor was empty. Even so, he had lowered his voice.

Jane Rodley shook her head. 'He hasn't been in since last week. Some of the children have told me he's run away again. What's he done now?'

He held out the copybook for her to examine and said, 'Perhaps this is the reason he did so.'

For a moment, she looked flustered, her brow furrowed as she looked at the scorched edges of the book.

'You realise I shall have to contact the police? Again?'

From the tone of his voice, she got the impression that somehow this was her fault. He was, after all, in her class.

'You've shown quite a soft spot for that miscreant, haven't you?' Again, the undertone of rebuke.

'I've shown a certain amount of sympathy for the child. His family background . . .'

He took the book from her somewhat snappishly. 'The influence of your fiancé, no doubt. This.' He held up the evidence so that it was inches from her face. 'This is the reward for such sentimentality, Miss Rodley. And now I shall have to do my duty once more.'

He swirled round and stormed off down the corridor, leaving Jane Rodley with an expression of concern etched into her features.

'It's very good of you to come at such short notice, Sergeant Brennan.'

'Not at all. I was about to pay the school another visit anyway.'

'Oh?'

'Yes, but as your messenger said the matter was most urgent, I put aside all my other duties and ran all the way.'

The cynical look on Weston's face was evidence enough that the man was far more appreciative of irony than Constable Jaggery.

'Quite.'

Before Weston could explain why he had sent for him, Brennan said quietly, 'Why did you lie to the police, Mr Weston?'

There was a silence. The headmaster suddenly went pale. 'I beg your pardon?'

'When I asked you for Mr Tollet's address.'

'I gave you his address.'

'But you failed to mention that he was staying at the Royal Hotel.'

'That wasn't a lie. You asked for his address and I gave it to you.'

'It was obstructing my investigation.'

'I didn't like your tone then, Sergeant, and I certainly don't like it now!'

Brennan could see the man's lips tighten in anger. 'Just a few more questions before we move onto the reason you called me in.'

'More questions? I thought . . .'

'I'd like to know where you were in the summer of 1879.'

Weston sat back and looked nonplussed. 'What on earth do you wish to know that for?'

'Please just answer the question.'

Weston coughed to clear his throat. 'If you must know, my father was a solicitor. In that year, if I remember rightly, he was practising in Cambridge. Not far from Petty Cury, as a matter of fact. You know Cambridge, Sergeant?'

'Never had the pleasure, sir. Does he still practise in Cambridge?'

'My father died several years ago. My mother died last year.'

'I see. I'm sorry.' Brennan scribbled a few notes in his notebook and then said, 'You ever been to Hawkshead, in the Lake District?'

Weston shook his head.

'It appears Dorothea Gadsworth recognised someone from her past.'

'Well I can assure you it wasn't I.'

158

'A little girl, Tilly Pollard, drowned when Miss Gadsworth was seven. It sorely affected her.'

'It would sorely affect anyone, wouldn't it?'

'Indeed it would.' He paused, then said, 'Well then. The reason for my current visit?'

Weston took a deep breath and exhaled slowly. Then he opened his table drawer and took out a curled book, which he slid towards Brennan. 'It's a boy's copybook. As you can see, the outer edges have been singed.'

Brennan read the name on the front cover. 'Where was this found?'

'In the coal cellar. Beneath a dwindling mound of coal. In my opinion, that is evidence of arson.'

Brennan shook his head. 'Not quite, Mr Weston.'

The headmaster sucked his teeth. 'What is it then? An attempt to smoke the damned thing?'

He looked at Weston closely. The sharp response was reflected in the expression on the man's face. He seemed to have the weight of the world on his shoulders. Perhaps the business of leading a school was harder than Brennan imagined.

Brennan spoke calmly. 'What I mean is, there was no arson, was there? So nobody can be accused of it.'

'Attempted arson, then.'

'A different matter.' Brennan flicked through the pages of the book, noticed the untidy scrawl that littered each page. 'Not one of your brightest scholars then?'

'If you must know, the boy is a dratted nuisance. Always claiming victimhood. And that . . . mother of his.'

'I'm no believer in coincidences, Mr Weston, but this is genuinely one of them.'

Weston looked nonplussed.

'You see, the other reason I was going to pay you another visit today was because of this very pupil. William Kelly. It seems he's gone missing.'

'So I hear. Miss Rodley tells me some of Standard 6 have been talking. Jungle drums, Sergeant.'

'Well there's one coincidence I am doubtful about.'

'What's that?'

'The fact that William Kelly is last seen on the very night Miss Dorothea Gadsworth is murdered.'

Again, the headmaster sucked his teeth.

Brennan spoke patiently. 'I've already been to speak with Mrs Kelly.'

'A delightful experience, I'm sure.'

He ignored the comment. 'And she tells me that, while she has little time for the school as a whole, there's one teacher who at least seems to show some interest in her son's educational welfare.'

At the slur on the school's good name, Weston bridled. 'My staff pride themselves on getting the best out of our pupils. Sometimes it's like nibbling at a rotten apple, but . . .'

'I'd like to see the teacher in question, Miss Rodley. If it's convenient.'

'Absolutely not. She is teaching Standard 6.'

'Only a few minutes, I can assure you.'

'Out of the question.'

Brennan made to stand up. 'Then if she can't leave the classroom, there'll be no objection to my going there.'

Weston also stood up, his face scarlet now with anger. 'You'll do no such thing! What sort of pandemonium would erupt if a member of my staff were interviewed by the police in front of thirty-eight children? Can you imagine the damage that would cause? The pupils would spread the news like water through a burst dam.'

Brennan, having goaded the headmaster towards his apocalyptic nightmare, sat down again. 'Then I'm sure if you send her to me, you can take the opportunity to re-sharpen your teaching skills by sitting with Standard 6 for the next five minutes.'

Thus outmanoeuvred, Weston stifled the response he'd been about to give and was about to leave the room when Brennan added, 'Oh and I might as well kill two birds, so to speak.'

'I beg your pardon?'

'I need to have just a minute of Miss Alice Walsh's time when I'm done with Miss Rodley.'

'This is outrageous! I'm running a school, not a doctor's surgery!'

'It would merely necessitate you swapping Standard 6 for – I believe – Standard 3? Once Miss Rodley returns, of course.'

The smile he offered the headmaster did nothing to take the sting out of the venomous look he was given.

A few minutes later, Jane Rodley sat opposite Brennan, who had now removed himself from the visitor's chair and placed himself behind the headmaster's desk. Once again he was captivated by the singular beauty of her features, despite the worried look that now showed itself.

'I gather you know about William Kelly, Miss Rodley?'

'It's never *William*,' she said with an attempt at a smile. 'I remember the first morning this term when I read out the register. He made it quite clear he was to be referred to as *Billy*. But yes, I knew he'd gone missing. The others are full of wild tales about him.'

'Such as?'

She glanced down at her hands, as if she'd said something she shouldn't. 'Oh, the usual childish nonsense.'

'Give me an example.'

After a pause, she said, 'He was apparently in a fight on Friday night with another of my pupils. Albert Parkinson. The two of them are, shall we say, rivals?'

That tallied with what Mrs Kelly had told him. And Billy's expressed fear of being hanged for something. He glanced at the copybook still lying on the desk before him. Had the boy tried to burn the school down and was afraid he'd be hauled before the courts? Attempted arson wasn't a hanging offence, and even if it were, Billy Kelly was ten. Brennan knew full well there was no minimum age for the gallows but he'd never heard of a ten-year-old child having his neck stretched. No, if the lad were afraid of being hanged, then it was entirely possible someone put that thought into his head.

If so, why?

The damaged copybook suggested he was in the school cellar at some time. Had he been there Friday night?

'I heard about their confrontation,' he said. 'Mrs Kelly seems to be very worried. It has been several days now.'

A trace of a sneer flashed across her face.

'You've met the mother, Miss Rodley? She speaks highly of you.'

'Such a pity I can't reciprocate.'

'She tells me you're the only one to show any sort of interest in the lad.'

'Including her,' came the snappish reply. Then she seemed to realise what she'd said, and a professional veneer replaced the scorn. 'I'm sorry, Sergeant. I shouldn't have said that. I don't know the full situation in that family. All I know is there's an air of casual brutality. I've seen bruises . . .'

'Had he spoken to you about likely hiding places?'

She examined him curiously. 'What a strange question.'

'If the lad has run away from home it stands to reason he's hiding somewhere. And if you've shown some interest in him . . .'

She slowly shook her head. 'I think you misunderstand. I've shown him some consideration, some understanding. I've even taken the time to sit beside him while he's working to help him through his sums or his grammar work. But that's as far as it goes, Sergeant. I wouldn't dream of engaging with him on a personal nature. Why, he's probably miles away from here. Gone off to seek his fortune.'

'I see. Well, just a few more questions, Miss Rodley. Then you can go and rescue Mr Weston.'

'I can assure you he's perfectly capable of holding Standard 6 in the palm of his hand,' she said with a smile.

'I'm sure. Well then, can you tell me where you come from?'

'I beg your pardon?'

'Where were you born? Brought up?'

She shook her head. 'Is this an attempt at humour?'

'No. I'd just like to know.'

She held his gaze for a few seconds before replying. 'Liverpool, actually.'

He looked surprised. 'Really? You don't have the Liverpool twang, shall we say?'

'That's because I've taken pains to lose it.'

'Why?'

'My work as a teacher means I have to try to train my pupils to articulate. A losing battle in Wigan, but I can't even *try* to do that if my vowels and consonants deviate from the norm. Can I, Sergeant?'

'Have you ever lived in the Lake District? Hawkshead?'

'No.'

'It's just that the death of Miss Gadsworth might well be linked to the drowning of a small child fifteen years ago. Tilly Pollard.'

She looked away, towards the window. 'The death of any child diminishes the world, Sergeant. Does it not?'

He nodded slowly then reached forward, picked up the copybook and slid it into his pocket. 'Well that's all for the moment, Miss Rodley. If you hear anything of interest from the children – rumours, gossip, that sort of thing . . .'

'I'll be sure to let you know.'

'Thank you.'

She left without another word, and Brennan sat there for a few moments, drumming his fingers on the desk and replaying the interview in his mind.

Barely a minute later, Miss Alice Walsh was standing before him, looking down.

'I much prefer to stand in front of my betters,' she replied caustically to his offer of a seat. 'Reminds me of my place.'

Brennan sat back. Once more, the expression on her face was one of defiance.

'I apologise for asking you to leave your pupils.'

'I wasn't *asked*.'

'Nevertheless, it's good of you to see me.'

She set her lips, preventing another retort.

'I'm just trying to find out a little bit more about the staff here.'

'Why?'

'Oh, it's the way I work. Your background, for instance.'

'What about it?'

'I'm particularly interested in a time fifteen years ago. 1879 to be precise. *Summer* of 1879 to be even more precise.'

'That's a long time ago.'

'You would have been what? Seventeen? Eighteen?'

'Give or take,' she said. She appeared to take the reference to her age as an insult.

'Well then. Where were you living at that time?'

She raised her eyes and looked through the headmaster's window. 'That would be the summer before I started my teacher training. So I would have been at home, still living with my parents.'

'And where exactly was home?'

'Preston.'

He gave her his most disarming smile.

'Can you tell me if you have ever been to Hawkshead in the Lake District?'

'Why?'

'To satisfy my idle curiosity.'

She turned from the window. 'In that case, absolutely not is the answer to your question.'

'Miss Gadsworth's death may be connected to the death of a young child back then.'

She gave a frown. 'That's very sad. How did she die?'

'The little girl drowned, Miss Walsh. Tilly Pollard was her name.'

She bowed her head for a few seconds.

'Thank you, Miss Walsh. You may now return to your pupils.'

She turned on her heels and left the room. He stared at the closed door for several minutes before it reopened and Weston walked in.

'I hope your time has been profitable, Sergeant?' he asked as Brennan vacated the headmasterial chair.

'Possibly, Mr Weston. Possibly.'

CHAPTER NINE

It was funny, Billy told himself. A rat had bit him and made his hand throb, but it was another rat – or it might be the same sly bugger as bit him for all he knew – that had showed him how to escape.

He'd heard it slithering around the cellar. But it hadn't come under the door, because he'd been lying there for ages shouting through the gap at the bottom for someone to open the bloody door. But nobody came. He'd been left here to rot away or be gobbled up by man-eating rats. He couldn't climb up to the ceiling where the small narrow ledge was that led out onto the street: there was nothing in the place to climb on, for one thing. And even if he found something, what would be the use? The hole was far too narrow for him to squeeze himself through. And although he'd yelled and yelled and yelled, nobody from the street above had even stopped for a second to find out where all the noise had been coming from.

But then the rat came.

There was a bit of daylight that crept in from above, and that helped him. He heard at first that usual scratching sound, but at the very moment a shaft of sunlight shone through the opening he saw something move in the wall opposite the door.

Along the bottom, a tiny bulge appeared as the rat – a huge bugger! – pushed its snout through and finally managed to force its body into the cellar. He watched it scurry around the floor a couple of times until it disappeared into the darker recesses of the place. Gingerly, he crept over to where the rat had entered and pressed his hand against the lower part of the wall. It was damp, and the plastering felt crumbly and soft. He shoved a finger into the wall and, instead of meeting hard brick beneath, it broke through. He felt plastering and damp bits of wood as he pushed his hand then his arm all the way through to meet fresh air.

He could feel the wind blowing against his bare arm!

His heart began to thump faster as he drew his arm back then plunged it hard into the section of the lower wall next to the hole he'd just made. Again, with a little effort, the plaster yielded and despite the splintering on his arm he managed to force that through, too. Soon he was tugging at the jagged edges of the wall, laughing as he heard it loosen and crack away from its mouldy base.

He peered through and saw uneven flagstones, weeds sprouting at various intervals where the flags had buckled free from the others. He could also make out the bottom step of what seemed to be a set of steps curving round and upwards to street level. A swirl of wind drifted through the hole into the cellar, bringing with it louder noises from the street above. He could hear a band playing, and cymbals clashing.

Invigorated by the new sounds and smells, he'd soon created a space large enough for him to heave his body through. He fell in a heap onto the cold, damp flagstones.

Outside!

Dust from the wall swirled around and sharp particles of grit stung his eyes. It was the dust, along with the glare of sunlight, that forced him to close his eyes then rub them roughly to take away the stinging sensation. When he opened them again, his sight was blurred and he felt strange, his head swimming as the fresh air filled his lungs.

Through a red-rimmed haze, he found himself staring at a pair of slender shoes, well-polished and gleaming in the brightness of the afternoon sun. Beside them, a pair of equally well-polished boots, although both boots and shoes were flecked with tiny bits of dust making him think of stars in a night sky. The right boot was tapping impatiently on the flagstones, causing a *clack-clack* sound. The left shoe beside it turned inwards, and he heard the right boot say in a stern voice, 'Folly is bound up in the heart of a child.'

Then the left shoe, in a gentler voice, said, 'Proverbs?'

The right boot replied, 'Proverbs indeed.'

It was almost two in the afternoon when Nathaniel Edgar arrived at school. He was normally well presented, his suit a trifle shabby perhaps, but collar and tie were always in place and his waistcoat buttoned with his timepiece showing from his side pocket. Today, though, he had a rather dishevelled look. His tie was loose and a little askew, while his waistcoat was only partly buttoned. There was no sign of the watch.

He appeared to be having an animated discussion with Alice Walsh. When she saw the headmaster approach, she moved quickly along the corridor to where her own class were waiting for permission to enter their classroom.

'What the blazes do you think you're about?' Weston hissed in his ear when he saw Standard 5 already filing into the classroom and appearing unprepared for work. There was some pushing and shoving, with the girls giving as good as they got from the boys.

'Bringing the sheep from the fold and into the pen,' came the hearty reply.

Weston glared at him. There was a smell of carbolic about him, but something lurked beneath – another, quite different odour.

'What was Miss Walsh doing here?'

'Scolding me for my unprofessional appearance,' Edgar said, buttoning his waistcoat.

'Are you able to teach?' he asked.

Edgar placed a hand on his headmaster's shoulder. His words were steady, unslurred. 'I'm always ready to teach, Headmaster. Have no fear about that.'

Without waiting for a response, he walked briskly into the classroom, bellowed an order for silence, and closed the door behind him.

Weston looked through the upper half of the door, where the glass was dulled and almost opaque. He saw Edgar standing at the front and issuing further commands, the pupils responding with a miserable groan but obediently raising their desk lids and taking out their books. The time was fast approaching when he would have to speak with Nathaniel Edgar. They'd known each other a very long time, and it would be no easy task.

He was about to turn away when he noticed the frame holding the glass squares of the door: the putty was chipped and missing in places, and he could see the edging of the glass with its narrow brown strip where the putty had been.

'Falling apart,' he muttered to himself as he walked away. 'Falling apart.'

'Until now, sir, we've been concentrating our efforts on the murder of Dorothea Gadsworth.'

'Arsenic is a vile substance.' Captain Bell frowned. 'Took the stuff myself once.'

Brennan raised an eyebrow, but before he could present his train of thought as to the murder of Henry Tollet, the man was in full flow.

'I was bitten once, you see, by a viper in India. At one stage the medics feared for my leg, which was threatening to turn gangrenous. So they administered a Tanjore Pill. Arsenic, quicksilver and other such delicacies, all ground together and rubbed with wild cotton juice. After a few doses of that they stuck warm chicken livers on the wound. I stunk to high heaven but kept my leg, Sergeant.'

As if to prove the limb's sturdy survival, he slapped his right leg with some force.

Then he sat back and stared at the ceiling. Brennan's heart sank as he waited for an elaboration of the anecdote.

Instead, the chief constable said, 'Still, despite the heinous nature of arsenical poisoning, it's to the murder of Mr Henry Tollet that you must turn your attention.'

'Exactly, sir, as I was about to—'

'I've just returned from a meeting of the watch committee in the Council Chamber.'

'Oh?' Brennan, irritated at the interruption, knew full well the power such an august body wielded. Captain Bell had even been heard to curse them in his less discreet moments.

'*Oh* indeed. First of all they insisted that I follow the recommendations of the recent inspection report and arrange for those members of my force who failed the ambulance class to attend another. They tell me that first aid is an essential weapon in a policeman's armoury. I would have thought a truncheon better fitted that description. So I am to coerce the police surgeon to set up another series of classes. *Then*, as if to rub salt in the wound and leave the worst till last, they wish to know if we have an epidemic on our hands. "We mean murder, Chief Constable," they said, "not smallpox." It hasn't helped that one of the victims is a school inspector. The national newspapers have shown an interest. After last year's coal strikes and the horrors that brought, this is the last thing the town needs. I've given them my assurances that you are well advanced in your pursuit of the guilty one. Well advanced.'

This wasn't the time to qualify such a judgement. Instead, Brennan said, 'The murders are undoubtedly linked. But as to *how* they're linked . . .' He spread his hands palms upwards to show how empty they were.

'Tell me what you have.'

'Dorothea Gadsworth was given arsenic in the classroom at George Street. By whom, we don't know yet. But we do know she was due to catch her train back to Bolton from Wallgate Station on Friday night, only she didn't. For some reason she went instead to the school.'

'Lured there?'

'Presumably.'

'Why go back to a place where you failed to gain an appointment?'

Brennan thought for a moment before replying. He chose his words carefully. 'As I have already mentioned in our earlier meeting, it's my opinion she recognised someone at that school. Before she fainted she said something that sounded to the witness, Mr Nathaniel Edgar, like "Of course . . . let's wait."'

Captain Bell, in order to show how carefully he listened to what his sergeant had told him, added, 'And when you spoke to the grieving parents, they told you a sad tale from the time Miss Gadsworth was a small child, living in Hawkshead. Near a small lake called Esthwaite Water.'

Brennan repeated the version of the tale told to him by the Gadsworths – the drowning of the little girl Tilly Pollard, the criminal lack of care shown by the seventeen-year-old Julia Reece, a dereliction made all the fouler by her lewdness in the church with the young man called David.

'And you suspect Miss Gadsworth recognised this girl Julia, now grown into womanhood?'

'Or the boy David, grown into manhood.'

Captain Bell once more examined the ceiling. 'So whoever she recognises *knows* he or she has been recognised.'

'Presumably.'

'And if she were to let it be known what this person had done . . .'

'Scandal, certainly.'

'It could be any of the teachers, you say?'

'Or the vicar.'

The captain's eyes opened wide at that. 'Good Lord, you're not suggesting that Reverend Pearl . . . I mean, if he were the young man, David, then to be discovered having such a secret hidden deep in the past . . .'

'It would make for an interesting sermon.'

Bell frowned. The idea upset him, Brennan could see. The man had firm religious principles and expected others, especially men of the cloth, to uphold the virtues espoused by the Church. 'For such a person,' he mused, 'even with the excuse of youth, to be found practising such foulness in a church . . .'

'And a belfry at that,' Brennan added.

'What the blazes does it matter where he did it? A church is a church, whether he does it in a belfry or on top of the altar . . .'

He stopped abruptly, and Brennan could see the poor fellow was appalled by the sacrilegious image his own words had created. He had actually turned white with rage and shame.

'But to return to the matter of the school inspector,' said Brennan gently, by way of rescuing the man from his own vision of hell. 'It may well be that Miss Gadsworth felt compelled to speak with him, to tell him what she'd discovered. I've gone through the papers he left in the hotel room, but they reveal nothing.'

Nevertheless, Captain Bell's spirits were raised. It would, after all, be more likely to be a teacher she'd recognised if she were to share that information with a school inspector. 'Let's say she did speak with him. Did he believe her?'

'Hard to say, sir. What would he do with such information if he did believe her?'

'He would be duty-bound to report such a dark secret to the education authorities.'

'Along with the other thing, of course.'

Captain Bell frowned, worried that some new horror was about to be unleashed.

But Brennan merely said, 'The deception. If it were a teacher, or even if it were the vicar, one thing is sure: he or she is working under a false name. None of the male teachers is called David, and the vicar is Charles. And none of the women has the Christian name Julia, nor the surname Reece.'

'Here under false pretences then?'

'It would appear so.'

'So if Miss Gadsworth *did* recognise someone and told Henry Tollet, it would mean that both she and the inspector would need to be silenced.'

'Yes, sir.'

'But how did he or she manage to get the fellow to wander down to Poolstock and take a stroll by the bridge?'

'Apparently, according to the Royal Hotel, a note was left for Mr Tollet at the reception desk.'

'Who left it?'

Brennan shrugged. 'They saw no one. The note was just left there.'

'That's a gross dereliction of duty by whoever was manning the desk.'

'The fact remains he did receive a note. Probably urging him to meet with whoever it was. Then when they do meet, he or she pushes him into the canal and makes sure he can't climb to safety by stamping hard on his hands until he can climb no more.'

Bell stood up and walked over to his favourite position overlooking King Street.

'We're dealing with a fiend, Sergeant.'

'It may well be, sir. And there's the missing child, too.'

Captain Bell whirled round. 'The one who goes to the school?'

'Yes, sir.'

'And what does he have to do with all this?'

Brennan told him about the finding of the singed copybook, the comment overheard by young Parkinson that he was determined not to be hanged. 'I think someone planted that thought in his head.'

'Why?'

'He may well have seen something on Friday night. The murderer with the victim, perhaps. He might not know its significance, but he would later on when he heard about Miss Gadsworth's death.'

'So you think the boy is dead?'

'I hope not, sir. At least his body hasn't turned up.'

'Thank the Lord for that.'

Brennan paused then said, 'There are a couple of things that bother me, though.'

'Go on.'

'Well, sir, the note found by the body, for one thing. It contained the single word "*FAILED*". It wasn't written by the victim, according to her parents. And it wasn't a suicide note anyway because we know it wasn't suicide. But whoever put it there did so to make us think it was suicide.'

Captain Bell frowned. 'A puzzle, certainly. You said a couple of things?'

'The murderer placed a bottle of Scotch by the body to make it appear that Miss Gadsworth had taken drink either with the arsenic in it or as some sort of aid to courage. But Doctor Monroe found no trace of the whisky in her stomach. So why was the bottle put there?'

'Again, to make us think it was suicide.'

'Correct. But once more, like the clumsy suicide note, it was a stupid thing to do. Any murderer worth his or her salt would know these pieces of evidence would be discounted as soon as we investigated them. So why place these things for us to find them?'

'I see what you mean.'

'Either the murderer is very stupid indeed, sir, or playing a very clever game, the object of which at the moment is beyond me.'

* * *

At first their uniforms struck terror into Billy. When he allowed his blurred gaze to drift slowly upwards, he saw the navy blue trousers with their sharp creases, and a scarlet jumper stretched taut over a stiff-necked shirt, far cleaner than any shirt he'd ever seen. The woman to whom the shoes belonged wore a long navy blue skirt and a high-necked tunic topped with white lace collars. The man had a thick black beard, and for a second Billy thought of pirates and walking the plank. It was only when he saw what the man was wearing on his head – a smart cap with a red band – and the woman – a navy blue bonnet – that his terror subsided, to be replaced with distaste.

'Now young fellow,' said the man as he bent down and held out a hand towards Billy, 'I'm sure there are easier ways of leaving a building.'

Billy declined his offer of help and stood up of his own accord. The dust was still stinging his eyes and he couldn't clearly make out the man's features, registering only the fact that his eyes seemed narrowed, suspicious.

When the woman spoke, her voice was gentler, containing a note of friendliness and amusement. 'And there are doors now that open at the merest turn of the handle.'

He wiped his eyes and tried to focus on her face: she had a small mouth, turned up at the corners with the suggestion of a smile.

'That bloody place doesn't,' he said with a backward jerk of the head.

The man tutted. 'There's no need for that.'

Billy, who hadn't a clue what he'd done to offend the man, started to move past them. As he did so, he caught sight of several people staring down into the basement well from railings above. All of them wore the same uniform he'd heard his dad mocking whenever they marched past blowing their trombones and clashing their cymbals: '*Imagine that lot on a battlefield, eh, lad? Some bloody good that army'd be.*'

Before either of them could stop him, he ran up the steps and made an attempt to rush out onto the street, where a group of onlookers were now gathering on the other side of the street. But one of the Salvation Army soldiers reacted quickly to block his path, placing one arm on the gated opening at the top of the steps, his other hand clutching his euphonium.

'There's no need to run, child,' he said. 'We aren't going to bite.'

He would rue those words. Once the idea was planted in his head, Billy leant forward on the topmost step and launched himself towards the man's right hand, sinking his teeth into the pink flesh and tasting the metallic warmth of blood.

The man howled in pain, emitted a curse that would have shocked William Booth himself to his very core, and clutched his right hand with his left, dropping the euphonium in the process.

Billy scurried past him, leaping over the fallen instrument, ignoring the raucous cheers from the onlookers across the way and hurtled headlong down the street as a small band of Salvation Army soldiers relinquished their instruments in more careful fashion and began to chase after him. There was such a pain in his head now, and his hand was throbbing where the rat had bitten him. He felt hot and clammy, but he knew he had to put all the pain to the back of his mind. He had to focus on one thing at this moment, and that was escape.

He didn't know this part of Wigan very well. He'd been told only that it was far enough away from where he lived – and near enough to the railway station – that it would be safe for him to be seen on the streets once the plan to get him out of town was under way. But as he tore along St Thomas Street and into Chapel Street all he could think of was why he'd not been brought out of that stinking cellar before now?

He heard the clatter of boots on the cobbles behind him and the shouts of 'Stop him! Stop that boy!' He was growing breathless; his mouth started to become dry and hot, and it was difficult to swallow, but he daren't stop. He didn't even take the time to turn round to see where they were as he swept past a small group of beshawled women standing outside a butcher's shop with their arms folded and looped through dangling baskets.

'What's the matter with yon mon?' said the butcher himself who had come to the shop doorway to see what all the shouting and clattering of feet was in aid of.

'Bet the little bugger's pinched summat,' said one of his erstwhile customers.

The butcher pointed at one of the pursuing Salvation Army soldiers who was himself growing red-faced with the effort of the chase. 'Looks like that mon needs a drink,' he said.

'Aye. A pint o' stout!' came the reply from another of the women, a comment that seemed to amuse them a great deal for they all started to chortle and urge the young boy to run faster.

Once he reached the end of Chapel Street, Billy stopped for a second to catch his breath and assess his options. As he leant back against the wall of the house on the corner, he felt a wave of sickness wash through him. He leant forward, placing both hands on his knees, and vomited into the gutter.

'Dirty little bastard!' came a hard voice from behind. He turned his head and fully expected to see one of his pursuers standing there. He breathed a sigh of relief when he saw it was a man standing at his front door, staring with disgust at the pool of vomit at Billy's feet.

Billy ignored him, wiping his mouth and spitting out the rancid taste. The road facing him – Queen Street – swept to right and left for quite a distance, flanked on either side by a row of houses and shops. He chose right and had managed barely twenty yards when the ones chasing him turned the corner.

'They'll drag me to the rozzers and then I'll be jailed for bitin' an' all,' lamented Billy. He could feel his legs grow weary now, and his breath was coming in short, frantic bursts. He started to sob and felt the tears slide down his face.

'*You'll hang for sure, Billy. Unless you let me help you.*' That's what he'd been told.

Ahead, he could see a rag-and-bone man, a bowler hat planted askew on his head, his cart built high with a vast array of clothing of every description, clothing only slightly more soiled than the ones he himself was wearing. He was bent over his horse, patting his head as he devoured the contents of his feed bag. The man, a rough-looking individual, glanced up as Billy rushed down the street towards him. He took in the three men chasing him, whispered something to his horse, who studiously ignored him, and stepped away from the cart and directly into Billy's path, clenching his fist as he did so.

CHAPTER TEN

Richard Weston had so many things weighing him down now that he felt breaking point was growing closer by the hour. He waited until the end of the school day and the last of the pupils had left the building to summon up the courage for what was going to be a most difficult meeting. Still, this was something he couldn't ignore any longer: Nathaniel Edgar's drinking was growing worse, and it was only a matter of time now before he did something that reflected badly on the school.

When the knock came on the door, swiftly followed by Edgar's breezy entrance, he sat behind his desk looking composed and amenable. The last thing he wanted was a stand-up row.

'You know, Nathaniel, that this last week has been hellish.'

Edgar sat down and said, 'It would have broken a lesser man, Headmaster.'

'God knows the place has a less than satisfactory reputation as it is, and now, with the supposed murders of two people, that reputation is being dragged further and further into the mud.'

'I hardly think that's fair,' said Edgar in the school's defence. 'What annoys me is the unfairness of it all. Both of the victims were only tangentially connected to the school, weren't they? Neither of them had ever been to the place before Friday. All this nonsense about a child drowning fifteen years ago. No. They can't tar us with that particular brush, can they now?'

Weston sighed. This wasn't going exactly as he'd planned.

'Look, Nathaniel, it's the school's reputation we need to focus on.'

'I agree.'

'And while I'm the last person to throw wild accusations around . . .'

Edgar sat forward. From the expression on his face it was fairly obvious he had an idea where the conversation was leading. Weston leant forward and picked up a ruler, tapping it once on the desk.

'It's the drinking, Nathaniel.'

'The drinking?'

'I know why you were late today. Why you only arrived at two this afternoon. Most unprofessional.'

'And why was I late?' Edgar's voice had taken a harder, more defensive tone.

'I mean, this thing about your neighbour . . .'

'Being ill, you mean?'

Weston slowly shook his head. 'It isn't so long ago you told me the man was unpleasant to you. Sneering at the fact you're a teacher.'

'The man is unpleasant, and he does sneer.'

'So?'

'His wife doesn't.'

'I beg your pardon?'

'She knocked on my door and asked me to send for the doctor. She had a fever, or so she thought.'

There was a heaviness now in the pit of Weston's stomach. He knew absolutely that Edgar was lying.

'You told me a few weeks ago that the man was a widower.'

The room was filled with an uneasy silence that hung in the air. Sounds drifted in through the open window: snatches of conversation from passers-by, the caretaker whistling in the playground.

Finally, Edgar said, 'It seems I've been caught out.'

Weston gave another sigh.

'So what do you propose to do, Richard? Give me the cane?'

Weston stood up and walked over to the window, his hands clasped behind his back. The caretaker Prendergast, who was sweeping leaves from the gated entrance, had the audacity to pause mid-sweep and give him a wave. Was the entire structure of order and respect crumbling? He whirled round.

'Even if I were to give you one final chance, who's to say we won't be in this position in, say, two months' time? By which point you might have done something to bring the school's reputation plummeting down.'

'Even further, you mean?'

Weston ignored him. 'I cannot make the decision on my own, of course. Reverend Pearl must be . . .'

Before he could finish, Edgar too had stood up, the expression on his face now very dark and menacing. So much so that Weston's words dried in his throat.

'Well, Headmaster,' said Edgar with a grim smile slowly spreading on his lips. 'I'm sure you won't need to involve the good reverend.'

'And why not? As school manager he would . . .'

'As school manager, he would need to be informed. Of course he would. But what if the matter of a teacher occasionally having a little too much to drink were to pale in comparison with what another, more highly regarded member of the school had been up to? Wouldn't that have the same impact as the blowing of the trumpets outside the walls of Jericho?'

One of the lessons Reverend Charles Pearl learnt early in his life was the power of language. 'It goes beyond saying,' he was told early in his ministry, 'that we in the Church are educated to a far higher degree than the ones who will sit in their Sunday morning pews waiting for the weekly sermon. A sermon only has power if it is accessible. Talk about *grandeur* and *omnipotence* and the parishioner will start scratching for fleas. No, Charles, far better to use the language and the images they can relate to. The challenge, then, of course, is to render an everyday image in such a way as to reflect the glory of the message. The warm glow of the sun is cooled and made dull, is it not, by the opaqueness of a stained-glass window? You must show them Heaven's beauty in a lump of coal.'

However, he was struggling, at the moment, to find the words to fit any image or to urge a contemplation of Heaven's beauty or the infinite mercy of God.

The little girl was lying in bed, the room dark and curtained to keep out the rays of late afternoon sunlight, and her mother and father were sitting either side, each clasping a hand with uncharacteristic gentleness, as if any pressure they exerted would squeeze the last drops of life from her emaciated body. On her face and the upper part of her chest, dark, purple eruptions were clearly visible, rendered all the more sinister by the redness around the base of each swelling, the inflammation evidently taking its putrid hold and refusing to relax its grip. Occasionally, the child's tongue protruded, and the vicar was repulsed by its thick, dry blackness.

'Doctor told us to give her beef broth,' the mother whispered, her voice weak and hopeless. 'But the poor little mite couldn't keep owt down.'

Reverend Pearl gave a small cough. These people – two of his loyal parishioners who sat in the same pews each Sunday and gave every appearance of heeding his admonitions on sin and the evils of intemperance – had sent for him not out of any desire for spiritual comfort but as a sign of their helplessness. The doctor had been and gone, and now it was his turn.

'She reminds me of a child I once knew,' he began, slowly and in hushed, sepulchral tones. 'She, too, suffered a great deal and was taken early from the comforting arms of her family. And I remember the pain they felt when she finally left this wicked world. But their pain, their grief, was nothing compared to the look of sheer elation – I mean, of sheer delight – that suddenly spread itself across the child's face when the moment came. It was as if suddenly the storm clouds had opened and revealed the brightest of heavenly skies, all filled with little angels with arms open just waiting to welcome another one into their presence. It was a beautiful sight, like emerging from the pit to a beautiful summer's day.'

They blinked and flashed a look at each other across the damp and crumpled bed. This wasn't what the good vicar normally talked about in his sermons, the look said. There, he gave them a weekly vision of the other place, a lowly place all ablaze with the fires of Hell, with the leering grasping menace of unspeakable demons all ready and willing to snatch you from the world after your evil sinning.

'Happen we should give the lass a bit of a wash, like,' said the father, a stoker on the railways with broad and muscular arms.

'Why?' his wife asked.

The man gave Reverend Pearl an embarrassed glance. 'Just in case, that's all.'

'In case what?'

'In case them angels come. Poor little wench wants to be spotless for them.'

Before his wife could respond – whether to mock his gullibility or accede to his request it was impossible for Charles Pearl to know – the little girl opened her eyes. They were black, and deep, and sightless.

'Water,' she said in a hoarse whisper.

'Please, allow me,' said the vicar and stood up before either of the parents could prevent him. 'I'll get the child some water from downstairs. You'll both need to be by her side.'

With that, he left the room with what appeared to be indelicate haste. As he closed the door behind him, he placed his head against the jamb and closed his eyes tightly.

He wished Jane were here at this moment.

It had been an easy matter to escape the clutches of the Salvation Army once the rag-and-bone man hit the first of them with his huge fist. The sight of the uniformed soldier falling flat on his backside had a varied impact on those watching: the ones across the street, including the butcher and his customers, were secretly pleased that the man had ended up in such an undignified position, for none of them espoused the evangelical temperance that the Salvation Army made such a fuss about. The other soldiers, following closely behind their colleague, stopped abruptly and stared in wonder at the most undignified way he had removed his cap and was rubbing his jaw.

One of them said, 'I'll go on. That boy needs help.'

The others shrugged, conscious that their view of *salvation* lacked their colleague's ardour.

'Get gooin', yer little bugger!' the rag-and-bone man had yelled, and Billy hadn't needed telling twice.

He fled down Queen Street, unaware of the single figure now following him, and at last entered a road he was familiar with. Turning left into Chapel Lane he began to slow down. He looked round. No sign now of the ones chasing him. He walked quickly, blending into the number of people making their way mainly in the one direction, towards the spot where Darlington Street and King Street blended into one.

He knew full well that he couldn't venture anywhere near King Street. That was where the police station was, and for all he knew they were already building the gallows where they'd hang him till his neck stretched.

No, he'd make his way along Chapel Lane, past the cattle pens where sometimes he and his pals had goaded the cattle till they stomped and snorted and mooed, then sneak up the long alleyway that ran the length of the goods sheds beneath the railway bridge. That would bring him to the sloping embankment. The plan was to scramble to the top of the embankment and, when the right moment came along, stretch up and clamber aboard one of the many goods trains that rattled along. He'd done it before, just for a short time, for they all knew the trains were slowing down by this time: Wigan Wallgate and Wigan North Western were only some two hundred yards away. He'd climb into one of the wagons and hide himself beneath the canopy. Hadn't they done that too before now?

He smiled to himself. Soon, he'd be safely hidden. Soon he'd be out of Wigan and free of the hangman's noose.

Soon, he'd be really on his own. He shivered as the implications hit home.

Home.

Fifty yards further back, the Salvation Army soldier began to increase his pace.

At that moment, Jane Rodley had other worries to contend with. She had been late leaving school – the caretaker Prendergast had spotted her as she walked out of the main entrance and had immediately made his way towards her. He was pointing at the school building.

'Lucky it's still standin', eh?'

She blinked, unaware of his meaning.

'The school,' he went on, leaning on his brush as if their conversation were quite a natural, everyday occurrence.

'I don't follow you.'

'Ah, his lordship's not told you then?'

'Told me what?'

'That brat you've allus taken a shine to.'

'Which brat?'

Her tone implied there were plenty brats to choose from.

'Kelly.'

She pursed her lips. 'The boy's gone missing, Prendergast.'

'Oh aye. He would. After tryin' to burn the place down.'

He spent the next few minutes embellishing the tale of the copybook, which she already knew, its finding and its condition, along with its significance. She stood there, lips pursed, unwilling to share in the caretaker's condemnation of Billy Kelly.

The foolish child!

'That's what comes of you offerin' the lad a helpin' hand,' he went on. 'Gets bitten clean off.'

Another voice behind them said, 'What gets bitten clean off?'

They both turned round as Emily Mason approached. She looked quite startled by the caretaker's comment.

Prendergast gave a superior sniff and began to sweep the flooring of the entrance. He was muttering something about someone being 'only a bit of a child herself.'

As he disappeared inside the building, Emily turned to Jane Rodley, her face ashen. 'He's referrin' to me, miss, ain't he?'

'Well,' said Jane with a frown on her forehead, 'firstly, remember what I told you? I'm Jane, not miss. Not any longer.'

Emily flushed a deep scarlet. 'I know. I know. It's just hard sometimes. You havin' taught me a few years ago an' all.'

'And secondly,' Jane went on, placing a hand upon the pupil-teacher's arm, 'you must never say *ain't*. Remember it isn't a word. It's a colloquialism. I'm sure the headmaster has explained that to you in your mentoring meetings. But,' she added quickly when she saw the girl's head drop, 'you're doing very well indeed with your aitches. You hardly drop any now. That's very good.'

'Thank you, miss. I mean, Jane.' She said her goodbyes and walked through the playground to the railings beyond, her head still fixed on the ground.

Jane too started to leave. At the school gate, she stopped and looked back at the building. Soon she would leave this place for the last time, and a new world would open for her. She often thought about what that would mean. Now she only had children to deal with; in a short while it would be the worries and tribulations of all Charles's parishioners. The children would fade into the background. That would be hard to accept, she knew, for she had such a desire to save them all.

Suddenly she heard whistling and saw Nathaniel Edgar emerging from the building.

'Nathaniel?' She saw the expression on his face. It held just a glimmer of suppressed excitement. 'Are you feeling all right?'

'I've never felt better!' he declared. He gave a nod backwards. 'We should do it each and every day. What a better world it would be, eh, Miss Rodley?'

'What do you mean?'

He swept past her with an ironic touch of the forelock.

'Clear the air, my dear. Clear the air.'

The eight wheels of the LNWR coal engine were still rotating at a fair speed as they approached Wigan Wallgate in the distance. Along the side of every coal wagon two white diamond shapes were painted above the initials LNWR that were written along the solebar beneath. Once upon a time, Billy and the others would race alongside the rattling wagons, seeking out the safest way to get on board. Once they'd managed to clamber onto the slowing wagon by grabbing the long metal levers that operated the side doors, they'd heave themselves over the rim of the wagon and into the body of the wagon itself. Sitting on top of a mound of coal, seeing how deep they could force their legs to sink into the pile and waving to bemused onlookers, gave them all a bloody great laugh. But the best time came when the wagons were empty of coal, for that brought different challenges to Billy Kelly and his pals. There, they'd struggle to slide the lower lever that operated the wooden planks of the flooring that lay beneath the solebar and raise a cheer when their efforts were rewarded and the door beneath their feet dropped open.

Only problem was the state of their clothes when they'd dropped through the floor and onto the railway tracks once the train had stopped. If the wagons were empty, often the engine didn't slow down and stop at the station, which meant they'd have to risk jumping from the moving train onto the grassy embankment just beyond the station. That was risky, but they'd tumble around for ages living off the experience and clearing themselves of coal dust in the process.

Now, though, as he stood on the embankment watching the coal engine getting nearer, his heart sank a little. The trail of wagons behind the engine were all piled high with coal. That meant he'd have nowhere to hide and would be forced to risk being spotted as the wagons rattled through the station.

What should he do?

He could wait for another goods train, he supposed. Passenger trains were no good; he'd run a far greater chance of being caught by some stuck-up inspector even if he managed to scramble into a carriage. And there'd be the problem of other passengers creating merry hell if he suddenly pulled the door open and pulled himself into the compartment.

No, he told himself. He'd have to be patient and wait for the right goods train to come along. He'd even jump a cattle wagon and put up with the cow shit.

He looked down at his hand where the rat had bitten him, and was shocked to see how red and swollen it had become.

No wonder the bastard's throbbin', he thought. His vision

blurred once more, and he saw the two puncture marks, where the rat's teeth had sunk into his flesh, suddenly become four. He felt his head grow light and dizzy; his mouth felt hot and dry, and he closed his eyes for a second to steady himself.

When he opened them again he saw the train getting closer now. He watched the steam belch from the chimney, drifting a few feet above the engine and billowing around the trailing wagons. Just before the loaded goods train drew near to where he was standing, he heard the crunch of footsteps close behind him.

He whirled round.

One of the Salvation Army soldiers was a mere yard away, his arms outstretched as if ready to snatch him and take him back to St Thomas Street.

'Don't worry,' the man said. 'I won't hurt you.'

'Fuck off!' said Billy and turned to flee.

The man behind him screamed as Billy stepped onto the railway track, his legs appearing to buckle beneath him as he fell into the path of the approaching train.

CHAPTER ELEVEN

Brennan sat in his office, deep in thought.

He'd dealt with quite a few murders in his time. Last year, for instance, during the miners' strike, he'd been faced with quite a complex murder case until he finally fixed the pieces of the puzzle together. But there was something about the two murders that bothered him. The first victim – Dorothea Gadsworth – was poisoned. Very often, poisoners were found to be women, the crime being almost without the confrontational violence that occurred, say, in a stabbing or a vicious assault. The poisoner could be miles away when the effects of the deadly substance were felt and the task completed.

Yet the second murder – Henry Tollet – was very different. This involved no subtle and furtive dissolving of poison. No, this crime was of a violent kind, stamping hard on the poor man's hands as they tried to claw their way back onto the canal bank. More of a man's crime?

With two murders of such different characteristics, he might well consider the possibility of two separate killers. One male, one female.

And that would suggest a collaboration.

He went through the list of possible suspects, the ones who had been present at the school when Miss Gadsworth came for her interview.

Richard Weston. Nathaniel Edgar. Reverend Charles Pearl. Jane Rodley. Emily Mason. Alice Walsh. Esther Ryan. Florence Hardman.

One of them? Two of them?

Or none? Was he completely on the wrong track?

The last two weren't in the staffroom when she fainted, although recognition could have been delayed. Yet those two were somewhat older than Julia Reece would now be.

He was convinced of one thing, though: the missing boy, Billy Kelly, had been at the school last Friday night. What had he seen? It was highly likely he'd tried to set the school ablaze – from what he'd discovered about the boy, he was continually in trouble and endured several beatings recently. If he were receiving the same treatment at home from that harridan of a mother . . .

What a life the child had.

But now he was missing. Had he run away? Or was he even now lying at the bottom of the canal or in some shallow-dug grave somewhere in the woods? The thought made him shudder.

There was a knock on the door. Constable Jaggery entered.

'Sergeant.'

'What is it?'

'Messenger from the Victoria Hotel.'

Brennan grew irritated. 'Get to the point.'

194

'He's brought a message from the Gadsworths.'

'What message, Constable?'

'They want to see you. Said they'd remembered summat.'

As they turned into King Street, they could hear some shouting from a distance behind them, from Darlington Street.

'What the bloody 'ell's all that?' said Jaggery, turning round and noticing a small crowd gathering and pointing upwards towards the railway embankment.

Brennan kept on walking. 'We have more pressing matters to deal with, Constable. If it's a clog-fight there's plenty constables in the station can deal with it. Now keep up.'

'I boil the fruit for an age, you see, Miss Rodley. An age. Nothing to cover it. Then it's best to skim it. No sugar at that point, oh deary me, no. You see, the scum from the fruit rises. *Then* you add the sugar.'

As if to demonstrate her point, Mrs Flanagan, the vicar's housekeeper, emptied a bag of sugar into the preserving pan.

'See? Three quarters of a pound. Pound of fruit, three quarters of a pound of sugar. It's gettin' them proportions just so, Miss Rodley.'

The kitchen was small, with a single oven enclosed in a small range. Mrs Flanagan stood back and offered the wooden ladle to Jane Rodley. ''Ere, miss. You give it a stir.'

With a deep breath, she took the ladle and sunk it into the glutinous mess that would miraculously transform itself into strawberry jam. Inwardly, she cursed the housekeeper. When Jane called at the vicarage, she was told by Mrs Flanagan that the good reverend had been unexpectedly called out to an ailing child, and

195

that she was to come in and wait for him as he didn't expect to be too long, and wouldn't it be a good idea for his housekeeper to take the time to show his wife-to-be some of the secrets of the kitchen?

'A little bit more bant, miss,' said Mrs Flanagan in a gently disapproving tone.

'A little more what?'

'Bant, miss. Sorry. I forgot you weren't from round 'ere.'

'No.'

'Bit more effort then, miss. Preserves is a sticky thingumajig.'

'Indeed,' she agreed. Then she immediately breathed a sigh of relief when she heard the front door open and close and Charles's familiar footsteps echo along the small corridor. She quickly handed the ladle back and said, 'An enjoyable lesson. It makes a change to be on the receiving end of education, Mrs Flanagan.'

Before the housekeeper could respond, she swept out of the room. Mrs Flanagan tutted as a small globule of preserve dripped from the ladle to the kitchen floor.

As soon as Jane saw her fiancé's face, she knew something was wrong.

'What is it, Charles?' she asked when they had sat down in the living room and he had removed his outer clothing.

He looked at her for a while then said, 'I've just watched a young girl die.'

'How horrible.'

'Yes, it was.'

'What was the cause?'

'Measles.'

Jane remained silent for a minute, while the dying light of early evening settled upon the room. Finally she said, 'Do you wish to be left alone?'

He gave her a look of infinite pain.

She spoke in a low, hushed tone. 'You feel the helplessness of death too much, my dearest. What's done is done. Far better to look to the future and let the past be at rest.'

He held her hand tightly. 'You are my strength, Jane,' he whispered.

Since they last spoke, Brennan noticed a marked deterioration in Mrs Gadsworth's complexion. Inside their hotel room, without the social necessity of a mourning veil, her face was even paler than before. Her eyes, too, although red-rimmed from crying, were dried and cracked. He wondered if she'd cried so much that she had nothing left, and the sockets were now sore reminders of a time when grief had given her some slight relief from the knowledge of what had happened to her daughter. Gadsworth himself stood beside his wife, who was seated on one of the two chairs the room possessed, with a protective hand on her shoulder. Brennan noticed the man's hand was shaking.

Constable Jaggery stood by the window which overlooked Wallgate itself, although the curtains were closed as a mark of respect for the dead.

'You asked us to let you know if we remembered anything,' Gadsworth said.

'Anything at all,' agreed Brennan, anxious to find out if the information was of case-shattering importance or merely recollected trivia from a time gone by.

Mrs Gadsworth gave a small cough and covered her mouth with a handkerchief. When she removed it, she examined the cloth for a second and looked up at her husband, giving him an almost imperceptible shake of the head. He seemed heartened by it.

'We were talking last night – the usual things people talk about in circumstances such as ours, I suppose. Memories of a far happier time, of the countless instances of mischief and antics Dorothea got up to.'

'And the things she used to say,' added his wife. 'Don't all parents treasure up those little bits of childish nonsense? Save them to be brought out and shared, like a box of photographs?'

'Indeed we do,' said Brennan gently, with a fleeting memory of his son Barry asking why the priest kept saying 'Dominoes for biscuits' during the mass. It was far easier to shrug and pat him on the head than to explain why Father Clooney was speaking Latin and that *Dominus vobiscum* had nothing to do with biscuits.

'Well,' Gadsworth went on, 'we remembered what she said that summer, when poor Tilly was drowned. One day, not long after the accident, she suddenly told us that she thought Julia Reece must have been a witch.'

Brennan frowned. He glanced over to where Constable Jaggery was furtively peering through a narrow gap in the curtains. He caught his sergeant's gaze and turned back into the room.

'And why was that?'

'She told us that she and Tilly had one day sat in the graveyard while David was clearing the graves for the vicar. Julia Reece was there, and the two of them were talking about religion, and good and evil. Julia told David that she had once saved a witch from being burnt at the stake, and of course David laughed. But Dorothea and Tilly didn't laugh. After all, talking about witches in a graveyard . . .' He allowed his voice to taper off, perhaps to imply the evil that even then lurked inside the girl.

Mrs Gadsworth continued. 'Later, when my sister came over to Leeds to stay with us for a while – she needed to spend some time away from Hawkshead and the tragic memories it held – we told her what Dorothea had said. About Julia claiming to have saved a witch. And to our surprise she said that, in essence at any rate, the claim was true. Apparently, a few years before the accident, Julia had befriended an old woman, a curmudgeonly old thing, who often asked Julia to run errands. Then some of the dogs and cats in the village took ill and died. A disease, like as not. But when the old woman's cat survived, the more superstitious of them claimed it was witchcraft. They took to threatening her, even stoning her house. Then Julia organised a group of the children and they took to standing defiantly outside the woman's home, holding hands and singing hymns. Silly sort of stuff, but it did the trick. Later the veterinary surgeon from Windermere discovered that the rotting carcass of a dead pig had caused the disease which killed many of the animals. So I suppose the Reece girl played some part in saving the woman, certainly from persecution. Although I think the threat of burning her at the stake was the girl's invention.'

'Probably means nothing at all,' said her husband.

'I disagree,' Brennan replied. 'Anything that helps to give us a clearer picture of the girl is of immense value. Thank you both.'

As they left the hotel, Brennan filled his lungs with the cool evening air. Somehow he'd felt stifled in that sad room, and it felt good to be out on the street where a tram had stopped and people were disembarking.

Jaggery, who saw the lines of concentration along his sergeant's brow, said, 'Witches, Sergeant? Bit of a let-down, eh?'

Brennan slowly breathed out. 'Well, we know more about the Reece girl now than we did before.'

'What? That she saved an old bat from burnin'?'

Brennan didn't feel like correcting him.

* * *

'You seem in a better mood!'

The speaker, a clerk in a local bank, stood beside Nathaniel Edgar who was watching some of the members on the green through the clubhouse window. The Wigan and District Bowling Club lay on the outskirts of town. It was founded in 1852, and many of the older members recalled a time when the green was first built. Back then, they'd had to retire to a local public house, the Three Crowns Inn, until the members managed to secure a loan from the bank to build their own clubhouse. Now it was thriving, despite recent criticisms of the standard of the green and the possibility of a re-turf.

None of which bothered Nathaniel Edgar, who saw the place more as a place of refuge, of companionship, rather than a venue for gentle exercise. He turned, held up his glass in acknowledgement of the greeting, and recited some lines in a slurred voice:

'"*Small clouds are sailing, Blue sky prevailing, The rain is over and gone!*"'

His friend took one look at the half-drained glass and smiled. 'Shakespeare?'

'Oh, dear me, no. I couldn't see Shakespeare waxing lyrical at the foot of a bridge in Ullswater as Wordsworth did.'

'So what's brought on this change of mood? Last night you were in as black a mood as I've seen you. When I took you home you were mumbling about having lost something. Did you find it?'

Nathaniel took a long draught and emptied his glass. 'We all lose something, Patrick, my young friend. And then we have to go looking for something else.'

'Why don't we go out on the green? Get some fresh air. There's enough light for fourteen ends.'

'Not at all.' He raised a finger and pointed to the fading

light outside. 'Just look at that sky. *"Good things of day begin to droop and drowse."'*

'Wordsworth again?'

'No, dear boy. Shakespeare.'

It had taken Alice Walsh a long time to be accepted. At first, with her alien accent and her more refined mode of dress, not to mention the fact that when she went to work the only substance to sully her hands was chalk dust, the women who worked on the pit brow had the distinct impression that she looked down on them, that she sometimes stood outside the colliery gates with leaflets and petitions of all sorts in her delicate hands only to expect gratitude from them and perhaps even a curtsy or two.

But gradually, as she engaged them in conversation and suffered the ribald comments of the miners as they passed the small group of women at the gates, Alice Walsh was at least tolerated. One or two of them began to acknowledge her in the street when they passed her in town. Some of them even came along to the meetings of the Wigan branch of the Manchester National Society for Women's Suffrage, where she and others would make every effort to elicit their support for the franchise and exhort them to spread the word at every colliery in the borough. She knew there was an appetite for protest in the women. It had only been seven years ago that twenty three of them had travelled to London to lobby the then Home Secretary against the threat of abolishing their right to work at the pits with the proposed new Mines Regulation Act. The government had even touched upon their practical mode of dress – black flannel trousers – as unsuitable, and Alice had been especially pleased when told the women had turned up in London wearing their working attire.

One in the eye for the toffs.

It was that steely and dignified resolve, to fight against Westminster tyranny, that she admired so much. If only her fellow members of the Wigan branch could harness that sense of defiance and righteousness in the cause of suffrage!

Tonight's meeting had gone well, and over twenty pit women had turned up to hear what the society was proposing. Once the last of them had left the hall, Alice spent a few minutes with the other members of the committee before saying goodnight.

When she got outside, she headed towards the nearest tram stop. All thoughts of suffrage were now replaced by other considerations. She prided herself on the ability to do that, to immerse herself in one thing then section it off and turn to something else.

Now, she thought of the other problem facing her. The other night, admittedly, she'd lost all track of time and completely forgot what she had promised. That wouldn't happen again. It would be unpleasant, she knew, but sometimes when things had gone as far as they could go and there was no other way out, then you just had to take the bull by the horns, so to speak. She would do it tonight.

Once she was settled in the tram, wrapping her coat around her to ward off the growing chill of the night, she allowed her mind to think forward, to what was to come. Not backwards, at what had been.

Sometimes, no matter how hard she tried, it proved very difficult for Mrs Flanagan to block her ears and deaden the sounds of conversation. She knew the good reverend had been unsettled in his mind these past few days, and she also knew that the recent visit to a dying child had sorely troubled him. That he was essentially a good and decent man, she had no doubt, even though his choice of future wife –Jane Rodley – wouldn't have been her choice for the sainted man. No, she had far too much to say for herself, for one thing. And that was a consequence of being a teacher and used to having instant obedience. But the other thing was the way she had recently been speaking to him, as if he were inferior. A man of faults.

The first thing that surprised her this morning as she arrived at the vicarage was the fact that Miss Rodley was already inside. Mrs Flanagan had a deep sense of propriety, and while she had no doubts whatsoever about the nature of the woman's visit – the vicar must have been appalled when he opened the door and saw her standing there as she must have appeared, in a swirl of mist – she nevertheless felt it was a breach of some code or other for her to pay such an early morning visit.

And then, once Mrs Flanagan had accepted her presence with a sniff and gone immediately to the kitchen for the reverend's breakfast, she had accidentally left the kitchen door ajar, thus rendering it possible to hear some of whatever was being said along the corridor. To close the door might bring attention to the fact that it was open in the first place. And in the second place . . . well, it was clear, once she moved into the corridor itself, that words of a heated nature were being exchanged.

'. . . *Sure it won't come to that* . . .'

'. . . *Hardly slept for worry* . . .'

'. . . *You must do what you have to do* . . .'

'. . . *There will be no going back* . . .'

When the voices grew louder, and it appeared that the row was reaching its crescendo, the housekeeper crept back into the kitchen and made suitable noises with a saucepan.

It was fortunate that she did, for a minute later she heard the living-room door swing open and petulant footsteps echo down the corridor. Nothing else was said – it would have been indecorous for the vicar to pursue his fiancée and continue their exchange in more public surroundings, as it were. Still, when Mrs Flanagan heard the front door slam shut, she waited for a few moments until she heard the living-room door close once more, gently this time, and then she stepped to the hallway where she glanced through the window that overlooked the path. There she just caught sight of Miss Rodley's back before the thick morning fog consumed her.

Poor children, she thought. They'd be in for it today.

Damn this fog! Richard Weston thought as he waited for the tram into town. It always seemed to find its way onto his chest, and so he covered his face with his thick muffler in a vain attempt to keep its stale metallic pungency at bay.

He hadn't slept well at all. It seemed that the fates were conspiring against him in all manner of ways: the dreadful events of Monday morning, which he thought he'd coped with in a most professional way considering how circumstances had worked against him; the almost scathing manner he had been spoken to by the obnoxious detective; the finding of Tollet's body; Nathaniel Edgar's stubborn and chronic leaning towards the bottle – not to mention that foul child's attempt to burn his school down!

And Emily Mason. What on earth was he to do about her?

What ordinary mortal could bear such tribulations?

Once on board, he sat downstairs in the bogie car at the rear and studiously avoided the company of the other passengers who chattered away in lively tones and whose conversation he invariably found to be trivial and mundane. When one nodded at him he nodded curtly back, and when another observed how chilly the morning was he merely added the single comment 'Autumn'. They were familiar faces, of course, catching the same tram every morning and dispersing once they reached the reversing triangle in Market Place, off to fill their places behind shop counters and bank desks and market stalls. One or two recognised him, of course, but they kept their distance, a combination of respect and painful memories of their own schooldays when they'd endured the punishments meted out by people such as Weston.

As the tram shunted to a halt at its terminus, he alighted, drew his muffler close around his face once more and made his way down Market Street towards George Street. The fog was still thick here, and as he walked down the slight incline he noticed fancifully how it seemed to swirl and wrap itself around his legs like phantom spirits urging him to stay where he was and give school a miss today.

He smiled at the thought and muttered to himself, 'If only I could!'

Carriages rattled past, their lanterns appearing suddenly, lit and spectral in the morning gloom, before vanishing into the thick greyness, a disembodied whinny momentarily filling the rancid air. Someone brushed past him from behind, but there was no muttered apology as the figure moved quickly ahead of him before disappearing.

At the bottom of Market Street he turned left into Frog Lane and sighed, wondering what fresh complications would be waiting for him once he stepped into the building.

Perhaps, if I'm extraordinarily lucky, it will be a normal day.

But in less than a minute, his day would turn out to be anything but normal.

* * *

It was time, Brennan thought as he whisked up sufficient lather to shave, to go on the attack. Up until now, he'd been following the course of events rather like the local street cleaners scooping up horse manure well after the steaming deeds had been done. He scraped the razor against his day-old stubble, careful to avoid his thick moustache that he was quite proud of.

He gazed at his eyes in the mirror and allowed his thoughts to ready themselves.

Dorothea Gadsworth had recognised someone from the past, someone who had been involved in the tragic drowning of young Tilly Pollard. That involvement, of course, wasn't a crime in itself, although if he had his way, leaving seven-year-olds to amuse themselves while the one in charge allowed carnal lust to replace such a responsibility should be regarded as neglect and punished with the unfortunately defunct cat o'nine tails.

But the one she recognised, whether the girl Julia Reece or the boy David, would have a great deal to lose if the truth of that dereliction of duty came out.

Enough motive to kill twice?

He reached down and swirled the razor in the cold water, before once more returning to his daily task.

How difficult would it be to find out about each of the ones present that day? The one she recognised had at one time lived in the Lake District. The girl Julia had lived in Hawkshead until her shame and the pressure of daily accusations had forced her and her family to flee the village. The boy David, with no surname to speak of, had once lived in Windermere, and he was no longer seen in Hawkshead after the child's death. Had he too fled the area, or had he remained in Windermere, merely avoiding the ferry and the shame he too would face if he ever set foot there again?

Although he had questioned them all about their past, about where they were brought up, about their parents and where they had lived, he had done so more out of a desire to see how they reacted than any real prospect of the truth coming out. No one would admit to a connection if they were involved, and he had neither the time nor the resources to follow up on their backgrounds. Captain Bell would never sanction such a wide-reaching and probably futile investigation. Even as he'd considered that course of action and actually and momentarily grown excited about pursuing it, he realised with a sinking of the heart that whoever the guilty party was, he or she had spent years covering their tracks and creating a new life for themselves, a life that involved a change of identity and a total denial of the past.

As he gave his reflection in the mirror a consolatory smile, he felt a sharp nick on his throat and watched the blood begin to slither out, turning the shaving lather pink.

The hammer attack on Richard Weston had been helped and hindered by the fog.

Although any assault would be all but invisible in this fog – it was impossible to see across the street, and even on the pavement this side of Frog Lane visibility stretched only a few yards – yet it was difficult to make out anyone's features until they were up close, and then it might be too late, or the wrong person might get the hammer blow. Good job he was a creature of habit, and brushing past him on Market Street to make sure it was actually the headmaster had been a very clever idea.

Still, you make the best of what you're up against. And Weston needed to pay for what happened to the child, right enough.

Weston got to within a yard of his assailant when suddenly

he stopped and was seized by a coughing fit. He doubled up, the racking cough deadened by his muffler.

It had to be now!

From the swirling grey mass, a figure loomed towards him, its arm held high, something dull and metallic clutched in its right hand. Weston thought for a split second that this was some kind of prank, but the inhuman screech that accompanied the hellish vision, followed immediately by the crashing blow to his temple, brought the grim reality of the attack into his consciousness seconds before he lost it.

CHAPTER TWELVE

By nine o'clock that morning, it was evident that something was wrong. Richard Weston was invariably at his desk a good half hour before the rest of the staff came into school. He had never taken a day off through illness, and the talk in the staffroom had made optimistic references to the thickness of the fog and the distinct possibility that the trams had stopped running.

'He'll doubtless be sitting impatiently in a hackney carriage,' said Nathaniel Edgar with languid indifference, taking little notice of the concerned expressions on the rest of them.

Emily Mason, in particular, seemed most distressed. Weston was, after all, her mentor, and the prospect of him failing to attend school on any day would have filled her with consternation. This morning she had sat waiting patiently outside his office for him to arrive for their pre-school meeting where she showed him her plans for the day and he inspected the work the class did the previous day. This break from routine had upset her, and it was just one more example of how things were going badly for her.

Jane Rodley was seated by the window gazing out. Florence Hardman, in charge of Standard 2, was attempting to engage her in conversation, but it was clear that Miss Rodley was in no mood for idle speculation. It was unusual, for she was normally a most amenable colleague. Not today, though.

'I don't know what all the fuss is about,' declared Alice Walsh. 'Just because our esteemed headmaster is always on time, it doesn't mean that he is perfect. Sometimes,' she added with a sly glance at Nathaniel, 'we put these men on a pedestal and find we are surprised when they fall off it. It's that magical moment when we see their feet are made of clay, and not marble.'

He responded by miming the lifting of a glass, but the look he gave her was one of pure venom.

It was Miss Ryan, as the acknowledged deputy to the headmaster, who finally clapped her hands sharply and declared, 'Well it's obvious the headmaster has been delayed. We should therefore attend to our classes before they allow their baser instincts to surface.'

'Like bubbles from a gaseous swamp, you mean?' said Edgar, but as they all left the staffroom, nobody so much as smiled at his imagery or his cynicism. Alice Walsh, standing at the door, made a point of holding the door open until he had passed through. He gave a nod of appreciation at the irony of her gesture.

For the rest of that morning, the atmosphere at George Street Elementary School was subdued. It was as though the staff, trying hard to keep things as normal, somehow transferred their concerns to the children, who were quick to detect any sort of change in mood from their teachers and were uncertain how to proceed – with tacit obedience or rebellious nonconformity. The result was confusion and a resignation, knowing well that any overstepping of the boundaries might this day produce overly enthusiastic responses from the teachers.

When the bell monitor trotted along the school corridors signalling the end of morning school, there was a collective sigh of relief. Outside, as the children made their way home for their dinners, there was slightly more noise than usual. Some of them huddled in whispers as word got round that the headmaster had failed to turn up, and there were lurid speculations about the reasons for his absence.

Although the staff weren't huddled together in the staffroom and were making an effort to proceed as if this were just another school day, they too were prey to speculation. The difference between staffroom and playground, however, was one of invention: pupils created ever more colourful fates for their headmaster – many of them involving dismemberment – and shared them with giggles and gasps, whereas the teachers kept whatever images they had formed to themselves. Yet with two murders inextricably linked to the school, and the disappearance of the Kelly boy, it was hardly surprising that they fully expected to hear of another tragedy.

'So I suppose we sit here and wait?' Nathaniel Edgar declared to the small group sitting or standing around the room. There was a smell of crusted bread, of stale tea and coffee in the air.

'The fog's cleared,' Miss Ryan observed.

'Typically British,' Edgar said without humour. 'While the world all around us is collapsing, we observe the niceties by commenting on the weather.'

Miss Ryan turned and gave him the basilisk glare that Standard 4 knew all too well.

'I was about to point out, Mr Edgar, that the fog clearing might well bring the headmaster to us. If the trams had been suspended . . .'

'But they weren't, were they?' Edgar replied snappily and with a certain viciousness. 'I caught the tram. Most here did too. You, of course, always arrive by broomstick.'

Suddenly, from the far corner of the room, Emily Mason, who had been sitting there gazing wistfully through the window, burst into tears.

'Why are you always so 'orrible?' she sobbed, standing up to give her words added force.

'I beg your pardon?'

Not only Edgar, but the other members of staff also stared at Emily in shock. The pupil-teacher had never been known to express any sort of opinion on anything before now, cowed as she was by the proximity of those who used to teach her not all that long ago. But she hadn't finished.

'After all Mr Weston's done for you. For *you*!' She raised a finger and pointed it unwaveringly at Nathaniel Edgar. 'Aye. All you can do is sneer an' sit yonder lovin' it.'

It was Jane Rodley who moved quickly to the girl's side and placed an arm around her shoulder. 'Now, now, Emily. We're all overwrought by this. Best to sit back down over here with me.'

'Aye, lass,' said Edgar mockingly. 'Sit thiself down before I say summat I shouldn't.'

Jane Rodley whirled round to remonstrate with such unpleasantness.

Alice Walsh, having moved quickly across the room, helped sit Emily down. 'The man isn't worth the bother, Jane,' she said.

Edgar was about to snap a response when he was stopped in his tracks by the staffroom door opening.

'What on earth is going on?' asked Richard Weston,

standing with one hand on the door handle and the other adjusting the bandage that was wrapped around his head.

'It was most definitely a woman,' Weston said, somewhat shamefacedly.

'What makes you so sure?' Brennan was sitting in the headmaster's office at the end of the day.

All the staff had left, except for Miss Mason who was due to begin her mentoring session with Weston. He had insisted that the session go ahead, despite the pupil-teacher's misgivings. Weston sat back and gingerly touched his head. The grain of opium powder he had been given by the doctor was now losing its effect, and a dull throbbing threatened to develop into something much more painful.

'No man would ever make such an unholy shriek just before the attack.'

'Have you any reason to suppose someone might wish to harm you?'

'None, Sergeant. All I know is that the blow rendered me unconscious.'

'You suffered a single blow.'

'Correct.'

Brennan frowned. None of this made any sense. If the one who murdered Dorothea Gadsworth and Henry Tollet were the one wielding the hammer, then surely she would have finished the job as he lay there defenceless? Unless she was disturbed. But again, this was a completely different modus operandi. Poisoning. Drowning. Now a hammer attack?

What the hell was going on?

'Can you remember anything else about the attack? Anything, however insignificant you might think it.'

The headmaster gave the question some thought before replying in the negative.

'I think that's all I can tell you, Sergeant. Not much help, I know.' He stretched out his arms as if to conclude the meeting. At that point there was a timid knock on his door. 'Come in, Miss Mason,' he called out with an apologetic smile to Brennan.

The pupil-teacher came in slowly, her eyes still red from lunchtime and the unsavoury confrontation with Nathaniel Edgar.

'Please, sit down. Sergeant Brennan is just leaving. I hardly think he's desperate to learn the fundamentals of teaching, are you, Sergeant?'

Brennan admitted that it wasn't on his list of priorities, gave the pupil-teacher a nod of acknowledgement and left the room.

As he did so, Weston reached into his desk drawer and took out an old, dog-eared volume. She was familiar with its contents, as it provided the bulk of their tutorials. She read its title: *A Manual for Good Teachers*.

'You must be very wary, once you become a fully qualified member of the profession, when people start talking about how best to educate the young. I spoke last time about Froebel, the German who brought us the word "kindergarten". All very well and good, but to encourage children to learn through play, with little regard for the importance of discipline, is to my mind nothing short of catastrophic. Listen to this, Emily.'

He opened the book and extracted a slip of paper on which he had written some text.

'"*Play . . .is the free expression of what is in a child's soul.*" What do you think of that for an educational philosophy, eh?'

Emily shifted uncomfortably in her seat. 'What should I think?'

'You should think that such nonsense should never have left

Germany. Play indeed! The only path to learning lies in two things: the establishment of good discipline, and the ability to explain and encourage. *Play* discourages both. Now note, I am not saying there is no place for play, far from it. Healthy mind and so on. But there's a place for that sort of thing and it isn't the classroom. There the atmosphere should be orderly and structured. Out there . . .' He waved a hand towards the window and the playground beyond. 'Out there they can let off steam. That is all. Now, I want you to read the section "Strategies for Discipline". In particular we'll discuss the relative merits of immediate punishment as opposed to the implementation of a cooling-off period. Later, by way of light relief, we'll practise the conjugation of the verb "*aimer*".'

Emily, suppressing a sniffle, opened the volume at the relative chapter and began to read, or give a show of reading.

Weston, meanwhile, stood up and walked over to the window. He saw the playground railings, women walking past clutching shawls around them to ward off the early evening chill. But it was the railings he focused on as his head began to throb with more insistence. For the first time, he began to see them not as a practical means of keeping children in, but as a way of keeping demons out.

When he got back to the station, Brennan was met by Constable Jaggery, who seemed in an excitable mood.

'You'll never guess, Sergeant!' said Jaggery in the corridor leading to Brennan's office.

'That's true,' Brennan replied and walked on.

'No, I mean, we might've found him.'

'Who?'

'The lad what went missing. Billy Kelly.'

Brennan stopped in his tracks. From the enthusiastic sparkle in his constable's eye he knew the answer to the next question but asked it anyway. 'Alive?'

'Aye!'

'Where is he?' Brennan looked round the corridor as if expecting the boy to be produced at any moment like a rabbit from a top hat.

'Ah,' said Jaggery with a slight lowering of his voice.

'Ah what?'

'Well, when I say alive . . .'

'You mean dead?'

'No, Sergeant. Oh no. The lad's alive, right enough.'

'So where is he?'

'The infirmary.'

'He's been attacked?'

'In a manner o' speakin', like.'

Brennan was beginning to feel this was a conversation he'd never escape from.

'Constable Jaggery. If you don't tell me in as few words as possible what the matter is with young Kelly, then I'll personally see to it that you're on night patrol in Scholes every Saturday for the next month.'

The threat of patrolling that particular area of Wigan, especially after the events of last winter during the miners' lockout, was more than enough to render his prose succinct and eloquent.

'The lad was bitten by what looks like a rat or rats, Sergeant. He was saved from fallin' in front of a goods train by the Sally Ann. Doctor says the lad's got a fever an' isn't conscious.'

'How do we know it's the missing boy then?'

'He's got red hair. How many red-haired lads . . .'

'Thank you, Constable. Now come with me.' He patted the

216

man's broad shoulders and turned towards the exit. As they left the station in search of a hackney, he prayed that this was the breakthrough he'd been hoping for.

Once he'd seen the boy for himself – still unconscious and hand swathed in bandages – Brennan gave orders for Constable Jaggery to inform the boy's parents that their son had been found. 'Use discretion and sensitivity, Constable. I don't want them running up here expecting to see their son sitting up in bed eating porridge.'

'Don't think that's likely, is it, Sergeant? Judgin' by the state of 'im.'

Brennan gave a heavy sigh and waved his dismissal.

'Well?' he asked, turning to the doctor who was standing by the boy's bed and consulting his notes.

'No,' the doctor replied, deliberately misunderstanding him. 'Not well, Sergeant. Not well at all. The boy has been bitten by a rat, and he is running a dangerously high fever. See here?'

He lifted the boy's bare arms and indicated an irregular red rash; smooth in places and dotted with lumps in others.

'And here, you can see the joints in his knees are swollen. So too are his feet, which also contain a similar rash. These are not good signs.'

'Will he survive?'

The doctor shrugged. 'I don't know where he's been for the last few days, but the boy stank to high heaven when he was brought in. The nurses washed him. But he has had a rough time of it, I'd guess. Which of course might mean that, ironically, he's used to surviving in less than satisfactory conditions. He might live. He might die.'

'I hear he was saved by the Salvation Army.'

A half-smile crept on to the doctor's face. 'Isn't that their raison d'être?'

'Their what?'

'It's French, Sergeant. It means their reason for existing. They aren't called the *Salvation* Army for nothing.'

'He almost got killed by a train,' Brennan said, ignoring the doctor's attempt at humour.

'So I gather.'

'Then what was he doing on a train track?'

'I have no idea.'

'And what was the Sally Army doing on a train track?'

Again, the doctor gave a hint of a smile. 'Apparently, according to the ambulance driver who brought him here, the boy was being chased.'

'Chased? By who?'

'Why, Sergeant, by the Salvation Army.'

I'll need to speak to that lot, he thought.

Brennan stared at the boy's expressionless face. If this child had been the one to attempt arson at the school, and if he were there on Friday night, then he might well have seen Miss Gadsworth and whoever gave her the poison. It would help his investigation no end if the lad were to wake up and give him a name. But then again, he might never wake up, never speak again.

'If the boy does come round, Doctor, I'd like to be informed. Immediately.'

The look the doctor gave him showed how unaccustomed he was to being told what to do. He gave a curt nod and moved along the ward to the next bed.

As Brennan turned to leave, he was surprised to see the double

218

doors at the far end of the ward swing open and two familiar figures enter in some haste.

They spoke briefly to the nurse on duty seated at a small table by the entrance, and she pointed down the ward to where Billy Kelly was lying. They both looked up and saw Brennan who had stopped at the foot of the bed. Both figures seemed hesitant, uncertain whether to proceed down the ward or turn round and leave.

But I've seen you now, thought Brennan. He gave them a wave to underline the fact.

Reverend Charles Pearl and Jane Rodley approached him slowly and with as much dignity as they could muster.

'Sergeant Brennan!' Miss Rodley said. 'An unexpected pleasure.'

'Ma'am. Vicar.'

Reverend Pearl gave a slight cough. Of the two of them, he seemed most discomforted by the policeman's presence. 'We were visiting some of my sick parishioners,' he began.

Miss Rodley took up the tale. 'And we bumped into your constable. The rather large one.'

'Hard to miss,' Brennan agreed.

'We exchanged pleasantries and I asked how your investigations were progressing and he simply suggested we ask you ourselves.'

'So here we are!' Reverend Pearl added, unnecessarily.

To forestall any questions, Miss Rodley moved to the boy's bedside and gazed down at his unconscious form. Brennan was surprised to see her reach down and stroke the boy's hair.

'He gets into more fights because of this,' she said, holding his red hair in her fingers. 'Children can be so cruel. Anyone who is different in any way . . .'

'How is the boy?' asked Reverend Pearl.

'He has a fever,' said Brennan.

'But he'll be all right?' Miss Rodley asked.

Brennan held up his hands.

'The poor child.'

After a few moments, she moved away and stood beside her fiancé, whispering something in his ear that Brennan couldn't quite catch. The vicar gave her a questioning look, then gave a nod of acquiescence before moving to the boy's bedside and kneeling down. Miss Rodley placed herself on the other side of the bed and she too knelt down. Both of them bowed their heads and Reverend Pearl began to pray.

'Heavenly Father, tender shepherd of the sheep, you gather the lambs in your arms and cherish them to your bosom. We commend to your loving care this child, William. Relieve his pain and guard him from danger. Restore to him your gifts of gladness and strength. Through Jesus Christ our Lord. Amen.'

Brennan whispered 'Amen' and watched them both stand up. They bade him farewell, Miss Rodley stroking the boy's hair one last time. As they walked slowly, almost funereally, from the bed, Brennan heard her say, 'It's *Billy*. He hates *William*.'

When he alighted from the tram on Park Road, Constable Jaggery glared enviously at the two colliers across the road who were entering the vault of the Pagefield Hotel. They were still coated in coal dust, and he could imagine how, in a few minutes' time, their thirst would be quenched by a cooling pint of bitter. He promised himself, as he turned down Gidlow Lane, that he would soon be doing exactly the same once his shift had finished in an hour's time.

As he made his way towards Diggle Street, he wondered

whether the news he was bringing the Kellys would be deemed good or bad. It was certainly good news that the lad had been found, but it was also bad news that he was lying in the infirmary unconscious. He wondered how he'd respond if his own lad were lying there. But then he told himself the situations wouldn't be the same at all, because he and his missus thought the world of their boy and wouldn't have left it four hours, let alone four days, before reporting him missing.

Still, they were his mam and dad after all, and surely they'd welcome the good news if not the bad.

When he got to number 23 he took a deep breath and knocked on the door.

The curtain in the front window twitched and he heard a muffled conversation from beyond the front door, but instead of the sound of a key turning or a door handle rattling, all he could hear was the sound of something heavy being knocked to the floor and a volley of curses followed swiftly by the slamming of another door inside.

'Open the door!' he shouted. 'Police 'ere. I got news about your lad!'

He hammered on the door once more. He heard heavy footsteps from inside and suddenly the door swung open. The giant of a man who stood there glowered at him with murderous intent.

'What dost want?' he growled.

Jaggery wasn't cowed by the man's size nor his obvious strength. He took in his red hair and recalled seeing him arguing with Sergeant Prescott at the station. 'It's about your lad.'

'What about 'im?'

'We've found him.'

Tommy Kelly cast a glance behind the policeman, as if he were shielding the child. 'Where is he then?'

By now a couple of doors along the street had opened, and curious heads peered out.

'Happen it's best if I come in,' said Jaggery.

But Tommy Kelly stood his ground on the doorstep. 'Happen it's not.'

'But I've got summat to tell you, an' it might be better if I told you inside. Is your wife in?'

'Aye. She's up t'chimney.'

Jaggery looked surprised at that. 'Well, if you could get her down . . .'

Before Kelly could respond, another voice piped up from number 19.

'If tha lookin' for Edith Kelly tha're out o' luck.'

Jaggery whirled round and saw a sharp-featured woman standing on her doorstep now, arms folded and staring back at Tommy Kelly in brave defiance.

'Why? Where is she?'

The woman gave a harsh laugh. 'Gone tearin' down t'backs as if tallyman's after 'er!'

With that she stepped back inside and slammed her door shut.

Jaggery looked at Kelly with interest now. 'Why's she buggered off then?'

Kelly shrugged. 'Gone for some milk. We've run out.'

'Wrong, pal. *She's* run out, not your bloody milk jug.'

For a second it seemed that Kelly was about to launch himself at the policeman, but whether he was afraid of the criminal consequences of such a move, or he remembered why the policeman was standing there in the first place, he managed to control himself and said, 'Just tell me where me son is, eh? Then I'll go fetch him.'

222

Jaggery shifted his stance. He reckoned it didn't really matter one jot if the Kelly woman had run off or not. He'd come to give them the news and that was what he'd do. He'd given him the good – now it was time for the bad.

Brennan decided there was little point in contacting the headmaster again to inform him of the boy Kelly's situation. There was nothing he could do, save create a great fuss about having the boy arrested for attempted arson. No, it was better to let sleeping boys lie for the time being. Today was Friday, and Miss Rodley would doubtless inform him and the rest of the staff on Monday morning at school. So once he got back from the infirmary, he decided to sample an evening pint at the Crofter's Arms before heading home. He sat in his usual corner, where he was assured of some degree of solitude, and took a long, slow draught.

Before he could take a second swig, Constable Jaggery, now out of uniform and clearly in the mood for a drink, came in and made a beeline for Brennan. The expression on his sergeant's face had no effect on Jaggery, who wanted to share the information about the Kelly woman as soon as he could.

'And she didn't say a word?' Brennan asked when Jaggery had finished the tale.

'No, Sergeant. She just ran off. Didn't know what to make of it but I thought you should know.'

Brennan took another sip. 'You did the right thing, Constable.'

'Thank God for that. I thought you might've expected me to run after the bitch.'

'Not at all. There's no warrant for her arrest, is there?'

'None that I know of.'

'Still, there must've been a reason for such strange behaviour.'

'You can never tell wi' women.' Jaggery shook his head as if he were pondering an imponderable.

'I wonder . . .'

'Wonder what, Sergeant?'

Brennan didn't reply for a while, merely swirled the remaining beer around in his glass, watching it form tiny froth patterns around the rim. Finally, he said, 'We know Mrs Kelly has already been visited by the police last week.'

'Do we?'

Brennan nodded. 'She'd gone into school to complain to the headmaster about young Billy getting beaten.'

'Little sod must've deserved it.'

'Agreed. But she caused a scene, and it was reported by the head. Then a few days later Billy Kelly disappears. Possibly murdered like the Gadsworth girl and Tollet, the school inspector.'

'Aye. I'm with you so far.'

'She's had several days now to scour the streets for her son. We know the boy's father's been up and down looking for him.'

'As any dad would.'

'So over the last week, who do you think she blames for him running away?'

'But we thought the lad was dead.'

'I know. But as far as she was concerned he'd run away because of the school. He's done it before, remember?'

Jaggery thought for a while as Brennan drained his glass. Then he said, with a note of triumph, 'Well then, she'd blame the headmaster!'

'Exactly!'

But Jaggery's elation at getting to the right answer was short-lived. 'I still don't see what you're getting at though, Sergeant.'

'This morning the headmaster was attacked in the street on his way to school by someone wielding a hammer.'

'I know.'

'And we imagined it was another attack by our murderer.'

The light in Jaggery's head finally hissed into life. It had taken a while, thought Brennan, not for the first time. It was like putting a match to a damp wick.

'You mean you think Mrs Kelly was the one who attacked Weston?'

'It's a possibility.'

'Why,' said Jaggery as the flame started to flare, 'that must be why the bitch ran off! She saw me uniform and thought, *Bugger that.*'

'Well done, Constable. Now as reward for your impeccable exercise in logic, I'll allow you to buy me another pint.'

'A pleasure, Sergeant!'

CHAPTER THIRTEEN

The next morning – Saturday – Brennan was up early, knowing that it would be the best time to find the ones he wished to speak to.

It had always struck him as fitting that the Salvation Army Hall was to be found in Hope Street. Indeed, the hall took its name from the street – Hope Hall – and he supposed that *hope* was what the Sally Ann brought to many of the town's inhabitants. While not subscribing to their philosophy about drink – his family hailed from Tipperary, after all – he couldn't doubt the sincerity of their mission and the support they offered to the ones who found themselves in need of a helping hand.

The tall and imposing building stood facing Wigan Market Hall in the centre of town, and at that time of the morning there were several people making their way along Woodcock Street heading for the indoor stalls and the fresh produce to be had at this early part of the day. Saturday was a good day for the market, with the freshest produce going early, and the cheapest being sold off late on.

He climbed up the steps of Hope Hall and saw that the door was half-open. He entered the cavernous building and saw small clusters of men in various states of dishevelment, each of them with a bowl of steaming broth in his hands. A Salvation Army soldier, who had been moving among the groups, saw Brennan standing in the entrance and made his way over.

'Good morning, brother,' he said with a dubious glance at Brennan's clothing. 'Do you need some sustenance?'

'Actually, I need some information.'

He introduced himself and explained the reason for his visit.

'Please,' said the soldier. 'I think you need to speak with Sergeant Hammond. He's the one who found the poor child. I'm just the one he bit.'

Brennan blinked a few times, and was about to ask for an explanation, but the young soldier had already spun round and was leading the way to a room at the rear of the hall where he knocked on the door, opened it and spoke to the one inside. Then he stood to one side and waved Brennan into the room. There, seated behind a desk and writing into what appeared to be a ledger of accounts, was a stockily built man of middle age and sporting a large black beard, greying a little in places and reminding Brennan of paintings he had seen of Moses wielding the tablets of the Ten Commandments. An imposing figure.

'Please. Take a seat. I'm told we share the same rank, Sergeant?'

'Indeed, sir.'

Brennan sat opposite the man. He saw, ranged along the side of the desk and enclosed by metal bookends, a series of volumes, the most prominent of which carried the title *In Darkest England and The Way Out*.

Sergeant Hammond gave a slight chuckle. 'I see you are drawn to the general's great work.'

'The General?'

'General William Booth. The founder of our humble organisation.'

'I've heard of him, yes.'

'You may find its title strange.' Without warning he leant forward and plucked the book from its place in the row and flicked it open until he came to the page he was looking for. 'Now then. This should explain things, Sergeant.' He began to read aloud. '"As in Africa, it is all trees, trees, trees with no other world conceivable; so is it here – it is all vice and poverty and crime".'

He closed the book and stroked its dark leather cover. 'But then, as a policeman in Wigan, you'll immediately recognise the sentiments expressed here.'

'It's not quite as dark as you paint it,' Brennan replied, feeling the need to offer some defence, at least, of his fellow Wiganers.

As if in direct challenge to his visitor's words, the man again picked up the book and chose another section.

'"Darkest England has many more public houses than the forest of the Aruwimi has rivers".'

Brennan shifted in his seat. He hadn't come for a lecture on drink. 'I'm afraid I've never visited the forest of the Aruwimi, Sergeant Hammond. It's much closer to home I'm interested in.'

'I'm sorry,' he said, closing the book and returning it to its slot on the desk. 'It's easy to get carried away. Now then. Concerning the young scamp.'

'Yes, sir. Where exactly was it that he bit your colleague?'

'On the left hand.'

'My fault, Sergeant Hammond. I meant, where were you both when the assault took place?'

229

'Oh I see.' The man gave a huge grin, lighting up his features and making him seem at once much more affable. 'Let me see. We were playing "I'm a Soldier Bound for Glory". One of Richard Jukes' finest, if I may say so. At any rate, once we'd finished we heard a tremendous crash that seemed to come from one of the derelict basements nearby. Myself and a colleague went to see if anyone needed help and there he was. The child covered in dust and appearing dazed and half-starved. Naturally we offered the boy assistance but he repaid the kindness by biting the soldier's hand that was about to feed him.' He indicated the closed door and the soldier Brennan had met.

'Where was this basement?'

'Let me think. Ah yes. It was St Thomas Street. The last house on the corner opposite St Thomas church. There's a small row of them. All empty.'

Brennan sat upright, as if someone had jabbed him with a sharp knife. 'St Thomas Street? Are you sure?'

'Yes, I am, Sergeant. Does it surprise you?'

But Brennan had stood up and, after offering a hasty *Thank you*, left the room and the Salvation Army building.

This is bloody embarrassing! he thought as he made his way back along Woodcock Street, passing the growing number of people heading for the indoor market.

St Thomas Street was the next street to where he lived.

He went alone, deciding that Constable Jaggery might well let it slip to all and sundry at the station that Sergeant Brennan lived not a stone's throw from where the missing boy had probably been hiding. He could imagine him regaling the canteen:

An' the lad were there, right under his lordship's bloody nose!

When he got to St Thomas Street, he looked up at the church's tall spire, and compared it with the one at St Catharine's in Lorne Street on the other side of town, where Reverend Pearl was the incumbent. Here, the spire, with its cross above braving the elements, stood tall and erect, no deviation from the perpendicular here.

He sought out the last house on the corner, as indicated by Sergeant Hammond, and when he found it his heart sank. The neighbouring houses were, as the Salvation Army man had told him, all empty – no possibility of questioning curious neighbours then – and the one he was interested in had no curtains, the glass of the windows so smeared with dust and grease that it was impossible to see inside. He looked over the railings and the rusted iron gate that led down to a small basement area, and saw the debris from where the boy had smashed his way out through the wall. He pushed the gate open and stepped carefully down the cracked stone steps and over the rotted plasterwork on the flagged floor. There was a door sunk into a recess in the wall. He tried the handle but it was locked.

Then a voice from above shouted down, 'If you're after money you're wastin' your time. Buggered off months ago, they did.'

He glanced up. A man, middle-aged and wearing a bowler hat cocked to one side, was leaning over. Through the railings, Brennan could see a smock that had once been white hanging below his waist, and he heard the impatient whinnying of a horse from the street above. He gave the door one last look before climbing back to street level and coming face-to-face with the man, whom he now recognised as a familiar sight – and a familiar smell – once he caught sight of the open cart which displayed the numerous varieties of fish the man usually hawked around town.

'Whose house is it?' he asked, deciding against offering him a handshake. He could see slivers of fish skin clinging to his fingers, and scales stuck to his smock where he'd continually wiped his hands.

'Dunno the owner,' he said with a shrug. 'All's I know is the ones who rented it did a moonlight months ago. Owed me a fair bit, too.'

'Have you seen anyone round here recently?'

The fish hawker shook his head. 'Not seen, as such.'

'What then?'

'Heard things.'

'What things?'

'Set off early t'other mornin', get to Fleetwood, see?' He turned and nodded towards the contents of his cart: already they were depleted, with smaller cuts of cod, plaice and herring laid out on what looked like a stretch of tarpaulin. 'Anyroad, we're trottin' past this place an' I heard somebody wailin'.'

'A child?'

'Aye. Could've been. All I know is, it gave Bessie yonder a scare.' He pointed to his horse, whose head was now bobbing up and down. 'I thought at first they were back, them as left. But when I got to the door there were no signs o' life anywhere, no light, nothin'. An' after I knocked the wailin' stopped an' I heard nowt else. But the place was in darkness. An' what wi' Bessie takin' boggarts, well, I reckon what I heard wasn't human at all.'

'What do you mean? Like a ghost?'

'Aye. You hear strange things in a mornin'. So I got back on me cart an' we buggered off to Fleetwood.'

With that, the man climbed on board, took up the reins and flicked his wrists. Bessie trotted off quickly, seemingly anxious to get away from the place.

Brennan turned back to the house and went down the steps to

the basement door. Ghost or no ghost, he'd get inside, even if he had to break the bloody door down. He glanced down at the gaping hole in the wall where the boy Kelly must have burst through, but he decided it was much too small a gap for him to squeeze through. Besides, he didn't like the idea of getting his suit filthy and having to face Ellen with dust and God knows what else marring his appearance. So he placed a shoulder against the door and pushed hard. He heard the door jamb creak. The wood around the frame must be rotted, he thought, and stood back, pressing both hands against the lower wall behind him and launched his feet against the middle of the door. Both feet went crashing through, but as he withdrew them, his left calf tore itself on a jagged row of splinters, and the curse he let rip would have made Constable Jaggery blush.

Still, as he stood up and examined the flesh – deep scratches that stung when he stroked a tentative finger along their uneven length – he realised it could have been far worse. What with the scar on his neck from shaving, and now this . . .

Gingerly he stepped into the basement of the house, and found that it was nothing more than a cellar. The light from outside failed to penetrate here, and he was hard pushed to make out anything in the room. But he knew for certain one thing the cellar contained, even, thankfully, without seeing it.

The place stank of human excrement.

Carefully he moved forward into the cellar, peering down at the floor in the forlorn hope of seeing what he needed to avoid stepping in. He took out a box of matches and lit one, but the light it gave off was weak and reached only a yard in front of him.

If only I had a bullseye with me, he thought.

Still, the matches were the best he could manage, so he moved the light around, catching sight of small mounds of excrement scattered around the floor. Somehow, now that he could see them, he felt a wave not of revulsion but of sorrow, and sympathy. The poor lad had spent some time here and, unless he had light, he must have been desperate indeed to stay in this place for any length of time. Then he saw a dried pool of vomit, and stepped carefully around it. He heard something, too. The skittering of tiny feet, and the high-pitched squeal of rats disturbed in their endeavours.

This is where the lad was bitten.

He made a methodical search of the place. From the crunching sound his shoes made, he knew this had once been merely a coal cellar, and when he stooped low he did indeed see tiny fragments of coal glistening in the light. Built into the wall opposite the door he had smashed open lay another door, and this one too was locked. He frowned as a thought suddenly struck him. Quickly he retraced his steps back to the door he'd come through. There was sufficient light here from the street level above for him to examine the inside of the door, and in particular the lock mechanism. He looked at the keyhole, then at the area surrounding the door, meticulously picking at the wooden splinters that had dropped onto the floor inside the cellar and moving them to one side. But what he was looking for wasn't there.

The key.

Which confirmed what he'd already suspected, that the boy wasn't so much hiding in this place as being kept here against his will. There were no signs of him breaking into the cellar but every sign of him breaking out.

Now who would want to keep a ten-year-old child prisoner?

CHAPTER FOURTEEN

The following Monday morning, Jane Rodley declared to the rest of the staff before school that young Billy Kelly had been found.

'As in dead?' asked Nathaniel Edgar.

Several of them gave him a look that revealed how insensitive they regarded the question. Emily Mason, sitting in the corner and gazing through the window, gave him a venomous glance.

'No, Nathaniel. Not dead.' Jane paused and cleared her throat. 'Although the doctors at Wigan Infirmary fear that may only be a matter of time.' She told them what she knew – that the boy had been bitten by a rat and was suffering from fever. She and Reverend Pearl had called at the infirmary twice over the weekend to see how Billy Kelly was, only to be informed with what she deemed a pessimistic air that there had been no change in the boy's condition.

'How did you know he was at the infirmary in the first place?' he asked.

'Not that it's any of your business, but I was with Reverend Pearl, who was visiting a sick parishioner. We saw the poor child then.'

'Where has the boy been?' Alice Walsh asked. 'Has he said anything?'

Jane shook her head. 'I have no idea. But at least he's alive.'

'Do the police know he's there?'

Jane looked at Alice and nodded.

Richard Weston entered at that moment. 'What's this about the police? Haven't we seen enough of them for one term?'

They all looked at him. It was only Friday that the man had been viciously attacked, and now he stood there with the same dignity and firmness he always showed at this time of day.

Nathaniel Edgar told him.

'And do the police know?' asked Weston, unaware that the question had already been asked.

Jane said, 'We saw Detective Sergeant Brennan at the infirmary yesterday. He has arranged for a policeman to stay by the boy's bedside.'

'Good. Still, it's strange that he hasn't informed me in an official capacity.'

'I think he presumed I would do so. The point is, the boy's alive.'

'I wasn't talking about the boy's survival,' he said curtly.

Everyone looked at him in surprise.

'I was talking about the boy's arrest.'

'Arrest?' asked Miss Hardman. 'What on earth for?'

'For attempted arson. Miss Rodley, as teacher in charge of Standard 6, already knows as I have shown her the irrefutable evidence that he tried to burn the school down.'

'Not irrefutable, Headmaster,' she corrected him. 'The evidence suggests his copybook was used to try to light a fire. We don't know it was young Billy.'

He glared at her. 'That young vandal will soon be under arrest. I intend to pursue his prosecution with all vigour. This is *my* school, and no one will attempt to burn it down and then sail away freely into the sunset.'

Leaving his staff with such an unlikely image, he clapped his hands together and said, with a nod in the direction of the raucous sounds emanating from the playground, 'Now, I think it's time we brought order to chaos, don't you all agree?'

With that, he turned on his heel and left the staffroom.

When he got to the station that morning, the first thing Brennan did was to sit at his desk and place his leg on another chair. The deep cuts were healing right enough, but he'd made Ellen a promise to give the leg as much rest as he could, which included refraining from kicking down doors. She had spent the weekend applying a simple water dressing to the wounds on his calf. He remembered what his ma had told him years ago, when he got up to all manner of scrapes resulting in scratches of varying depth and severity:

'Sure, there's nothin' quite the same as the natural powers o' water. Ye can keep your ointments an' the like. Water does the job well enough.'

So Ellen had taken some lint from their small medicine chest, soaked it in water and then applied it to the wound, making sure to cover the lint with a larger strip of oiled calico. When he'd announced his intention of going up to the infirmary to see how the boy was progressing, she'd pointed at the recently applied dressing and said, 'If that develops gangrene and the leg drops off, don't come running to me for sympathy.'

'Wouldn't be able to,' he'd replied with a wink that turned into a frown when little Barry gave forth a loud scream.

'What on earth's the matter?' Ellen had said, holding her sobbing son in her arms.

'Don't want Dad's leg to drop off,' he simpered.

'Don't worry,' she'd responded quickly. 'If it drops off I'll be sure to catch it. Then I'll just sew it back on.'

He was smiling at the memory when a voice broke the silence.

'Feet up already, Sergeant?'

He placed his left leg on the floor and stood up as Captain Bell strolled into his office without knocking, something he often did. 'Not quite, sir.'

He proceeded to explain where he went on Saturday and what he'd discovered.

'The house is derelict, you say?'

'Yes sir. Has been for a while, according to the fish hawker I spoke to. Said he'd heard someone crying. A child, probably.'

'And the fool didn't think to report it?'

'No, sir. Thought it was a ghost.'

Captain Bell sneered, then said, 'I gather from Constable Jaggery that the boy's mother may be guilty of that heinous assault on the headmaster?'

'Yes, sir.'

'Does it follow then that she might have something to do with the two murders?'

'Not really, sir.'

'And why not? She attempts to kill one teacher and may have succeeded with the other. Not to mention the school inspector.

238

It may be that she bears a grudge against all things educational.'

Brennan sighed. 'I think it highly unlikely that a harridan like that should have the intelligence to persuade Miss Dorothea Gadsworth to meet her in an empty school. And the idea of Mr Henry Tollet being persuaded to meet her on a canal footpath . . .'

Captain Bell gave an embarrassed cough. 'Quite so. Still, she must be brought to justice for the assault on Mr Weston.'

'It might be difficult to prove it was her.'

'Not difficult at all if she confesses.'

He forbore from pointing out how unlikely that would be.

With his customary advice to 'bring this matter to its conclusion, Sergeant', the chief constable left the office. No sooner had Brennan relaxed when the door burst open and a breathless Constable Jaggery came rushing in.

'Is knocking on doors going out of fashion?' Brennan asked.

'No, Sergeant. His lordship told me you were in 'ere, like.'

'Not really an explanation.' Before Jaggery could attempt one, Brennan added, 'What do you want me for?'

Jaggery took a few deep breaths to regain some sort of equilibrium. It was obvious the man wasn't accustomed to haste. Then finally he said, 'I was on me way to the infirmary, like you asked me to do. See 'ow the lad was.'

Brennan's heart sank. 'And?'

'I met Constable Hardy on Wigan Lane comin' this road an' I says to 'im, "What you doin' 'ere? Ain't you supposed to be waitin' on the ward watchin' over the lad?" An' guess what he says to me?'

'Just spit it out.'

'No, Sergeant. Not that. He says he was on his way to tell us. The lad's fever's dropped an' he's opened his eyes. Asked for a bacon butty.'

* * *

'He's *what?*'

The matron in charge of the ward was usually the one to inspire fear into her nurses. Her word was law and woe betide any shirkers. It was therefore a unique experience both for the matron and her acolytes when Detective Sergeant Brennan not only raised his voice at her but glowered in a most disrespectful manner.

She gave a slight cough to ensure her words betrayed no trace of what she was feeling at that moment. Constable Jaggery, however, standing by his sergeant's side and observing the woman closely, could only thank the Lord that she wasn't armed.

'I shall repeat myself, Sergeant, only out of sympathy with your poverty of hearing.'

Brennan shifted his gaze from the stiffly erect figure of the matron to the empty hospital bed at the far end of the ward.

'As I have already told you, the boy Kelly has left. He has not been discharged. He has left under his own volition.'

'He was unconscious not an hour ago.'

'That is incorrect. He was *asleep* an hour ago. There is a distinct clinical difference between the two states.'

'One of my constables was given strict instructions to let me know when his condition changed.'

'His condition changed during the night when he awoke briefly. Your constable was slumped in that chair beside the bed. As to whether *he* was unconscious or simply asleep we have no way of knowing as we didn't examine him. We gave the boy a drink and he then slept. There was little point in disturbing your constable.'

'But the boy is an important witness in a double murder case.'

The matron, regaining her equilibrium, sniffed and dismissed the small group of nurses who had seen fit to attend to patients nearest to the ward entrance, thus rendering it easier to eavesdrop. They scurried away.

Brennan took a deep breath. 'And the lad had no clothing. The rags he was found in have surely been incinerated?'

'Indeed they have. The ones who came for him this morning brought some clean clothes.'

'Who came for him?'

Again she sniffed. 'Do you think we're in the habit of letting children loose without appropriate guardians?'

'Perhaps I should repeat the question, Matron, out of sympathy with *your* poverty of hearing. *Who* came for him?'

A nurse sniggered a few yards away. The glare she got from Matron was a sore reminder of a coming retribution.

'The boy's parents. They came to see him yesterday – very briefly I might add – and returned this morning. When they saw he was awake, they wasted no time in dressing him and removing him. They were not the sort of people we like to see in such a place. That woman . . .'

But before she could express more fully what she thought of Edith Kelly, Brennan had whirled round and was marching through the door, oblivious now of the pain from his leg. Jaggery, who followed as quickly as he could in his wake, struggled to keep up with him as he made rapid strides along the corridor towards the entrance, where Constable Hardy was waiting in great trepidation.

'Give me a reason not to put you on cell duty for a month!' Brennan said when he found him standing by one of the portico pillars that marked the entrance to the infirmary.

'Sorry, Sergeant. Only I was doin' what I was told to do.'

'Which was that, might I ask? Falling asleep on duty or deserting your post?'

'No, Sergeant. Lettin' you know he'd woke up.'

'So you left him unguarded?'

'No, Sergeant. Ward were full o' nurses. I tried to find a lad to bring you a message only I couldn't find one. So I thought I'd run down to the station, like.'

Brennan pursed his lips and hurried down the steps to the main courtyard of the infirmary. A couple of hackney carriages were waiting just inside the main gate, their cabbies making idle chat while they waited for business. Brennan hailed one and waited impatiently for it to turn and approach the steps. Jaggery fetched up beside him.

'Where we off to, Sergeant?'

'Diggle Street.'

Jaggery could see he was in no mood for further explanation. When Sergeant Brennan got in this state, it was best to keep quiet and let him deal with the thunderstorm in his head on his own.

As they clambered aboard the carriage, Brennan's mind was indeed in turmoil. Young Billy Kelly could well have seen who was with Dorothea Gadsworth that Friday night. And he'd been so close to speaking to him and clearing things up quickly. Now, he'd slipped away, and he felt a wave of frustration overwhelm him. But he was also consumed with another thought.

Why would the Kellys be in such a hurry to get their son – their sick son – away from the infirmary, away from the police?

When they reached Diggle Street, Brennan asked the cab driver to wait. The two of them stood at the Kellys' front step and Jaggery hammered his fist against the door. After a few moments, the door swung open and Tommy Kelly loomed in the doorway, his huge frame almost filling the gap. He took in Jaggery's uniform and his lip curled.

'What the bloody 'ell's gooin' on? What are thy doin' 'ere agen?'

Brennan said, 'Where's the lad?'

'What lad?'

'Your Billy.'

Kelly sneered. 'Nowt to do wi' you lot. You lot couldn't find your arse in a petty, let alone my lad. Bloody Sally Ann what found 'im, eh? That's a soddin' laugh an' all.'

He was about to close the door when Jaggery stuck his foot in the gap.

Kelly glared down at the offending foot and said in a low growl, 'If tha doesn't shift that in one second I'll brast thee.'

But Jaggery remained steadfast.

Kelly gave a roar and lunged at him with his huge fists flailing. Jaggery moved with surprising speed for one with so large a frame, ducking to his left and swinging his right hand upwards with such force that when it struck Kelly in the throat it stopped both his progress and his roar so completely that Brennan thought for a moment the man was dead. But then he staggered backwards, clutching his throat and whining like an injured dog. Jaggery helped him on his way, pushing him back into the small front room and onto an armchair that had definitely seen better days.

'I see you haven't lost your speed or power, Constable, when it comes to the art of pugilism.'

'Aye,' said Jaggery, rubbing his fist, 'but me accuracy's gone to buggery. I were aiming for his snout.'

Brennan moved into the kitchen at the rear of the house, then ran quickly upstairs to examine the two small bedrooms. When he came down he shook his head. 'Not here,' he said. 'Neither son

243

nor mother.' He bent low on his haunches to gaze into the dulled eyes of Tommy Kelly, who was still holding his throat and making a hoarse rattling sound as he attempted to breathe through the bruised windpipe. Brennan wondered if this big moron had ever been treated like this in his life. Perhaps he should have warned him that his constable had been area boxing champion for a number of years.

'Now then, Mr Kelly. I have some questions and I'd appreciate it very much if you answered them. Is that agreeable?'

Kelly's face was purple with rage, but in his eyes there were traces of shock and fear, too. He gave a sharp nod and continued to rub his throat.

'Good. And before you offer, no, we won't have a cup of tea or a sugar butty.'

Brennan heard Jaggery snigger.

'It's your son Billy we need to talk to, you see?'

Another nod.

'Can you tell us where he is?'

For the first time since the assault, he moved his hand from his throat and swallowed several times before trying to speak. When he finally managed to do so, his voice was hoarse and rasping.

'He's not 'ere.'

Brennan smiled. 'I can see that. I didn't ask you where he wasn't, but where he was.'

After taking deep breaths and swallowing painfully several times, Kelly found he could speak more easily now. 'You think I'd tell you lot? You're after blamin' 'im for tryin' to burn that soddin' shithole down.'

'By "soddin' shithole" I presume you mean George Street Elementary School? If so, let me assure you I have no intention of charging him with arson or even breaking and entering, which I'm sure he also did last Friday night.'

Kelly's eyes narrowed. 'But we got told yon 'eadmaster were after doin' our Billy for it.'

Brennan looked askance at his constable. 'Who told you that?'

'Vicar.'

'Which vicar?'

'Reverend Pearl. Him an' his fancy bit called round.'

'Jane Rodley, the schoolteacher?'

'Aye. Th'only one 'as 'ad any time for our Billy.'

'What did they say?'

'She'd 'eard th'eadmaster say my lad would be charged wi' arson. She said it'd be best if we got some clothes an' took 'im out of yon infirmary . . . put 'im out of 'arm's way.'

'Where did you take him?'

Kelly shifted in his chair. 'Can't tell thee.'

Brennan stood up. 'Then I'm arresting you for kidnap and for aiding and abetting a fugitive. I'll think of a few more charges once we get you down in the cells.'

Kelly shook his head. 'Tha can arrest me all tha likes, but my lad is where you lot can't touch 'im. In sanitary.'

Brennan took in the meaning of his words and the sudden flash of confidence that spread across his face. 'You mean the vicar is sheltering him?'

It was as though Kelly had suffered another blow. He sank back with his head against the back of the armchair. Then he said, 'Awreet, aye. But tha can't touch 'im. Vicar said he could claim sanitary.'

Jaggery blinked and looked at the man as if his brain had been dislodged with the blow he'd suffered.

245

But Brennan understood. 'You mean "sanctuary"?'

'Aye, that's it.'

'Come on, Constable,' said Brennan with a note of urgency, moving quickly to the front door, beyond which a small group of neighbours had gathered and were sharing a wealth of speculation.

'We leavin' 'im, Sergeant?'

'We are indeed.'

'So where are we off to?'

'To church.'

Jaggery halted as Brennan climbed back into the carriage. 'But you heard what that bugger said. His son's claiming sanctuary.'

As he sat down inside the cab, Brennan said, 'There's no such thing, Constable. There hasn't been for over three hundred years. For whatever reason, Reverend Pearl has told that lumbering fool back there a pack of lies. So let's see exactly what the good vicar and his fiancée are up to, shall we?' He called up to the driver. 'St Catharine's Church, cabbie. Fast as you can!'

Richard Weston felt as if everything he had built up over the last five years was rapidly crumbling before his eyes. Nathaniel Edgar's drinking, his lateness and absences were bad enough, but despite the threats the man made against him, he had remained confident that the situation was under control, that he could ultimately ward off any danger to his reputation and carry on as normal.

But this . . .

He read the letter once more in the forlorn expectation that somehow the words would scramble themselves into something far removed from what they were currently saying:

Dear Mr Weston,

It is with great regret that I must tender my resignation today, with immediate effect. The last few years have been a delight and I wish you and the school every good wish for the future.

Miss Jane Rodley

No reason given for such a traitorous act. The letter was simply lying in wait for him on his desk that morning. *She must have been in very early to put it there*, he mused. But why resign now? She would be leaving once they could advertise and arrange for another interview. How long would that take? A few weeks? A month? Certainly by Christmas they would have a replacement. Why on earth leave him in the lurch when he needed her the most?

There was a knock on the door.

'Enter!'

Miss Ryan came in, her face a picture of concern.

'What is it, Miss Ryan? I'm rather busy at the moment.'

'I think you should know that there is complete pandemonium in Standard 1.'

'Why? Miss Mason should be doing sums with them. Abacus time.'

'Miss Mason isn't doing sums or reading or anything else for that matter.'

'What is she doing then?'

'Having a breakdown would be my guess.'

Weston stood up. He was fast reaching the end of his tether.

Within thirty seconds he was standing in the doorway of Standard 1. The youngest children in the school – a mere five years old – were wreaking havoc, chasing each other around the desks, hurling whatever missiles they could get their hands on, and whooping like savages while Emily Mason sat at the front of the classroom with her head in her hands and sobbing uncontrollably.

'Sit down!' Weston boomed. 'Any child not in his or her place by the time I count to five will be caned so hard you won't be able to pick your nose for a month!'

The dreaded, resounding sound of the headmaster's voice, reinforced by his glowering and menacing presence in the doorway, ensured that every child was back where he or she belonged well before he got to five. Emily Mason's sobbing also died down, to be replaced by intermittent sniffling and the application of a handkerchief.

'Now.' He turned to Miss Ryan who was standing behind him with pursed lips and ice in her eyes. 'Miss Ryan will set your work and will leave this door and her own door across the corridor wide open. You will complete the work to her satisfaction and you will make no sound whatsoever until I return.' He glanced at Miss Ryan to ensure she understood the import of what he'd just said. Then he turned once more to the now silent class. 'If you fail to complete the work set, or if you make any noise at all, then I will return and cane the lot of you. Every single snivelling one of you. Is that clear?'

'Yes, Mr Weston,' they all chimed in unison, some already with tears in their eyes at the prospect of punishment.

'Miss Mason. My office.'

The pupil-teacher for Standard 1 pushed herself to her feet slowly and held the handkerchief to her face. Then, once she had stepped from behind the teacher's desk, she ran from the room and out into the corridor.

When they arrived at St Catharine's Church, Constable Jaggery's first comment was a most irreligious *Christ Almighty*. The cabbie took the fare and, as his carriage trundled off towards Scholefield Lane and the centre of town, he could be heard chuckling to himself. The unlikely source of his amusement was plain for all to see: the area outside the church was filled with onlookers as a hearse was being emptied of its contents. The family mourners were garbed in black, the men with mourning suits and crape bands around their headwear, the women wearing black gowns, faces shielded with veils and hands covered with black gloves, all waiting respectfully and tearfully in line as the coffin was brought forth beneath the canopy of ostrich feathers that stretched above the hearse. There was the sound of weeping, gentle, subdued signs of grief as the pall-bearers took up their burden.

'Somebody wi' a bit o' brass, eh, Sergeant?' Constable Jaggery whispered as the two of them stood respectfully across the narrow street, Brennan with his hat removed and Jaggery clutching his helmet in his hands.

'Not that it'll do the poor soul much good,' Brennan replied.

'Aye. There is that.'

Brennan glanced over to the entrance to the church, where Reverend Pearl was standing with a sombre expression on his face.

'Suppose we'll 'ave to wait till the poor bugger's six feet under, eh, Sergeant?' Jaggery nodded upwards, to the thickening clouds that were gathering overhead. 'I just hope that lot blows over.'

Brennan said nothing. The good reverend had spotted him, and a dark expression spread across his brow.

'I've tried an' tried an' tried but it's no use. No use at all.'

Emily Mason sat facing the headmaster, her tear-stained face making her look far younger than her fifteen years.

'You need to take a deep breath,' said Weston gently. Despite everything that had been laid at his door this last week, he retained a well of sympathy and support for this former pupil of the school. 'You need to realise that we all go through such doubts. I certainly did when I was training.'

But Emily shook her head. 'It's all too much. Too much.'

Outside, he could see flecks of rain dotting the window. *Even the elements are conspiring*, he thought morosely.

He sighed and lifted his leather-bound blotter. The resignation letter from Jane Rodley lay open, one end of the paper folded into a corner of the blotter.

'You've worked too hard, Emily, to give up now.'

'You're half-right, anyroad. I've worked too hard. But it's all gettin' too much. I can't cope any more, what with . . .'

Once more the tears came, this time a whole flood of them. Weston stood up and came round to where she sat. He placed his arm across her shoulder, lowered his head to hers and pulled her towards him. He whispered, 'I hate to see you cry, Emily.'

She leant her head against his, sniffling all the while and reaching for her handkerchief once more. Then he kissed her, very gently, on the forehead.

CHAPTER FIFTEEN

Brennan didn't like being kept waiting, especially when he needed to find a key witness urgently. He suspected that Reverend Pearl had spent more than the usual amount of time comforting the bereaved and listening with apparent enthusiasm and respect to the various anecdotes about the deceased – a manager in one of the larger banks in Wigan. But Brennan was nothing if not dogged, and he and Jaggery waited for over an hour, firstly at the rear of the church during the service and then on the periphery of the graveyard as the man was finally laid to rest. There, a number of umbrellas were now open as the rain began to fall, and beside him Constable Jaggery pulled his collars close to his cheeks with a muttered curse.

When Brennan saw that the vicar was engaging all and sundry in conversation, he went over and almost physically drew him to one side.

Reluctantly the man nodded and arranged for them to wait in

his study while he 'showed the family the respect they deserved'.

It was another fifteen minutes before the door to the study swung open and Reverend Charles Pearl came in, wiping his damp face with a handkerchief.

'I trust Mrs Flanagan has made you comfortable?' he asked, moving to the window and gazing out, his hands clasped behind his back and, to Brennan's mind, fidgeting nervously. 'I always think rain most suitable for funerals, don't you think so, Sergeant Brennan? As if the good Lord Himself is sharing in the grief. But I suppose one could equally make out the case for sunshine, too. The celestial glow of welcome from a smiling God, eh? Perhaps substance for a sermon. "God in His Elements." What do you think?'

'I think your housekeeper has been most informative, Vicar.'

At that, Reverend Pearl turned round and cast a momentary glance at the closed door. 'In what way?'

'Oh, she tells us, for instance, that the person we are looking for has been here this morning.'

'And who is that?'

'The boy, Billy Kelly.'

There was a moment's hesitation, as if the man were considering bluff and denial. Then he said, 'Indeed. He was here.'

'You offered him sanctuary, I believe?'

The vicar laughed. 'I see you've been speaking with the concerned parents?'

'We have.'

There was a pause, during which Reverend Pearl clasped and unclasped his hands, looked fleetingly out of the window, then with a heavy sigh of surrender sat down behind his desk and brought his hands together as if in prayer.

'Why did you tell them you were prepared to give the boy sanctuary when you know full well it does not exist and hasn't existed for centuries?'

'You know the kind of people they are?'

Brennan and Jaggery exchanged glances. 'I do.'

'Well then. We needed to get the child away from them.'

'We?'

He looked at Brennan levelly. 'You know very well who I mean.'

'Mrs Flanagan tells me that your fiancée left with the boy an hour after arriving.'

Reverend Pearl shrugged.

'Where has she taken him?'

'Somewhere safe.'

'Where?'

The vicar unclasped his hands and sat back in his chair. 'Why is it so important that you speak with this child?'

'That is my concern. Let's just say he may have vital information.'

He licked his lips. 'I'm not at liberty to tell you what you wish to know.'

Brennan saw the renewed determination in the vicar's eyes. He stood up. 'Well the first part of your statement is about to come true.'

'I'm sorry?'

'You have just forfeited your own liberty, Reverend Pearl. You're coming with me and my constable here down to the station.'

'What?'

It was Jaggery who explained. 'You're under arrest, pal.'

It began as a hazy drizzle that soon turned into a heavier downpour. The children always seemed to be much more badly behaved whenever they returned to school wet. Richard Weston stood before Standard 6 and waited until the fidgeting had completely ended. Sometimes, he felt a certain sympathy with the view being espoused in some circles that the provision of free school meals for the deserving poor, which embraced his entire school, should become universal and not left simply to the discretion and humanity of the local school boards. They would remain in school, for one thing, and their return to class would be organised and marshalled – and dry – after they had eaten sufficiently well to ensure their concentration would stretch through the afternoon.

The Lord only knew what they had actually eaten this dinner time – if anything.

'This morning you were taken into Standard 5 and taught by Mr Edgar,' he said.

There were no sounds in response to what they'd already experienced, but he could sense what they felt about the morning's experience by looking at their eyes.

'Miss Rodley was feeling unwell this morning and she will not be in this afternoon.'

Again, he could see their feelings expressed through the lowering of their eyes and the beginnings of a communal groan which he quickly stifled. If he told them the truth, that the wretched woman had resigned forthwith, then there'd be no telling what their response would be – or the reaction from their parents. Miss Rodley was well liked by the community.

'As a consequence, therefore, of this unfortunate situation, I have some good news.'

They all looked up, some of them casting a glance at the closed door to the classroom, as if they expected Miss Rodley to sweep through the door like a magician's assistant.

'You will not be sitting on the floor in Standard 5, as you were this morning. You shall be sitting in your own seats this afternoon. And I shall be taking your lessons.'

He hadn't expected a round of applause, and they were far too young to appreciate the inconvenience to himself and his overseeing of the school as a whole, but he did expect some expression of approval – the occasional smile, perhaps, at this rarest of treats. But once more the eyes went down. He looked at the classroom window, and the rivulets of rain cascading down the glass.

'Daisy Roper?'

The girl, who was seated in the middle of the room, sat up straight and looked terrified. 'Yes, sir?'

'Go to the cupboard and take out *Arithmetic for Schools*. Give them out one between two.'

He saw their eyes again, dulled and disconsolate, as Daisy Roper carried out his commands. Within minutes, all heads were bowed and the only sounds that could be heard were the scratching of pens on paper and the *drip-drip* of rain against the window.

Silently, he cursed Jane Rodley. As soon as school was over he would go to see her in her lodgings and demand an explanation. That was the least he deserved.

'Have you taken leave of your senses, man?'

Brennan saw the veins on Captain Bell's neck bulge quite alarmingly. He had reported to him the events of the morning as a matter of courtesy, although the apoplectic reaction now developing was something he had feared would happen. The chief constable grabbed a pen and held it tightly in his right hand, as if it were his sergeant's throat.

'I had no choice, sir. The man was being obstructive.'

'You have arrested a man of the cloth? A *vicar*? How do I explain *that* to the Watch Committee, eh?' He leant forward across the desk where he was sitting and narrowed his eyes. 'Who just happens to be of a different persuasion from yourself, does he not? If it were a Catholic priest now . . .'

'It wouldn't matter a jot if he were Protestant, Catholic or Orthodox Jew!' Brennan snapped back. He bitterly resented the implication.

Captain Bell sat back, the expression on his face now one of instant regret. 'I take that back, Sergeant.' He paused. 'But you understand my anger?'

'Yes, sir, I do. It's not every day we do such a thing. But this man knows where the boy Kelly is, and it's my belief the boy knows something of great relevance to my investigation. We know he was at the school on the Friday night.'

'Yes. Trying to burn the place down.'

Brennan ignored the comment. 'And we also know he was kept prisoner on St Thomas Street. I think the murderer did that, to keep him from telling what he saw.'

'But why should the murderer do that? Why not kill the boy as well and have done with the matter?'

'That's the crux of the matter, sir. Whoever held him prisoner didn't kill him because they couldn't. He's a child. The other two were adults. Necessary victims. The boy was an accidental witness. He might even now not be fully aware of what he saw. He might well have seen Dorothea Gadsworth in the classroom with the killer, but that might be all. Perhaps he didn't see the poor woman actually die. Just saw her in the company of someone he knows.'

'So why take him prisoner?'

'Because once he found out the woman died on Friday night,

he might open his mouth and say what – or who – he saw. The killer couldn't take that chance.'

Captain Bell steepled his fingers. 'But he couldn't be kept prisoner for ever.'

'Whoever took him must have thought it worth the risk. Possibly filling the boy's head with tales of escape, a new life somewhere. He's ten, remember. You'll believe anything at that age.'

'And you tell me Reverend Pearl and the Rodley woman offered to take the child from his parents?'

'The headmaster is determined to have the boy prosecuted. It was a simple task to persuade them. Especially as there doesn't seem to be what we would consider the normal bond of love between parents and child. It's a brutal environment.'

'Why then does the vicar not tell you where the boy is?'

'That is the reason I brought him in, sir. If he won't talk at the vicarage, perhaps he might find the cells below more conducive to confession.'

Captain Bell stood up and eyed him, not sure if he were being deliberately and irreligiously provoking. 'You tread very carefully, Sergeant. Very carefully indeed. And I don't want that lumbering bovine anywhere near him. Do you hear?'

Brennan nodded. It wasn't the first time the chief constable had referred to Jaggery that way.

As Weston was leaving school later that afternoon, he caught sight of Nathaniel Edgar who appeared deep in conversation with Alice Walsh at the school gates. She appeared a little flustered and was shaking her head slowly, as if she strongly disagreed with something he had just said. He sighed. After the emotional events of the morning, when it had taken him a long time to calm Emily Mason down and give her the encouragement she needed to return to the classroom and face the children she'd left in tears earlier, the very last thing he needed was for Edgar to upset another of his teachers.

He approached the two of them affably enough. 'At least the rain has stopped. I thought it was set for the night.'

Alice turned to him coolly. 'We were talking about Miss Rodley. Is she unwell?'

Nathaniel Edgar added, 'Most unlike Saint Jane, failing to show up for her lessons. It's *unprofessional*. We both think that, don't we, Alice?'

Weston blanched, having his own words thrown back at him. The man was positively gloating over the misfortunes of the day. Thank God he'd kept her resignation letter to himself.

'I am on my way to her lodgings now,' he said primly, 'to see how she is.'

At that point, Emily Mason emerged from the building.

With a nod in her direction, Edgar said, 'No tuition tonight, Headmaster?'

Weston turned and raised a hand in greeting.

'Miss Mason is *most* concerned, Headmaster,' Edgar went on with a smile. 'She feels you have the makings of a martyr after today.'

As she neared them, Emily was about to say something but held it back. Instead she turned to go.

Weston said, 'If you're going to the tram, Miss Mason, perhaps I could walk with you?'

She gave him a curious look and glanced at Nathaniel before looking away. 'Very well,' she said.

'Goodnight, Miss Walsh. Nathaniel,' said Weston, touching his hat. He and the pupil-teacher walked through the school gate and onto the pavement beyond.

Edgar watched them go, an unpleasant grin spreading across his face. Then he turned to Alice and said, 'Well? Have you reconsidered?'

But before she could give an answer, they both felt a presence behind him. Prendergast, the caretaker, was standing there leaning against the railings.

'He thinks a lot o' that girl, don't he, Mr Edgar?'

Edgar swung round and smiled. 'Oh, he thinks a great deal of her, John. It's the kind of man he is.'

With that, he took Alice Walsh by the arm and escorted her to the school gate. John Prendergast watched them go. She removed Edgar's arm with some violence and slapped him across the face.

'Just who do you think you are?' the caretaker heard her say.

He watched Edgar lean close to her and whisper something in her ear. She made to strike him once more, but he dodged the blow and walked quickly away.

'Bloody teachers,' Prendergast muttered as he walked back into the building.

'Now then, Vicar, why don't you give the answer to a simple question and then you may leave?'

Reverend Pearl sat on the only chair in the cell – a rickety wooden contraption that had proved a most unreliable seat in the past, with prisoners tumbling from its base with painful regularity. Brennan knew that, in this interview at least, such an accident would be unthinkable.

'If the simple question involves the boy's whereabouts then I must decline to answer. There is a greater authority I must answer to.'

Brennan pointed upwards. 'Does He condone lying to the police?'

The vicar smiled ruefully. 'I wasn't aiming that high. I was referring to my fiancée.'

'Ah yes, the one who has absconded with the child. A crime in itself.'

Reverend Pearl reached into his waistcoat pocket and brought out a silver watch.

'You have an appointment, Vicar?'

'No,' he said quietly, replacing the watch. 'But my fiancée has.'

'Please explain.'

He leant forward in his chair, occasioning a tremulous creak from the weakened legs. 'I have sworn to say nothing. At least until . . .'

'Until what?'

'Until Jane has done what she has promised to do.'

'And what is that?'

The man smiled. 'Her duty,' he said, opening his palms. 'Her God-given duty. She has taken him to a far better place. And he won't be coming back. You can accept my solemn assurance on that.'

Later that night, as Nathaniel Edgar made his way home, he pulled his coat collar close around his face. It had grown considerably colder since the early part of the evening, when he'd stepped through the double doors of the Bowling Club and begun the first of his many drinks. At first, he'd been sullen and uncommunicative, grunting monosyllabic responses to those who made any attempt to engage him in conversation. But gradually, as the night wore on, and as the whisky began its soothing magic, he joined in with the rest of them, the small group at the bar who had eschewed the bowling green – far too wet to play any sort of wood. The tales grew bawdier by the drink, and soon he was telling them of his time as a youth when he'd deflowered more than one delectable rose and no mistake. Some of what he told them caused general uproar and some claims of exaggeration:

Nay, Nat, not even you would do summat like that!

Didn't know that sort o' stuff was even possible!

Ye rum bugger!

It nevertheless ensured that the night went swimmingly, and that laughter – bawdy or otherwise – was the best medicine for the ills of the day.

'An' I'll tell ye what,' he said, swaying a little at the bar and grateful for its sturdiness. 'Tomorrow mornin' this bright chappie might well have a lie in. Who's to kick me out of bed, eh? Answer me that!'

'You'll get caned, ye daft sod,' one of the group's more sober members pointed out.

'Ah,' Nathaniel replied with a knowing wink. 'That bugger knows that *I* know. He'll keep his cane hanging on its peg.'

'An' what dost know, Nat?'

But Nathaniel merely touched his nose and gave another wink.

Now, as he weaved his way along the street, he smiled at the recollection. He crossed over to the entrance to the park, his usual shortcut and a necessary one on a night like this. He found he needed to pass water, so he threaded his way through the iron gate and entered the park. He looked around. There was no one in sight, so as he made his way along the path, surrounded by bushes on either side, he unbuttoned his flies and took out his member. At first it was difficult – the cold made it a challenge – but he walked on and came alongside the small pond in the centre of the park.

When he finally managed to pee, he said aloud, 'Look, I'm passing water while passing water!' and he giggled, thinking it a wonderful joke and one which he would share with his friends the next time he stood at the bar of the Bowling Club.

But he would never again stand at the bar of the Bowling Club.

The one who crept from the bushes behind him would see to that.

Jane Rodley unlocked the door to her lodgings and carefully entered, closing the door quietly behind her, sliding the bar across. It was late now, and the last thing she wanted was to disturb her neighbours. The house she rented was in Upper Dicconson Street, to the north of Wigan town centre, within easy walking distance of school.

She closed the curtains and gave a shiver. Although the rain had been intermittent throughout the day, tonight it had been replaced by a chill in the air, a precursor to worsening weather, she thought ruefully. She sat in her armchair and let her head fall back in an attitude of exhaustion. It was too late now to make the fire, but it was equally too cold to remain where she was. After a while, during which she could feel her eyes grow heavy, she forced herself from the armchair and moved to the gas mantle where she struck a match and lit the gas. The front room was bathed in a yellow glow that gradually grew stronger until it was casting sufficient light for her to see the sheet of paper on the floor behind the front door.

She picked it up and read its contents.

So Richard Weston had called round to see her, no doubt to try to persuade her to change her mind and tear up her resignation. She tore up his letter instead and placed the pieces in the empty grate. After what had happened today, it would be impossible for her ever to return to George Street again.

She went into the kitchen at the rear to make herself a warming cup of tea. She watched as her hand shook, and the water slopped around the mug.

Control yourself!

As she glanced through the window that overlooked her small yard, she thought she saw some movement by the gate that led to the narrow alley beyond. But then she shook her head. The darkness playing tricks. After what she'd done today, and seen the expression on Billy Kelly's face, it was hardly surprising that she should be jumping at imaginary shadows.

It was as she returned to the armchair, clasping her mug of tea in both hands to ward off the chill and steady her nerves, that she heard the knock on the door. It alarmed her so much she spilt some of the hot liquid on her dress and yelped in pain. Then the knocking came again.

'Who's there?' she asked with some trepidation. Her heart was beating fast, and her throat suddenly felt dry.

'It's me, Miss Rodley,' came a familiar voice.

She unbarred the door and pulled it open. The sight of Detective Sergeant Brennan standing in her doorway was enough to make her catch her breath.

'Good evening, Miss Rodley. It's bitterly cold out here. Mind if I step inside?'

She stood to one side and gave him a look compounded of anger and puzzlement.

Once they were seated at the kitchen table, Brennan told her quite simply that her fiancé was at that moment enjoying the hospitality of the Wigan Borough Police cells.

'I wish to know what you have done with Billy Kelly, Miss Rodley,' he added. 'But let me first assure you that I have no intention of having the boy prosecuted for attempting to burn the school down. For one thing, there's no real evidence that any crime was committed, not in that cellar at any rate. A few sticks of wood and a singed copybook? It would be laughed out of court.' He leant forward, anxious to impress upon her the importance of what he was about to say. 'No, I have much bigger fish to fry. It's my belief that Billy Kelly saw something that Friday night, something that might have appeared innocent until he would later hear about Dorothea Gadsworth's body being found. Then he might have said something. So he was kept hidden in the cellar of a derelict house, until he managed to escape. It was his misfortune to be bitten by a rat, and it was his good fortune to be saved from a horrible death by a member of the Salvation Army. The lad has suffered a great deal over the last week.'

He stood, and she gazed up at him, feeling the full force of his personality.

'What have you done with him, Miss Rodley?'

CHAPTER SIXTEEN

Constable Higginson was patrolling the park and cursing his luck that he should be on night duty, tonight of all nights. If it wasn't raining it was blowing a gale and rendering the cape he wore useless. His wife of less than a year was tucked up in bed with that firm tempting body wrapped round itself rather than him. He could spit.

He was about to hide himself behind a bush near the duck pond and light up a cigarette – there was no one around at this time of night, surely? – when he heard something a few yards away.

What is it? A man groaning?

If some fool were tomming a prossy under cover of bushes then he was about to get a bloody big shock and a shameful day in court under the charge of gross indecency. Following the direction of the sounds, he literally stumbled over a man curled up in agony and making a low moaning cry. Higginson bent low and leant over him, taking out a match and striking it to get a better look.

What he saw shocked him.

The man had been stabbed in his lower back, the blood already congealing and forming a thick and sticky mess. But it wasn't that that revolted him. It was the sight of the man's member protruding from his flies and lying limp across his thigh.

'Don't need no detective to find out what you've been up to, pal,' said Higginson in a low whisper. 'Looks like you got what was comin' to ye. Dirty bastard.'

'And where exactly is Elm Lodge?'

Jane Rodley sighed. 'It's in Seaforth, Liverpool. It's run by the Waifs and Strays' Society, under the auspices of the Church of England. I was present last year at the dedication service conducted by the Bishop of Liverpool. His daughter performed the official opening.' She held her hands steady, palms down, on the table. 'I've been very concerned about young Billy Kelly, Sergeant, for a long time. The poor soul comes regularly to school underfed, bruised and wearing not much more than rags. You've met both of his parents. Hardly shining examples of virtue and parenthood, are they?'

Brennan said nothing. He knew very well the sort of life young Kelly would be living.

She went on. 'At Elm Lodge they run lessons to teach the boys a trade. But that wasn't what we have in mind for young Kelly. One of the ways in which the society offers practical help – help that changes lives, literally – is the existence of the emigration system.'

'Emigration?' It was a word close to Brennan's heart, for his parents were both emigrants from Ireland, escaping abject poverty for a better life in Wigan.

'Many of the children are found homes abroad – Canada,

mostly – and there they are given a life and a set of opportunities they couldn't even dream of here.'

'So you've been planning this for a while?'

She nodded. 'We'd discussed it even before the events of last week. Billy's life was being stunted and brutalised in that place they laughingly called *home*. When he went missing we feared the worst. Not that he might be the witness to a crime but the victim of one. It wouldn't have surprised us if that harridan of a mother had done for him. It really wouldn't.'

Brennan frowned, trying to arrange things in his mind. 'So, once you'd discovered he was in the infirmary, you and the good reverend persuaded his parents to remove him and place him in your hands on the pretext of sanctuary? You took him from his home. In effect, you stole him.'

'That isn't the word I would use, Sergeant, but yes. In a nutshell.'

'And in so doing you removed a vital witness. One who could identify his jailer.'

She looked up. 'The boy is still very weak, Sergeant Brennan. I took him to Seaforth on the train and he slept most of the way. We were the object of much speculation and concern, I can tell you. One woman passenger in the carriage even whispered the word "typhus". He spoke very little, and he seemed to grow even weaker as we neared our destination.'

'Well he would, wouldn't he? Removed prematurely from his hospital bed?'

She looked down, her face growing warm and flushed. 'As soon as we arrived on Seaforth Road the superintendent there sent for a doctor, who gave him a strong sedative and ordered that he be confined to bed.'

She let her words drift into the cold air of the kitchen.

Brennan spoke firmly. He needed to deal in facts, and certainties. 'Did the boy say anything at all about the one who kept him in that cellar?'

She shook her head. 'He said only two words the entire time I was with him.'

'What were they?' he asked with a sliver of hope in his voice.

'He kept saying "bacon butty" . . . "bacon butty" . . . but when I bought him a sandwich at the railway station, he ate a few mouthfuls and was then sick.' She paused then said, 'You will now let my fiancé go? He has spiritual strength, Sergeant, not physical.'

'I'll consider it,' he said, standing up. Inside he was seething and sorely tempted to let rip and blast her for the stupidity of what she'd done. If the boy failed to recover, he'd see to it that the good vicar and his fiancée would spend some time at Her Majesty's pleasure. As for now, he would have to travel to Seaforth and hope against hope that the boy would somehow undergo a miraculous recovery and give him a name.

He needed a bloody name.

The following morning, he was forced to put his travel plans on hold when he received a report of a stabbing in Mesnes Park. When he saw the name of the victim, he felt the veins in his head pulsate violently.

Nathaniel Edgar.

Another victim linked this time directly to the school. The sound of angry footsteps clacking down the corridor, and the way his door swung open without the courtesy of a knock, told him that the chief constable shared his feelings of outrage.

'Another one?' was Captain Bell's manner of greeting him. '*Another one?*'

'Well, not quite, sir,' said Brennan in his best straw-clutching voice.

'What do you mean by that?' Bell snapped, at least having the decency now to slam the door shut. 'Are you saying the assault was a coincidence? That the perpetrator was a one-legged rag-and-bone man? Or maybe Jack the Ripper on tour?'

'No, sir. What I meant was, well, according to this report, Mr Nathaniel Edgar is still alive.'

'Oh hallelujah and rejoice!'

'I'll go immediately to the infirmary and see if he is well enough to be interviewed.'

'This has to stop. Do you hear me, man? Whatever demons are swirling around that godforsaken hellhole in George Street must be caught forthwith. Do I make myself clear?'

'Yes, sir. I think things are heading in that direction.'

Captain Bell gave him a long, hard look. 'They had better be.'

Brennan stood up to show his sense of urgency and single-mindedness. The chief constable opened the door and stood to one side, a gesture not so much of common courtesy but of impatience.

'Oh, and by the way, Sergeant,' he said as Brennan reached for his hat behind the door.

'Yes, sir?'

'You might also, in the course of your interview, enquire as to why Mr Edgar had his manhood dangling from his trousers for all the world and his dog to see.'

Richard Weston had no choice but to send a child to the vicarage at Lorne Street with an urgent message. In the first place, Reverend Pearl was the school manager, and as such he had to shoulder much of the burden arising from the situation the school now faced: with Nathaniel Edgar having failed once again to show up for his lessons this morning, the position was critical. In the second place, the good reverend would be able to furnish him with some sort of reason why his fiancée chose the previous day to resign with no notice given. And in the third place, it might well galvanise the man into some sort of action – perhaps sending word to Miss Rodley that things were at a desperate state here at George Street, and an appeal to her sense of duty and loyalty might well bring her back, at least on a temporary basis.

And things *were* desperate.

Nathaniel Edgar's class – Standard 5 – were squeezed into Standard 4's classroom, much to the outrage of Miss Ryan, who was heard to mutter, as they filed out of the staffroom that morning, that 'this ship is sinking fast.' And he himself was taking Jane Rodley's Standard 6.

As he walked down the corridor to the classroom, he had cause to thank the frosty-featured Miss Ryan, for she had given him the idea for the core of the lesson he would teach in the first hour: he would have them recite *A Greyport Legend*, one of his personal favourites, wherein a rotting hulk filled with children at play is parted from its moorings in thick fog and they disappear, often to be heard in fogs playing in ghostly ignorance on their phantom ship. He even felt buoyed by the irony of the poem, and when he passed Emily Mason's classroom, its door not yet closed, she was surprised to hear him reciting a fragment from the poem:

For the voices of children, still at play
In a phantom hulk that drifts alway
Through channels whose waters never fail.

She marvelled at the indomitability of his spirit as he moved past her classroom. She had felt so sorry for him this morning.

It had seemed that everything was conspiring against him, but she felt sure he would come through this trial. His strength had certainly helped her these last weeks. She turned to Standard 1 and clapped her hands loudly. They all immediately stood to attention.

Half an hour later, she thought she heard a yell of anguish from along the corridor. That couldn't have been Mr Weston's voice, surely? It had sounded wild and unrestrained. Every child in Standard 1 looked up from their copybooks and their struggle to write the alphabet neatly, and a few of them began to whimper.

'Carry on with your work!' Emily Mason snapped, but she was as disturbed and worried as they were. Still, ten years separated her from the pupils sitting in front of her, and, despite her histrionics of the previous day, she was learning to keep her emotions under some sort of control.

Then, after a few minutes of tense silence, she heard footsteps along the corridor. Through the glass partition in her door she saw the headmaster walk briskly past, his face ashen. Alongside him, Reverend Pearl and the large police constable who had been here with Detective Sergeant Brennan. All three of them had grim expressions on their faces.

'Miss?' one of the children asked.

'Yes, Vera, what is it?'

''As Mr Weston bin 'rested?'

'Bin what? I mean, *been* what?'

''Rested, miss. By that fat bobby.'

Emily shook her head. 'Don't talk nonsense, Vera. Now get on with your letters. You haven't got to haitch yet.'

Brennan had been at the bedside of Nathaniel Edgar for hours now, waiting for him to recover from the surgery he'd undergone earlier that morning. He knew, according to the surgeon, that the knife had penetrated his spinal cord in the lumbar region, and that it was highly likely that he would suffer paralysis and impairment of sensation below the injury.

'In plain words, Sergeant, the poor chap might well never walk again. Still, from another point of view, he was lucky that your constable found him. If he'd been left there, he wouldn't be here.'

Brennan hadn't challenged his definition of lucky, even though he could think of nothing worse for a single man like Nathaniel Edgar than to be housebound and totally dependent on others. For a while, he gave thanks for his own health, and more so for that of Ellen and Barry.

He'd asked Captain Bell to send a telegram to the Seaforth police, requesting their assistance by despatching an officer to the Waifs and Strays' Home at Elm Lodge on Seaforth Road to check on the boy's welfare until Brennan could make the journey to Merseyside. He'd also sent Jaggery down to the school to let the headmaster know of what had happened. He realised the man couldn't be expected to drop everything and come up to the infirmary. He had a school to run, and now, with Edgar totally incapacitated, Weston had a huge problem on his hands.

He heard a groaning from the bed. Nathaniel Edgar opened his eyes slowly, then closed them again as the light from the ward disturbed him.

'Mr Edgar?' Brennan said quietly. 'Mr Edgar?'

Edgar licked his lips. They looked cracked and dry. 'Water,' he said in a weak voice.

The contrast between the man now and the last time they spoke was marked. As he stood up and walked to the small cabinet by the bed where a jug of water had been placed, Brennan wondered how

Nathaniel Edgar would find the strength to cope with the devastating news he would soon be given. He filled a small glass with water and held it to the man's lips. He tried to raise his head but found the effort too much, so Brennan held the glass there, pouring the soothing water into his mouth little by little until he shook his head.

'Do you feel like answering a few questions?' Brennan asked as he sat back down.

Edgar gave a feeble smile. 'Not going anywhere.'

'Do you remember what happened?'

A pause while he screwed up his face in an effort to recollect the dark events of the previous night.

'Wanted to piss.'

Brennan nodded. That, at least, gave him the answer to one question. He'd make a point of haranguing Constable Higginson back at the station for the lurid image he'd painted of the man getting his just deserts for flashing his old man at all and sundry.

'Did you see who did this?'

Another pause. Another contortion of the face. 'Too dark.'

'Did you hear anything? Something that might give us some inkling as to who did it?'

Slowly, with great effort, Edgar turned his head to face Brennan. His eyes were open now, and there was a tearful intensity in them.

'Nothing . . . But I may know . . .'

Brennan caught his breath. 'What?'

The man's eyes closed tightly, as if a wave of pain was sweeping through him. Then, after a few moments, he said drowsily, 'I may know someone . . . who'd want me to disappear.'

CHAPTER SEVENTEEN

Richard Weston returned to Standard 6 and listened to some of them mangle Bret Harte's haunting poem. None of them could pronounce the final word 'anchorage', being unable to grasp the concept of *ch* transforming itself into a hard consonant sound, and no matter how many times he corrected them, once they returned to the beginning of the poem, '*They ran through the streets of the seaport town*', they had forgotten the pronunciation or the divine symbolism of the word at the end: '*Drawing the soul to its anchorage.*'

After the sixth mangling of the word he tore into them, ordering each and every disobedient devil to stand while he marched along the aisles swinging his cane and showing them the error of their ways. When the only sounds in the classroom were snivelling and sobbing and groans of pain, he sat down and commanded that they read the poem in silence until the end of morning school, and to reflect on the fate of the children on the hulk who were blissfully unaware of the rotting ship slipping its moorings and floating into a fog-filled oblivion.

'That will be your fate in life!' he barked.

While they strove to make sense of the poem and its import, Weston sat at the front, staring out of the window and reflecting on what Reverend Pearl and Constable Jaggery had told him. They had met coincidentally as they arrived at the school. The vicar brought good news: he had been in touch with Jane Rodley and she had agreed to step in and continue with Standard 6. She would be there within the hour. But that information paled into insignificance with the news that Nathaniel Edgar had been attacked in the park the previous night and was even now in a poor condition at Wigan Infirmary.

But the man had survived!

A knife in the back and he had survived!

He could muse all he liked about the indomitability of the spirit in the face of overwhelming odds. He could even think back with fondness on the happier times the two of them had shared together when they were both starting out at George Street and enjoying a post-classroom drink at Nathaniel's Bowling Club. But neither of those thoughts lasted long in his head. No, the only thing in his thoughts, like a worm eating away, bit by bit, at his peace of mind, was what the man would say to the police when he – or indeed *if* he – regained consciousness.

It would be the end of everything.

Brennan felt a huge wave of frustration sweep over him. Edgar had drifted back to sleep, saying nothing more. He had been about to give Brennan a name, though he'd admitted he saw nothing to indicate who his assailant was.

Still, sitting by an unconscious man's bedside gave him the opportunity to review what he knew about this strange case and its sequence of events, events which, he was convinced, began not at George Street Elementary School but up in the Lake District, in Hawkshead, the parish church of St Michael and All Angels, and the tragedy of a little girl's drowning in Esthwaite Water.

It was beyond doubt that Dorothea Gadsworth recognised someone that day at George Street Elementary. Her words before she fainted, which Nathaniel Edgar thought sounded like 'Let's wait', must have been referring to Esthwaite, and the telegram she sent to her parents confirmed it. What had she written?

Seen one responsible for Tilly's death. Past inescapable.

The phrase 'one responsible' could refer to either Julia Reece or the youth David. If it were Julia Reece that Miss Gadsworth had seen, then that meant she had changed her name, for the only women she met that day were teachers at the school, none of whom was called Julia. Emily Mason, at fifteen, was too young anyway – she wouldn't have been born when Tilly Pollard drowned. Jane Rodley was around the same age as Julia Reece – and, he suddenly realised, she had the same initials: *J. R.*

He decided to follow that thought for a while. *If* Jane Rodley were Julia Reece, then is it possible that Reverend Charles Pearl, her fiancé who was also present when the unfortunate Miss Gadsworth fainted, was the youth *David* who had desecrated the church with such tragic consequences all those years ago? The Gadsworths said that David was around seventeen at the time, which would make him thirty-two. The vicar was around that age himself. Were Jane Rodley and Charles Pearl really Julia Reece and the youth David?

But there was something wrong with that supposition: Miss Gadsworth had written in her telegram that she had seen *one* responsible for Tilly Pollard's death – wouldn't she have written *the ones* or *both*?

Still, that didn't preclude the possibility that *one* of them had been in that belfry all those years ago. And the one who would stand to lose the most if the truth of such sacrilegious and lewd behaviour came out would be a man who now called himself *reverend* and preached hellfire sermons every Sunday.

It was true that the two of them had taken the boy Kelly away from his parents and away from Brennan himself. Were they indeed acting out of the best of motives? Or had they fooled him into thinking that way? He only had Jane Rodley's word that she took him to Seaforth.

The sooner he got to Seaforth to check for himself the better.

He thought, too, of something else that the Gadsworths told him: that young Julia had been outspoken in her defence of a local woman accused of witchcraft by her more superstitious neighbours.

Alice Walsh was an outspoken supporter of women's suffrage. Had the girl's childish defence of an old woman's right to live in peace translated itself into the defence of all women's rights, including the right to vote?

A coincidence? He didn't like coincidences.

He thought of another coincidence, one that had been bothering him for some time ever since those early interviews.

Something that one of them had said came back to him now with a clarity that both alarmed and excited him. *Had* it been a coincidence? Or was that person having a gruesome joke at his expense?

Surely not?

He frowned and looked down at the sleeping form in the bed. *Wake up, man.*

* * *

Jane Rodley had arrived in school later that morning and immediately took over her own class, Standard 6. She was somewhat surprised to hear them raise a cheer when she walked into the room and had to maintain a professionally stern expression on her face when Richard Weston silenced them with a dire threat to render their earlier punishment the merest of tickles in comparison with what he would mete out if the caterwauling continued. Still, it was good to stand there once more, having thought that she would never do so again. That might still be the case, she reflected, if Detective Sergeant Brennan took it into his head to arrest her for what she did with young Billy Kelly.

At dinner time, with the pupils out of the building and walking home for their lunches, Misses Hardman, Walsh and Ryan – Standards 2, 3 and 4 respectively – were seated in a huddle in the staffroom and discussing the lamentable course of events that were slowly but surely sinking the ship. Jane sat in the furthest corner of the room and was engaging in conversation with Emily Mason, telling her about young Billy and the place of safety she had taken him the previous day.

'The poor boy,' said the pupil-teacher. 'He must be very weak.'

'He was being seen to by a doctor as I left.'

Emily shook her head slowly at such misfortune.

At that point the door opened and Richard Weston entered, closely followed by Reverend Pearl.   Both men had stern expressions.

It was the headmaster who spoke.

'There is no easy way to tell you all this. You are all aware that Nathaniel Edgar didn't arrive this morning. I assumed it was part of a pattern that I was in the process of dealing with. I was wrong.'

He paused then said, 'Nathaniel was viciously attacked last night in Mesnes Park, the victim of an assault with a knife.'

Alice Walsh whispered, 'Oh dear Lord no!'

Miss Ryan asked, 'Did Mr Edgar survive the attack?'

Reverend Pearl spoke up. 'He survived, yes. But it is feared the poor man may never walk again.'

Suddenly, Alice stood up and walked from the room, head held high.

Emily Mason said, 'Why is all this happening?' and let forth a series of sobs. She was immediately comforted by Jane Rodley, who looked at both men and her eyes rebuked them for bringing such devastating news while a pupil-teacher was present.

'Do the police know who did this?' Miss Hardman asked.

Weston shook his head. 'I shall, of course, go to the infirmary once school has closed for the day,' he said in a sombre voice. 'And I'm sure you'll wish me to take your very best wishes for his recovery.'

'I'm sure he'd much rather you took him his favourite bottle of Scotch,' said Miss Ryan with some asperity, prompting everyone in the room to stare at her in disbelief. 'We are all aware of Mr Edgar's little peccadilloes. Perhaps it would be better if in future we all spread our little secrets on the table, like a pack of cards,' she added before standing up and leaving the room.

Reverend Pearl gave Miss Rodley a questioning look, but she subtly shook her head and indicated the sobbing girl beside her. *She needs my attention now*, the expression said.

Weston said, 'I shall expect the school to be solemn and silent this afternoon. A *respectful* atmosphere. So the children will work in total silence throughout.' He was staring directly at Emily Mason with that last sentence. The significance wasn't missed by anyone.

With that, he turned on his heels and left the room, Reverend Pearl following behind him.

Nathaniel Edgar awoke later that afternoon, much to the delight and relief of Detective Sergeant Brennan. The doctor had been round to see him earlier, and had told Brennan that he seemed to be sleeping more soundly now, and his pulse was growing stronger. When he finally opened his eyes, he stared at Brennan for a few seconds, as if he was wondering what on earth the policeman was doing by his bedside. Then the memory must have returned, for he gave a wan smile and said, 'Now where were we, Sergeant?'

'You were telling me someone might wish you to disappear.'

Edgar sighed. 'Richard Weston is about to fire me.'

'Why?'

'You found the evidence yourself.'

'The bottle of Scotch?'

Edgar gave a slow nod. 'It is a friend and a traitor, all wrapped up in one.' He remained silent and closed his eyes. Brennan thought he was drifting back to sleep, but then, still with his eyes closed, he said in a low voice, 'It's the reason – or shall we say, one of the reasons – my wife left me. Or, would it be more truthful to say that it became my bosom companion when she deserted me? Whichever it is, the bottle became shall we say, essential?'

'And Mr Weston warned you about it?'

A nod.

'Was it affecting your work?'

Another nod.

281

'And you think that is sufficient grounds for him to attack you with a knife?'

Edgar smiled. 'Oh, probably not. It's simply not in his nature. But he was angry with me. I'd failed to show up for my class and that made things very awkward for him. So we argued and I threatened him.'

'*You* threatened *him*?'

Edgar swallowed and licked his dry lips. Brennan stood up and poured him some water, which he sipped slowly, savouring its coolness. 'If only water could make you forget, eh, Sergeant? Who would have any need for whisky?'

'Indeed.'

He handed the glass back to Brennan, then lay his head back on the pillow and spoke to the ceiling. 'If I were to lose my teaching position I would be very much in dire straits. I wouldn't get another, that's for sure, not when they asked about my reasons for leaving. Weston and the good reverend would make sure that any reference would include a comment on my relationship with the bottle. It's as well they know nothing of . . .' He broke off there and paused before adding, 'We all know Charles Pearl's views on anyone deviating from Christian virtues.'

Brennan wondered what he would say if he knew that the vicar had colluded in a child abduction and was released from police custody only last night.

'So I decided to fight back. And you only fight with weapons that you can trust. I told Richard if he dispensed with my services then I would send a letter to the school board informing them of what I knew.'

'And what do you know, Mr Edgar?'

He turned his head and looked Brennan straight in the

eye. 'I told you once that I knew the man behind the mask.'

'I thought it a curious thing to say.'

'He would have exposed my relationship with the bottle. So I fought fire with fire.'

'How?'

'I threatened to expose his relationship with Emily Mason.'

Brennan's jaw dropped.

CHAPTER EIGHTEEN

'Oh, I see!' said Nathaniel Edgar, and even managed to force out a laugh of sorts. 'No, Sergeant Brennan. That's not what I meant at all. Good God, man! The very idea of Richard Weston . . . No. That's not what I meant by *relationship*.'

'Then what did you mean by it?' Brennan wasn't accustomed to being laughed at. His darkening brow told the prostrate teacher what he thought of that.

'I meant exactly and literally what I said. By *relationship* I mean the link, the *relation* between them. Do you have relations, Sergeant?'

Again, Brennan scowled. 'I do.'

'A child, perhaps?'

'A son, yes.'

Now it began to dawn on him what Nathaniel Edgar meant. 'You mean, Emily Mason is *Weston's daughter*?'

'Yes.'

Brennan sat back and took a moment to assimilate the information.

Edgar went on, pausing occasionally in his narrative to take a breath and wait for the pain to subside.

'Quite a few years ago now, at Christmas time it was, Richard and I went to the club. He wasn't headmaster back then, of course. He was in a sulky sort of mood and I asked him what the matter was. He wouldn't tell me. Not at the beginning of the night, at any rate. But as the night wore on, and the drinks became more and more frequent, he began to loosen. He said, "Do you know Emily Mason in Standard 2?" I said yes, of course. It isn't a big school and we know most of them by name. "A very bright girl," I replied, curious as to where this conversation was leading. And then he did something I've never seen him do before or since. He started to cry. That stage of drinking when a man is easy prey to maudlin thoughts and memories. And it was Christmas, too, don't forget. I asked him what the matter was and he finally said, "She's my daughter." As simply as that. I was dumbstruck. I mean, he's unmarried for one thing. For another we'd all known about her father, who apparently was a bad sort. She had not long been at George Street, I think, back then. Her father had died, and they'd moved from Manchester to Wigan. Fresh start. Then, not a year later, her mother died, too. Terrible time for the girl. Eventually she was looked after by her grandmother. Still is, by all accounts.'

'But if she already had a father, how could Weston claim to be her father?'

Edgar shrugged. The action caused him further pain, and he winced and closed his eyes. After a few moments, during which the pain apparently subsided, he opened his eyes again and said, in a weaker voice this time, 'He denied what he'd said the next time we met. But he'd said it. And meant it. I didn't pry. But he knew that I knew. And it has remained an unspoken secret, once shared, ever since. I suppose I should feel ashamed for using it as a weapon, but the simple truth is I am past all shame, Sergeant.'

'Just one more question, Mr Edgar.'

'Go on.'

'What is your opinion of school inspectors?'

Edgar gave him a curious look. 'Why?'

'Humour me.'

'No opinion,' he said. 'A necessary evil, I suppose.'

Before Brennan could ask his next question, Edgar let out an agonised groan and his face became contorted with pain.

'Get . . . a . . . nurse!'

Brennan moved quickly, guiltily aware that the past five minutes had exhausted the man. The morphine he'd been given was apparently wearing off, too. He returned with the nurse, who advised him curtly that it was time for him to leave. Brennan thanked the man for his cooperation, realising that the pain was becoming almost excruciating and he was now clutching at his bedsheets and gasping for air. There was nothing he could do. He walked down the ward towards the doors at the end. There, he glanced back and saw another nurse had joined the first and they were both tending to him as best they could. He felt dreadfully sorry for Nathaniel Edgar, who had once stood proudly before thirty or so children and, at one time at least, had seemed a powerful and awesome figure. He would never experience that feeling again.

Once outside the infirmary, he gave Constable Hardy, who had been waiting there for hours, strict instructions to stay with Mr Edgar and under no circumstances allow anyone to visit him at visiting time.

'What about family, Sergeant?' asked Hardy, anxious to perform his duties to the letter now.

'He has none that I know of. I repeat: no one gets to visit him. Do you understand, Constable?'

Now that the orders couldn't be misinterpreted, he said eagerly, 'Not a soul, Sergeant.'

As the constable re-entered the infirmary, almost running up the steps in his eagerness, Brennan saw Constable Jaggery turning into the driveway of the infirmary.

'Glad I caught you, Sergeant,' he said with a slight wheezing of breath.

'How did things go at the school?'

'Oh the vicar was there so he sort of took over.'

'How was the headmaster?'

'Usual self. Miserable as sin.'

Brennan frowned. 'You might have hit the nail on the head, Constable.'

'Eh?'

Brennan took out his watch. 'Four-thirty. We'll give ourselves a treat and take a hackney carriage.'

'We packin' in early, Sergeant?' Jaggery asked with a rising note of optimism in his voice.

'Perish the thought, lad. We're going back to school.'

'Bloody hellfire!' said Jaggery under his breath.

Once inside the school building they made their way along the corridor towards the headmaster's office. The school was empty now, and when they reached Weston's office Brennan knocked and waited, but there was no response from within. He frowned. After school, the man often held what he referred to as monitoring sessions with his pupil-teacher who was also his daughter, according to Nathaniel Edgar. He opened the door and found the room empty.

'If you're lookin' for Mr Weston you're lookin' in t'wrong place.'

The caretaker, Prendergast, was standing in the corridor with a mop and bucket in his hand. He placed them down and walked towards them.

'Where *can* he be found then?' Brennan asked, closing the door behind him.

Prendergast shrugged. 'Saw 'im leavin' not ten minutes ago with Miss Mason. Place 'as been like a morgue this afternoon. Hear a pin drop.'

'Why was that?'

'Respect for Mr Edgar, I suppose. They was all upset. Apart from Miss Ryan. She saw it as a punishment from God cos Edgar 'as a drop now an' agen.'

'Does Mr Weston ever leave early?'

'Never.' Prendergast rammed his mop into the bucket and water splashed over the rim. 'Never seen 'im so quiet. Like one o' them funeral mutes. Did some shoutin' earlier when Miss Walsh was in a state over what happened to Mr Edgar. Everyone was a bit cowed by 'is mood, apart from Miss Walsh. She give as good as she got. Bloody teachers.'

With that pronouncement he proceeded to mop with a vigour that expressed his feelings far better than his words.

'What do we do now, Sergeant?'

Brennan sighed. 'I've asked the chief constable to send word to Seaforth. They should have replied by now. I want you to return to the station and see what message is waiting for me there. I'll be back in an hour.'

'What do we do about 'is lordship? Weston?'

'Nothing at the moment.'

'But you said him an' Edgar had argued. Might be a motive.'

'Possible. But is it sufficient motive to attempt murder? Whoever tried to kill Edgar has already killed twice before. There's something I'm missing and I can't quite put my finger on it.'

As they walked back along the corridor and out into the early evening gloom, Jaggery said, 'So where are you headed, Sergeant?'

'Here and there, Constable. Here and there.'

Before Jaggery could get him to elaborate, he was already heading for the school gates.

From the list of addresses Weston had given him, Brennan made his way to where Alice Walsh lived. Chatham Street lay just off Darlington Street East. Brennan noted with interest that the street was within walking distance of St Catharine's Church in Lorne Street, and he wondered if Miss Walsh were the churchgoing type. Somehow he doubted it.

She answered the door on his third knock and looked surprised to see him.

'Sergeant Brennan?'

'A few questions, Miss Walsh. I won't take up too much of your time.'

She stood to one side and invited him in. The tiny hallway was neatly presented: a small polished stand bearing a bowl of flowers, an oval mahogany mirror, and hanging alongside, a framed cartoon depicting three evil-looking witches sitting around a bubbling cauldron with disembodied hands reaching up through the thick stew holding cards which read 'Votes for Women'. Around the cauldron ran the words 'New Woman's Demands'.

'You know that's the latest phrase,' she said, indicating the cartoon with an attempt at bitterness that didn't quite ring true. 'They call us the "New Woman". I think I prefer that to other names we've been given. Especially the "Shrieking Sisterhood". The picture reminds me of what we're facing. The way we're regarded. Interesting that it's the contents of the cauldron that have our demands. As if they're somehow poisonous.'

Brennan could tell by the way she was talking that her words hid something deeper, more personal. Alice Walsh was upset and shielding it, very badly. And it had nothing to do with women's suffrage.

'Perhaps if we sit down?' he said gently.

'Of course. My manners.'

She led the way into the living room, a small but compact area with room for two padded chairs, a small table set against the wall, and taking pride of place it seemed, a small ornament resting in the centre of the mantel, a beautifully styled butterfly encased in glass, its blue and yellow wings spread wide as it rested on a small tree branch, the artist capturing almost the moment of flight.

As they both sat down, he saw that her eyes were red, and he wondered if she had been crying.

'You know, of course, that Mr Edgar was attacked last night?'

She held her hands on her lap and gave a nod.

'I gather you were somewhat distraught by the news?'

She looked him straight in the eye. The old defiance had returned, if only momentarily. 'He's a colleague. Isn't it usual to respond in that way when someone you work with is attacked?'

'Of course. But I'm told you had words with Mr Weston this afternoon.'

'Who told you that?'

'Does it matter?'

She glared at him and once more lowered her eyes. 'I asked the headmaster if I could have leave to go and see Mr Edgar.'

'What? During school time?'

'Yes.'

'But if Mr Edgar is only a colleague . . . ?'

She raised her head and looked at the ornament on her mantel. 'You see that butterfly, Sergeant?'

'Yes. It's beautiful.'

'You think so?'

'You don't?'

'I think it's horrible.'

'Why?'

She stood up and went over, touching the smooth glass surface and stroking her finger along its curved edge. He coughed uncomfortably.

'It *is* beautiful, Sergeant Brennan. That's true. But look at it closer. Look at its wings, all ready to take flight and flutter around a garden in the bright sunshine, free and unfettered. Unconfined.'

He could see the symbol she was presenting but wondered what it had to do with Nathaniel Edgar, if anything.

Then she said, 'Are you bound by the same restrictions as a priest?'

'What do you mean?'

'In Confession, you can say what you like and the priest is bound to keep it to himself. Or share it with God – if that's what you happen to believe.'

He wondered why she was using an example from the Church in one breath then mocking it in the next. He said, 'If you're asking me if I can keep my mouth shut . . . ?'

She laughed at that. 'Well? Can you?'

'Within reason. I won't reveal what you tell me as long as I don't break the law or allow you to.'

She gave a slow nod, as if accepting what he said. 'Well then. I wanted to go to see Nathaniel Edgar because at one time we were lovers. Even when he was living with his wife.'

'I see.'

'You aren't shocked?'

'I see many things as a policeman, Miss Walsh. I might not agree with the morality of what you say, but it doesn't shock me one bit.'

'Sometimes I used to think of him as this butterfly. Trapped behind a glass case. Beautiful.' She gave another laugh, this time a slightly more bitter one. 'But he wouldn't fly, even when I offered to set him free.'

'How?'

'I asked him to come here and live with me.'

Brennan tried not to show his shock. It was one thing conducting an immoral relationship with a man who was still married – that sort of thing was usually done under cover of darkness and subterfuge anyway – but to live together openly, while both teaching in a local elementary school? They would have become lepers. Unemployed lepers.

She gave a sharp laugh, a curious sound, for it managed to convey her mockery of both Brennan and Edgar – one for his morality, the other for what she regarded as his cowardice.

'You still have feelings for Nathaniel Edgar?'

For the first time her confidence failed her. Instead of answering him directly, she simply asked, 'How is he? Is it true he'll never walk again?'

Brennan remained silent for a few seconds, realising that it wasn't his place to give her any information as to the man's condition. Still, he could see by the flicker of her eyes that his silence had carried bad news.

When she next spoke, it was barely a whisper. 'Who would do such a thing, Sergeant?'

'An unstable mind, miss. I don't suppose you have any idea of who could be responsible?'

She shook her head. 'There's a maniac loose, isn't there?'

'Whoever it is, he or she seems to be growing more desperate. If there's anything you can think of, anything at all that might indicate a motive? I'm positive all this dates back fifteen years, to a time when a small child was drowned because of a young girl's negligence.'

Alice gripped the glass case tightly. 'And what on earth does that have to do with Nathaniel? What does it have to do with anyone? The past should remain buried, should it not? What possible good . . .'

For a second he imagined she was about to hurl the butterfly at him, but then she relinquished her grip and her shoulders sagged.

'I apologise, Sergeant. Whoever did this to Nathaniel should learn to live with the past and all its mistakes. That's what life should be, isn't it?'

'Perhaps.'

He stood to go. As he reached the hallway he turned and saw that she still stood by the mantel, her hand once more caressing the glass that rested between her touch and the butterfly. She spoke softly, not meeting his gaze.

'Nathaniel Edgar is a man, with all the weaknesses that sex carries. But he didn't deserve a knife in the back, Sergeant. Whatever he has done. Or not done.'

'Oh, I almost forgot,' he said. 'Perhaps you could clear up a little niggle I've been having with myself.'

'Is it contagious?'

He smiled. 'I doubt it. It's just something you said when I first mentioned the child's death to you back at school.'

She gave a nervous swallow. 'Go on.'

'I used the phrase "small child" to describe Tilly Pollard. I've just used it again.'

'So?'

'Well, back at school I gave no indication of the gender of the child, yet you assumed it was a girl. You said, "How did she die?"'

She took a deep breath. 'And you think that was an incriminatory slip of the tongue?'

'Perhaps.'

'Well, *perhaps* Mr Weston mentioned it to me when he came to relieve me of my class. Then again, *perhaps* I simply made the right guess. Who knows?'

'Who indeed, Miss Walsh.'

He made no further response but left, closing the front door quietly behind him.

He had another visit to make before he could finish for the day. One which required a delicate touch.

CHAPTER NINETEEN

Brennan knocked on the front door where Emily Mason lived with her grandmother and waited. He knocked once more, and continued to wait. But no one came to the door. He stepped back and looked at the small terraced house, at the upstairs windows to see if young Emily was gazing down, too distraught to answer the door.

'You might want to go round the back an' stand at the kitchen window,' came a voice from his left. A woman in her mid-thirties was standing in the doorway of the house next door. 'She'll not 'ear you wi' knockin'. Deaf as a doorpost, is old Peggy.'

That must be the grandmother's name, thought Brennan. He thanked her and looked up and down the street for an alleyway to take him round the back. There was no sign of one, and the woman, still standing there with arms folded, understood his predicament.

'It's a long way round right enough,' she said. 'I've never met a fella what wasn't lazy.' Then, with a backward throw of her head, she said, 'Come on then. You can get through 'ere, but don't take all day cos tongues might start waggin', me being widowed an' all – at my age, too.'

'Thank you,' said Brennan, slightly nervous at the twinkle in her eye.

'I'm Mrs Houghton,' she said. 'But Brenda to them as knows me.'

'Thank you, Mrs Houghton.'

She sniffed and stood back to let him in before glancing up and down the street to check they hadn't been observed. 'Is it rent you're after?' she asked as she closed the door.

'Not at all.'

She nodded the direction he should go, through the living room and into the small kitchen at the rear.

'I reckon you could do wi' a strong cup o' tea,' she said, moving in front of him and quickly scooping up small articles of clothing that were hanging over the mantelpiece above a roaring fire.

'No, thank you.'

'Or summat a bit stronger. It's nippy out yonder.'

Brennan could feel the heat, and it wasn't coming from the fire.

'In a bit of a hurry, miss.'

'Mrs as was.'

'Through here, you say?'

He saw the slight lowering of her eyelids as she walked over to the back door and swung it open. Her tone had changed slightly now, as she said, 'Out yonder, through the gate an' right. Her gate's opposite the privies.'

'It's much appreciated,' he said and moved quickly into the back yard.

'Bye then,' she said, and closed the back door with just a little too much force, he thought.

He stepped out into the alley and saw the row of privies the woman had spoken of. A stale and unpleasant odour drifted towards him. He turned quickly to the gate to his right and pushed it open. The small back yard was identical to the one next door. He approached the window and peered through. A small woman, perhaps in her late sixties, was sitting at the kitchen table eating what looked like beef stew. She was facing the window and he tapped quite forcefully on the glass but there was no reaction. She really was stone deaf. It was only on her third mouthful of stew that she deigned to glance up at the window. When she caught sight of Brennan standing there watching, she dropped the spoon and almost fell from her chair in shock.

He held his hand flat against the window pane to show he was no threat to her. He also mouthed a few words in an exaggerated fashion in the hope that she could lip-read.

I want to speak with you. I am a policeman.

He had to repeat that last sentence several times before the truth finally dawned on her and she reluctantly left the table and came to the door. She opened it and let him in.

'What do you want?' she asked uncertainly, returning to her food and sitting down again.

He spoke slowly, and she cupped her right ear so that she was able to hear some of what he was saying. The conversation was at times strained and he had to repeat himself several times, making sure she registered his exaggerated pronouncements.

'I wish to speak with your granddaughter, Emily.'

'What's she done?'

'Nothing. It's to do with school.'

She nodded, as if that explained everything. 'She's not here.'

Brennan looked quickly round, saw the single place at the table opposite her laid for one, could hear – and smell – the rest of the stew simmering in a pot by the small kitchen range.

'Where is she?'

'Had to go out. Something to do with books.'

'Books?'

'Said she needed to get some books before the library closed. She'll be there for a while. Always is. Loses herself in her books, she does.'

He stepped closer so there would be no mistake in her hearing what he said. 'Does her father give her books?'

The woman's eyes narrowed. She turned round and went back to her plate of stew.

'Emily's father is dead.'

He looked at her, saw her pick up the spoon and began to eat once more. If what Nathaniel Edgar had told him was correct, then Emily's father was still very much alive. He wondered if he should ask her about Emily's parentage, but decided that it would take too long to make himself understood. Moreover, her response would very likely be an angry one. *Meddling in family matters that don't concern him.*

'Well thank you. I'm sorry for disturbing you. I'll be going. When she returns, ask her to come to the station. I want to speak with her.'

She watched him as he moved to the door but said nothing.

It was as he closed the front door behind him and stood on the pavement, watching two women across the way standing in their doorways and talking as their children played with an old buckled bicycle wheel in the middle of the street, that something struck him. Something the woman next door had said to him.

Perhaps it was just another coincidence.

* * *

At the station there was no sign of Constable Jaggery, so he went directly to Captain Bell's office but was told he had left for the day.

'But he left this for you, Mick,' said the desk sergeant when he came back.

He handed Brennan an envelope which he tore open and read the contents:

Liverpool Constabulary informed. They have agreed to keep an eye on the boys' home in Seaforth Road. I have arranged permission for you to travel to the Waifs and Strays' Home to speak with the child. I wish to be informed immediately of any developments. God speed.
Alexander Bell.

Brennan looked at his watch. Five-thirty. It was too late to travel over to Seaforth at this time of night – he'd never get back, for one thing, and for another, by the time he arrived at the boys' home on Seaforth Road the place would be shut up for the night and presumably all the boys tucked into their beds. Billy Kelly would be in need of special care, but the authorities at the home would take care of that. No, he would wait until the morning and catch the first available train to Liverpool.

He folded the letter and replaced it in the envelope. 'I'll head off home then,' he said to the desk sergeant.

'Oh aye,' he replied with a knowing wink. Brennan was a creature of habit, and he'd be sitting in his usual seat in the Crofter's in five minutes.

'By the way,' said Brennan, turning at the doorway, 'where's Constable Jaggery?'

The desk sergeant laughed. 'Went through that door not ten minutes ago, cursing like a pitman.'

'Why?'

'Oh they sent word down from the infirmary about a scuffle up yonder. Constable Hardy asked for assistance. And Jaggery had been rubbing his hands about finishing early once you got back.'

But Brennan was alerted by the news. 'What scuffle?'

'No idea, Mick. I just sent him up yonder. He'll sort the buggers out. Drunks, more like as not.'

Without a word more, Brennan was through the doors and marching up King Street in search of a hackney.

When he got there, whatever scuffling had taken place had ended. As he raced up the steps of the infirmary he was met by a dishevelled-looking Constable Hardy who was making a valiant effort to readjust his uniform to something like normality.

'What's been going on, Constable?' Brennan asked.

'Well sir, I was guarding the victim like you asked, stood just outside the ward I was cos that matron wouldn't let me get any closer to him. Then that headmaster turns up and demands to see him. Tries to come it all high an' mighty wi' that matron. She tells him he can't go in till visitin' time an' I chips in an' tells him he can't go in even then. He says why not so I tells him it's me orders an' more than me life's worth. Family only, I says. But there is no family, he says. An' I says that's nowt to do wi' me, pal.'

He stopped to take a breath. His face was still flushed and Brennan could guess what came next.

'So then he tried to barge his way in?'

'Aye. *Tried* anyroad. I grabbed him back an' he swung round an' we ended up rollin' down the ward like two drunks on a Saturday night. All I could hear was screamin' from the nurses an' jeers from the men in the beds. 'Course they was all cheerin' the headmaster on, like. Me wi' me uniform on an' all. I managed to get him down an' told the matron to send word down to the station on account of me not bein' able to leave me post, like you said.'

'Quite right, Constable. You did well.'

'I had to hold the bugger all that time, an' him wrigglin' like a bloodworm.'

'Where is he now?'

'Room down yonder. Sort of store cupboard. Freddie Jaggery's with him.' Constable Hardy laughed. 'Shit hisself when he saw Jaggery come bouncin' down the ward like a circus bear!'

Brennan turned to go, then stopped and said, 'So who's guarding Mr Edgar?'

Hardy's face went scarlet. 'Them nurses, I reckon.'

'You reckon? If you're not back outside that ward in ten seconds you'll be inside it in twenty. In a bed of your own!'

Hardy rushed off down the corridor while Brennan went to the store cupboard. He knocked on the door then opened it. Richard Weston was slumped in a corner, his head in his hands, while Jaggery was examining a box that bore the legend 'Urethra Dilators'. When he saw Brennan, he smiled and nodded towards the disconsolate figure on the floor beside him.

'Feelin' a bit out o' sorts, is Mr Weston.'

Weston slowly raised his head and looked at Brennan. He gave a cough and stood up with some effort. Brennan noticed he had the beginnings of a black eye, and his lip was swollen.

'Now, Mr Weston. What's this all about?'

Before he could answer, the door was pulled wide open and Matron stood there, a dark and forbidding expression on her face.

She glared first at Weston, then Brennan, but settled her basilisk gaze on Constable Jaggery.

'Are you having difficulty passing water?'

Jaggery looked nonplussed.

'Or perhaps the blockage in your urethra is caused by gonorrhoea. Whichever it is I would be more than willing to apply that instrument under local anaesthetic.'

Jaggery looked at Brennan for explanation.

'I think she's asking you to put that box down, Constable. In her own inimitable way, of course.'

Jaggery placed the box back on the shelf as if it contained a deadly viper.

'Good,' said Matron. 'Now I'm sure you would all be much more comfortable away from this infirmary so that I could re-establish some semblance of order and restfulness.' She stood to one side and the three of them trooped out, like recently chastised schoolboys.

Once outside the infirmary, Brennan motioned for Weston to sit on a bench by the entrance to the building. It was with some discomfort that the man sat down. Brennan sat beside him, and then turned to Jaggery.

'I think you've earned that pint, Constable.'

'You mean I've done for the day?' His eyes lit up.

'All the earlier tomorrow.'

'As bright as a budgie, Sergeant.' With that unusual simile ringing in Brennan's ears, Jaggery almost fluttered his way through the infirmary gates.

'Now, Mr Weston, what's this all about?'

The headmaster took a deep breath. 'I came here with the best of intentions, Sergeant Brennan. To visit my colleague. I wished to see him, speak with him, so that I could let my staff know in the morning. They're all very worried about him, you know. Then your constable became very heavy-handed and spoke to me with a lack of respect.' He gingerly touched his swollen lip.

'He was acting on my orders, Mr Weston. If someone has made one attempt on Mr Edgar's life they could well try again.'

'But I'm the man's headmaster, for God's sake!'

Brennan leant towards him and said quietly, 'Mr Edgar told me about Emily Mason.'

It was as if the man had been shot. 'What do you mean?' he asked sharply, swallowing hard to regain his composure.

Brennan sighed. 'You told him once that she was your daughter.'

'Well, it's nonsense.'

'She'll confirm that, will she?'

Weston looked ready to launch into a staunch denial of the relationship, but one look into Brennan's eyes told him how futile that would be. The man had cast-iron certainty in those eyes.

'I don't see how this is of any concern,' he said finally, with an air of resignation.

'It's possibly of no concern at all. But I've been to her home. The one she shares with her grandmother.'

The expression on Weston's face told its own story. A smile of resignation, all hostility now fled from his eyes, to be replaced with something akin to fondness. Finally, he said, 'It's a wonder you made yourself understood with old Peggy.'

Brennan remembered the feeling he'd had after his visit, as he stood outside the old woman's house and recalled what the neighbour, Mrs Houghton, had called her.

Old Peggy.

He had that feeling again. And although he didn't believe in coincidences, perhaps there were times when they just happened. Still, he had to ask.

'Interesting name, *Peggy*.'

Weston looked at him curiously. 'Is it?'

'Women called Margaret are often given Peggy as a sort of fond nickname, aren't they?'

'And what if they are? I don't really see what you are talking about.'

'When she was a little girl, Dorothea Gadsworth was under the care of someone called Julia Reece.'

Weston looked away and gave his attention to a small group of people who were waiting outside the main entrance for the doors to open for visiting hour.

'Dorothea's parents told me that Julia Reece and her mother were forced to leave Hawkshead as a result of the shame Julia's lewd and blasphemous act had brought upon them.'

'A sad story,' said Weston in a low and trembling voice.

Brennan sighed and carried on. 'They told me her mother's name was Margaret. Margaret Reece.'

'Is it such a wonder that Emily's grandmother is named Margaret? Is it an unusual name? An exotic one? Peculiar to the rickshaw-pullers of Yokohama, perhaps?'

He could see the man was rattled, his voice rising as a growing sense of outrage contended with a feeling of entrapment.

'Perhaps if you took a deep breath, Mr Weston, and allowed me to finish?'

The headmaster was about to retort but thought better of it. From the growing queue outside the infirmary entrance, heads were beginning to turn.

'The boy – young man – who was caught with Julia Reece was known only by the name of David.'

Weston said nothing but his head began to droop, and he examined his hands, which were now clenching and unclenching.

'Your name is Richard.'

'How observant.'

'But on the sign outside your school it reads "Richard D. Weston". What does the *D* stand for, Mr Weston?'

In barely a whisper, he replied, 'David.'

Brennan sat back, satisfied.

Richard Weston was the one Dorothea Gadsworth had recognised.

Probably not straight away, but the recognition developed, much like the image on a photographic negative plate, until the moment he entered the staffroom alongside Reverend Pearl and Henry Tollet, the inspector.

It was a long time before Weston answered. Then he began to speak. 'I assure you, Sergeant, that I had no idea who Miss Gadsworth was. The name meant nothing to me. What happened in Hawkshead was a very long time ago.'

'Yet she recognised you.'

'Apparently so.' He paused and seemed to gaze into the middle distance, back to the past itself. 'What we did that day in the church at Hawkshead, and the thing that happened because of it . . . caused both of our lives to change for ever. Julia's mother – a widow – was forced to leave the village because of the scandal, and I went back to Windermere.'

'You lied to me.'

'How so?'

'When I asked you where you were in the summer of 1880 you told me Cambridge.'

'If you recall, I answered by telling you about my father and his solicitor's practice in Cambridge.'

Brennan thought back to the interview. *Clever*, he thought. *Very clever*.

'I was actually spending that summer on my uncle's farm. I had plenty of time on my hands back then. I was quite wild. Carefree and wild. A combination not uncommon, but when it meets someone equally wild, equally carefree . . .'

He paused for a while as the past drifted before his eyes.

'It doesn't matter now, of course, but it was her idea. The belfry. She even suggested tugging on a bellrope once we'd finished as a sort of demonic sign of what we'd done. Only we never got the chance. We were both castigated, although it was easier for me. I could catch the ferry back to Windermere and leave my uncle's farm early. Return to Cambridge unsullied, as it were, by the scandal of what we'd done. The tragedy of what we'd done.'

He looked up, and Brennan saw now there were tears in the man's eyes. Humiliation? Regret? Fear of being exposed?

'But the shame of what I had done was compounded when, a few months later, I received a letter from Julia, informing me that she was with child. Our child. They had moved in with a distant relation in Manchester. I suppose in a way that news changed me more than anything else. Made me realise what dangerous creatures we really are. We had created a life at the same time as destroying one. But she also told me she was engaged to be married to a man named Sidney Mason, who had accepted a sum of money from Julia's relation so that the child would be born in wedlock.'

'What did you do then?'

'I decided to go to Manchester, to speak with Julia and offer my hand in marriage. But it was too late. By that time her condition was common knowledge and Mason acknowledged locally as the father. That brought her shame enough, but can you imagine what damage would have been done if another man suddenly arrived claiming *he* and not Mason were the father? No. They had done with shame, done with fleeing its consequences. So the wedding was rushed through and Julia Reece became Julia Mason. And Emily was born.'

'He was a bad father?'

Weston nodded. 'The very worst kind. Violence. Women. Gambling. And all the while my beautiful daughter was witness to every kind of wickedness. I knew little of this at the time. All I could do was continue with my own life, training to become a teacher. When I qualified I moved to the north, to Wigan. Not that I could ever see either of them, just to know that I was close by if they needed me. Then, one night, the swine came home blind drunk, so drunk, in fact, that he fell down the stairs, but not before giving poor Julia the beating of her life.'

Brennan could picture the scene, the horror of the violence that poor little Emily had grown so accustomed to in her short life.

'By that time I was working at George Street – I started at the same time as Nathaniel Edgar – and once I'd heard what had happened I went over to Manchester and persuaded both Julia and her mother to move over to Wigan, to make a fresh start – another one – and send the child to the school I was working in. I would be sure to keep a very close eye on her and make sure she had the best of teaching. When I became headmaster and Emily was of an age, I encouraged her to become a monitor and work towards pupil-teacher status.'

'Did Emily know you were her father? Her real one?'

Weston shook his head. 'Not at first, no. But then, in what might be seen as another dreadful blow of retribution, Julia became ill.'

Again he paused, and Brennan could see how painful this was for the man.

'She became ill because of that swine.'

'Mason?'

'His – shall we say? – fondness for female company. He passed on to Julia what he had contracted himself. Syphilis. "The consequence of impure connexion". Ironic, isn't it, that he failed to kill her while he lived and succeeded once he'd died. He murdered her from the grave. Her end was slow and painful and utterly humiliating. I was with her when she died, when she begged me to care for her darling child – *our* darling child. It was then, with almost her last words, she told Emily the truth.'

There was silence between them, as both men seemed to realise the enormity of what Weston had just admitted.

'You know what this means?' said Brennan.

Weston stood up and his shoulders drooped. 'Miss Gadsworth recognised me. I had no idea who she was. Fifteen years is a long time to recall a small girl who tagged along with Julia. But then when she fainted and was cared for by Henry Tollet, I overheard her mention my name, and what I'd done in Hawkshead. I simply couldn't allow her to spread that information any further.'

'So you had to silence both of them?'

'There was no other way.'

'How did you lure her back to school?'

Weston gave a sad smile. 'I think I've told you enough, Sergeant. One mustn't make things too easy for you.'

'And Nathaniel Edgar? Did he know of Hawkshead and Esthwaite Water?'

At first, Weston looked nonplussed. Then he said, 'What Miss

Gadsworth and the school inspector knew would have destroyed my reputation. If Nathaniel told Reverend Pearl about Emily being my daughter, as he threatened to do on more than one occasion . . . why, the result would have been the same. Scandal. Humiliation. So he too had to die.'

'But he isn't going to die,' said Brennan. He allowed the silence between them to stretch before adding, 'In that case we had better find you a comfortable cell for the night.' He led Weston over to where a hackney carriage was waiting.

As they stepped aboard, Weston said, 'Do you still have those addresses? For my staff?'

'I do indeed.'

'Then would it be possible to get a message to Miss Ryan? She's my deputy and she will be taking over in my absence. I should just like her to be given forewarning of my detention so she can be prepared.'

'I'll see to it, Mr Weston.'

As they made their way down Wigan Lane back towards town, Weston leant his head back against the rest and closed his eyes. It was clear that the pressures of the last week or so had brought him immense distress. Brennan gazed out at the passing scene: people taking an early evening stroll along the lane, a customary practice that transcended the classes. These were people who laughed and chatted and shared frivolous tales of the day they'd had, unaware of the agony that was passing them in a hackney carriage.

'Just one thing more, Mr Weston.'

The headmaster opened his eyes wearily, as if disturbed from a troublesome slumber. 'Yes?'

'The boy. Kelly. Exactly what did you hope to gain?'

Weston gave a nervous gulp. 'What do you mean?'

'Well, you couldn't have kept him incarcerated for ever, now, could you?'

Weston was about to say something but thought better of it. He set his lips firmly shut and uttered not one word until they reached King Street. Even then he offered only a subdued 'Thank you' as he was escorted into the building by Sergeant Brennan, who asked the cabbie to wait for him.

Once the man was charged and led down to the cells for the night – he had no intention of conducting any sort of formal interview at this time of night – Brennan didn't repair to his office but asked Sergeant Prescott to advise Miss Ryan of the situation and then left the station in some haste.

It was usual, at around this time of night, for him to pay the Crofter's a short visit before heading home, but he would forego that pleasure for tonight.

He did not believe in coincidences, and this case had been riddled with them. But the one he refused to believe above all others was the coincidence swirling around *motive* like a pestilential fog.

According to Weston, he had been prompted by not one but *two* motives to kill.

Dorothea Gadsworth and Henry Tollet had to die because they could destroy the reputation he had painstakingly built up over the years – that of highly respected disciplinarian, headmaster and pillar of the community – in his eyes, at least.

Then along comes quite a different motive: Nathaniel Edgar threatening to expose his illegitimate link with his pupil-teacher. So he too had to die.

Two motives? Quite a coincidence was that. What an unlucky chap he was.

But it didn't fit. And when he had asked him how he'd lured

Miss Gadsworth back to the school the night she was poisoned he refused to answer.

Why? Because he couldn't. He had no idea.

And when he'd mentioned Billy Kelly in the carriage he'd reacted strangely. As though he hadn't a clue what Brennan was talking about.

No. If you get rid of the idea of *two* motives and leave yourself with *one* only – namely the exposure and subsequent disgrace of Richard David Weston – then you were left with one clear suspect.

But he still needed Billy Kelly to confirm whom he saw that night with Dorothea Gadsworth. The one who kept him prisoner to prevent him from revealing what he'd seen the night he tried to burn the school down. The boy's testimony would be a powerful weapon in the hands of the prosecution.

He climbed back into the cab and gave the driver the address he'd been to once already that day. As they pulled away from the station, a brief image flickered across his mind like a magic lantern slide: a beautiful butterfly in a glass case, fluttering its wings in a panic as he reached inside to grab it.

When he reached the house he'd visited earlier that day, he was surprised to see the neighbour, Mrs Houghton, standing on her doorstep with a small cluster of women. In the midst of them, Emily Mason's grandmother was sobbing, several of them offering words of comfort.

'What's happened?' Brennan asked as he leapt from the cab.

It was Mrs Houghton who stepped forward. 'It's the young lass, Emily. She's gone missin'.'

'What?'

'Peggy yonder says she went to t'library for some books

an' she's not come back. An' what with all that bother at that school where she works, well. It makes you wonder, don't it?' She moved very close to him, placed an advisory hand on his arm and gripped it a little too tightly. Then she leant into his ear and whispered, 'Happen she's been done away with, eh? Just like them others. Somebody as 'as a grudge against teachers. Canal's up yonder an' all.'

He asked her to take the woman back inside, assuring her that he would do all he could to find the girl. But even as she closed the door and he heard the neighbour speak words of comfort to a sobbing grandmother, he felt a heaviness weigh him down. Emily Mason was missing. He had a good idea where she could be found, and it didn't involve the Leeds–Liverpool Canal.

First thing in the morning, he would catch the train to take him to Seaforth, and the Waifs and Strays Home on Seaforth Road, where Billy Kelly was lying in a sick bed.

He hoped to God he wasn't too late.

CHAPTER TWENTY

There was a thick fog shrouding the platform at Wigan Wallgate railway station. Brennan stood waiting for the seven-thirty Lancashire and Yorkshire train that would take him on the first leg of his journey to Seaforth, to Southport. From there he would catch the 10:10 L&YR train to Seaforth, following the contours of the coastline until he reached his destination.

'Will you see the sea?' Barry had asked, his eyes sparkling with the possibility of an invitation to join his dad.

'I should think so,' he'd said, rubbing his son's hair, a practice the little lad hated.

'And will you see the tower?'

Brennan had laughed. 'No, lad. The tower's in Blackpool.'

'But it's near the sea!'

'I know, but the sea's a big place. I'm going first to Southport then to Liverpool.'

'I bet if you look hard you'll see it. The tower. An' they might

315

'ave built a tower at Southport by now. And at Liverpool.'

'I'll tell you if they have. How's that?'

Barry had beamed a huge smile that had kept Brennan warm since he walked from his house to the station through the fog. Now, as he stood on the platform peering into the grey gloom to his left for any sign of a lamp heralding the train's approach, he felt a growing despondency wrap itself around him like the fog itself.

There were several what ifs.

What if the boy Kelly had given up the fight for life and was even now lying on a slab in the mortuary?

What if the Seaforth police had failed in their duty to watch over him?

What if Emily Mason had made it all the way to Merseyside to silence him before he had the chance to speak with the child?

And what if, after all his efforts, Billy Kelly refused to tell him the name of the one who'd kept him hidden away for days out of some misguided sense of loyalty?

Suddenly, a yellow light penetrated the swirling heaviness around him, and he stepped back as the seven-thirty chugged and steamed its way into the station, doors swinging open and passengers disgorging themselves from its innards like minnows from the leviathan.

When he clambered aboard, Brennan was disappointed to find the carriage was already occupied by a well-dressed man who gave him a flinty smile of acknowledgement, as if he too resented the intrusion to his privacy. That was fair enough, thought Brennan. He didn't feel like making any kind of polite and meaningless conversation anyway, preferring to gaze through the grey mass of nothingness outside and let his thoughts meander over the intricacies of the case.

A blasphemous and immoral act in the church belfry at St Michael and All Angels had set in motion a wave of consequences that even now was still in frantic sway, like a violent sea-storm.

Dorothea Gadsworth had fainted when Weston, Henry Tollet and Reverend Pearl entered the staffroom. She had said, 'Of course, Esthwaite', a reference to Esthwaite Water, where the young girl Tilly Pollard had died. But it had been the phrase, 'Of course', which meant, he now realised, that she had finally confirmed who Richard Weston was – or who he had been. It must have been playing on her mind since she met him that morning. It cost not only her life but the life of the school inspector, Henry Tollet.

Emily Mason must have overheard Miss Gadsworth tell the school inspector what she knew.

And that meant her father – her real father, who had rescued her from ignominy – was in grave danger of losing everything he had built up.

So both of them had to die before Tollet could bring his information to the proper authorities.

He saw odd shapes through the still-heavy fog, trees on a nearby embankment, stretching branches now growing devoid of leaves, resembling skeletal figures pleading with the heavens for some kind of mercy. As they rattled and swayed past a colliery, he could just make out the pithead winding gear, the wheels seemingly disembodied and still, no sign of life anywhere in the grey mass that eddied around it.

The world of nature. The world of man.

Had Emily's life been damaged beyond measure? Scarred by what she had seen whenever Sidney Mason rolled in drunk, and violent, and without mercy?

317

Brennan shook such thoughts from his head.

When they got to Gathurst Station, another man climbed into the carriage, carrying a strangely elongated travel bag. He wore a check suit, a bowler hat, and beamed at the two occupants. The other man merely nodded and held up a newspaper which he had been reading since they left Wigan, which meant that the new arrival would direct his bonhomie at Brennan.

His opening gambit told Brennan at once what the man's profession was.

'You look a man of taste, sir.'

Brennan smiled but then returned his gaze to the window, where the fog seemed to be finally clearing. He needed to continue his reflections on the case.

But the newcomer had different ideas. He immediately lifted his bag onto the vacant seat beside him and opened it with a flourish. 'Here, sir, are the finest walking sticks you will ever set your eyes on. I can see that you're a discerning sort of chap. You look like a silver knob to me!'

Brennan's eyes widened as the man slid out from a slender sheath an elegant walking stick topped with a silver globe. When he saw Brennan's unenthusiastic reaction, he quickly replaced it and took out another of his exhibits.

'You're quite right. This is more you, my friend.'

He held a cane in his hands as if it were the crown jewels. At its summit was an eagle's head, carved elegantly in brass, and the highly polished wood of the cane gleamed even in the dull light of the carriage lamps. 'Thirty-five inches of elegance, sir. With the eagle's head in your hands, what power, what grace, as you stroll down Lord Street on a Sunday afternoon.'

'Why would I be strolling down Lord Street, Sunday or any

other time?' said Brennan growing bored with the man's excess of enthusiasm.

'Southport, my dear sir. Southport!'

'But I live in Wigan, friend. Not much call for silver knobs in Wigan.'

The man looked crestfallen. But not beaten.

He took another sample from his bag. 'Now this is truly unique. The only one of its kind in the world. Or at least, Lancashire!'

He held it out for Brennan to examine. It had at its summit a white billiard ball, the cane embedded in its base.

'Hmm,' Brennan said at last, 'it might prove useful at that. How many skulls would I crack with one swing, do you reckon?'

'Skulls?' said the salesman, his voice weakening as it dawned on him that he might be offering a violent weapon to a madman.

'Only in the case of a refusal to be arrested, of course.'

The man hurriedly replaced the canes and fastened his bag. As they approached Newburgh Station, he saw the newspaper-reader offer him a conspiratorial smirk.

For the rest of the journey, Brennan was left mainly in peace. Stops at Bescar Lane, Blowick and St Luke's Road ensured that the carriage was filled to its capacity, and that, ironically enough, rendered conversation difficult. *People are reluctant to converse*, Brennan mused, *when their comments have a large audience.*

At Southport, he was cheered to see the fog had lifted completely, and the morning was one of glorious sunshine. There was a smell of sea in the air too, which he inhaled deeply, a salty contrast to the heavier, dustier atmosphere of his home town. He had a little time to spare before catching the 10:10 to Seaforth, so he took the opportunity to take a stroll along the magnificent boulevard of Lord Street, minus the perambulatory advantage of a walking stick, with its wonderful array of shops that had so enraptured – and frustrated – Ellen the last time they came, bringing Barry with them for the first time.

It was strange, he reflected after gazing idly at a number of shop displays, how the street was already crowded with people rushing to work – shop hands and clerks and office workers – or those better dressed members of the leisured class simply beginning the day with a stroll around the shops and perhaps around the marina later.

He felt lonely without Ellen and Barry – Ellen marvelling at the latest unattainable fashions, and Barry moaning that he couldn't see a tower anywhere. It made him realise, not for the first time, how important his family was to him, and that thought led inevitably to the circumstances of the case that was so pressing on his mind. How many lives had been affected by that monstrous act of neglect by Julia Reece, lustfully supported by Richard David Weston?

How many families blighted?

Perhaps he was wrong to think Emily Mason was headed for Seaforth. What would she gain now by silencing the boy?

But her crimes had shown what a dark and troubled mind she had. She might be thinking even now that she could still be free if only the boy were silenced. Yet when she had had the chance to kill him, she hadn't.

As he returned to the station, his mood was rather sombre now. He looked up at the skies, but all he could see was a clear fresh blue, no cloud to share his feelings.

The journey from Southport to Seaforth was uneventful. At Formby, the carriage emptied and Brennan had the place to himself for the rest of the time. He looked at his watch several times and grew impatient for his business to conclude. He needed the boy's testimony to help build the case against Emily. He needed him to regain his strength so that he could give evidence to that effect in court.

He needed him alive.

As he stepped into the bright sunshine once more at Seaforth Station, he hailed a hackney cab and gave his instructions.

They moved sedately along the vast stretch of Seaforth Road until, in the distance, he saw a commotion ahead, with people running across the road from what appeared to be a long driveway to his right. It swept in a curve towards a building set back amid a cluster of trees.

'Somethin' goin' on down there!' the cabbie called out.

Indeed there was. Standing across the road from the entrance, a huddle of young boys seemed nonplussed by what was taking place, several masters holding out their arms and shepherding them away from the immediate vicinity. A uniformed constable was emerging from the driveway carrying a small boy still in his nightgown, and a woman, wearing the garb of a nurse, was by his side and speaking gently to the child. A huddle of onlookers stood there, arms folded and watching the proceedings with a prurient interest. But what captured Brennan's interest far more than any of this were the fire hose wagon with 'Waterloo and Seaforth Fire Brigade' emblazoned across the base of the wagon, its horses standing patiently in the driveway, and the thick plumes of smoke that were emanating from Elm Lodge Home for Boys.

CHAPTER TWENTY-ONE

As soon as he alighted from the cab, Brennan went over to the policeman who had passed the child he was carrying to one of the masters. He introduced himself before asking with some abruptness, 'What's gone on, Constable?'

'I was told to keep an eye on the place. So I've been callin' in every so often, like. This mornin' I hears screamin'. Somebody shouted there was a fire near the front door an' when I get there the bloody place is full o' thick black smoke. The superintendent, Mr Laidlaw – that's the bloke over yonder talkin' to the fireman – orders everyone outside an' across the road. I got told there's a young child on the top floor so I ran up there an' there he is, shiverin' his socks off!' He pointed to the child in the nightgown with some pride.

Black hair.

'Where's the boy Kelly?'

The policeman – whose name was Clarke – shifted his stance

and looked back towards the building. 'There was a lot o' panic, Sergeant Brennan.'

'So I gather. But I'll ask again. Where's Billy Kelly?'

At last, the constable shrugged his ignorance. 'I was told to watch the place, nothin' else.'

Brennan left him and walked quickly over to the man identified as the superintendent of the home, Mr Laidlaw, interrupting his conversation with the fireman. He told him who he was and asked the same question.

'I'm sorry, Sergeant,' said Laidlaw, 'but we have no boy of that name at Elm House.'

For a moment, Brennan was taken aback, then realised that Jane Rodley might well have had him admitted under another name.

'Ginger-haired lad,' he explained.

The superintendent took a quick look round the group of boys, many of whom were coughing from the smoke they'd inhaled then pointed at one boy standing on the edge of the group. 'He's the only one with ginger hair.'

Brennan looked over at the boy, a thick-set youth of about thirteen.

It wasn't Billy Kelly.

'The boy was brought in yesterday,' Brennan said, a note of urgency and growing panic now in his voice.

Mr Laidlaw shook his head. 'I'm sorry. No boy was brought in yesterday.'

'You sure?'

'I'm the superintendent. My signature must be on the admissions form.'

'But he was brought here by Miss Jane Rodley. From Wigan.'

Mr Laidlaw held his hands out in a gesture of ignorance. 'I'm sorry.'

Before Brennan could say anything else, another fireman approached them and addressed his colleague.

'There was a sort of makeshift incendiary device, sir – looks like some clumps of straw and old matting.'

The superintendent said, 'There's straw and matting stored in the boys' playing shed. We keep toys and things for the lads there.'

The second fireman wiped his eyes. 'Looks like somebody slept in that shed last night. Old sacking on the floor, straw piled up like a makeshift pillow. Must've gathered the stuff and stuffed it through the letter box this morning, lit it and then ran off. There's street rats round here who'd do such a thing.'

The superintendent nodded. 'They poke fun at the lads that live here. It's very upsetting. So there's no fire?'

'A smouldering pile dragged outside by my men. It's quite harmless now, as long as you don't go near and breathe the fumes in.'

Brennan turned once more to Laidlaw and clutched at one last straw. 'Is it possible that somehow a boy could have been brought here without your knowledge?'

'No, Sergeant. It isn't.'

Brennan sighed heavily and thanked the superintendent. As he moved away, he caught sight of the nurse stooping low to attend to the small boy the constable had carried out. He went over, introduced himself and asked her the same questions he'd just put to Mr Laidlaw.

She glanced up, took in the concerned expression on his face and said, 'I can assure you, Sergeant Brennan, that we have had no such boy admitted.'

'But he was ill. Perhaps . . .'

'Then he would have been attended to by me in the first instance. And I can assure you I attended to no sickly child yesterday.'

Jane Rodley had lied to him.

He thought about her, the cool way she had given him the information, the utterly believable tale of salvation, even down to the address and purpose of an establishment designed to provide practical help to boys such as Billy Kelly.

Why had she lied?

Had he been completely and hopelessly wrong about Emily Mason?

Was she indeed at the bottom of the canal back in Wigan, or some similarly dark, deadly place?

Was Billy Kelly down there with her?

The nurse's words broke into his line of thought. 'And I hope now that *that* is the end of the matter.'

'I beg your pardon?' He took a step back, surprised at the strength of feeling in her response.

'I told the one who came last night and I'm telling you the same thing.'

'You told who last night?'

'The one who marched up to the front door and demanded to see this fictitious child.'

'Who was it?'

'She told me she was his sister and that it was her right – her absolute right – to see her brother. I told her that she had no rights whatsoever at Elm House whether her brother was in residence or a mere phantom. She accused me of lying, became most agitated and so I had her marched from the premises. If you're looking for someone who caused that smoke then you've no need to look any further.'

Brennan suppressed a violent curse. 'Can you describe this *sister*?'

'I certainly can.'

And she did.

To Billy Kelly, the world was filled with new sensations: he had never seen the sea, and he was almost struck dumb by the sheer size of it, how it stretched away into the distance as far as he could see. What amazed him, too, was the way the sea, at its furthest point, was a straight line, unmoving and perfect, far straighter than anything he'd ever managed with a ruler in his copybook. And yet, despite how still it looked out yonder, the closer the sea got the more it was in motion.

And the waves! He went dizzy watching wave after wave, each one topped with white foam that splashed and melted into itself the closer it got to the sandy beach.

Then there were the smells! How fresh, how salty was the breeze cooling his face and turning his late fever into a fading memory. The salty air was flavoured with something familiar and for a few moments he tried to work out what the smell was. He didn't want to ask the one who brought him here, not until he'd worked it out for himself . . .

Of course!

'Vinegar!' he shouted out, and the people who were strolling past the two of them seated on the wooden bench facing the Irish Sea stared at him, some of them giggling. But he didn't care. He didn't *care*.

'And what about vinegar?' she asked.

'I can smell it!' Billy replied, looking round for the source of the aroma.

'Look,' she said, turning round and pointing to a wheeled

stall on the promenade behind them. 'Cockles. Mussels.'

'I've never 'ad 'em.'

'Well we'll get you a big bag full of cockles later. First we'll go up *there*.'

He turned to follow where she was pointing. He'd already told her that he was scared and didn't really want to go so high.

'But you'll see the whole world from up there,' she said, smiling to reassure him.

A tram rattled past the promenade, filled with sightseers. Across the wide road, he saw the sign that read 'Aviary and Aquarium'.

'What does that say?'

She told him.

'What's it mean?'

'An aviary is where they keep birds and an aquarium is where they keep fish.'

'Can't we just go in yonder instead?'

'Billy. You know this will be the last time you'll ever come here, don't you? I explained that to you, didn't I?'

'Yes, miss.'

'So we're going to the top of Blackpool Tower and you'll experience something you'll remember for the rest of your life.'

'What if it falls down? While we're up there? It's windy, ain't it?'

She gave him a reassuring smile. 'You mean "Isn't it"?'

He gave an obedient nod and smiled weakly.

She stood up and held out her hand. 'Come along. You'll be perfectly safe, Billy. You're with me, remember?'

He was filled with a desperate sense of urgency now. The nurse's description of the so-called sister of Billy Kelly only served to confirm what Brennan already knew – that the one responsible for the murders of Dorothea Gadsworth and Henry Tollet – and the attempted murder of Nathaniel Edgar – was Emily Mason. She had tried to pass herself off as Billy Kelly's sister, and when that didn't work she must have slept in the shed and started the smoke this morning that brought about the wholesale evacuation of Elm Lodge. He explained as quickly as he could to Constable Clarke what the situation was.

'She started that smoke earlier, which means she might still be in the area. We need to find her, Constable.'

The constable turned and went to every staff member in turn, describing Emily and asking each of them if they had seen her. They all shook their heads. Brennan looked up and down Seaforth Road. She could only have been gone a matter of thirty minutes or so, for that was when the smoke was detected and the fire brigade sent for. The building, the shed and the gardens had already been searched by the members of staff for any child lurking there, and found no one.

Where would she go?

Constable Clarke had by this time crossed the road and was speaking to the passers-by whom Brennan had noticed as he arrived. Brennan crossed over and got there just in time to hear one woman say, 'Only a matter of time before something like this happened.'

'Like what?' the constable asked.

'Bringing that sort of child here. They'd have burnt the place down sooner or later. Now it's sooner, isn't it? The place has only been in use a year and look what happens. It's fate, that's what it is.'

Brennan coughed. The woman looked him up and down and sniffed.

Before she could add further to her tirade, another of the

group, a tall, bespectacled man clutching a book under one arm, said, 'A young girl, you say?'

The constable nodded.

'It just so happens I did see someone like that. I thought it was strange that she was in some sort of distress. She was crying, you see, and I offered to help her. I thought it was something like a lost dog.'

'Should have had him on a lead,' the woman said with another sniff.

'Where was she?' Brennan asked.

'Let me see,' said the man, gazing down Seaforth Road. 'Ah yes. I was walking along Church Road. I'd just been to the book shop on Rawson Road, you see?' He held up the book he was holding as evidence of his veracity. 'Well, I turned left into Church Road and was making my way along when I saw her.'

'Heading which way?' asked the constable.

'Why, in the opposite direction, Constable. Towards the Shore Road and the estuary.'

'Thank you, sir.'

Brennan was glad to see the constable was now infused with the same sense of urgency. 'We'd best get a move on, Sergeant Brennan. If she's headed towards the river . . .'

The sentence remained unfinished. There was no need to complete it.

They left the group of passers-by looking open-mouthed at the uniformed constable and the plain-clothes detective running down Seaforth Road and turning right into Church Road.

'You don't think she'd do herself in, Sergeant?' Clarke yelled as they rushed along, bringing curious glances from the ones they passed.

'I've no idea!' Brennan shouted back.

'Bloody lunatic!'

They came to a wide road – Brennan read a sign that said Crosby Road – and Constable Clarke pointed to a road opposite.

'Shore Road!' he yelled above the clang and rattle of a tram shuttling its way past them.

As they rushed along Shore Road, Brennan kept his eyes open for any sign that Emily might have scurried through an alleyway or small entry, but he soon came to realise that this wasn't Wigan, where alleyways were as frequent and as twisted as veins on an old crone's hand. The road was well-kept, with few buildings set back from the pavement and a sign that pointed to Seafield Convent to his right.

When they reached the end of the road, Brennan saw that they were close to a wall that overlooked a sloped stretch of sand leading all the way to the coastline and the water beyond. He leant over the wall, glanced to his left and right where the grassy stretch could be seen for quite a distance. Then he scanned the horizon and pointed to the land across the water.

'Where's that?' he asked.

Constable Clarke said, 'New Brighton.'

The wall ran alongside a narrow walkway. 'You go right,' said Brennan. 'I'll go left.'

'What if she's not here?'

Brennan, who had already started off, stopped and said simply, 'Then we look somewhere else.'

They both went their separate ways, Constable Clarke taking out his whistle and blowing hard to attract the attention of other policemen. Brennan rushed down the path, his heart pounding now and cursing out loud. He prayed to God he wasn't too late, but the sight of the water stretching to his right filled him with a deep sense of foreboding. Although he searched the road and the coastline that lay in front of him with all the watchfulness and concentration of a bird of prey, he could see no sign of Emily Mason. Further ahead, he could see people strolling along the sand, enjoying the early afternoon sun, chatting inconsequentially and occasionally letting out a hoot of laughter.

In the far distance he saw the steel pillars of the overhead railway that seemed to follow the path of the coast all the way back to the city of Liverpool itself, a train approaching the broad curve that ran to his left and inwards. For a fleeting moment he harboured a wild image of Emily standing on a platform ready to leap in front of the train.

Then, suddenly, he heard a shrill whistling from behind, followed by a yell that was drowned out by the rattle of the oncoming train. He whirled round, moved to the wall and peered to the right. He could see nothing at first, as the coastline curved slightly and blocked his view, so he ran back in the direction he had come.

And suddenly, he saw Constable Clarke rushing along the sand, his progress hampered by the dampness underfoot.

Brennan followed the direction the policeman was heading: far out, almost at the point where the sand met the water, he saw her.

Emily Mason was walking slowly, her arms almost stretched forward to greet the oncoming waves. The hem of her skirt lifted as the water swept towards her, welcoming her.

Constable Clarke was still a good hundred yards away.

Brennan climbed over the wall and ran as fast as he could towards the girl, but he knew that he could only watch as Clarke made his way towards her.

He only prayed that the man would reach her in time.

Then he saw Emily lunge forward, tumbling into the water with a splash and almost forcing her head below the surface of the waves which now greedily swept around her. As he got closer, he saw the froth gushing around her head like the drool of a madman.

Constable Clarke had now reached the water. He held his arms up high to avoid the waves that swirled all round him, fighting against the flow of the Mersey to reach a figure that was now floundering a matter of yards away, the small head seeming to give up the ghost and sink below the waves with a final bow of resignation.

CHAPTER TWENTY-TWO

After paying for a fortifying lunch in gratitude for what Constable Clarke had done, Brennan sent a telegram to Captain Bell requesting the release of Richard Weston. He then made his way to Seaforth Bridewell, where it had been decided by Clarke's superiors that Emily Mason would be released into Brennan's custody after enjoying the dubious comforts of a few hours drying off in the cells below street level, where she was able to ponder the folly of trying to commit suicide – a crime for which she would have been charged if it hadn't been for Brennan's persuasive argument that she faced far more serious charges back in Wigan.

After signing the formal papers of release, he declined the offer of handcuffs.

'What if she decides to make a dash for it again?' said the Bridewell sergeant with a scowl in the prisoner's direction.

'Somehow I don't think that's going to happen,' Brennan replied. He looked at her, head bowed low and simpering, clothed in a plain calico dress and scuffed shoes that clearly weren't her own.

When Constable Clarke had rushed into the water to save her, he had fought with commendable courage and tenacity against a rising current, diving and surfacing, diving and surfacing, several times before finally finding the girl and heaving her to the surface and dragging her, arms flailing in violent protest, back to the shore where Brennan was standing, hands on hips and trying to regain his breath.

'Come along, Emily,' he now said gently. 'We'll take you back to Wigan, eh? It's a bit of a journey so we can talk on the way. Wouldn't that be best?'

Two other people were heading for a railway station at that moment. Not the same one, of course. Jane Rodley and Billy Kelly had spent the night at the home of a friend of Jane's who lived in Poulton-le-Fylde, a few miles from Blackpool.

Billy had slept better the previous night than he had done for many months. He had experienced the thrill of his young life as he and Miss Rodley had stood at the very top of Blackpool Tower. How small the people looked! And the trams!

'Like worms, miss, them trams!' he'd yelled above the strength of the wind.

Later, she paid the 6d entrance fee for Dr Cocker's Aquarium and Menagerie, and she had felt such a lifting of her spirits watching Billy's reaction as they passed cages where lions, tigers and panthers prowled with their fierce scowls and occasional deep-throated roars. It was only when he said, 'Bet they'd scatter if me dad were 'ere!' that her spirits flagged. It would take the boy quite a while to leave everything behind, including his spaniel-like trust in such a brute.

Now, as they walked up the steps to Poulton Station, Jane spied the man standing just beyond the gates. She gave him a wave and placed a hand on Billy's head.

This is the boy, the gesture said. *The one you'll soon be taking to Liverpool Docks and the first stage of his new life.*

The two of them passed through onto the platform. She saw the boy shrink back when she introduced him to the man.

'Don't worry, Billy. This is Mr Laidlaw from the society. He's going to take you on a long and exciting journey, just as I told you. You'll be safe with him, and you'll have a life beyond your wildest dreams. Canada is the most beautiful country in the entire world.'

Mr Laidlaw gave her a nod.

'You met Detective Sergeant Brennan?' she asked.

'I did indeed. And you were right. He struck me as a tenacious character. He would have taken this child back with him.'

'All the same, I'm sorry I lied to him. About Billy's whereabouts. And his state of health.'

'For a greater purpose, Jane,' came the reply.

She was silent for a while as Billy wandered along the platform, keeping an eye out for the promised train. Then she said in a low voice, 'He finally told me last night as we tucked him into bed. That it was Emily Mason, our pupil-teacher, who kept him safe.'

'Why would she do that?'

Jane shrugged. 'He just said she kept him safe from the police. A strange girl.' She gave a long sigh. 'She too had a troubled childhood. Perhaps if I'd been there when she was suffering . . .'

Laidlaw patted her shoulder and smiled. 'You can't save them all, Jane. Don't be greedy!'

'I suppose Sergeant Brennan will wish to speak with me when I return.'

'If you need my support . . .'

She smiled in gratitude. 'You've done more than enough already. Besides, Charles will be there.'

He shrugged and touched the brim of his hat. 'In that case . . .'

'Thank you,' she said as the boy was led away to the waiting room.

When it was clear she wasn't coming with him, Billy turned and ran back to her, throwing his arms around her waist and clinging to her so tightly she found it difficult to breathe. He muttered something she couldn't quite hear, so she managed to push him from her.

'What did you say, Billy?'

The boy sobbed and said, 'I want me dad.'

Emily Mason remained doggedly silent as they took the train from Seaforth to Southport, gazing through the carriage window with her head resting against the glass. The other passengers gave her – and Brennan – curious glances, but when he faced them and held their looks with a challenging expression on his face, they soon turned back to their newspapers or their thoughts. At one stage, as they were passing through Ainsdale, she raised her head and gazed out at the expanse of sandy beach with the glimmer of water reflecting a dying sun in the distance, a reminder, perhaps, of the fate she had planned for herself. Or was it the view of a horizon of escape, a vision of a future denied her?

It was the same on the platform at Southport, head bowed, sullen and silent. They sat on a bench and waited for the L&YR train back to Wigan. It was only when they boarded the train and found an empty carriage that Emily began to speak.

'What'll happen now?' she asked.

Even though she had murdered two innocent people and tried to kill another, he still felt a pang of pity for this girl. For that was what she was. A girl.

'You'll stand trial for the murders of Dorothea Gadsworth and Henry Tollet.'

'And then?'

'If you're found guilty, you could well hang.'

There was a pause as the awful truth of that sentence – in both senses of the word – struck home.

'Do you want to tell me why you did it, Emily?'

She shook her head.

'Then let me do it for you.'

He watched as she once more rested her head against the window.

'Your father is Richard Weston.'

She closed her eyes.

'And your mother was Julia Reece.'

A sigh. Nothing more.

'You know what happened between them? In Hawkshead?'

She said in a low voice, 'They fell in love.'

'Yes, I suppose they did. But they were forced to leave, weren't they?'

'Yes.'

'Because they did a wicked thing.'

She gave a rare smile then. 'You mean they *produced* a wicked thing? She didn't know then she was expecting. When she did, Grandmother told her in no uncertain terms that she'd made her bed and should now lie in it. Before she once again brought shame on the family. I was that shame, you see?'

'She married Sidney Mason.'

For the first time since he'd brought her from Seaforth she showed real anger, her eyes flashing a venomous look at the mention of the name.

'That pig! He beat my mother, he beat my grandmother. You don't think she was born deaf, do you? He was a monster. More than you can imagine.'

A cold shiver ran through him.

Then she said quietly, 'It wasn't only my mother he did things to.'

Brennan went cold. He recalled what Weston had told him – that Sidney Mason had infected Julia with syphilis. She had died relatively quickly, but he had heard of cases where that vile contagion festered, sometimes for years and years, before rendering the innocent victim insane. If Emily had been infected too . . .

Suddenly, he said, 'He was your *first* victim, wasn't he?'

The expression on her face showed relief more than fear. This policeman *knew*.

'He came home drunk one night – nothing new there – but he began on me, fumbling, pawing, as he always did. But my mother caught him this time, and he hit her so hard I could feel the draught as he struck her and struck her, and she was sinkin' to the floor at the top of the landin' beggin' the swine to stop. But even then she was thinkin' o' me. "Don't let little Em see this, Sid. Don't let little Em see this!" But he just laughed and snarled and swung an' swung until I could bear it no more, so I ran at the bastard as hard as I could an' I caught 'im right in his balls an' he doubles up an' I runs again an' heaves 'im down the stairs like the sack o' shit that he were.'

As she spoke, he could almost hear the schoolteacher diction fade away and the rawness of that moment bring its own brutal clarity of expression.

'What happened on the Friday, when Dorothea Gadsworth came to school?'

She lowered her head. She had expended so much energy on remembering the distant past that the present had misted over for a while. He gave her time to recover her senses. By this time they had reached Parbold, and he looked out at the fine rolling hillside, at the way the small clouds were now drawing shifting shadows on the green slopes of Parbold Hill.

'I heard her. She told that school inspector she recognised Richard only his name weren't Richard it were David an' he'd done a really bad thing a long time ago an' was it right he should be headmaster now?' She too looked through the window. 'It was as much news to me as it was to him. I'd never known about that.'

'What did the inspector say?'

'Said it were a grave matter she were talkin' about an' he could only make mention in his report. Let others deal with it. So I had to do summat. Since Mason died, Richard Weston – my dad – came back an' did all he could to look after us. I owe him everythin'. Everythin'.'

'How did you lure Miss Gadsworth back to the school?'

Emily Mason had tears in her eyes now. 'Simple. Just waited for her at the station an' told her the inspector wanted to see her. Wanted her to sign summat. She jumped at the chance. 'Specially after she'd messed up the interview earlier.'

'And the poison?'

'John Prendergast don't care much about keepin' stuff like that locked away.'

'It was the bottle of whisky that made me curious,' said Brennan. 'I mean, you gave her a mug of tea with the arsenic in, right?'

'Yes.'

'So why remove the mug and put the Scotch in its place?'

Emily shrugged. 'It's what people who kill themselves do, ain't it? Get drunk before. I thought it might make it more realistic. Only that poison didn't work straight off. I thought she'd just take it and drop. Only she didn't. So I locked her in the classroom.'

'But you wrote the word "FAILED" to make us think it was suicide?'

'Yes. Wrote it an' slid it under the door after I'd locked it. An' it was easy droppin' that key Monday mornin' so they all thought she'd locked herself in. I thought that was clever of me.'

There was a child-like tone in her voice, almost a plea for adult praise.

With a heavy sigh at the sloppiness, the childish opportunism, of the crime, he went on. 'You left a note for the inspector at his hotel?'

Emily nodded. 'I'd heard him tell my father he was staying there for another inspection. So I wrote the note, tellin' him I had definite proof Miss Gadsworth was tellin' the truth.'

'And he came to meet you.'

'I'd pushed one man down the stairs when I were nowt but a babby. It were easy pushin' him in. Only after he'd told me he'd not put it in the report yet.'

'And Nathaniel Edgar?'

'I missed me aim in the dark. He'd threatened my father, said he'd tell everyone I was his daughter. I was listenin' after school. His window was open and I was passin' my father's office. The caretaker saw me an' waved. I think dad thought he was wavin' at him. As if he would!' She curled her lip. 'They'd have sacked him. An' Mr Edgar's nothin' more than a drunkard. They get what they deserve, drunkards.'

Brennan laid his head back. They would soon be arriving at Wallgate Station, and making the short walk down King Street to the police station.

'How did you know it were me?' Emily asked.

He thought about it for a second, then said, 'I don't believe in coincidences, Emily.'

'What do you mean?'

'When I interviewed you, before we knew the school inspector, Henry Tollet, was missing, let alone dead, you said to me that all school inspectors should be "drowned at birth". When he *was* found drowned it rankled with me. Either a coincidence or you were having a quiet laugh at my expense. Besides, the crimes themselves, they were too haphazard, too unplanned. There was no consistency of thought behind them. A poisoning, a drowning and a stabbing? People – even criminals – are consistent, they prefer to follow one route. You were all over the place.'

He didn't add that it was also a sign of the madness that was surely tightening its grip on her mind.

Silence now. Only the rhythmic rattle of wheels on the tracks beneath them.

'One final question, Emily.'

She looked at him through tear-filled eyes.

'Why didn't you silence young Billy Kelly when you locked him up?'

She thought for a while before replying. 'He'd done nothin' wrong, had he?'

'You could say the same for your victims.'

She shook her head. 'They knew what they were doin'. All of 'em wanted to do some harm to a good man. Billy didn't. All he'd done was see me wi' Miss Gadsworth. Heard us talkin'. I caught him after I'd locked her in the classroom. So I couldn't risk him tellin' anyone. Besides, you've seen the bruises on the lad. Reminded me of the life I led when little – so no. I couldn't do Billy any mischief. Just wanted him out of the way.'

'But why go to Seaforth to see him?'

'Miss Rodley told me where she'd took him. Said he'd be emigratin' soon. I just wanted to see the boy, tell him how sorry I were, wish him well. When I found out he weren't there, I just . . . I'm so tired, you see?'

There was a sad simplicity about the girl, Brennan thought. That, and a growing insanity.

As they walked down King Street, the light was fading fast, and there was a chill in the evening air. He felt none of the elation he normally felt when a case was solved. Somehow, he told himself with a furtive glance in Emily Mason's direction, a silly and immoral act by two foolish lovers fifteen years ago had begun a sequence of events that brought devastation to a number of people. And for this girl, the suffering wasn't over, not by a long way. The only one who'd deserved to die was the bastard Mason.

As she was led down into the cells below, he caught sight of Constable Jaggery emerging from the canteen.

'Howdo, Sergeant!' he hailed as he approached. 'I see you've got the little bitch then?'

Brennan didn't reply, but turned on his heel, walked out of the station and headed for home, where his family would be waiting for him.

George Street Elementary School, Wigan
Extracts from school logbook December 1894
[Completed by Miss E. Ryan, Acting Headmistress]

Monday 10th December

Very cold day. Many children absent because of thick snow. Lessons continued notwithstanding. Albert Parkinson brought to my office for swearing at Joe Marshall and breaking a slate over his head. He was strapped six times on each hand. Letter sent home warning of the consequences of any repeated behaviour. I took the opportunity to speak with the temporary assistant teacher of Standard 6, Mr Boland, to ensure he maintains the strictest of discipline with a most unsatisfactory class.

The girls in Standard 3 produce far superior dictation work than the boys. Reports have also reached my office of the appalling behaviour of those same boys during the dinner hour, many refusing to go home and loiter in the street outside. I have spoken with Miss Walsh and demanded the issues be addressed as a matter of urgency. While promising to do so, she has also told me that the children are not her responsibility once they leave through the school gates. She intends to make a complaint to the school board concerning my running of the school in general and my 'vindictiveness' towards her in particular. It will be for the board to make a judgement as to the evidence.

Tuesday 11th December

The pupils have begun the decoration of their classrooms for the Christmas festivities, apart from Standard 6, whose continued misbehaviour has convinced me to withhold permission for the classroom to be decorated. It will be a salutary reminder to them of what the holy season is all about.

Several of the children have colds and I have received a number of requests to allow them to sit nearer to the classroom stove. This has been granted within reason.

Wednesday 12th December

A most distressing morning. Reverend Pearl addressed the entire school and informed them of the death of Emily Mason through an unspecified illness. Naturally, I objected to such an announcement, almost sanctifying a foul and evil murderess. Miss Rodley, who has been assisting with Standard 5 since Mr Edgar's absence, leapt to her fiancé's defence and caused a most unseemly scene in the staffroom, supported, one must say inevitably, by Miss Walsh.

Thursday 13th December

Miss Walsh came to see me and said she would petition the school board for my removal as headmistress. I wished her good fortune in such a futile endeavour.

Friday 14th December

Reverend Pearl gave the children much joy when he brought in a lantern slide show which included a presentation of Charles Dickens's *A Christmas Carol*, and a set of Christmas scenes. The children were genuinely afraid when presented with the image of Scrooge at his own graveside with the Ghost of Christmas Yet to Come hovering over him. As Reverend Pearl commented, it was a salutary reminder of our own misdeeds and the punishment we shall all receive unless we take steps to mend our ways. I gave a strong speech in front of almost the entire school – and those members of the school board who came along in support – praising the excellent manner in which Reverend Pearl had brought such edifying material into the pupils' lives. A great pity that Standard 6 were not allowed to see the slide show, for with hindsight I feel they would be the ones who would most benefit from its lessons.

A letter arrived this afternoon informing me that, as our most recent inspection ended so tragically, with the concomitant lack of reporting so necessary for the machinery of education and its monitoring, a new HMI has been assigned to our school and he will be visiting next Wednesday. This will enable our 1894 annual report to be completed. I have called an extraordinary staff meeting for Monday evening.

AUTHOR'S NOTE

George Street Elementary School is of course a fictitious establishment, and for those interested in the geography of Wigan, George Street is not to be confused with Great George Street off Wallgate.

ACKNOWLEDGEMENTS

Once again I have people to thank. My agent, Sara Keane, of the Keane Kataria Literary Agency, is always supportive and unfailingly cheerful! Sophie Robinson, Editor at Allison & Busby, has once again helped me avoid embarrassing errors and made insightful comments. Any mistakes are therefore her fault – sorry, I meant to put my fault!

Finally, I should like to thank all those teachers who taught me at both primary and secondary school. Admittedly some of them wouldn't have felt out of place at George Street Elementary, especially where good old-fashioned discipline is concerned! Yet they taught me well, inspired me to follow in their footsteps and prepared me admirably for when I started at the chalk-face!